The Rejected Mate Games

Game Of Wolves: Book 1

Lindsey Devin & Skye Wilson

© 2023

Disclaimer

D0886128

This is a work of fiction. Names, places, characters, and events are all fictitious for the reader's pleasure. Any similarities to real people, places, events, living, or dead are all coincidental.

This book contains sexually explicit content that is intended for ADULTS ONLY (+18).

Contents

Chapter 1 - Kira

Rivulets of condensation trickled down the side of my glass as I glanced around. The restaurant wasn't empty, but it wasn't busy, either, which was perfect. I wasn't surprised my target had chosen this location. It was upscale but not too expensive—the exact type of place I assumed he always took his victims. He was late, though, which didn't fit his style.

"Kira?" the voice in my earpiece said. "Any sign?"

It was Douglas, one of the other Tranquility operatives assigned to this sting. We had a two-man team plus the bait. I was, of course, the bait. Douglas sat in an unmarked van three blocks away. The second member of the team, Carter, was hidden in the line of sight of the restaurant with a camera. I'd chosen a seat by the big bay window so the team would have a good vantage point.

The earpiece was small, virtually invisible unless you were incredibly observant, and more silent than regular tech allowed. The fae had created the magical device for the council. The spell ensured no one but the wearer could hear anything being broadcast through it. It was incredibly helpful when we went into ops with creatures like shifters, who had significantly enhanced hearing. As small and hidden as the earpiece was, I had my hair down, covering my ears just in case. Thankfully, my hair was long enough to hide my ears, coming to the tops of my shoulders. For some operations, I dyed it or wore wigs, but I'd gone with my natural blond today.

I lifted my drink to my lips to hide my mouth. "Nope. I'm not sure what's taking so long," I whispered.

Carter's voice broke in. "I've scanned the surrounding parking lots and see nothing. I think this guy's a no-show."

We were here to take down a lion shifter by the name of Leon Marx, who targeted human women for sexual attacks. Three months ago, when reports came in of over a dozen women who'd been assaulted or stalked by the same guy, the Tranquility Council got involved. Interspecies mating wasn't outlawed per se, but it was frowned upon, especially by more traditional creatures. Wolf shifters, like me, did frown upon it.

"I'm still confused," Douglas said. "Why is the council so worried about this guy?"

"Because, dumbass, he's sexually assaulting humans. What more do we need to know?" Carter retorted with a derisive laugh.

"Watch the language on the comms," I muttered, letting my lips move as little as possible. I didn't need people knowing I was talking to anyone when I was supposed to be alone.

"Sorry. Dumbass was a bit aggressive," Carter said. "I meant to say moron."

"I get that," Douglas replied, ignoring Carter's jibe. "But when we were briefed, they said it was a pretty cut-and-dry case. Like, can't the human authorities take care of this? Seems overkill to bring in Tranquility operatives to take down a date-raping scuzzball."

"It's the old guard and all their backwards rules," I said, resting my chin in my palm to cover my mouth with my fingers. "The alphas are up in arms because this lion shifter is stalking women of other species. Favors have been called in. That's what's going on. It's old-school bullshit, but who cares? Like you said, he's a shitheel who needs to be neutered. We're here now, so we do the job. Got it?"

Unlike other wolf shifters, I'd never had a problem with interspecies relationships, but the old men who ran most of the packs were skittish about it. So much so that when something like this popped up, they called in favors to the council to have it dealt with.

"Right." Douglas sighed. "I'm still saying this dude is a no-show. Maybe he sniffed us out. How good is a lion shifter's sense of smell, anyway?"

"We wait," I hissed through gritted teeth. "You guys know how things are right now. The fact that this guy is hunting victims in a wolf-shifter territory should be enough to get the point across. We wait. That's final."

My team had express orders to take this guy down and do it fast. There was currently some volatility within wolf-shifter society between those who wanted our species to remain insular and pure and those who were more liberal in their ideologies. I didn't want to think about what would happen if this guy got away and began to prey on people of my own species. Something as simple as a rogue lion shifter could tip the scales toward the war that had been brewing for months now. Some packs just wanted a reason to fight.

"I still say I should have been the bait," Carter said. "I look good in a cocktail dress. I mean, minus the bulge between my legs."

I sighed in irritation. I'd volunteered to try smoking out the lion shifter. As one of the few operatives in the entire organization who could seamlessly pass for human, even among other paranormal creatures, jobs like these were right up my alley. I couldn't even remember the last time I shifted into my wolf form. It had been years. That suppression made me almost indistinguishable from human women. Even my scent had changed after all these years. I was perfect for this.

My team had created a fake dating profile on the same app Marx used to find his last three victims. I'd tried not to roll my eyes as I took revealing, sexy selfies to entice him. I had to grind through dozens of unsolicited dick pics and equally creepy come-ons before Leon finally made contact and swallowed the bait. We'd scheduled to meet up at a restaurant in Cullman, a small town near the Eastern Wilds where the majority of the population was human. I was not about to give up so easily. By the goddess, I deserved this bust after seeing all those pictures of men's genitalia. Catching this piece of shit would make it all worth it.

"Let's give it a few more minutes," I whispered.

"Copy that," Douglas said.

"Yeah, ten-four. I'm moving closer for a better vantage," Carter said with a grunt.

With nothing to do but wait, I pulled out my phone and turned on the forward-facing camera to check my makeup and hair. If the guy did show, I wanted to look as irresistible as possible. Zoe had done a damn good job on me. Switching from the camera to my messaging app, I shot her a text:

Hey girl, love the makeover you gave me. I think this guy's gonna drop dead when he sees me.

The reply came within seconds.

Good! How do you like the dress?

I glanced down at the scarlet dress. It was low-cut and form-fitting. From the way the other operatives had been doing their best to look anywhere but my chest, my boobs must have looked great in it.

It's fantastic. The guy's going to be drooling on himself when he gets here.

Too bad he's a scuzzball. Otherwise, I'd say give him a shot. Better him than that flaky-ass mate of yours. He never appreciates all the work I put in to make you look adorable. Maybe I'll just enchant him and force him to stop dragging his feet.

She was probably only joking. Probably. Zoe and I had been best friends for years, and she'd been my personal cosmetician for as long as I could remember. She was a fae, and if she wanted to, she *could* enchant my future mate. Not only was it slightly illegal, but I also didn't want that. Our pairing was one of convenience and opportunity, nothing more. It would almost certainly never lead to love, but I'd come to terms with that.

My friend's affection and support sent a pleasant warmth through my chest. It was nice to know at least one person had my back. I needed to stay focused, though. I couldn't get too deep into a conversation when this lion could show up any second.

Gotta go back to work. Talk to you later.

Zoe replied with a thumbs-up emoji, and I slipped my phone back into my purse. In my ear, Carter and Douglas were going over mission parameters. I blocked most of it out since none of it really pertained to me. But then a surprise voice broke over the chatter. That voice most *definitely* pertained to me.

"Kira, we need to call it. We'll regroup later and see what went wrong."

I gritted my teeth. Even the sound of his voice set me on edge.

"Wyatt?" I put my hand in front of my mouth to cover my words. "What the fuck are you doing here? You weren't assigned to this operation."

Wyatt Rivers was a fellow Tranquility operative and my brother's best friend. He was also the biggest pain in my ass. He was like a pebble in your shoe— annoying, ever-present, and right when you thought you'd gotten rid of it, it was back again.

"Kira, we're in the same division. You know we share resources. I read this guy's file and thought you might need the backup. I'm in a sedan about a hundred yards from the restaurant. Like I said, let's call it. We can drop back and punt. Maybe use another fake profile. Try again."

I rested my chin on my hand again to cover my mouth. "Screw that. He's coming. I know it. I could tell from the messages he sent me that he was basically humping his keyboard. This is what we do. We maintain the balance between humans and the paranormal. This guy is preying on human women, and I'm going to stop him. Let me do my damned job and get off this freaking channel."

Before Wyatt could say anything in reply, Carter's voice interrupted us. "Heads up, target is incoming. Repeat, target is incoming."

Forgetting all about Wyatt, I snapped my head up and looked toward the entrance. Carter was right. I'd studied Leon's pictures for weeks, and that slick son of a bitch had just walked in. He took a few tentative steps through the door, scanning the room. When his eyes fell on me and the ample cleavage I was displaying, he grinned. He was a lion shifter, so it shouldn't have been a surprise, but that smile reminded me of the Cheshire Cat. It was uncomfortable to look at, but I plastered a similar smile on my own face and stood to greet him.

Wyatt gave another warning. "Kira, give us a signal if you need help."

Through a smile of gritted teeth, I murmured, "Shut up."

Leon stepped over, giving me a chaste hug and a peck on the cheek. "Gods, you look good enough to eat."

It was time to play up the ditzy hot chick angle I'd used to snare him.

Giggling, I put a hand on his chest. "Oh, stop."

Leon took his seat opposite me, then raised a hand and snapped his fingers at the server. He actually snapped his fingers. Good lord, what an ass. The vapid smile never left my face as he ordered a bottle of wine and our entrees. He didn't bother to ask me what I wanted. After the server had gone, he turned his attention back to me.

His gaze slid across my shoulders and chest, then up to my face. "I must say," he said, "you're hotter in person."

I waved a hand at him playfully. "You probably say that to all the girls."

His grin grew hungrier. "Only the ones that look like you."

"Kira, I don't like the look of this guy," Wyatt said in my ear. "We need to pull you out."

In answer, I scratched the side of my head facing the window with my middle finger. Hopefully, Wyatt would get the message. He was surely tapped into the telephoto camera feed. He hissed a curse but went silent.

Leaning across the table, I slid a hand across the thick muscles of Leon's arm. "Oh my goodness," I breathed. "So hard and thick. Do you have anything else like these arms?"

Leon's entire body responded. His eyes went wild with desire, and I could smell the pheromones wafting off him.

"Oh, I've got a few surprises. If you play your cards right, maybe you'll see."

I cocked an eyebrow. "Is that a promise?"

He nodded and slid his tongue across his lips. "Bet on it."

One of the reasons for the in-person meeting was to get a DNA sample. The plan was to have Carter slip in as soon as we left the restaurant and snatch Leon's drinking glass before the server cleared it. That, along with the human testimony, should be enough to take him down. Unfortunately, I'd have to live through this awful act for at least another hour. Stroking this guy's ego was nauseating.

The conversation continued for another five minutes before the server brought our wine. Leon had already commented on my breasts twice and had even asked if I shaved or waxed my vagina. It was hard for me to keep a straight face at his sheer gall and arrogance. We'd only met each other in person less than ten minutes before.

For my part, I was a good actress. It was another reason I usually went on undercover operations like these. The act I was putting on in the restaurant was worthy of an Oscar. I did my best to ask him about past relationships or girls he'd been with before, anything to get a little more incriminating evidence. The conversation invariably veered back to my body, his body, and various sexual positions.

"Can I try your dish?" Leon eyed the steak that the waiter had just brought me.

I grinned. "Absolutely."

Leon leaned across the table and cut a piece of the steak. When he pulled back, he bumped my wine glass, and it wobbled precariously. With lion reflexes, he snatched it and righted the glass with both hands before handing it to me. I took it with a nod of thanks.

"What the hell was that?" Wyatt barked in my ear. "Did anyone else see that? On the feed? Kira, don't drink that wine."

But the warning came too late. I'd already sipped the liquid. Something was off. The smell and taste were different, the flavor on my tongue a little bitter. The fucker had slipped something into my drink. I couldn't figure out what, though. My shifter senses were powerful, but the substance was too subtle for me to place. If I had to guess, it was probably a roofie or another human drug. It wouldn't work on me, but the fact he'd even tried to use it meant my ruse was working.

I blinked as a warm, fuzzy sensation settled over my eyes. Even though it had been years since I'd felt it, I knew my brown irises had turned a faint shimmery yellow. Leon's smile vanished in an instant, almost like it had been turned off with a light switch. With his eyes locked on mine, his lips turned up in a sneer of disgust and anger.

"Lying cunt," he hissed and leaped from his chair, flipping the table toward me as he did.

He sprinted for the door. Pushing the table off me, I jumped to follow him.

"Target is on the loose! Repeat, target is on the loose!" I yelled into the microphone.

Chaos erupted around me. The other diners were yelling, running, or pointing. I tugged a small pistol from my thigh holster and ran after Leon. I couldn't let him get away. We'd probably never find him again. The chatter in my ear was almost indecipherable, with the entire team going back and forth. I ripped the earpiece out and tossed it to the ground.

Outside, I saw Leon sprinting to the restaurant's back parking lot. Gritting my teeth, I ran after him. I shouldn't have, but I was enjoying the chase. It was much more enjoyable than it should have been. I wasn't sure why, but I had no time to think about it. He was right there, and I knew I could catch him.

As I rounded the corner of the building, I had a single instant to realize my mistake. I was in trouble. Leon had run around the corner but then stopped, lying in wait for me. He knew I was too fast, and he wouldn't get away. So, he decided to take me out.

A knife blade lashed out, slashing across the air less than an inch from my eyes. I could feel the wind off his hand, hear the faint hiss as the weapon cut the air in front of me.

Instinctively, I jerked my head back, away from the blade. That gave Leon an opening. His reflexes were almost as fast as mine. His foot shot out, kicking my gun out of my hand. The metal clattered against the ground as the gun bounced and spun far out of reach.

He snarled at me, his face contorted with rage as he surged forward and jammed the tip of the knife toward my stomach. He was fast and strong, but the council trained its operatives well, and I was one of the best. I whirled away from the knife and snapped my fist, punching Leon with a backhand. The momentum from the stab propelled him toward the brick wall. I kicked him in his back, and he slammed face-first into it. I could hear the muffled crack as his nose broke.

Instead of slowing down, he spun away from the wall, screaming in anger, and dived at me. He was still clutching the knife—the familiar and noxious scent of silver was like a slap in the face. I twisted sideways and caught his foot with my own, sending him sprawling onto the pavement. When he rolled over, I straddled him and gripped the wrist holding the knife. He was honestly making this too easy. He was used to holding women down who had never learned to defend themselves. Well, I was about to show him what a woman was capable of.

Holding his knife hand away, I raised my free hand, ready to slam my elbow into his pretty face. A sudden flush of heat radiated through me. The surge was powerful enough that I forgot all about Leon. Fire—lava—coursed through my veins. My vision went blurry as my head spun.

Leon wrenched his hand free from my grip and jammed the silver blade toward my chest. The barest warning of danger flickered through my mind, and I managed to turn at the last second. Instead of the blade burying in my heart, it slid deep into the meat between my shoulder and collarbone. A scream tore from my throat as I rolled off him and fell to the asphalt. He scrambled to his feet and bolted. I was still holding my shoulder when he disappeared into the forest.

Carter and Douglas came skidding around the corner, their weapons drawn. They saw me on the ground, a knife sticking out of my shoulder, blood spreading from the wound. Carter took a step toward me, but I waved frantically at the forest.

"He went that way. Dammit, hurry. He's getting away," I growled.

Douglas shook his head. "Kira, you need a medic–"

"It's a shallow wound, I'll be fine. Go after him. Move!"

Reluctantly, they sprinted into the woods. What the hell was going on with my body? It had to be whatever he'd put in my drink because I'd never experienced anything like it. That, along with the agony from the silver in my shoulder, was driving me mad. There was more blood than there should have been. I wasn't sure if the blade had nicked an artery or if the silver was preventing my blood from clotting. Either way, it added a new wave of fear.

Wyatt sprinted toward me, his hair in sweaty disarray. His face was still as chiseled as it had been all the years I'd known him. He was opening his mouth to chew me out, but when he saw the wound, all thoughts of chastising me vanished.

"Holy shit, Kira. Are you okay?" he asked as he dropped to his knees beside me and cradled my head.

The smell of him hit me: musk and man, pine trees, sawdust, and whiskey. A single thought burst through the pain. *Heat.* I was in a heat so powerful and beyond explanation. I tried to understand what was happening to me, but it was as if my thoughts were thrown into a blender at the highest speed. All that was left was my inner wolf howling and snapping as it blocked out all coherent thought. A growl purred out of my throat as I turned and clutched at Wyatt. Running my hands through his messy dark hair, I gazed into his green eyes. It was like a fire had been lit between my legs, and all rational thought took a backseat to desire. All I wanted was to have him inside me. The thought of Wyatt filling me, thrusting into me, had saliva pooling in my mouth. Nothing had ever made me feel so animalistic, at least not for a long time. I didn't just want him; I *needed* him. My very nerves begged to have him, and the warmth between my legs engulfed me in flames that I knew only Wyatt could quench. Like water in a desert, Wyatt was what I needed to survive.

His eyes widened in shock as I pawed at him, clutching his shirt and yanking him toward me, my injury forgotten.

Chapter 2 - Wyatt

Kira's pheromones pulsed off her in palpable waves that overwhelmed my senses. It was so strong and unexpected that I was at a loss for words until she lunged at me, yanking at my shirt. There was nothing but lust and need in her eyes.

"Kira?" I shouted at her, trying to snap her out of whatever daze she was in, but it was useless. Her hands continued their path over my chest.

"What the hell?" I gently tried to push her away, but she batted my hands like she would an annoying gnat and leaned forward to kiss my collarbone.

With a heavy force of will, I pulled away. "Hey, Kira. Stop."

I grabbed her wrists, but she was strong and highly trained. She flipped her hands out of my grasp and pawed at me again. The scent of her was quickly draining my self-control. Kira was always searching out danger, taking on the most treacherous assignments and ops, trying to prove herself and generally being a pain in my ass. She got under my skin, irritated the crap out of me, and was the only person who could ever get my control to slip. My calm, carefully cultivated demeanor cracked when she was in the vicinity. And this was not helping.

Kira leaned close, eyes half-lidded with desire. "Fuck me, Wyatt," she moaned.

Shock and surprise had me gaping at her even as my traitorous body responded. Despite my best intentions, I was hard in an instant—partly from her words but mostly from the pheromones and the thick smell of her heat surging around me. For the barest second, I had the urge to rip off her clothes, yank my cock out, and take her right there on the pavement in front of the goddess and anyone else who might see.

I squeezed my eyes shut and tried to pull myself together. I managed, though barely, to reign myself in. Opening my eyes, I tightened my grip on her wrists and pinned her to the ground. Kira's hips bucked in the air as she tried to rub her crotch against me. What the fuck was going on? This was out of character for her. Had I not been able to see her face, I would have assumed this woman was not Kira.

I remembered the video feed, remembering seeing that jackass slip something into her drink. Could that have caused this? There was no other feasible explanation. Whatever he'd given her had forced her into an insanely intense heat.

The knife was sticking out of her shoulder, the weapon's silver cloying in my nostrils. Panic and anger roiled within me as blood oozed out of her at an alarming rate. He'd not only poisoned her but almost killed her. Who knew which veins or arteries the knife might have hit? It must have hit something important to produce so much blood.

Again, Kira pulled her hand from my grip. Her arm shot forward, fingers grabbing and gently caressing my crotch through my pants.

"Please," she whined. "Give it to me. I need it."

The sensation of her hand on me, rubbing and massaging, nearly had me losing control. My mind flipped and short-circuited. If we were anywhere else, at any other time, would I be able to stop myself? I imagined how this would go if she were unhurt and acting this way in a quiet secluded area. I imagined her pulling my cock out and taking it into her mouth. Ripping her dress away and pulling her body to mine as I worshipped her nipples with my lips and tongue. The fiery heat of her pussy as I plunged into her. The echo of our moans and screams as we fucked.

"No," I hissed to myself, shaking my head again. "No."

It took all I had to ignore her pheromones, her words, her actions, and focus on what needed to be done. The mental images I'd allowed myself filled me with guilt. She was seriously hurt, and here I was, daydreaming about sex. It made me feel like shit.

Kira pounced on me again, but the handle of the knife bumped against my chest. The blade jammed deeper into her, and she screamed. For a moment, the pain seemed to overcome her desire. Grimacing, I took hold of the knife and yanked it out of her flesh, then quickly covered her wound, putting pressure on it as more blood spilled out between my fingers. She looked down and saw my hands.

"Gods," she whispered. "At least finger me. Give me something."

Her voice dripped with desperation. It was almost like she was so horny that it was causing her physical pain. Maybe I *could* help? If she was in pain, and she was begging for it...my cock was rock hard and throbbing. I was caught in a haze of desire, all coherent thoughts impossible to find. I blinked the ideas away again.

"Carter? Douglas? Where the hell are you?" I yelled into my earpiece. "Kira needs medical attention."

Carter's voice, heaving with exertion, filtered into my ear a moment later. "We called in a med team. We're in pursuit of the lion shifter. Med team's ten minutes out."

"Ten minutes? Why the fuck will it take that long?" I growled.

"Closest one had a call about an operative who was attacked by a rogue demon. Bad timing and bad luck. They're on the way, though."

"Fuck," I snapped. "Fine."

I let them go back to their hunt. Kira had sat up and wrapped her arms around me, licking and sucking at my neck. She was not making this any easier on me. I needed to do something, or what semblance of control I had left would crack completely and fall apart. In mere minutes, we'd be screwing our brains out in a restaurant parking lot.

Kira let out a whimper of pain. The heat was causing her physical agony. If I ever got hold of that fucking lion, I would rip his head off and piss down his throat.

Kira climbed into my lap and tore my shirt open. It happened so fast, I couldn't have stopped it if I tried. She slid her hands across my chest, which was sweaty from the exertion of trying to hold her still. As she did everything she could to have sex with me, tears leaked from her eyes, a combination of pain from her wound and the heat.

Glancing around, I saw we were still alone. Dammit, I needed someone else here so I didn't give in to Kira's pleading. A small clutch purse hung crosswise over her chest. I dug into it and yanked her phone out, scrolling through the contacts for Jayson's number. Maybe hearing her future mate's voice would help snap Kira out of it.

"Hey, babe, what's up?" Jayson said as he answered.

"Jayson, it's Wyatt Rivers. I need you to–"

"Gods, I wanna suck your dick so bad. Please, Wyatt, just for a second?" Kira whispered.

I closed my eyes, wincing at what was coming next.

"What the fuck was that?" Jayson screamed. "Was that Kira?"

"It's not what you think," I said, hoping he could hear the honesty in my voice.

"Are you trying to fuck my girl? You piece of shit, I swear to Heline, I'll kill you if you touch what's mine."

"Jayson, there's no time for this. Kira's been stabbed and poisoned. I need you to get to the Black Pine Brasserie. It's a restaurant in Cullman. Hurry."

Kira whimpered. "Oh, gods. Damn, make me come. Make me come, and it'll be over. Please, Wyatt."

Shit. Jayson was screaming curses at me through the phone, completely ignoring the information about Kira. All he cared about was what he heard. The last five minutes had been some of the most stressful and ridiculous minutes of my entire life. I had no more patience. Especially not for Kira's douchebag of a fated mate.

"Jayson, please shut up and listen. Kira is hurt. She needs you. Get down here now, before I do something to take care of it myself." I ended the call and tossed the phone on the ground.

With every passing minute that I struggled with Kira, my self-control drained more. When Jayson appeared with a flash, along with Kira's fae friend Zoe,

I was both relieved and irritated. Of course, he'd shown up right as Kira leaned forward and licked my exposed nipple. I would have kept her away, but I was too busy to keep pressure on her stab wound.

Jayson's eyes flared as his hands curled into fists. Ignoring all the blood and the obvious pain Kira was in, he pointed at me. "You motherfucker!"

Zoe's face paled at the sight of all the blood Kira had lost, and she ran forward, putting a hand on the wound to staunch the bleeding. Having more people here did help. My own lust and desire were tamped down now that Zoe was helping, and my dislike of Jayson pushed my other emotions to the side. My guilt started to make a resurgence. Kira was my best friend's sister. Gods, I was a piece of shit for thinking all those things about her.

Jayson was still going on. "I can't believe this. I'll make sure my father gets you fired. He knows people. Powerful people. You'll—"

"Dammit, will you shut up? Here, take her." I twisted a bit to offer her to him.

Zoe shook her head. "Don't. She's losing too much blood." She turned and snapped at Jayson.

"Whatever she's been poisoned with must be highly toxic. Look at her."

He glanced at Kira's morbidly pale face, and his expression softened a bit, but not enough for my liking. He shrugged. "Yeah? Fix her. You're a fae, right? I want to get home," he said sulkily. Then he winced in disgust. "Gods, she reeks of his scent. I'll have to give her a bath when we get home to get the stink off her."

Flaming anger flashed across Zoe's eyes. I had the sense that if I hadn't been there as a witness, Jayson Fell might not have made it home alive.

Through clenched teeth, Zoe said, "I'll do my best, but I don't know a lot about healing spells. I think I can slow the bleeding."

Zoe placed her hands on Kira's shoulder and murmured a few words. Kira's head lolled to the side, and her breathing became heavy and slow. She'd been put to sleep. The oozing blood had slowed to a trickle, too. I sighed with a relief that settled through my every muscle. My body was exhausted from trying to keep Kira from attacking me.

Jayson, however, looked like he was more concerned with getting out of there.

He glanced at his watch, then back at Zoe. "Is she good now? Can you get us home? I want to watch the game that's starting soon."

Zoe sighed and waved her hand in Jayson's direction. His eyes rolled to the back of his head, and he slumped to the ground, smacking his cheek on the pavement, deeply asleep like Kira. I gaped at his wide-open mouth as he snored like a freight train. When I looked back at Zoe, she gave me an embarrassed smile and shrugged.

"He's a dick."

I smiled back at her. I'd always considered Kira's friend flighty and a bit of a loose cannon. Now I appreciated her. She'd take care of Kira, no matter what. I was certain of that after seeing what she'd done to Jayson.

My earpiece kicked back to life. "Wyatt? You there?"

"I'm here, Douglas. What's going on?"

"Med team will be at the restaurant in less than three minutes."

I sighed. "Thank the gods."

Moments later, the team swooped in. Zoe and I stepped back and let them work. One of the medics glanced at Jayson's unconscious form on the ground. "What about him? Does he need assistance?"

"Oh no," Zoe said, waving him off. "He's suffering from terminal asshole-itis. There's no cure. But thanks for asking."

The medic frowned but went back to getting Kira onto a gurney. Zoe looked back and forth at Kira and me before pulling me aside.

"Thanks for helping her. If you hadn't kept pressure on her wound, she would have lost even more blood. I think she'll be fine once they get her to a trained healer."

I shrugged. "No big deal. She would have done the same for me."

Zoe made a face. "Probably, but she would have bitched about it for weeks after. I know I'm supposed to be on her side all the time, including hating you." She rolled her eyes. "Gods know she makes that abundantly clear, but I still appreciate all you do to keep her out of trouble. Just remember, I can never say that when she's conscious. So, if I'm a bitch to you the next time I see you, know that I have to be that way."

Chuckling, I nodded. It was a good reminder that Kira hated me. It all went back to that one day so long ago. As far as I could remember, that was the last time I'd seen her covered in this much blood. There'd been more that day. I swallowed hard and shook the thought away.

"I understand. Thanks for coming, Zoe," I said.

My own emotions toward Kira had always been convoluted. I tended to worry about her and acted like an older brother at work. She was constantly in trouble, or so it seemed to me. Any other feelings I might have were kept under wraps, tucked and locked away, never to be pulled out and assessed. I refused to allow that. For one, she was my best friend's sister. For another, she was already spoken for. And most important of all, she hated me.

She despised me, yes. Still, the feel of her hands and mouth on me a few minutes before was fresh in my mind. The heat of her body, the wetness of her tongue...the things she'd said and asked for...it had almost driven me crazy. I was glad it was over. That drug, whatever it had been, was the only reason she'd behaved that way. I had to remember that if I wanted to stay sane around her.

Chapter 3 - Kira

My bed was damp with sweat. It was the first thing I noticed when I opened my eyes. Everything from the moment the target had walked into the restaurant until opening my eyes in my bed was one big feverish haze. I had no clue how long I'd been out, but it must have been at least a couple of days. The forced heat I'd been subjected to had drained all the strength from my body, leaving me weak and exhausted.

I'd drifted in and out of a burning sleep for what felt like days. I recalled flashes of fae healers, human doctors, and shifter medics working on me. Whatever had happened must have been bad.

Two IVs were attached to my arm. I glanced up at the bags. One looked to be some basic hydration solution, while the other had a dark purple color—likely some healing potion a fae had cooked up. Careful not to hurt myself, I tugged both tubes out of my arm. I hated seeing those things protruding from me. I could only imagine how I looked with tubes and wires covering my sweaty body as I moaned in my sleep. I despised looking weak. Feeling better than I had since taking that sip of wine, I decided it would be fine to try to look more like myself.

Easing up onto the pillows behind me, I glanced around at the familiar surroundings. I was at my family's home. Outside the window, the massive forest of the Eastern Wilds stretched beyond my father's property. The Eleventh Pack's land wasn't huge like some of the other packs', but it was still beautiful. I was glad I was here rather than at a hospital or operative clinic.

A few bottles of water stood on the nightstand next to my bed. Greedily, I snatched one. The room-temperature water was a heavenly elixir sliding down my parched throat. The IV had kept me from dying of dehydration, but nothing was better than a drink of water when you were thirsty.

After drinking my fill, I realized I wasn't entirely back to normal yet. The healers had fixed me fairly rapidly, and all the painful need from being forced into heat had vanished. My vagina had actually ached to be filled, and not in a good way. The residual effects were still in my body, though. An insistent desire still pulsed through me, and wetness pooled between my legs.

Maybe if I got myself off, the orgasm would flush the rest of the stuff from my system. Gods, I could barely think with the lust coiled in my belly. I'd need to be in full control of my body if I were to face the meetings, inquiries, maybe even reprimands that were par for the course after a failed operation.

I slid a hand under the covers, then under the waistband of my panties. A breath shuddered past me as my fingers slipped across the wet folds of my pussy. Glancing at the door to make sure no one was coming in, I closed my eyes and slid the tip of my middle finger across my clit.

Unbidden, a memory flooded my mind of Wyatt cradling my body. The scent of him, the taste of his skin, the rippling muscles of his body underneath my caresses. I was dripping wet at the mere thought. As I slid a finger inside myself, a moan escaped my lips. The sound of Wyatt's voice, deep and sexy as he'd been trying to calm me down, sent me into a frenzy. My hand worked furiously between my legs as a thousand fantasies played out in my mind.

I imagined us in that parking lot, but instead of waiting for help, Wyatt gave in to my begging. Gave me what I was desperate to have. A second finger slipped into my pussy as I thought of him ripping my dress open, my breasts free and aching for the touch of his hands and lips. He would slip his tongue over my nipples as I feverishly tugged at his zipper until his thick cock was finally in my hands.

It was wrong—no, it was beyond wrong—to think about this, but once I started, I couldn't stop. The drug or potion that lion shifter had given me was still messing with my head, and all I could do was ride it out.

I rubbed at my clit with my free hand as the other continued to work in and out of me. My breaths left me in short, shallow gasps. The next image that flashed through my mind was Wyatt's hard and defined muscles coated in a sheen of sweat, strong hands clutching my hips as he fucked me. His cock slipped deep into me, all the way to his balls, and it was like I was complete. Whole. After twenty-three years of life, this moment was the most intense I'd ever had. The sensation of Wyatt filling me should have been awful to imagine. Instead, I released a contented sigh and thought about how good it would feel to reach up and play with my nipples while he took me.

For a few brief seconds, I wished it wasn't a fantasy. If imagining it made me feel this way, what would the real thing be like?

Before I could dive into that thought, a violent tremor shot through me. An explosion of rapture was building deep inside me, like I was being lifted high into the air, rising and preparing to crash down into ecstasy.

In my fantasy, Wyatt started fucking me faster, almost like his life depended on making me come. Sweat dripped from his brow onto my stomach, and I slid my fingers through it before cupping my breasts.

Then, like a bomb going off in my mind and body, pleasure surged from my pelvis, up my chest, and across my whole body. I kept pressing my fingers into myself, riding the wave. For a moment, I thought it would never end, but then it tapered and ebbed, leaving me a gasping and shivering puddle on my bed.

There was one last image of Wyatt, groaning and slamming his hips into me as his own orgasm struck. Smiling, I watched it in my mind's eye. The smile faded as quickly as it had come. My eyes snapped open, and I looked around, an immense and immediate guilt tinged with disgusted horror descending on me.

Sitting up, I took a deep breath and shivered. My skin crawled from my fantasy of the person who was my biggest nemesis, the one man who always managed to get under my skin.

He did more than get under my skin a moment before, I thought, then winced at my lame joke.

The worst part was that Wyatt was an inherently gorgeous man. Any other woman would be drooling and tripping over herself to get him to so much as look at her. That was not something I could ever imagine myself doing. We had too much history, too much baggage. No. I needed to forget I'd ever slipped and had those thoughts.

I blamed the drug. It had messed with my head and forced me into heat. If a fat, tottering old man with one leg and fungus on his face had found me instead of Wyatt, I'd have been all over him as well. It had nothing to do with Wyatt himself. That made sense, and it's what I told myself. What I repeated over and over, swearing I'd never have another unholy thought about Wyatt until the day I died.

Once I was mostly under control, I checked my nightstand and found my phone plugged in and ready. When I checked the home screen, I had to blink and double-check, then triple-check the date. I'd been out for three days? Holy shit. If that was true, then my mating ceremony was the next day.

I sagged back onto my pillows. Jayson and I had finally picked a date a few weeks before, but it might have been postponed due to my accident. I had a very faint memory of him being at the parking lot where Wyatt had found me. I closed my eyes as I tried to remember if that had been real or part of some fever dream I'd had over the last few days. No matter how hard I tried, all I could remember was Wyatt.

I gave up, not wanting to go down that path again. The guy was seared into my brain, and I needed to stop thinking about him. I hoped to the goddess that Jayson hadn't been there. That would make things even more awkward between him and Wyatt. The two had never liked each other.

After a few minutes, I decided to test out my legs. Swinging my feet out from under the covers, I stood. I didn't feel dizzy or too weak. What I did feel was disgusting. I could tell I hadn't bathed since the day of the operation. A shower would probably make it all a little better. Once I was cleaned up, it would be easier to face whatever blowback came from the failed operation.

In the bathroom, I stripped off my T-shirt and panties, then studied myself in the mirror. I'd lost a little weight, which accentuated my muscles more. A fresh, small white scar adorned my shoulder close to my clavicle. The fae healers had done a good job with it. It was faint enough that you wouldn't even notice it unless you knew it was there.

After showering, I dressed in a loose top, leggings, and sneakers, then dried my hair. It was amazing how much better I felt after getting cleaned up. As soon as I stepped out into the hallway, I heard a small gasp and saw Zoe leap to her feet. It looked like she'd been keeping vigil on a chair outside my room. Gods knew how long she'd been there.

She ran to me and wrapped her arms around me, tears streaming down her cheeks. "Oh my gosh. You're okay, you're really okay."

She burst into sobs, and all I could do was hold her in my embrace. Guilt trickled through me. Obviously, I hadn't done anything wrong, but my injury was causing Zoe's, which made me feel like crap.

Once her tears slowed, I patted her back. "Zoe, it's okay. I'm fine. It's all over."

Zoe released me, wiping at her eyes and nose. "Yeah. Your dress isn't okay, though. You ruined it," she said, chuckling slightly.

I smiled back at her. "Yeah, a knife to the shoulder and about a pint of blood will do that. I'll owe you one. How's that? Maybe a week straight of girl's nights? Mud masks, wine, sappy movies, and lots of chocolate?"

"Make it white chocolate, and you've got a deal."

I wrinkled my nose. "Weirdo. Fine."

"Oh, thank the goddess!" a voice called from behind us.

I turned to see my mother hurrying toward me. My father was walking behind her, a relieved smile on his face.

"We were just coming up to check on you," Mom said. "We've been worried sick."

Mom pulled me into an almost back-breaking embrace. She didn't weep like Zoe, but I could tell by how she clutched me that she'd been just as worried as my friend, if not more. When Mom finally released me, it was Dad's turn to hug me.

"We got the best doctors and healers the pack could afford," he said.

"And I told each one that if they messed anything up, I'd kill them," Zoe added.

Dad nodded. "I can confirm that."

My brother Kolton came jogging up the stairs, looking frantic. "Kiki?"

I rolled my eyes. "I nearly died, and you're still gonna call me that?"

Ignoring me, he scooped me into his arms and swung me around. I laughed, despite myself.

"I was really worried we'd have to put 'killed by lion-shifter roofie' on your tombstone," he said. "I'd never be able to visit your grave out of sheer embarrassment."

"Oh, shut up," I laughed, shoving him away.

"Kolton, you probably shouldn't be swinging the little brat around like that. She's still recovering."

The voice sent a wave of irritation through me. Wyatt. All the sexy thoughts I'd had twenty minutes ago had vanished. Shoving the memories of what I'd done in the parking lot out of my mind, I did my best to fight the shame even as heat began to rise in my cheeks and ears. We were back to our old feelings of disdain for each other.

I nodded to him. "Wyatt."

He cocked his eyebrow. "Kira."

I looked at Dad and Kolton. "I didn't know the Eleventh Pack was running with lone wolves now."

If the slight dig hurt Wyatt, he didn't show it. If anything, he looked pleased that I'd pointed out his status as a lone wolf.

Dad sighed and glanced over his shoulder at Wyatt before shaking his head. "You know Kolton and Wyatt are friends, Kira. Wyatt and his lone wolves have been a real help to us the last few years."

"Sure, but do we really want them in the house? How can we trust them? Are all his scraggly band of outsiders doing their best to intrude on families, like he is?" I asked with a curt nod toward Wyatt.

I could cut the tension in the air with a knife, but I couldn't stop myself. I hated relying on anyone or asking for help. The fact that Wyatt, of all people, had found me and called for help stuck in my craw and made it impossible for me not to try knocking him down a notch or two. My anger wasn't even directed at him, really, but at myself for having fantasized about him.

Kolton rolled his eyes. "I took Wyatt on a run, then came by to check on you. Chill the hell out."

"On a run?" I asked. "Now unofficial pack members go on runs?"

"Oh, stop. Both of you," Dad said. "Can't we all just be happy that Kira is okay?"

"Right," Kolton said. "I mean, shouldn't you simply be happy that Wyatt saved your life?"

I scoffed at him. "Zoe saved my life, not Wyatt."

"Uh, well..." Zoe cleared her throat. "I wouldn't have really known anything was wrong if Wyatt hadn't called Jayson. Then Jayson called me a few seconds later and demanded I get him there fast. You would have bled out and died. So, um, Wyatt did kinda save you."

I loved my best friend more than anything, but at that moment, I could have strangled her. She was telling the truth, but I'd have preferred her to go along with my memory of events.

Wyatt looked like he was trying to hide a smug smile. From the look on my parents' faces, I needed to end the argument. I sighed internally and steeled myself for what I was about to say.

"Umm, yeah. Thank you, Wyatt," I said through gritted teeth.

Wyatt waved a hand at me. "No problem. I'm sure one day you'll find a way to repay me for all the times I've stepped in to save your sorry butt."

The words struck me like a volley of flaming arrows, sending rage swirling within me. My eyes widened, but before I could unload on him, Mom interrupted us.

"Now that Kira is on the mend, we need to make sure everything is in place for the official mating ceremony tomorrow."

My mouth dropped open. I'd pretty much told myself the ceremony had been postponed. "So, it's still on?"

Mom nodded. "Yes. And a good thing, too. The rumors of war are intensifying each day. The sooner we bind our packs through this ceremony, the better. We'll need a strong ally to survive, so we decided to keep it on schedule. We didn't want to postpone unless you were still unconscious or in bad shape. That was actually what we were coming to check on." She smiled at me, a big beaming grin that spread across her entire face. "I'm so happy you and Jayson are finally becoming official."

"Yup," Zoe said in an emotionless monotone. "Really happy."

Kolton had vanished at the mention of the ceremony, disappearing back to his room downstairs. Wyatt, for some reason, was still standing there, acting like he was part of the conversation.

I lifted my hand and shooed him off. "If you're looking for another thank you, you'll be there in a few decades. Can we have some privacy?"

He scowled and opened his mouth to say something, but Mom continued gushing about the ceremony.

"I'm sure Jayson will be so happy to finally have you as a mate. Goodness, you'll be gorgeous in that dress. I bet you'll be more beautiful than the Moon Goddess herself."

Wyatt left while she spoke. I breathed a sigh of relief. Neither he nor Kolton was happy about my betrothal to Jayson, but it would help our pack's standing, and I was ready to do whatever I needed to make that happen.

Lower-ranking packs were desperate to maintain the ancient status quo and prevent the mingling of species, whereas higher-ranked packs were more open to changing things. What should have been a simple disagreement between neighboring factions was rapidly becoming a raging inferno of dissent. There'd already been some incursions into pack lands by rival packs. Even out here in the Eastern Wilds, Tranquility operatives had their hands full quelling small fights between the packs that had broken out. War was coming—everyone could feel it—and if my mating with Jayson could help my family and packmates survive, I'd do it a hundred times over.

"Where did your brother go?" Mom asked when she finally realized he was gone.

"Didn't want to stick around and hear all about tomorrow's festivities," Zoe said. "He's not Jayson's biggest fan." She shrugged. "Honestly, I can't say I am, either."

"This is about more than happiness," Dad said. "Kira is binding our pack to the Ninth Pack. It's important for us to ally ourselves. We're on the outskirts and nowhere near as strong as the higher packs. The Ninth's strength will be more than we can defend against if another war breaks out between packs. Like your mother said, the rumors are intensifying."

Little skirmishes were always breaking out between packs, but there'd been more drama and aggression going around in the last few years. There was a definite sense that things might escalate to an all-out war. That's why my family had been so happy when I'd matched with Jayson as my fated mate.

"This way," Dad went on, "Kira is at least doing something to make our pack proud."

That stung. It was a point of contention in the pack that I was a latent alpha. But I refused to let my wolf out and had suppressed it as deeply as I possibly could. It was *not* normal and a badge of shame on my family—one I happily ignored, even though I knew my parents had always hoped a strong alpha would emerge from our family.

Suppressing my wolf had been my decision. Even thinking about letting it out brought back dark memories that were better left buried. The pack could be displeased all they wanted, but they didn't get to tell me what I could and couldn't do with my own body. Mating with Jayson was the best way for me to give Dad what he'd always wanted: a stronger pack.

The unrest between the packs did not inspire confidence. Dad was right when he said there was no way the Eleventh Pack could defend against a full attack by something like the Fourth or Fifth packs, or gods forbid, the First Pack. That thought sent a shiver of fear through me. I would do whatever was necessary to make sure we were strong enough to fend off an attack.

"Kira, sweetie, do you want to go practice on your hair and makeup for tomorrow?" Mom asked, pulling me out of my thoughts.

"Yeah," Zoe said with a smile. "I've got some ideas. When I'm done with you, Jayson will want to rip your clothes off."

Dad grimaced and walked away. "My cue to leave," he said over his shoulder.

"Sure," I said. "Let's give it a shot."

I followed my mother and Zoe back into my room. I wasn't excited about the mating ceremony at all. Jayson was fine, but not who I'd have chosen for myself—not by a long shot. All I could do was put the worry out of my mind and let Mom and Zoe fuss over me. Tomorrow would be a big day, and I needed to be ready.

Chapter 4 - Wyatt

Kolton sat across from me. He'd retreated to his room after his mother had started talking about the ceremony, and I'd joined him not long after. Even after three damn days, I was still stewing about that jackass Jayson. Kolton was working on a college assignment as a muted basketball game played on the TV. I was pretending to watch the game, but I was pissed as hell.

I prided myself on being able to forgive and forget. The past was the past. Mistakes happened. That was all fine and good, but Jayson's selfishness and childishness when he'd seen Kira's rubbed me the wrong way. She'd nearly bled to death in my arms. While she was crying from the agony of her forced heat and stab wound, all Jayson had done was bitch and moan about wanting to go home—and rage about me touching what was his. Like Kira was a car or a pair of pants that belonged to him.

He was a lazy piece of shit, a pampered rich kid—but what more could one expect from the spoiled son of the Ninth Pack's alpha? Kira's parents were excited about her being matched to him and strengthening their pack's standing. I tried to be happy as well, but the guy had dragged his feet on setting a date for the ceremony. Five freaking years? Kira had done the mate-matching bloodwork and paired with Jayson half a decade ago, and he'd only now decided to have the ceremony. What sense did that make?

The day Kira had matched with Jayson, Kolton had told me. Apparently, she hadn't been super enthused by the idea. Not even a little bit. Still, she'd put on a brave face for her parents because they were over the moon that their daughter's fated mate was the son of a pack alpha.

After getting to know Jayson, I could see why Kira was emotionless about it. On paper, Jayson was a prize. In reality? He was the cheap plastic toy at the bottom of a cereal box. Pretty to look at but dull, spoiled, and boring.

Being a lone wolf gave me better insight into how our world worked. Most other creatures had a more romantic way of finding mates. Humans, fae, merpeople, and all the others? They fell in love, and that was that. It was much less pragmatic than the way wolves went about it. Blood shouldn't direct the rest of your life. Getting stuck with a jerk like Jayson who couldn't look past his own needs to see how much danger Kira was in the other day? It didn't sit right with me.

In my opinion, a blood test was no way to find a mate. But who the hell asked me? The Tranquility Council wasn't knocking my door down for suggestions. If they ever did, though, I'd give them an earful.

"Bro, you good?" Kolton asked.

Shaken from my thoughts, I looked up. He was staring at me with a look that bordered on worry and confusion. My internal thoughts must have shown on my face.

I gave a slight shake of my head. "Just thinking about how your parents are pretty much the only ones looking forward to the mating ceremony. I mean, if that's the case, why don't they call it off?"

Kolton barked out a laugh. "Good luck convincing Kira of that. Trust me, I've tried. We've talked about it. She's not all starry-eyed about Jayson—I could see that from day one—but she's so fucking stubborn. Initially, it was about going along with tradition, but she'll do whatever it takes to make the pack and this family proud, especially with the building tensions of the last year. She wants our pack to be stronger so we can survive whatever fight ends up breaking out. You know how rare it is for inter-pack mating to happen. Kira sees this pairing with Jayson as a blessing for the Eleventh Pack, not for herself." He shrugged in defeat. "It is what it is."

His acceptance made me even angrier. I leaned forward, elbows on my knees. "Kira's being unreasonable. You wouldn't do something like this if you were in her shoes. Why can't she see reason? She's about to ruin her life and mate with a total dick."

"I'm not saying you're wrong, but she's maniacally driven to prove herself and make something of herself in the pack's eyes because she can't shift. She's got this chip on her shoulder, like she's somehow lacking because of that."

I kept my mouth shut. He had a point, but there were things he didn't know, and it wasn't my place to say anything. I looked down at his textbook, feeling a sense of pride in my friend. Kolton had been hustling his ass at a local community college with the goal of transferring to Talbot University in Fangmore City, the wolf-shifter capital of the world. His parents, however, were adamant that he needed to finish his education in the Eastern Wilds and stay close to home. They wanted him ready and willing to take over as pack alpha. I thought that was dumb. Kolton and Kira had no autonomy to do as they liked. Their parents were treating them like little kids.

Kolton slapped his book closed and rubbed his eyes. "Okay, I need a break. I'm going to go cross-eyed if I study anymore. Want a snack or something?"

I stood and stretched. "Yeah. Then I need to check on some stuff with some of my guys. I've been here for days. I should make sure they're good."

I was a lone wolf, but over the years, I'd grouped up with a small group of guys. We were all the same—guys who'd lost their packs in some way and were now on their own. I was the de facto leader of the group, but Kolton's parents had taken us in a long time ago. Back in the day, that had been a minor scandal, but we'd done our best to prove we were worth it. Most shifters looked down on lone wolves with disdain, which was one of the reasons I didn't make my opinions overtly known to anyone but Kolton. We would never be official Eleventh Pack members, and that was fine with us, but the support of a pack kept us safer than we'd be on our own.

I followed Kolton down the hallway to the living room but came up short when I saw Kira sitting on the edge of the couch. Zoe was painting swirling symbols on her face. Kira looked so serene and calm that I couldn't help but see how beautiful she was.

Another flush of anger burst in me. I'd been here for days, slept on the couch in Kolton's room every night, waiting for Kira to wake up, to be okay, and Jayson hadn't stopped by once. The guy couldn't even be bothered to check on this beautiful woman who was supposed to be his fated mate. I gritted my teeth but kept my face impassive as Zoe caught sight of us.

"Hey, guys," Zoe said. "How does the lovely bride look?"

Kira opened her eyes, and irritation flashed across her face when she saw me. Before I could answer Zoe, Kira said, "Save it. I don't need to hear your opinion, Wyatt. It means less than nothing."

Taking a calming breath, I said, "I'm glad I hold a place of such high esteem. It's too bad your soon-to-be mate doesn't care enough to stop by. He apparently isn't concerned about your appearance, either." I shrugged nonchalantly. "From the looks of it, he doesn't give a damn if you're alive."

Kolton snorted a laugh, but Kira glared daggers at me. "Shouldn't you be out there checking on your little band of misfits?" She arched a curved eyebrow. "Aren't you supposed to be working today? Or did the Tranquility Council kick you out of the operatives?"

I crossed my arms and looked at the ceiling, pretending to make some very careful calculations before looking at her again. "Oh, yeah, that's right. The operative schedules got all mixed up when one of our agents allowed herself to get drugged and nearly killed. If only one of the operatives had shown up and told everyone to abort the mission. Man, things would have turned out way better if they'd all listened to that guy's gut instinct."

Zoe's cheeks puffed up. "Okay, maybe we should talk about something a little less—"

"What exactly are you getting at Wyatt?" Kira demanded.

I gave her a mock look of surprise and confusion. "Who? Me? I'm just saying you're a magnet for trouble, and I constantly have to swoop in and save your ass."

Kolton whistled through his teeth, knowing I'd stepped on a hornet's nest. Everyone was well aware of her background. Kira was a fierce operative, with tons of awards and accolades to prove it, but her fearlessness had put her in dire predicaments more than once before—enough that even she had to know it was a problem. She tended to get very defensive about it. The irritation on her face was quickly skyrocketing to full-blown rage.

"Okay, guys, I still need to do her nails," Zoe said, stepping in before an explosion of curses and shouting started. "We're about to watch last season's rerun of *The Reject Project*. You can stay, but then there needs to be a truce. Got it?"

Kolton made a derogatory noise with his tongue. "That's like watching cock fighting. The whole show is barbaric. Zoe, how do you not get sick watching it?"

I was with Kolton on that. The show was too much. I'd actively refrained from watching it my whole life because it was not my cup of tea, but it seemed Kolton and I were in the minority.

Zoe folded her hands in her lap and gave Kolton a sickly-sweet look. "Well, Mister Wolfboy, the show has been on for thirty years, which means I'm obviously not the only one who likes it."

"You're saying that because it's been on since before we were born, it's moral?" Kolton asked with an incredulous look.

Zoe laughed. "Who said it was moral? You could argue porn is immoral, but millions of humans and creatures watch that."

Kolton pointed at her. "So you admit that the show is like torture porn or something?"

"No. I know I used big words, so I can see how you got confused. I was comparing moralities. What I'm saying is that the whole world is mesmerized by it, not only wolf shifters. *The Reject Project* is the highest-rated show in *every* demographic. If you've got something that even fallen angels want to watch, you know it's good."

"But–"

Zoe held up a hand to stop Kolton. "Now I will admit, if you think too long about some of the stuff that happens, it is awful. I mean...I don't *like* watching people die, but they all signed up for it, and it's more of a cultural thing. In the past, wolf shifters went through similar trials to find their mate, and lots of them died. It's part of why you all do the blood test thing now. It's a show, and that's that. Watch it or don't. I, on the other hand, love the drama. It's sort of romantic. A bunch of rejected alphas competing to win the heart of a rejected female. The whole thing where the Moon Goddess comes and blesses their new union at the end." Zoe sighed and smiled, her eyes glassy. "It's dreamy. And honestly, if I knew I was going to find a lifelong partner, I'd think long and hard about taking part in the dangerous missions and tasks they go through. It's exciting to watch."

Kolton laughed and shook his head. "Okay. You do you. I'm gonna grab something to eat."

He was gone before I had a chance to say anything. Zoe and Kolton always picked at each other like they were siblings. I usually found it entertaining, but I hadn't enjoyed it this time. I was still stewing about Jayson and how Kira was about to ruin her life. The guy was a piece of work and spoiled rotten— always had been. He clearly didn't give a shit about Kira, but either no one else saw it, or they were too blinded by the prospect of aligning the packs.

I was almost out the door when I stopped and turned back to Kira.

"Hey, can you debrief your team at some point? I gave them a basic rundown, but they still need your account. The big wigs aren't too happy about what went down."

Kira held out her hand for Zoe to paint her nails and rolled her eyes. "Thanks, Wyatt, but I'm a big girl. I'll take care of it. I can handle things without you being anal about everything."

I suppressed a groan of annoyance and walked out before we started sniping at each other again. As much as Kira and I disliked each other, she was still my coworker and my best friend's sister. I couldn't help but worry about her. I couldn't simply erase my concerns, no matter how much I wished I could.

Tomorrow, I'd have to watch her bind herself to an unworthy piece of dog shit. She'd have to spend the rest of her life waking up next to Jayson Fell. Lord, how would I ever be able to watch that happen? Maybe I should just vanish. Leave my unofficial pack, resign from the council, and go out into the world as a true lone wolf. As terrifying and dangerous as that prospect was, I thought it might be preferable to watching Jayson and Kira together all the time. Especially knowing he viewed her as nothing but a piece of arm candy.

She was more than that. It was too bad her mate didn't see what I saw.

Chapter 5 - Kira

The forest around me had gone completely still. There was no chirping of insects or trilling of birds. I glanced around and wondered if the animals were being silent as a form of respect...or mourning. A bitter grin crossed my lips. Maybe the forest creatures shared Wyatt's opinion on what was about to happen.

Wyatt? Why was I thinking about him at a time like this? I sighed and gritted my teeth, chastising myself for letting my mind drift to him on the day of my mating ceremony. My mind drifted to the fantasy I'd had, but I slammed the door on it before it could fully form. Today was about Jayson and me.

Not Wyatt.

I turned my focus back to the present. My dress really was beautiful. The gauzy red fabric trailed behind me, flowing atop the rose petals that had been strewn about. But the simple thoughts of my dress were drowned out by the hammering of my heart as the moment I'd step out of the forest grew ever closer. The murmurs of the crowd drifted toward me.

As I leaned out from behind a tree trunk, I could see the entire Eleventh Pack gathered for the ceremony—hundreds of attendees, all with their faces painted in traditional tribal markings. The swirling patterns and runes symbolized fated mates and fertility.

Mating ceremonies were ancient occasions everyone looked forward to and celebrated. It was supposed to be a time of great happiness and revelry. From the look on everyone's faces, they were excited and ready. It made the lump of depression in my chest even heavier. I didn't love Jayson. I'd come to that realization years ago. This was a pairing of power, nothing more. I wished I did love him, but it was what it was. I was doing what I needed to for my pack.

Lots of shifters mated without loving each other. You were fated to whom you were fated. Simple as that. One thing that excited me was the fact that my parents and the rest of the pack would gain a huge amount of influence once I bound myself to the Ninth Pack. The pride that gave me pushed the depression aside. I was finally doing something that made them all proud. I'd give Jayson as many pups as he wanted, even though the thought of mating with Jayson wasn't incredibly pleasant. I felt no desire or sexual connection to him, and the idea of him fucking me made me cringe a bit. Still, I'd be the best mate imaginable, and I'd do it all with a smile.

Though...maybe things would be easier if I could get my hands on whatever drug that lion shifter had slipped me. The idea was tempting. At least then, I might want to do it with Jayson. But anything was worth throwing off the stigma of being a latent alpha.

Nervously, I smoothed my dress for the hundredth time. The color was a deep crimson, almost the color of blood. Zoe had picked it out for me. It was the second dress she'd chosen. The first had been a bright white dress with lots of tulle and satin. I'd gaped at it in horror. It took nearly an hour to explain to her that white dresses were only worn at human and fae weddings. Shifters—wolves at least—never wore white for weddings. There was no reason behind it; it was simply tradition. Red, violet, and other dark colors were used for these ceremonies. I'd never seen Zoe as confused as when I'd explained that to her.

Honestly, I understood where she was coming from. The entire thing was confusing even to me. Official mating ceremonies weren't necessary per se. It was a show, a public display of what was supposed to have already taken place in the heart. Fated mates were so intrinsic and sacred that the Moon Goddess Heline herself sanctioned them. The only thing Jayson and I had to do to seal the bond was recognize that our souls were bound together and claim each other in a way that attached our souls forever.

That had set Zoe into a fit of laughter, and she'd had a hard time catching her breath. Once she'd gotten herself under control, she'd told me she couldn't imagine Jayson ever feeling anything as sappy as that. My mother had frowned darkly at that, and Zoe had gone ahead and painted the symbols on my face. My friend disliked Jayson, but that was fine. She wasn't the one who needed to prove herself. I was.

I took a tentative step forward; it wasn't time yet, but I couldn't help wanting to catch a glimpse of the mating circle. I'd attended dozens of ceremonies here, but it looked so different when you were the one who would be stepping out there. The Ninth Pack had joined my pack, and together, they surrounded the clearing. The mating circle was an ancient and sacred area that had been used for mating ceremonies for centuries. I'd known I'd be stepping out into this place five years ago when the blood test had confirmed our pairing. All I wished was that this had happened sooner. Five long years of Jayson and I going back and forth on when to do it had caused my parents intense stress.

I gave a little sigh as, finally, the alliance would now be forged in blood. Both packs could rest easy knowing they were stronger with the specter of a coming wolf-shifter war.

A camera crew stood at the very far radius of the clearing. The ceremony would be broadcast to the world since the general population found wolf-shifter fated mates spell-binding for some reason. It was part of why *The Reject Project* was so popular. I couldn't fathom why any other creature or species would care how another chose their mates. A blood test had replaced the ancient battles waged for mates—battles that had caused all the wars in our history. At this point, choosing your mate had become as simple and boring as a dentist visit.

Mom was excited, though, which was nice. I wanted her to enjoy this. It was pure duty for me. Jayson would probably be a good father, a strong alpha, and would take care of my people. The match was suitable and exactly what my pack needed. But other than that, I was bereft of any exultation. Even my inner wolf was quiet, which was strange. All my life, I'd heard how excited my wolf would be to bind herself to her fated mate.

Perhaps things would get more exciting when my heat came in. My real heat, not whatever that lion had done to me. If it was anything like that experience, Jayson and I would be much more emotionally attached. If the way I'd felt toward Wyatt, someone I despised, was any indication, things would be even better with my actual mate. Or so I hoped.

In the distance, I watched Jayson walk out of the crowd into the center of the circle. That was my cue. A massive flutter of butterflies swarmed in my stomach, but I took a steadying breath and took my first step out of the forest. At the very edge of the circle of wolves stood Zoe, hands clasped beneath her chin and a huge smile on her face. She wasn't a wolf, but she had been granted access to watch on the condition that she stay well back, like the camera crew.

All I could concentrate on was not tripping over my dress. The last thing I wanted was face-plant in front of everyone. As I moved closer to the crowd, I saw my parents. Mom swiped at her tears, crying from happiness. Dad stood tall, doing his best to look as regal as possible.

The Eleventh Pack were all watching with excitement and happiness, but the Ninth Pack seemed much more stoic. Their alpha, Jayson's father, watched me walk toward the circle with an expression that bordered on disinterest. Jayson's younger brother Gavin looked like he'd rather be anywhere but here. I held my head high, trying to ignore the dark looks. It seemed some of Jayson's family had the same opinions of me that Kolton and Wyatt had of Jayson. That was their prerogative. No matter what our families and friends thought, Jayson and I were fated to each other.

Wyatt was standing next to Kolton, and a flicker of anger flashed through me when I saw him. He wasn't officially part of the Eleventh Pack and shouldn't have been there, which meant my father must have made an exception for him.

The sudden flash of anger vanished when I noticed a small group of Tranquility operatives at the outer edge of the circle. Douglas and Carter were there with several high-ranking council members. Wyatt had been right about my superiors being unhappy with me. The lion shifter had gotten away, and part of that blame was placed on me. They thought it had been careless of me to ingest whatever drug he'd slipped me. It had all happened so fast, and, in my defense, that asshole had been really smooth about it. He'd drugged my wine as seamlessly as a human magician made a coin vanish.

I gritted my teeth and forced myself to focus on what was important: my ceremony. When I looked at Jayson, I almost faltered. He didn't have the customary runes and symbols painted on his face. I kept walking but wondered why. Maybe the Ninth Pack wasn't as traditional as others. Still, he was dressed in some of the nicest clothes I'd ever seen, and as I approached, he stepped forward to face me. My worries quickly faded.

We stood facing each other for several awkward seconds. Traditionally, the male mate spoke first, but Jayson was looking around, almost as if he was uncomfortable. Had I ever attended a Ninth Pack mating ceremony? Did they do things differently? Maybe.

Inwardly rolling my eyes, I decided to take the reins and get things started. I was sure the goddess would overlook such a small change to protocol.

Pulling my shoulders back and lifting my chin, I began. "I, Kira Lana Durst, bring myself to bestow my body and soul to my fated mate, Jayson Chadwick Fell. My future is his, as his future is mine. Every full moon, every breath, and each day, I will be held under his sway as he will be under mine. I claim him as my mate fully and completely. I do this under the eyes of my pack and his. I speak these words beneath the gaze of the Moon Goddess Heline herself. May she bless us if you so claim me as well."

Throughout the entire recitation, I'd tried to keep my eyes on Jayson's, but his gaze had fixed on a spot in the crowd. A quick glance showed me he was looking at Wyatt. Nervous energy suddenly flicked through me. Sweat gathered in my armpits, and my palms became clammy. My inner wolf burrowed even deeper into the shelter I'd built around her, almost like she was trying to hide from the entire spectacle. Her worry was overwhelming.

Jayson looked uncomfortable, like he wasn't sure what to do next. My gods, had he not learned the words? Was that the problem? My irritation and worry gave way to anger.

I leaned forward and hissed, "You can start anytime now."

Jayson cleared his throat, then cast an uncomfortable glance over his shoulder at his father and brother. The knot in my stomach quickly clenched into a stone of doubt. This was not how things were supposed to go. Something was wrong. Something was very, very wrong.

Jayson's father gave an imperious nod. Jayson turned back toward me, though he still couldn't look me in the eyes. I was suddenly very nauseous.

"I, Jayson Chadwick Fell, son of the alpha of the Ninth Pack, under the gaze of the Moon Goddess Heline, do reject this mate as dishonorable and lacking in devotion." His voice boomed out across the crowd.

My whole world tilted on its axis. My stomach dropped. Shock and disbelief overtook me, and it was all I could do to keep my legs from giving way. A sharp, stabbing pain shot through my chest, almost as bad as the knife wound. It settled into my bones, my guts, my heart. That was when I knew he was serious.

He'd truly severed the fated bond between us. This wasn't his idea of a stupid, ill-timed joke. The magical connection had been broken.

Angry shouts erupted from the Eleventh Pack. Curses and screams of rage came so fast, they turned into a single sound, almost like static. My entire future had been upended in an instant. I was still trying to get Jayson to make eye contact, to see if I could read something there, but he turned away and walked back to his father's side.

Ignoring the shouts, Jayson's father stepped forward and shouted over the commotion.

Pointing an accusatory finger at me, he shouted, "We were willing to overlook this woman's bizarre inability to shift, but we cannot allow the future alpha of the Ninth Pack to tie himself to a woman who is loose with her body. A whore is not an acceptable mate for an alpha."

"Fuck you, motherfucker!" Kolton's voice rang out, audible above anyone else.

A whore? Loose? I was losing my battle with my legs and slowly sliding to the ground. It was like I'd been kicked in the chest. My breath wouldn't come. I couldn't breathe. Was I suffocating? Everything had been shattered in an instant.

Zoe's voice broke through. "She's not a whore! If you think that, you're an idiot."

Her chastising the alpha of the Ninth Pack was met with angry jeers from both sides. As neither a member of either pack nor a wolf shifter, Zoe had no place here and no right to speak. I worried for her safety, but I couldn't shake myself out of this haze.

Jayson's father spoke again. "She went into her heat in the arms of another shifter. A filthy lone wolf, of all people. The very fact that the Eleventh Pack is weak enough to align with such rabble is more evidence that they are beneath us and unworthy of our alliance."

The ceremony devolved into chaos. High-ranking members of the Eleventh Pack shouted that they'd banish me from the pack, expel me as a lone wolf, whatever it took to get back into the Ninth's good graces. Some of these people were relatives, some I'd thought were my friends. Now they were offering me up as a sacrifice. I glanced around and saw Kolton shoving one of the men who'd shouted out the offer. My father, face gray and eyes dazed, stared at the ground in shock as if it had vanished under his feet. Mom sobbed into her handkerchief, her eyes never meeting mine.

The council members, looking disgusted, turned away; Carter and Douglas had a mixture of pity and disappointment in their eyes as they turned their backs on me. Everything was falling apart. It was like my entire life had been a balloon and Jayson's words a pin. I had to fix it. There had to be a way. This had been my one chance to make my pack proud.

Steadying my legs, I lunged forward, grabbing Jayson's sleeve and tugging him around, making him look at me.

"Jayson? Please, we can fix this. Don't do this. It wasn't my fault. Please." The last word came out like a pitiful whine. I was ashamed of the way I was begging, but I couldn't stop myself.

Jayson's lip curled up in disgust. "Don't touch me, you filthy whore."

He yanked his hand from my grip and vanished into the forest. His words slammed into me. All I'd ever tried to do was bring pride to my family and pack. Being rejected like this, in public, was almost more than I could take. Some of my packmates were still shouting at the Ninth Pack, but everyone was moving away into the surrounding woods. I was left in the clearing, disgraced and on my knees. Humiliation cascaded over me, followed by shame, horror, and a sick feeling swelling within me.

A pair of eyes caught my attention. Striking green and incredibly intense. Wyatt. Pity and hurt radiated from his gaze. Pity for me.

It was too much. I couldn't bear it. Not from him.

I ran. My dress tore under my feet as I sprinted into the woods, the screams of anger and shouted arguments fading behind me. As I rushed headlong into the forest, my heart shattered more with every step. I'd ruined everything, even though I hadn't done anything wrong. The physical pain of the rejection became a throbbing ache inside me. My mind flashed back and forth between shame, anger, and despair. I had to fix this. Somehow. For the first time in twelve years, the searing burn of tears stung my eyes.

Chapter 6 - Wyatt

Kolton paced back and forth across my living room. His rage hadn't abated an ounce since the disaster the day before. He'd become intimately familiar with one of the pillows on my couch. Every hour or so, he'd grab it and either slam it to the ground or kick it across the room. It bore no resemblance to Jayson Fell, but my friend must have mentally imprinted that jackass's face onto it.

I let him vent. Better he did it here instead of at his house. That place was like a mausoleum. I'd gone over there four times since the ceremony had burst into metaphorical flames to check on Kira, but there'd been no sign of her. She'd still not returned home after escaping into the forest.

My own anger was running as hot as Kolton's, but it was simmering under the surface. If Kolton was a tornado, shouting and cursing into the void, then I was a volcano—hot, boiling molten rock, ready to erupt at any time. I still couldn't believe what I'd witnessed the day before. Not only the rejection but the way it had affected Kira. She'd cried. *Actual* tears. It hadn't been the same as the tears of pain she'd cried after being stabbed and drugged. No, she'd cried true tears of anguish. I'd only been witness to that once in all the time I'd known her. That day had been hell, and it looked like Jayson's rejection had hit her almost as badly.

It agitated both Kolton and me that she'd shed a single tear for that spoiled piece of shit. Sure, he was the heir to the Ninth Pack, but other than that, what did he have to offer? A substandard IQ, a pissy attitude, and an unwarranted sense of self-importance. I clenched my jaw, my teeth creaking as I remembered the look of relief on his face when he'd rejected Kira. The relief *and* the smug glint in his eyes.

I tried to remember if I'd ever heard or read about a rejection as public, embarrassing, or brutal, but I couldn't come up with anything. No legends mentioned anything close to what Kira had gone through, and if there was one thing people in the past had loved, it was drama and heartbreak. He'd had ample time to reject her in private instead of doing it in front of the gods and everyone. Nothing would change my mind that he'd done it purposefully to rip away her every shred of dignity. To eviscerate her ego and ensure she could never recover. I wasn't sure what I'd do if I ever came face to face with him again, but it would be a moment Jayson Fell would regret for the rest of his days. Of that, I was one hundred percent sure.

Kolton, spotting my poor throw pillow again, picked it up and threw it across the room. It struck the wall with a muffled *whomp.*

"I don't think that's going to help," I said.

Kolton turned, fists clenched. "It makes me *feel* better."

I shrugged. It probably did, but he needed to get himself under control. This wasn't about our anger or hatred. His sister had just been shamed in front of two packs, members of the Tranquility Council, and her family and friends. One good thing was that the film crew had been stopped and their cameras destroyed. At least the video of the entire fiasco wouldn't be sent out to the entire world. The only saving grace was that it hadn't been broadcast live.

Even so, word was spreading like wildfire. Fated-mate rejections were incredibly rare, especially when an heir of a pack was to be paired with the eldest alpha daughter of another pack. Even though Kira was a latent alpha, she was still an alpha. The whole fiasco was being talked about everywhere.

Kolton flopped down on the couch beside me and hung his head. He stared off into space, then shook his head.

"I'm usually on the same wavelength as Kira. We've sort of always been able to help each other through things, but I have no clue what to do now. I feel so damned guilty about it all. That's why I'm mad. This is partly my fault."

I frowned at him. "Where'd you get that idea from? That's some pretty crazy mental gymnastics."

"No, it's not. I was born first. I'm tabbed to be the next leader of the Eleventh Pack. Kira's an alpha, too, though. Super rare in a female, and even though she can't shift, she constantly made sure my parents knew she would lead the way. Kira's always known I had no desire to be the pack alpha, that I had other dreams. She took the entire burden of my parents' expectations onto her shoulders. She was determined to find a match that would strengthen the packs, either by combining us with another or creating a powerful alliance that would keep me from having to take the mantle."

Kolton was very intelligent and had also been born an alpha. With Kira's shifting ability suppressed, he was expected to take over. Kolton wanted that about as much as most people wanted a root canal. It all made sense now. Kira had latched onto the idea of mating with Jayson to bring pride, power, and prestige to her pack and save her brother from a life of misery. It made what happened the day before sting all the more.

"Those motherfuckers," Kolton hissed. "Gods-damned Ninth Pack motherfuckers. I'm willing to drop everything—school, Fangmore City, all of it—if it means wiping those smug bastards off the earth. No one humiliates my sister like that and gets away with it."

Kolton's reaction was out of character. In all the years we'd been friends, I'd never seen him so angry and full of hate. This betrayal had done more than harm the Eleventh Pack; it had devastated both Durst siblings. I wanted to see Kira and find out how she was dealing with it.

"I'm going to check in with Zoe. Maybe she's talked to Kira and knows how she's doing," I said, standing up.

Kolton blew out a breath. "Sounds good. I think she's still waiting for Kira at my parents' place. It's possible she's made contact with her. Even at the best of times, Zoe spends more time at our house than at her place in the city."

We decided to walk instead of drive. The Dursts' house was only half a mile from my place, and Kolton and I needed the fresh air. As we walked, I tried to think what I'd say to Kira if I found her, but everything I came up with sounded hollow and silly. How did you console someone who'd had their whole future ripped out from under them? Especially when that person wasn't your biggest fan in the first place?

Upon entering through the front door, Kolton and I froze and sniffed at the air. Kira's scent was there, and it was fresh. It was the first time I'd scented her since the ceremony. It meant she'd finally come home. Hope mingled with worry on Kolton's face. I probably looked the same way.

I heard Zoe's voice coming from the den. It sounded like she was ranting about something. Preparing myself for the worst, I headed toward the room. My imagination flicked through a dozen different scenarios. Kira, in pajamas, crying on the couch. Kira, still wearing her ceremony dress, staring off into space. Kira, with a tub of ice cream in her lap, binge-eating and watching TV.

Kolton and I stopped short as we stepped into the den. Zoe stopped talking, her face red and flushed, but she quickly schooled her expression at the sight of us. Kira, for her part, looked totally calm. What was even stranger was her clothing. She was dressed in her field gear. Full Tranquility ops uniform. My brow furrowed as I took in the sight. She looked more irritated that we'd interrupted her conversation with Zoe than anything else.

"Come on in," she said.

When Kolton and I exchanged another confused look, she huffed, "I'm not glass. You aren't going to break me."

Kolton walked over to sit beside her on the couch. "Kiki? Are you okay? How are you holding up?"

The nickname he used for her was usually said with such sweetness, it made my teeth hurt. But this time, his voice sounded so sad and hesitant that all I could think of was the two of them as children. For a moment, I didn't see two adults on the couch. Instead, they were two kids, one trying to console the other.

Kira nodded. "Oh, life's just peachy."

The words were stated flatly. Kira didn't even try to make it sound believable. That worried me. The look in her eyes worried me as well. I'd known her long enough to know when she was planning something dumb or dangerous. Hell, I'd spent years trying to prevent her from doing dumb and dangerous shit.

Kolton gestured at her clothes. "Um...why are you in your ops gear?"

Ignoring the question, Kira stood. "Anyone want a snack?"

Without another word, she walked through the arched doorway into the dining room and then into the kitchen. I shot Zoe a questioning glance, but she only rolled her eyes and shook her head. The three of us followed Kira into the kitchen, where she was pulling a loaf of bread and a jar of peanut butter out of the pantry.

Kolton watched her go through the motions of making the sandwich. I could tell by his expression that he was confused and concerned. Kira's face was set in stone as she smeared her knife across the bread.

"Still pining over Jayson?" I asked.

Kira spared me one sharp glance over her shoulder. "Oh, I bet you'd love that, wouldn't you?" She made a *pfft* sound. "No time to think about that shithead. I've been too busy with work."

"Work?" Kolton and I say almost in unison.

The knife clattered to the plate as she tossed it down and whirled around to glare at us. "Yes. Some of us have to work to make money and get douchebags off the street."

"You almost died a few days ago," I said, taking a step toward her. "There is no reason for you to be going on missions when you're not fully healed. You need to recover physically...and mentally," I added with a shrug.

Her eyes flashed. "What I do, and how I choose to recover, is not your business, Wyatt."

"It is my business when I'm always running around and saving you from danger."

Kira grabbed her sandwich and hurled it in my direction. I dodged, and the sandwich hit the wall with a sad little thump and slid to the floor, leaving a trail of peanut butter in its wake.

"I guess you haven't heard the good news. You won't have to worry about saving me anymore. I've just been terminated as a Tranquility Operative. Effective immediately. I've been fired."

My eyes nearly popped out of my head. What? The council fired Kira? The words didn't make sense. All the ribbing about having to be her white knight and swooping in to save her was mostly my way of getting under her skin. Kira was the best operative in our region. She'd had over a hundred successful operations and arrested countless perpetrators. There'd been the fiasco with the lion shifter, yes, but that was a blip. I was sure we'd eventually catch his trail again and bring him in. Surely it wasn't because she'd been drugged. Any operative could have fallen prey to that. The guy had slipped the drug into her wine so swiftly and discreetly, I'd barely seen it. None of the others had seen it, either.

"Why would they fire you?" I asked incredulously.

Her eyes narrowed, her lip curling in disgust. "Think about it, Wyatt."

My face must have looked ridiculous as my brain churned. Suddenly, something clicked into place. Something I'd never thought about because it wasn't pertinent to my job. Tranquility's district commander was mated to Jayson Fell's aunt. That meant family ties, backroom deals, and dirty deeds.

"Son of a bitch," I whispered.

Kira smiled at me bitterly. "Worked it out, did you?"

"What the hell's going on?" Kolton asked.

I glanced at him. "Jayson Fell has family high up with the council. He got Kira fired. His fucking aunt and uncle pulled strings to have her terminated."

"Shitheel," Zoe muttered under her breath, but she didn't look surprised. It was probably what she'd been railing about when we walked into the house.

Taking a few deep, angry breaths, I strode to the door. "I'm going to go have a word with the Fell family."

I'd managed to get out the front door when Kira suddenly grabbed my arm and spun me around to face her.

"I don't need you fighting my battles for me."

"That's not what this is about," I snapped. "Someone has to do something. I can't let them railroad you without repercussions."

"Oh my gods," she said with a roll of her eyes. "You're such a control freak."

That comment hurt more than it should have because I could see through her false bravado, see the cracks showing in Kira's legendary armor. She was truly hurt and falling apart inside, and there was nothing I could do to help her. She was too stubborn to let any of us in. Too angry and bitter to do more.

"Kira—"

"No, Wyatt. I'll confront the Fells when I feel the time is right. But right now, I'm fucking tired. Okay?"

The conviction in that last word calmed me down a bit, even as shame cascaded over me. This was partly my fault. This had happened because Jayson had seen Kira all over me. If I'd been more adamant about calling off the operation, if I'd been quicker getting to Kira...if I'd done any of the hundred things I could have done, none of this would have happened. I had helped ruin Kira's life.

The usual enmity between us wavered as we looked at each other. Her stony expression crumbled, and all I could see was a woman whose hopes and dreams had been ripped away. It took me back to that moment behind the restaurant. She'd been bleeding out and broken. Drugged out of her mind. Weak—the one thing she'd never wanted to be.

I stepped toward her, my arms open to hug her. We could bury the hatchet and move on. We could be friends and figure out where to go next. But as Kira saw what I was getting ready to do, all the old barriers sprang up. The angry fire in her eyes blazed back to life, and she stepped back, slapping my hands away.

"I don't need your pity," she spat, then stomped back inside, slamming the door behind her.

I stared at the door. All I'd wanted was a truce. For a fleeting moment, I'd really believed it could happen. With everything that had happened the last week, I'd thought it possible. After seeing her reaction, though? It was time to accept that things would probably never change. I needed to get over that idea once and for all.

Chapter 7 - Kira

I lay in bed a few days later, doing what I'd been doing for the past week: assessing the world and trying to figure out whether the disaster my life had become was merely a nightmare. Invariably, the realization sank in that, yes, my life was a disaster. I debated staying in bed until I wasted away to nothing.

Unfortunately, my mind would never let me do that. Be it a blessing or a curse, I was too driven to ever sink into a pit of despair. As much as my body protested, I swung my legs to the side and heaved myself out of bed. One foot in front of the other. That's all I could do. At least until I figured a way out of this catastrophe.

As I prepared for the day and tried to ignore the physical ache from my rejection, a bitter sense of loss settled in my heart when I looked at my Tranquility ops gear in my closet. I'd never wear it again. The one thing I was really good at, the one thing that made me whole, and now it was gone, too. That hurt almost as much as letting down my family. If I still had my job, at least I could have buried myself in work. Catching bad guys was a surefire way to get my mind off everything else.

I'd tried that as soon as the mating ceremony fell apart. Within hours of Jayson rejecting me, I called my superiors and asked to get back to work. I had hoped I would get a new case, a new project that would preoccupy me. Instead, they terminated me over the phone. There had been no build-up, no fake apologies. Just a couple sentences about cutbacks, a week's severance pay, and a boot in the ass. I'd put my life on the line for the council for years, and then Jayson's bitch of an aunt pulled a few strings and ended it just like that.

Shoving aside the gear, I grabbed a sweatshirt and pulled it over my head. I didn't have any plans for the day and had no clue what to do with myself. The only place I would be welcomed and not ostracized was Zoe's place.

I grabbed my car keys and headed to the front door. I was one of the few shifters who owned a car. In wolf form, we could run nearly forty miles an hour. Almost no one drove. The very fact that I had a car was another badge of dishonor, but I'd never cared about that. And anyone who thought it was weird could go screw themselves.

I was only a few steps off the porch when I froze in place. My keys slipped from my hand, clattering to the concrete. My tires had been slashed. Deep scratches scored the car's paint right down to the metal beneath. My jaw slowly fell open at the words spraypainted on the side:

Real wolves don't need cars

I circled the car, reading the other profanities that had been scratched into the metal or painted. *Whore*, *slut*, *traitor*, and *fake* were a few. My vision blurred red at the edges, and I had to look away before my rage took control.

This was dead center in Eleventh Pack territory. Fifty feet from my house. This wasn't the work of another pack. My packmates had done this. My own people were turning on me. Gods, things were really bad if some of my packmates had the balls to do this. Anger was a strong drug. It made you do crazy things.

I was appalled, but part of me had expected something like this. The pack's hopelessness had been evident for days. Everyone was jumpy and distraught. My pairing with Jayson had been one of the biggest things to happen to our pack in recent memory. The Ninth Pack had better connections and more strength than we could ever have dreamed of. Being fated to Jayson meant that power and influence would have carried.

For the past five years, my pack had looked to me as a savior, as the person who would secure our future and raise our standing. Now that this dream had been ripped away, there were bound to be desperate and furious people who wanted to act out. Teenagers, probably, reacting to the terrible rumors floating around about me.

I kicked my keys aside. I could shrug off the vandalism, but it didn't mean I couldn't be pissed about it. I was already frustrated about losing my mate, my parents' pride, and my job. My car being destroyed was the icing on top of a shit cake.

Grabbing an old tarp from the shed out back, I tossed it over the car to hide the damage, then pinned it down with some rocks. I sent Zoe a text, asking her to come over. I was obviously not driving anywhere.

I'd hoped the tarp would hide my car and keep it from being a conversation piece. Except, it had slipped my mind that Zoe, as loving and loyal as she was, was equally nosy. She barged in twenty minutes later, dragging the tarp behind her.

"I'll kill them," she grunted, shaking the tarp for emphasis. "I'll kill every single son of a bitch if I find them. You hear me?"

Sighing, I took the tea bag out of the cup it had been steeping in. "It's fine, Zoe. Really. Let them vent. I did a pretty good job of screwing up everyone's life."

Her eyes widened. "Are you serious? You're letting these people blame you for Jayson being a dick? For almost dying? This pack has always expected too much from you and Kolton. You especially, though. And now, the one time things don't go perfectly, they turn on you? That's bullshit."

She dropped the tarp on the floor and strode over to me. Shoving her hand into her pocket, she pulled out a key ring. "Here. We'll fix this right now."

A moment later, the keys duplicated, and she handed them to me.

"What are those?" I asked.

"Keys to my car and apartment. Your own set of each. You need to get away from this place, Kira. Come stay with me for a few weeks until you get back on your feet."

As I looked down at the keys, I had a strong urge to agree. A lump formed in my throat. Knowing at least one person had my back was making me emotional. It was tempting to get away, get out from under the weight of expectation and hide at my friend's place for a while.

But as soon as the thought entered my mind, I pushed it away. I swallowed hard, reining in my emotions. I had to stay strong now.

I smiled warmly at Zoe. "Thank you. That means a lot, but I can't run away from this problem. I've got to push through. I need to fix this."

Zoe's mouth dropped open. "Kira, there's no way to fix it. Jayson, piece of shit that he is, rejected you. You've given all you could for your family and pack. You don't owe them shit. Why do you even *want* to make these people happy? Honestly, the only people who seem to understand how hard you've tried are Kolton and Wyatt and his band of lone wolves.

Everyone else is demanding a pound of flesh from you."

I groaned at Wyatt's name. He was where everything had gone wrong. I couldn't even think about him without getting depressed.

I held a hand up. "Let's please not talk about Wyatt. And let's not discuss Kolton, either. He's getting all these ideas about dropping out of school. He's close to giving up his dreams of starting his own business to stay here and take over as alpha. You and I both know that's the last thing he wants. He'll shrivel and die inside if that ends up being his fate. Gods, it pisses me off and breaks my heart."

Zoe's face softened. "I know, but..." She shrugged. "Being alpha is really his destiny. It sucks, but maybe that's what fate and the gods have planned for him."

I shook my head vehemently. "No. I won't let that happen."

My drive to fix the situation ran deep into my soul. Fixing it was the best way for me to cope with all that had happened. I was driven by guilt. Guilt over what had happened, guilt that I should have seen it all coming. Jayson had never really wanted to mate with me. It had taken *half a decade* to get him to even discuss a date for the ceremony. Talk about red flags.

I felt responsible for everything. Unfair or not, I couldn't help it. My career was over, my family had been shamed, all the packs were on the verge of going to war. Things had fallen apart around me.

I sighed. It would have been nice to have a white knight come riding in to save the day. I'd never entertained such fantasies in the past, had never wanted or needed to be saved. But right then, I would have welcomed it.

At that moment, I would have done anything to fix the disaster my life had become. Things would come to a head soon if I didn't do something drastic. The odds were good that as a rejected mate, I'd get kicked out of the pack. My parents would fight against that, but how did you fight thousands of years of tradition? I didn't want to go rogue or fall into some rag-tag group of lone wolves like Wyatt had. Although, it didn't look like he minded it. I'd never talked to him about being a lone wolf. Come to think of it, I'd never spoken to him about any aspect of his past. The way things were going, I might be forced to pick his brain about how to survive.

"Hang on, I need sugar," Zoe said.

I watched as she produced two bowls filled with ice cream, chocolate sauce, and toppings out of thin air. While she cast her little spells, my mind continued to spin through the issues to find a possible solution. Regardless of what my pack thought about me, it was my responsibility to protect them. I wouldn't let Kolton waste away his life in misery, nor would I leave my family forever.

Every option was worse than the one before.

Zoe handed me one heaping bowl. "Here," she said. "Let's zone out for a little, okay? Get your mind off everything."

The sight of the calorie bomb made my stomach rumble, and I gave Zoe a grudging smile. "All right, we can try that."

Grinning, she went to flop down on the couch and grabbed the remote. "We can watch some trashy TV or something."

I settled in beside her as she flipped through the dozens of channels. As I spooned ice cream into my mouth, I wondered how long it would be before my friend tried to convince me to move in with her again. I'd never lived outside the Eastern Wilds. I wouldn't even know what to do with myself.

"Oh, here we go," Zoe said.

She'd stopped on a channel. I recognized the guy on the screen immediately. Von Thornton, the vampire host of *The Reject Project*. He was dressed, as always, from head to toe in perfectly tailored designer clothes.

"Good day, everyone, " Von said to a live crowd. "How are my darlings today?" He flashed a brilliant smile, the tips of his fangs glinting in the stage light.

The crowd gave a small cheer and a ripple of applause.

Von took a seat on a blood-red velvet armchair, the only furnishing on the entire stage. "Wonderful, absolutely wonderful," he said. "Well, as you and the rest of the world know, it's almost time for the next season of our favorite show. *The Reject Project* is returning for a thirty-first season, and I don't know about you, but I am beyond excited for the drama." He raised a provocative eyebrow, and the crowd twittered with laughter.

Crossing a leg over his knee nonchalantly, Von went on. "For those who may not know, wolf shifters are the focus of our little program. Unlike any other creature, wolves are the most delectable when it comes to their love lives. Their souls flutter through life, desperately seeking the match that will make them whole. Romance by fate. The fated mate is a lovely tradition that wolf shifters search for to fulfill their lives, as well as the lives of their family and pack."

Von leaned toward the audience and put a hand to his mouth, pretending to whisper conspiratorially. "I, for one, enjoy playing the field."

More laughs from the audience. The guy was a showman, but then, he'd had a few centuries to hone his craft.

"Our show delves into what happens when one of these twin flames burns out too soon. When one wolf falls out of sync with their fated pairing, a reject is born. It is rare, but as our thirty seasons can attest, not *that* rare. Our contestants come to us to fight it out and try to claim a new partner and get a second chance at romance. We offer a path for two lucky wolves to find a new mate with the blessing of the goddess. And as fans of the show know, things can get *very* intense."

The crowd applauded again, but I barely heard them. I was staring at Von Thornton, my bowl of ice cream forgotten.

"I'm here for this special program to announce that there has been a bit of a wrench thrown into the production of season thirty-one. A wrench that, on first inspection, could have proven disastrous, but upon closer study, may be the greatest and most exciting wrinkle that's ever happened."

Von stood, smoothed his immaculate suit, and walked to the edge of the stage. "Our female star has, unfortunately, had to withdraw from the show."

A murmur of disquiet ran through the crowd. Zoe gasped and put a hand to her mouth. I'd never heard of a female contestant stepping down. I wasn't as huge a fan as Zoe was, but the show was an omnipresent part of life, an institution almost everyone followed—even if unwillingly.

Von held up his hand to silence the crowd, then flashed another bright smile. "Easy, everyone. This isn't my first rodeo, as the humans say. An exciting opportunity has arisen for one lucky female wolf. I and the other showrunners have decided to make things more exciting rather than simply elevating one of the several other females who were chosen as, shall we say, understudy to our lead. We all know how dangerous Bloodstone Island is, and as past seasons have shown, not every lead makes it home to tell the tale. Starting today at noon and running through tomorrow at noon, we will be holding impromptu auditions for our next female lead. How exciting is that?" he shouted, raising his arms over his head.

I stared at the screen and felt a lick of hope. Fleeting and tenuous as it was, it sat bubbling in the deepest recesses of my mind. It was a million-to-one chance, but it was still a chance.

After a moment of hesitation, the crowd cheered. Von strutted back and forth across the stage, seeming to bask in the glow of the crowd's adoration.

Once the noise died down, he said, "Any young lady is free to come to Fangmore City and audition for our casting directors in the next twenty-four hours. If you are a rejected mate between the ages of eighteen and thirty, we look forward to meeting you." Von sighed and cocked an eyebrow. "Oh, and of course, you better be *gorgeous*." After another round of laughter and applause, Von finished his monologue. "Twenty-four hours, ladies. Who wouldn't want to have a bunch of hot, muscled wolf hunks fighting over you? So I ask you this: do you have what it takes? I hope so. Our slogan at *The Reject Project* stands true. Everyone loves an underdog."

The special showing switched to a screen that showed the address and phone number for the casting director's office in Fangmore City, followed by a bunch of legalese about the dangers associated with the show. I was still staring at the screen when Zoe turned to look at me as if she could read the thoughts forming my mind.

"No way. No godsdamned way, Kira," Zoe said.

"'No way what?" I asked, but my voice was hazy, my mind deep in thought. This was the best thing I'd heard since Jayson rejected me. I was desperate to redeem myself in the eyes of the pack. What better way than being on this show?

"Don't even think about it. There's no chance in hell I'm letting you audition."

I turned and raised my eyebrows. "What do you mean?" Was I really that transparent?

Zoe pointed at me. "I can see what you're thinking. It's not a good idea."

Sighing, I gestured toward the screen. "But you love the show. It's your favorite thing to watch. You've seen all the reruns of every season like four times."

Zoe leaped to her feet. "That's exactly the problem, Kira. I'm obsessed with the show, which means I know for *sure* I don't want anyone I *know* on it. Don't you know how dangerous it is?"

I stared right into her eyes. "What do you get if you win?"

Zoe stared back. "You know. You've watched it."

Rolling my eyes, I said, "Indulge me."

She crossed her arms, but her shoulders sagged a bit, and her face softened. "You get a buttload of money, for one thing. Then there's the fame and stuff. Several winners have ended up getting modeling contracts or going into acting or music. You get granted immediate access to a home in one of the most prestigious neighborhoods in Fangmore City. And then..." Her eyes widened as she remembered the last part. The very thing I'd set my sights on. "You become an honorary member of the First Pack. The most powerful wolf pack in the world."

"Exactly." I jabbed a finger at her. "And you get a new mate. Plus, the Moon Goddess will bless the new pairing on live TV. It's like the rejection never happened."

Jayson and I *had* been fated mates, even though neither of us loved each other. Even then, the rejection hadn't only hurt emotionally and psychologically but also physically. The rejection had left me with a bone-deep ache, like part of me had been sheared away. It was something I'd have to live with forever. But if I won this show, the Goddess Heline would take away the pain. With one blessing, I'd be whole again, regain my standing in the pack, and create a connection between the Eleventh Pack and the First Pack. Such an alliance would blow the original pairing with the Ninth Pack out of the water.

The First Pack was the most powerful in the world. Everyone tried to gain favor with them. If I did this, if I won, then I could fix everything with my pack. That would be amazing, but there was something else I had my eye on. Something even more powerful than all that.

"Then there's the other prize," I said.

Zoe frowned. "Huh? What other prize?"

"The favor from Heline."

There were always two options for the prize. The money and prestige and glamor were huge, of course. But Heline always offered the winner a chance to forgo the new fated-mate blessing and ask her to grant them one favor instead. The Moon Goddess, one of the most powerful magical beings in our entire world, would give you one wish.

"Has anyone ever taken the favor?" I asked greedily.

Zoe shook her head, a deep frown marring her brow. "No. Why would they? Anything they could ask for is already there in the winnings. You get, like, a dozen different benefits from taking that. Heline's favor would be one thing, right? Why would anyone choose one thing over the very thing that got them on the show? Over having a new fated mate?"

"To shield your loved ones, stop a war, increase their pack's standing? There are things more important than money or living in a nice neighborhood." I explained.

"Well, none of that matters," Zoe said in a tone that brooked no argument. "I'm not letting you do it. My gods, do you realize how bad the survival rate is on this show? It's terrible. I'll be honest, the female contestants usually fare even worse. I won't let you get sucked into this. It's not worth it, Kira."

It sounded totally worth it to me. I could ask Heline for her blessing over my pack, basically making them untouchable, or I could ask her to stop any war that might be about to break out. The Eleventh Pack wasn't strong, and the last war fifty years before had devastated us and dropped our station even further. Not only that, but preventing a war would also help the other lower-tier packs that would get gobbled up or destroyed in a war with the larger, more powerful packs.

This was my chance. If I could guarantee our pack's safety, then Mom and Dad might allow me to take the lead and allow Kolton to continue his education and follow his dreams. Even if I didn't win, simply doing well would help bring a little pride back to my pack after being shamed.

I had a hard time thinking I wouldn't do well. Yes, some of the little games and twists the showrunners used were dangerous and life-threatening, but I was a trained Tranquility operative.

Was there anything they could throw at me that I couldn't handle? I doubted it.

The more I thought about it, the more excited I became. I could do this. All I needed to do was get the show to choose me. From there? It would be smooth sailing.

I tuned Zoe's voice out as she rambled on about all the dangers. My mind was made up.

Chapter 8 - Wyatt

The way my mind kept drifting back to what had happened to Kira annoyed me. I really needed to get my head out of her problems. There was nothing I could do to help. On top of that, she'd made it abundantly clear that she didn't want any help from me.

That didn't stop me from remembering the absolute devastation on her face that day out in the forest. The mating ceremony had been the worst moment in her life. Far above her near death at the hands of the lion shifter or anything else that had happened before.

I had gone out on runs with my unofficial pack, hunting and sprinting to expend some of my angry energy. It hadn't helped at all. If anything, I was even more furious after a run. Ready to rip Jayson Fell's head off all over again.

Work was even less helpful at getting my mind off things. Every time I went into the office, I was met with Kira's empty desk. To me, it was like a ghost was wandering the building. Kira was such a force of nature that her presence was still palpable even though she wasn't.

Being at work only served to increase my rage at the situation. My superiors were so emotionless about the entire thing, it set my teeth on edge. They were treating it like business as usual, like every organization fired their best employee for reasons that had nothing to do with job performance. It was like a trash collector getting fired because he'd let his library card expire. Kira hadn't done anything to warrant termination. Hell, she'd still been on council-sanctioned medical leave during the ceremony. They knew she'd been drugged. Yes, she'd gotten injured, and the suspect had gotten away, but that was usually followed by a stern briefing, a slap on the wrist, a pat on the ass, and words of encouragement to do better the next time. It was how things worked. Or had.

I'd always thought the council to be the pristine defenders of human and creature kind. Now I saw what they really were: corruptible, easily manipulated, and dirty. All it took was one family to make one phone call, and any of us could be out the door. The council was run on nepotism, money, and power.

The pencil I was holding suddenly snapped between my fingers. Glancing down, I saw I'd clenched my fist tight enough that it had broken in two. My thoughts had pissed me off so much, I couldn't help it. A glance around the office showed no one had noticed. Carter was on the phone, and no one else was near. I needed to be careful. Everyone knew Kira and I had a tense relationship, but they also knew Kolton was my best friend. No matter how much I despised what had happened, I still needed the job. At this point, it was all I had.

"I'm heading out," I said, pulling my jacket off the chair as I stood.

Shonda Makey glanced up from her cubicle. "For the day? It's only one o'clock. You'll need to put in PTO for the remaining hours."

I rolled my eyes. Every office had that one staunch rule follower who made sure everyone had their toes on the line and all their "i's" dotted. Shonda was ours.

"Yes, Shonda. I know. Thanks for reminding me. I'll take care of it."

"Good. Want me to let Jacobs know you're leaving?"

David Jacobs was our pod manager, overseeing three ops teams that made up one Tranquility operatives pod.

I blew out a frustrated breath. "Holy shit, Shonda, I don't need a fucking mother right now. It'll be fine," I snapped.

She jerked her head back and pursed her lips. "Well, damn. Fine, then. Be that way."

She hunched back behind her cubicle just as Carter turned in his chair and raised his eyebrows in question. Waving him off, I strode out of the office. In the elevator, my thoughts once again turned to Kira.

My own experience with rejected mates wasn't exactly like hers, but it did give me some insight into what she was going through. Looking back on my past, I realized I was happier now than I ever could have been before. All I could hope was that Kira came out of this stronger than when she went into it. I couldn't deny that I was happy she'd been rejected. Living her whole life with that piece of shit would have been a few steps away from hell. He'd never cared for her, never really wanted her, and was a lazy, spoiled brat. Probably would have cheated on her left and right regardless of the pairing. Knowing that prick, he'd be down by the ocean trying to find a mermaid to give him a blowjob while they were on their honeymoon.

I headed a few blocks down to a sandwich shop and bought lunch. I'd barely eaten in two days, but my metabolism was too high to go without food, and I was ravenous. My worry about Kira had damn near destroyed my appetite. I devoured the hoagie and chips while formulating a plan. My plan sounded crazy on the surface, but it seemed the best way to help both Kira and Kolton.

Kira was now a pariah in her pack. All that prevented her from being cast out was that her father was the pack alpha. Even that might not matter if the pressure from the other high-ranking families in the pack pushed the issue.

Kolton had no desire to lead the pack. Taking over would be the end of his dreams, and my friend would mentally waste away if he was forced to stay in the Eastern Wilds and watch over the pack. His parents had to know that, but tradition dictated everything they did, and they wouldn't hesitate to force him when the time came.

There was only one way to prevent them from both going through that. I'd ask them to leave the hierarchical pack system and join my own small pack. We weren't large, but we didn't have allegiance to anyone. For years, we'd been under the protection of the Eleventh Pack, but we didn't *need* it. We could go anywhere and do whatever we wanted. Kolton and Kira would never be in a pack that had the kind of influence theirs had, but they'd be able to live their lives the way they wanted. It was highly uncommon for a shifter to leave their pack voluntarily, and they would lose respect, power, and influence within shifter society. But in return, they were free to do as they wished.

I crumpled the sandwich wrapper and chip bag into a ball as I thought it over. They'd have a hard time adjusting, like I'd had, but it had worked out fine for me. I was so sick and tired of seeing them walking around with the weight of the world on their shoulders. The worry they carried with them was more than I could stomach. Their father was loyal to the dozens of families who were members of the Eleventh Pack, but that didn't need to be their worry. If they left, the pack would find a new alpha when the time came for their father to retire. It wasn't unheard of. Every twenty or thirty years, leadership in one of the twelve packs transferred to a new family. There were plenty of alphas ready to take up the mantle. The Eleventh Pack would be fine.

By the time I left the sandwich shop, I'd come to a decision. I'd go talk to them. Right now. Kolton would be the easiest to convince. I'd wait to speak with him. Kira would be the toughest nut to crack. She was unflinchingly loyal to her pack. It would take a lot of explaining to get her to realize leaving was the best option. I was ready for a fight, but I was determined to make her see the truth. She'd basically lost everything she'd worked toward her entire life. It would be better to start over with a new pack. A clean slate. She'd have to see the appeal when I explained it to her. Then, once Kolton agreed, it would be simple. Our unofficial pack would head out and look for a new territory.

I practiced what I'd say to her as I headed to her house. Shifting to my wolf form, I sprinted through the countryside outside the city and imagined how things would go when I spoke to Kira. There were a hundred ways she could turn me down, and I needed to plan a rebuttal to all of those before she said them.

Twenty minutes later, I skidded to a stop outside Kira's house, my paws sliding through the grass. My body morphed out of its wolf form. My clothes reappeared on my body as my limbs transformed. The fur receded, and my torso and head shifted back to human once more.

Staring in shock, I walked around Kira's car. My eyes narrowed to slits at the damage. This was deep in her father's land. The only people who could have done this were her own packmates. A muted growl rumbled through my teeth. This had to be enough for her. She had to see that this pack was done with her. Coming with me and my guys was her only option.

Stomping up the porch steps, I grabbed the knocker and pounded it on the heavy oak door. To my surprise, Kira's friend Zoe answered the door.

She smiled at me sweetly. "Hello, sweetie. I'm afraid we aren't in the market for any Girl Scout cookies today. Now, if you have any alcohol or painkillers, we'd be glad to take those off your hands."

"Where's Kira?" I asked.

Zoe grimaced. "She...um...already left."

"Where'd she go? I need to talk to her. It's important." I nodded toward the car. "She couldn't have gone far."

Now Zoe wouldn't meet my eyes. She seemed to be looking everywhere but at me. "Like I said, she's gone."

"Oh, good grief. Move," I said, pushing past her into the house. Kira had to be in there somewhere.

"Hey? Did I invite you in?" Zoe said as she shut the door.

"Kira?" I called out.

Stepping into the living room, I saw two empty bowls smeared with chocolate sauce and whipped cream.

I pointed at the bowls. "I suppose you ate both of these yourself?"

Zoe shoved her fists into her hips. "I didn't say she wasn't here a minute ago. All I said was she left."

"Where's everyone else?"

"Well, Mister Nosy, Kolton is at class, and Mr. and Mrs. Durst are out on the edges of pack territory. Some kind of dust-up. If I had to guess, they may be chewing someone's ass about what happened to Kira's car."

"If you aren't gonna help, I'll go find her myself," I said.

Zoe shook her head, "Kira's right. You are a bossy little shit."

"I heard that."

"I meant you to," she said, then stuck her tongue out.

She rubbed at her temples, and when I really looked at her, I could see she looked drained.

"You aren't telling me something," I said, suspicion crawling up my spine.

"I've just got this awful headache." She sighed with resignation and met my eyes. "It took a lot out of me sending her where she wanted to go."

I took a step toward her, raising an eyebrow. "And where did you send her, Zoe?"

Her face crumpled under the weight of my stare. I could see her at war with herself, maybe having an entire argument inside her head.

"Okay," she relented. "It's like this. Those ungrateful jackasses wrecked her car, and she needed to get somewhere. Kira was all like, 'I have to go, you need to teleport me, I don't have time to wait,' but then I was like, 'No way, chick, it's too dangerous.' Then she went all, 'But you're my best friend, who else will help me?' Then I had the guilt and stuff. Then Kira said, 'I'll find someone else to take me,' so then I *had* to. It would be safer if I did it. See? Does that make sense?"

I stared at her, trying to comprehend the rambling mess that had tumbled out of her mouth.

"Zoe!" I shouted in exasperation. "Nothing you said makes sense. Can you please just tell me where you sent Kira?"

Zoe sucked her lower lip into her mouth and chewed on it, giving me a sheepish look. "She went to audition for *The Reject Project*."

A thunderclap went off in my mind, and a red film descended over my vision. Anger, fear, and horror flooded through me in quick succession. No way. There was no fucking way Kira would do something so insane.

"Did you put her up to it?" I asked. Zoe was a big fan of the show. It wasn't out of the realm of possibility.

Her eyes bugged out. "Me? Fuck, no! I spent thirty minutes trying to talk her out of it. We were eating ice cream and flipping through the channels when a special announcement came on TV. The new season starts soon, and the female lead dropped out. Kira said she had to get on the show. She wants to bring some pride back to her pack."

"And you fucking let her go?" I growled.

Zoe's face clouded. "Listen, buddy, I did my best. She said if I didn't help, she'd walk to Fangmore City or hitch a ride. What would have happened if a Ninth Packer picked her up? Or one of the shitheads who trashed her car?"

Without another word, I shoved past her and stomped outside. Zoe's argument was valid, but there had to be another way. Anything to keep Kira from going on that show.

Buried memories tried to push to the forefront of my mind. That damned atrocity of a TV show seemed to haunt me everywhere I went. Between my past and its worldwide popularity, I knew exactly what awaited Kira. I couldn't let her do this. That show was even more dangerous than being a Tranquility operative.

Most shifters who competed ended up dead. They weren't easy deaths, either. For the thousandth time, I cursed the show. Even more, I cursed Jayson Fell and his father. This was his fault. If I could get my hands on them right now, I'd choke the life from those two fuckers. I'd gladly take whatever punishment came down. Anything would be worth it to see the life drain out of their eyes by my hands.

I was thrashing around in the front yard, trying to calm myself enough to shift, when Kolton came walking down the driveway. He'd had a bright, easygoing smile on his face until he saw me. My rage must have been palpable. I could feel practically feel my blood boiling in my veins.

"Wyatt? What's wrong?" His gaze drifted to Kira's car. "Shit. Who did this?"

"Doesn't matter," I snapped, raking a hand through my hair. "Do you have any clue what your sister just did?" I stepped close to him, my nose inches from his. "Did she ask you about it? Did you know she was going?"

Kolton's head pulled away in surprise. "Yo, easy, man. What the hell are you talking about? Go where?"

I could see from the confusion in his eyes that he was telling the truth. I relaxed a fraction, though my shaking fingers were still clenched into iron fists.

"Kira," I growled, "had Zoe send her to Fangmore City. She's auditioning for *The Reject Project*."

Kolton's face went gray, and his jaw went slack as the reality of what I'd said sank in. He slowly shook his head. "No way. She wouldn't."

I nodded grimly. "She did."

Kolton sprinted inside. Grudgingly, I turned and followed him. All I wanted was to go after Kira, but that would have to wait. Unless I could force Zoe to teleport me to Kira, it would take hours for me to get to Fangmore. By then, she would have already done what she'd gone to do.

"Zoe?" Kolton shouted.

I trudged into the house, but the sound of paws on gravel interrupted my stride. Looking over my shoulder, I saw two wolves sprinting down the driveway. Kira's parents. Sighing, I followed after Kolton. I wasn't in the mood to break the news to them.

I found Zoe and Kolton in the kitchen. If anything, Kolton looked even more tired and haggard. Zoe's face was flushed with supreme sorrow. She'd obviously confirmed what I'd told Kolton. My friend looked a solid two decades older than he had a few minutes ago. He understood the dangers of the show. He was the only person I'd met who hated the show as much as I did.

Alpha Durst and his mate walked in. They looked irate. Zoe's assumption that they had been trying to figure out who had vandalized Kira's car was probably correct.

"What's all this?" Kira's father asked, his face going even darker.

Kolton looked up at him, a look of utter and complete devastation on his face. "Dad...Kira's gone."

Alpha Durst took a step forward, looking wary. "Gone? Gone where?"

Kolton looked like he was going to vomit. "She's gone to Fangmore City. She's auditioning for *The Reject Project*."

Surprisingly—shockingly—Kira's father's face broke into a joyous smile. I frowned, horrified at his reaction.

"She did? She really did that?" The pride in his voice turned my stomach.

Kolton had the same look on his face that I had. Horror and disbelief. "Yes, Dad. Why the hell do you look so happy?"

Het shook his head. "She's trying to bring honor back to us. I never even thought of it. If I had, I would have suggested it myself." He pumped his fist like he'd won a hand of cards. "That's my girl," he whispered.

It took every ounce of my willpower not to slap the shit out of the man right then and there. Didn't he understand that Kira was going to her death? If she got on the show, the odds of her returning were probably less than ten percent. It was the grotesque allure of the program.

Alpha Durst looked up at the three of us, obviously confused why Kolton, Zoe, and I looked somber. "Why do you all look like that? Aren't you proud of Kira? She's finally putting her pack first."

"Finally?" Kolton barked. "She's *always* putting the pack first, Dad. What the hell are you on about?"

His father nodded, but it was more a placating gesture than anything. "Yes, Kolton, of course. Still, if she'd tried to be closer to Jayson, tried to strengthen their relationship, he might not have rejected her." His eyes flicked to me with a quick flash of irritation that he concealed quickly. I knew he was pissed at me, but he also understood that what happened had been caused by a drug and not through willing actions on my or Kira's part.

I'd need to be careful around him for some time. That would be difficult, since it seemed like Kolton and I cared more about her safety than her own parents did.

"Things could have gone differently," he went on. "Now? We're a laughingstock. Totally gutted. Our influence has all but dissipated like crazy in the last week. If a war broke out among packs now, no one would align with us. We'd be crushed. This is her chance. *Our* chance. The power and prestige? The blessing of Heline herself? It's all we could ever ask for."

Kira's mother looked much less excited. She patted his shoulder. "Yes, dear, but we have to remember that hundreds of rejected mates from all over the country will be trying to get on that show. She probably won't even get picked. We have bigger things to worry about than the show."

"Like what?" I said, my anger amping up by the second.

Kira's father seemed to come back to reality, and his face went grim.

"Well," Kira's mother went on, "we need to comfort Kira when she gets home. We also need to figure out how to deal with the other Eleventh families. They're all calling for her to be banished. It's tradition. A rejected fated mate has always been removed from the pack. The other families think we are bucking tradition because she's the daughter of the alpha."

"Oh, for fuck's sake," I hissed and stomped out.

I couldn't stand being in that house any longer. I'd always respected Kira's father and had been grateful that he'd let my pack reside in his lands. But all that gratitude and respect vanished when I'd seen his greed and excitement at the prospect of his daughter participating in a show where the odds were good that she'd die. Yes, his pack had lost a ton of influence and would be in dire straits if the rumored war actually happened, but she was his *only* daughter.

My only option was to make sure Kira didn't get on the show. Her mother was right—the odds were low for her to get chosen. The prize money, blessings, and fame that came from being on *The Reject Project* ensured tons of women would apply. But even so, the probability was low, not zero. And I knew that if she *did* get on that show, I'd have to do something just as crazy.

I'd spent years saving Kira from danger. No way in hell was I gonna stop now. If she managed to succeed with this psychotic venture, I'd need to be there to drag her butt back to safety. Like I had dozens of times before.

Chapter 9 - Kira

I hated Fangmore City. It was so *busy*, like barely contained chaos. The unending movement and activity reminded me of a bag of snakes. I never fit in when I was there, even though over eighty percent of the population were wolf shifters.

Perhaps that was why I hated it so much. All along the streets and alleys, shifters padded or sprinted along, getting where they needed to go in their wolf form. It made the giant city eerily quiet. There was none of the noise pollution from cars and buses that human or mixed cities had. Seeing them go about their day as wolves reminded me of what I was missing. Regardless of whether or not it was my decision, it was always a sore spot.

Zoe had teleported me to a spot a few blocks from the studio offices where the auditions were being held. That forced me to walk the rest of the way. The sounds of wolf feet on pavement, the panting of breath, and the smell of fur gave me the feeling of being inexplicably out of place.

A massive bus pulled slowly up the street. The magic-electric hybrid shuttled a few of the humans and other creatures who shared the city with the wolf population. I hurried alongside it. A massive vinyl-wrap picture was plastered on the side. Von Thornton's gleaming vampire smile and glittering eyes were aimed right at me. *Season thirty-one! Coming soon!* The bright-red letters beside his face proclaimed. Beside that was the signature logo of *The Reject Project*—a red full moon with a howling wolf's head in black silhouetted against it.

Gritting my teeth in determination, I quickened my pace and found the studio. Once inside the building, I finally took a breath. The male receptionist behind a large desk glanced lazily at me before turning back to his computer.

"Um, hi, I'm not sure if you're who I need to talk to, but—"

Without looking up, he cut me off by pointing to the elevators. "Top floor. Second door on the right."

I frowned. "I'm sorry?"

With a dramatic, heaving sigh, he pulled his eyes from his computer. "You're here to audition." It was a statement, not a question.

Taken aback, I blinked. "Well, yes. For *the Reject*—"

"*Project*. Yeah, yeah. Like I said, top floor, second door on the right. You'll need to sign a waiver. They have a whole stack of them up there. Have a good day."

He turned back to his computer, effectively dismissing me. I glanced over the counter to see what was so damned important. The ass was deeply enthralled in a game of solitaire. I wanted to shout at him but decided accosting one of the employees for being a dick wouldn't help my chances of getting on the show.

"Thanks for the help," I said sarcastically and strode to the bank of elevators.

After waiting for what felt like forever, the doors finally dinged and opened. Stepping in, I hit the button for the top floor. The wall on my right had a large poster emblazoned with the slogan for *The Reject Project* in bright, bold letters. *Everyone Loves an Underdog*. I hoped to the gods that was true.

A few minutes later, I was sitting in a room full of hopeful contestants. It did not help my self-esteem. The other women looked nothing like me. For one, several of them were gorgeous in that over-the-top, plastic way of the wives and girlfriends of celebrities or sports stars: flowing hair, perfect lips, tight and revealing dresses, but cunning and desperate eyes.

Others looked like they could handle themselves in a fight, like me. Those women were the ones I worried about. They glanced around the room, taking in all the others, judging them, grading them...dismissing them.

Hopelessness clawed at my insides. Why would they choose me? I wasn't special. I barely even stood out among these women. This was the stupidest idea I'd ever had. I never should have done this. And by now, I was sure people had asked where I went, and Zoe would have told them. When I was turned down for the role, I'd have to go back home, embarrassed and rejected *again*. It would be devastating. I resolved to go ahead and pack my shit to leave if that was the case. I wouldn't make Dad have to officially banish me from the pack. I'd do it on my own and save us both the humiliation.

A big, burly wolf shifter stood at the door leading to the office, making sure no one went through until they were called. One younger girl was leaning on the wall and talking to him, though he seemed to be paying her no attention. Without trying, I overheard their conversation.

"And then he said he couldn't be with me because he didn't think we were compatible. He actually said that. Said that there must have been a mistake, and we couldn't even be friends because he didn't feel *anything* for me. Can you believe that?" She shook her head in disgust, then grabbed her oversized breasts. "I had a fucking fae doctor give me these because he liked big boobs. Do you have any idea how much that costs? I mean, I could have gotten the fake silicone things some people get, but I wanted my mate to have the real thing, you know?"

Around the room, through murmured conversations, I heard other sob stories of rejections. Most of them revolved around the male not being attracted to the female or some weird pack-hierarchy thing coming into play. One young woman said her blood test had paired her with her own pack's alpha, who was already mated to someone else, forcing him to reject her for decorum's sake.

I was surprised by how many gorgeous women had been rejected by their mates—far more than I would have anticipated. It was always thought that rejected mates were incredibly rare, but if this room was any inclination, it seemed to happen far more often than anyone realized. Then again, rejection was so devastating and embarrassing to the packs, the true numbers were probably kept under wraps. It was stressful enough to be paired with someone you might not even know. There was no reason to throw in the worry that you could be rejected and turned into an outcast.

Gripping my fingers together, I squeezed my hands between my knees to keep from fidgeting. I was fighting to prevent my mind from going down a dark rabbit hole full of hopelessness and despair. There would be dozens of women fighting for the coveted role on the show, but I was the strongest. I *knew* I was. No matter what it took, I would make this work. I had no other choice. Nothing else would bring pride and honor back to my pack.

"Kira Durst," a voice called out.

My head snapped up in surprise. The door beside the security guy had opened. A small, bespectacled woman stood there, looking down at a clipboard. Before my body could freeze in fear, I leaped to my feet.

"Here," I said, walking toward her.

She glanced up from the clipboard, gave me a quick once-over, then shrugged. "This way."

I followed after her, and the door shut behind me. I felt strange, like I'd been cut off or crossed over into another world. It sent my stomach into nauseous flips. There was no going back now. I was in it. And if I was? Then by the gods, I was going to win it.

The woman led me to a large room shrouded in darkness except for a stool beneath bright studio lights. I scanned the room. A man and a woman sat at a desk directly in front of the stool. They were obviously supposed to be the talent judges, but my Tranquility operative training had honed my ability to read rooms. They were nothing more than figureheads. In the far back, almost completely cloaked in shadows, sat another man, legs outstretched, ankles crossed, dark sunglasses covering his eyes. He was the real power in this room. The decision rested with him—whoever he was.

"Another blonde, I see," the male judge said. He had the distinct look of a half-demon. I could see the faint outline of small horns on his forehead. "Kira? Is that right?"

I nodded. "Yes, sir."

"Well, go ahead and strip off the clothes. Let's see what we're working with."

My eyes widened, and I tilted my head. "Does that line work with all the girls?"

Both he and the female judge laughed in good-natured surprise.

The female gestured toward my body. "I know it's a strange request, but our show is about desire and need. We want to make sure you have all the, shall we say, physical prerequisites to be a good fit as the lead. We want the alphas to *really* yearn for you."

I hadn't planned on this, but it was what it was. Being an operative had required me to do lots of things I wasn't necessarily comfortable with. I'd run ops in fatigues, bikinis, bathrobes. Once, I'd even been naked. This was a piece of cake compared to taking down a scumbag incubus who'd infiltrated a nudist resort.

Shrugging indifferently, I peeled off my clothes, leaving my bra and panties on. I made a slow turn before facing the judges again.

"Happy?" I asked.

They were both scribbling on notepads. What the hell were they writing?

The half-demon glanced up and, in a very offhand way, asked, "What's your breast size?"

"I'm sorry?" Had he really asked that?

The female judge looked at the male. "Jurion, I keep telling you that's not important. If they're too small, we can get her a pushup bra or something."

As she talked, I quickly dressed.

The half-demon—Jurion—sighed as though she'd told him he wasn't getting a birthday gift. "Fine." Addressing me again, he said, "So, we're looking for someone charismatic. We need someone who will not only make the alphas want to fight for her but also get the audience to root for her. Do you think that is something you can convey?"

Cocking an eyebrow, I said, "Charisma comes from being honest, not fake. People can smell fake from a mile away. I'm not going to bat my eyelashes and shake my tits at the camera if that's what you're looking for. I am who I am. Either they'll like me, or they won't. I'm not about to change myself to make the viewers or alphas *want* me more. I'm here to win. At any cost." I stared directly at the judges. "I'm ready to move on to the next step of the auditions. I think you know I've got what it takes."

My bravado wasn't entirely false. I did think I had what it took, but being that forward might backfire spectacularly. It was a last-second decision on my part to differentiate myself from the other auditioners. I suspected the other women would all be falling over themselves to suck up or pander to the judges. Being different might work in my favor.

A relieved breath escaped me when I noticed the mysterious man in the back leaning forward, his elbows on his knees as he studied me. I had to fight to keep the grin off my face.

The female judge raised her eyebrows in admiration. "Bold. I like that." She looked at her clipboard. "How long ago were you rejected?"

"Less than a week ago." I said it as if I were reading from an encyclopedia.

Both judges snapped their heads up, pinning me with shocked gazes. Clearly, that was not a typical answer.

"You were rejected by your fated mate less than a week ago?" Jurion asked. For the first time since I'd stepped into the room, he looked truly interested in me.

"That's correct. In fact, I was rejected during my mating ceremony."

The female judge looked like I'd just slapped her. "At the ceremony? My gods," she gasped.

Jurion looked at his cohort. "You know, it could be a huge change of pace and a nice hook if we had someone who was freshly heartbroken. It also says here that she's from the Eleventh Pack. We've never had an Eleventh Packer as the lead. We've only ever had one from that pack as a contestant—a male trying for the hand of a female lead, and he died in the first episode of season nineteen."

They leaned toward each other and spoke in hushed tones. Even my enhanced shifter hearing couldn't pick up on their words. There must have been a privacy spell on or around their desk. I peered into the shadows at the stranger. Was that a smile I detected? I tried to convince myself it was a good sign. Hope started to flare in my chest, pushing back against the despair that had been growing in my gut from the moment Jayson rejected me.

The half-demon raised his head, sweeping his eyes up and down my body once more. "There is an entrance fee for all contestants, including the lead. You do realize that. Is that something you can afford?"

He must have been referring to my old T-shirt and jeans. The decision to come here had been spur-of-the-moment and desperate enough that I hadn't even thought to change into something nicer like the other women had. Gods, I knew the fee was steep. I'd checked my account in the waiting room to ensure I could pay it. It would basically deplete my savings, but I could swing it. Barely.

With a nod, I said, "That's no problem. I can pay." Throwing caution to the wind, I added, "Besides, I'm going to win. What's a little money now when I'll have that much more at the end?"

"Ooh." The half-demon smiled. "Cocky. We haven't had that in a while."

The woman pointed her pen at me. "Go ahead and shift. Let's see what the wolf looks like. We've had a lot of gray wolves in the last two years. I'd like something different."

Damn. The audition had been going so well. Now all the hope that I'd begun to grab onto was draining away. Thankfully, I was trained not to let my emotions show on my face. There was no way around it, but I'd need to play it perfectly if I had any chance.

Pulling my shoulders back, I said, "I don't shift."

The two judges looked at me as though I'd said the dumbest thing they'd ever heard.

"Um, wait...what?" the woman asked.

"Hang on," the half-demon said, voice vibrating with rage. "You silly girl, you do realize this is *The Reject Project*, right? Every contestant is a wolf shifter. What are you? A human who was adopted into an Eleventh Pack family or something? Why would you even show up if you weren't a shifter?"

I couldn't back down or show weakness. Not now. This was my only shot.

"I assure you, I am a shifter. A blood test will tell you I am. I was, after all, fated to a mate. I'm simply unable to shift. I've seen enough of the show to know that you don't *have* to shift to compete, win, or survive."

They both looked at me for several seconds before bursting into laughter. Having them laugh at my expense set my teeth on edge. I clamped my jaw.

Just as I was about to say screw it and unload on them, I saw the man in the back stand and walk toward me.

At the sound of his footsteps, the two judges abruptly shut up. That alone told me I'd been right about him being the true power in the room. He stopped about two paces from me, slowly slid the sunglasses off his face, and tucked them into the pocket of his tailored black suit.

His eyes pierced into me, and I had the strange sensation he was looking even deeper than surface level. There was a hint of something at the back of my mind, an idea of what this man was.

"My dear Miss Durst," he said in a deep baritone. "The mysterious and enigmatic owner of *The Reject Project* won't even look at your application if you can't shift. You must realize this."

Glaring at him, I said, "Then make them."

The two judges gasped at my audacity.

If the man was upset, he didn't show it. Instead, he gave me a sad smile. "I'm afraid I don't have that kind of pull."

My years of training kicked in. I watched the strange twitch in his cheek as he spoke, the barest flicker as he tried to avert his gaze from mine. He was lying. The tell was there, and I could read it.

"Bullshit."

I had to keep myself from rolling my eyes when the two judges gasped again. The strange man tilted his head and studied me more intensely.

"In what way am I, as you so eloquently put it, bullshitting you?"

"I'm a senior Tranquility operative. I can read a room, see deceit, smell a lie from a mile away. You wouldn't be sitting in the shadows, silently watching every contestant come through here if you weren't important. You're the one vetting the contestants, not those two," I said, gesturing at the two judges with a wave of my hand. "And if that's a job only you have, then it means someone *very* powerful assigned it to you. How am I doing so far?"

He stared at me with a stony expression before bursting into a good-natured laugh. Some of the tension in my chest evaporated, but not all of it. He could still tell me to get the hell out.

Finally, he said, "Fair enough, Miss Durst. Fair enough. I admit, I am...hmm, what should I call myself? The invisible host of the show, I suppose. Von is the face. I act behind the scenes. I'm here to hand-pick half a dozen serious candidates for the final pool."

He looked at me through half-lidded eyes before sighing with pleasure. "We've never had someone who couldn't shift or someone with such a strong psyche before. It truly is delicious."

That sealed it. Talking about my psyche had given him away. This man was a psychic. A mind reader. Quickly, I thrust up walls around a certain set of memories I didn't want him to access.

He grinned, and his eyes glittered. "Oh my. You *are* an operative. You know how to guard yourself. Hmmm. Now, I wonder what those memories you just hid contained. What else is in that..." He trailed off, and his smile grew even wider. "Well, well, well. A female *alpha*? You are full of surprises."

I stiffened at that but forced myself to nod. "I am."

He studied me for a few more moments, then gave a little shrug. "I'll put your name in the running. That's all I can promise."

"But she can't shift," the female judge said, looking scandalized.

The mysterious man's head jerked toward her, all good nature fleeing his face. "Did I ask your opinion? Did I even ask to hear your voice?" Ice dripped from every word.

The woman immediately bowed her head, her eyes locking on the desk. "No, sir. I'm sorry."

Straightening his lapels, he turned back to me, the calm smile returning as though nothing had happened.

"As this season will have male alpha shifters competing for a single female, you will be the only woman on the show if you are chosen. Along with the entry fee, you will be required to bring your own stylist. I recommend having someone picked out in case you are cast." He glanced at my slovenly attire. "We don't want our leading lady to look like a hobo." He nodded toward the door. "That will be all, Miss Durst. You'll hear from us by the end of the week."

That was it? I'd made it to the next round? With how important this show was and how many people were auditioning, I really thought the audition would take at least an hour. I took it as a good sign that I'd only been in there for a few minutes. The psychic man's tone told me he was serious about putting my name up for consideration. I couldn't help but smile as I thanked him and headed for the door.

All the way out of the room and down the elevator, my heart beat rhythmically in my throat. I hadn't felt excitement like this in days. I could only pray that the psychic wasn't just getting my hopes up. I didn't think I could survive another rejection.

Chapter 10 - Wyatt

It had been two days since I found out Kira went to Fangmore City to audition for that fucking show. I'd headed straight there after stomping out of the house when her father had been so happy that she'd gone to audition. By the time I found the show's offices, Kira was gone, and the auditions were over. I'd spent two hours stalking through the city, barely controlling my rage. I'm sure some people thought I was a raving lunatic hobo.

Back in the Eastern Wilds, Zoe had vanished. Kolton said she'd gone back to her place. Kira never went back home. I knew because I'd checked a dozen times. Kolton, tired of seeing me worry myself to death, finally admitted that Kira was bunking with Zoe.

I gritted my teeth. "You couldn't have told me this sooner?"

Kolton slapped his laptop closed. "Well, I kinda thought you'd let it go. But you're like a damned demon on a reliquary."

"Where does Zoe live?" I asked, grabbing my jacket and walking toward the door.

Kolton's eyes widened. "No way. Not a chance. If you show up on her doorstep, Zoe will know I told you. Have you ever been on a fae's bad side? She'll like...I don't know...make my dick vanish or something."

Heaving in a deep calming breath, I turned to my friend. "Fair enough. How about a general location? I can follow Kira's scent from there. Deal?"

Kolton mulled that over. He was equally horrified by Kira's decision, but being her brother, he understood that there was no way to change her mind—some kind of built-in social contract between siblings or something. I didn't have that issue. She wasn't my sister, and I didn't think it was a lost cause.

"Fine," Kolton finally said. "Zoe lives near her cosmetology shop. It's on the corner of Scott Street and Howard Avenue. That's all you get," he added, holding up a warning finger. "If Zoe asks? I don't know anything."

"Yeah, yeah, got it. Thanks."

"Hang on. I gotta ask you something," Kolton said.

I looked over my shoulder warily. I had a feeling I knew what was coming. "Yeah?"

"Is there a reason you're so hell-bent on finding my sister?"

There was a pause that went on for several seconds as I tried to figure out the best thing to say. Finally, I said, "Someone needs to. We have to make sure she's okay. You know what she's trying to do and how dangerous it is."

He nodded. "I do. But there's more going on here." He eyed me with suspicion. "You two fight like cats and dogs. Of everyone she knows, you're the person I thought would be least likely to be so concerned."

"Listen," I said as I headed toward the door, "it is what it is. If I don't stop her, no one will. Who cares what happened before? I gotta go."

Kolton looked like he was trying to figure something out, but I didn't have time to deal with what he did or didn't think. I needed to find Kira, talk some sense into her, and see if I could convince her to give up this crazy idea.

I found the shop fairly easily. Unfortunately, there were a ton of apartments nearby. I probably could have called in some favors with the council and gotten Zoe's address, but I didn't think that was a good idea. Zoe Helio was a known acquaintance of Kira's, and Kira's name was mud with the council right now. If word got out that I was helping Kira, I could be in deep shit. And I needed my connections to stay clean if I was going to help Kira get out of the shit-storm she'd dropped herself into.

With nothing else to do, I stalked up and down the streets, trying to catch her scent or Zoe's, though tracking a fae by scent alone was pointless. Their scent was too amorphous, changing with their emotions. I'd be walking in circles if I only had to go off Zoe's scent.

Fortunately, later in the evening, I had a breakthrough. I caught a faint waft of what I was looking for near the entrance of a bar. I'd know Kira's smell anywhere: hints of vanilla and honeysuckle, an undertone of seawater and birch bark, with the smallest hint of rose water. My heart stuttered when I caught it, and my feet instinctually led me toward the scent.

Music assaulted my ears as I stepped into the bar. It was barely past eight, but the place was packed. The deep bass thumped so strongly, it resonated in my chest. Colored lights flashed and strobed around the bar and dance floor. I was already in a shit mood, and this place did little to appease me.

With everything going on in her life, Kira had decided clubbing was the best way to let off steam? Her life was on the line, and she was getting drunk in a bar? It made no sense. She was usually reserved and rigid. It wasn't like her to hang out in a place like this, unless she was on assignment. But she also had what I considered a self-destructive streak a mile wide. That usually displayed itself by her taking risks and volunteering for dangerous missions. She was impulsive, but I'd be damned if I let that be the death of her.

There was a short line at the door, a bouncer checking IDs and taking cover charges. I skirted the line and ducked under the velvet rope.

"Hey, fucker, back of the line!" the bouncer called out, grabbing the sleeve of my leather jacket.

My lips peeled back in a growl. Without speaking, I lifted my wallet and showed him my Tranquility operative badge. The bouncer's face went pale, and he released my jacket, holding his hands up in surrender.

"No problem, bro. You do you."

"That's what I thought," I snarled as I entered the club.

There had to be a hundred people inside, their scents all intermingling. I'd have to search for Kira. I pressed through the crowd, eyes bouncing from face to face until I spotted her. There she was, at the far end of the dance floor, drink in hand, dancing with Zoe. Her halter top clung to her skin, her shorts short enough to display the curve of her ass. The clothes must have been Zoe's—Kira never dressed like that.

As I watched her dance, a strange feeling coiled in my stomach at the sight of her bare midriff. My eyes flicked from the creamy skin of her stomach to the curve of her ass to the outline of her breasts. A flash of the day the lion shifter had poisoned her burst through my mind. Kira's tongue on my neck, her hands pawing at me, her breathless voice asking me to fuck her, to make her come.

I shook my head, shoving the thoughts away. This was Kolton's sister. As hot as she looked, I needed to get my head on straight. Things had to be put into perspective. Plus, she'd gone through a lot of shit lately. This wasn't the time for me to have some thirteen-year-old boy's wet dream. Even if the situation was different, Kira hated my guts—always would. Anything else I might feel was a moot point.

The two women didn't notice me until I was standing right next to them.

"Hello, ladies," I said, raising my voice to be heard above the music.

Kira's eyes snapped toward my voice. Her nostrils flared, the muscles in her jaw flexing as she gritted her teeth.

"Oh, goody, we get to have angsty and uncomfortable conversations on our night out. How fun," Zoe said drily after seeing both of our faces.

"What the hell are you doing here? How did you find us?" Kira demanded.

"Don't worry about that," I said. "We need to talk."

"Uh oh!" Zoe shouted, "Emperor Killjoy has arrived. Hide the alcohol, stop having sex, and start praying to the gods for forgiveness."

"Zoe, please," I said.

She grabbed a couple of drinks from the bar and held them out to Kira and me. "Here, it'll help you calm down."

Kira took hers and gulped it down.

I cocked an eyebrow. "You'd better be checking that. Remember the last time you took a drink and didn't double-check? You don't want to put yourself in a bad position again."

I regretted the words as soon as they were out of my mouth, but it was too late. Kira's eyes flashed menacingly.

"And what position would that be?"

Again, my mind flashed with the memory of her skin pressed against me in the parking lot. Her fingers sliding across my chest, breathless moans begging me to do dirty things to her. I couldn't let those thoughts out. Instead, I changed the subject.

"Are you guys out here celebrating or trying to drown your sorrows?" I asked, trying to get a read on how the audition went without coming straight out and asking.

Kira gave me a sickly-sweet smile dripping with sarcasm and held her drink up. "Both," she shouted, then took another drink.

That told me nothing. Why had I assumed anything different? Kira was smart, and I was sure she knew exactly what I was trying to get at. She was probably being as obstinate as possible to piss me off.

Kira handed her glass to Zoe, then slipped into the crowd, vanishing into the dance floor. Shit. I'd lost sight of her.

Grabbing Zoe, I tugged her into a fairly quiet corner.

"Hey, Mister Grabby-Hands, watch it," Zoe snapped, looking down at my fingers on her shoulder.

"Did Kira get on the show?" I asked.

Zoe's eyes skirted to the dance floor where Kira had vanished, then back to my face. "Show? Like on stage? This isn't that kind of club. You have to go a few blocks down to see that."

"Dammit, Zoe, you know what I mean. *The Reject Project*? Did they choose her for the show?"

She cupped a hand to her ear and squinted. "I'm sorry? The Preachy Quartet? Is that some religious acapella band you're in? It's so loud, I can't hear you."

"Zoe, for fuck's sake. Can't you..."

I trailed off as I glanced over and saw Kira. The crowd had parted, and I glimpsed her getting hot and heavy with some guy on the dance floor. She had her arms around the guy's neck, and he had his wrapped around her waist, his fingers digging into her ass as they gyrated. Even in the flashing lights, I could see the outline of his hard-on against his pants.

Before I knew what I was doing, I was on the dance floor, pulling Kira away from the guy. I was unreasonably angry, and I didn't really understand why, but I despised seeing another man's hands on her. It set me off in a way I'd never experienced before.

"Are you insane? What the hell is wrong with you?" I asked Kira.

When she looked at me, I could see the alcohol had started to affect her. Her eyes had the soft, glazed look of someone who was on their way to being drunk.

She pushed me in the chest. "I've been rejected, Wyatt. Fuck. That's what's wrong with me. I'm about to be an outcast, like you and your pathetic little group of *bros*. I'm losing my pack. I've lost my job. Everything is fucked. All I want is one night to enjoy myself, and I can't do that with you."

She pulled away from me and tried to turn back to the stranger she'd been dancing with. The last thing I wanted was to see that douchebag's hands on her again. The flashes of memory returned. The music was too loud, the smell of sweat, the scent of sexual musk so intense that my mind couldn't work right. I couldn't push the memories of the parking lot away as easily. My impulses overrode my will, my desires crashing through my carefully built walls.

I grabbed her arm and pulled her back, pressing my face close to hers. "You damn well *can* have a good time with me." I reached forward and grabbed her ass like she belonged to me. "It's about time I showed you that."

Kira's eyes widened in surprise, but to my delight, she didn't pull away. Instead, she studied me for a moment. I could almost hear the calculations happening in her head, weighing the pros and cons of what I'd said.

"Okay," she breathed. "Show me what you've got."

With a growl, I pulled her into the shadows, ignoring the curses from the guy she'd left behind. We crashed into a wall, and I was on her a moment later, pressing my lips to hers.

Kira, desperate with need and a little drunk, slid her tongue into my mouth. My cock stiffened immediately. Feeling it, Kira pressed her hips into me, grinding against my hard length.

Spurred on by lust, I pushed all sensible thoughts away and decided to live in the moment. Fuck the consequences. I cupped her breast, letting my thumb slide over her nipple. Kira sighed against my mouth and slid a hand between my legs, gently squeezing my bulge.

Kira wrenched her lips from mine and looked at me. Her usually controlled look was gone. The slight distaste she'd always shown me had vanished. Instead, all I saw in her eyes was desire and need.

She squeezed me again. "I thought you were gonna show me what you could do."

My mouth went dry, and my heart hammered painfully against my ribcage. Was she serious? Was this about to happen? On my walk here, I saw a small boutique hotel a few doors down from the club. I could take her there, but she might change her mind on the way.

Kira leaned close and flicked her tongue over my lower lip. "Are you gonna fuck me or not?"

The decision already made, I grabbed her hand and led her out the front door. She chuckled as we exited onto the street. The air outside was cooler than in the club, but it didn't tamp down my excitement.

Kira leaned against me as we walked, still caressing my crotch. She looked wholly unconcerned with what anyone might think as they saw us.

At the door of the hotel, I pushed her against the wall and kissed her again. Our bodies pressed into each other, grinding and desperate. All of a sudden, my underwear was too tight, and my cock ached to be free. Breaking our embrace again, I pulled her inside.

The receptionist tried to hide a smirk. The way we were acting was obviously funny to him. Honestly, I couldn't blame him. Kira kept leaning over and kissing my neck as I registered and paid for a room. The agent kept glancing up at us, smiling knowingly at me. The entire time, I kept thinking Kira would come to her senses and realize she couldn't do what we were about to do. I imagined her slapping me and storming out. I'd have to trudge up to my newly paid-for hotel room and jerk off a half dozen times to release all this sexual energy. But to my joyous surprise, when the agent held out the key, it was Kira who snatched it from his hand.

"Do not disturb," she said, tugging me toward the elevator.

As soon as the doors closed, Kira slid her hand across my chest, looking at me hungrily.

"Are you gonna give me what I want? Like a good little lone wolf?"

Nodding, I cupped her breasts. "I'm gonna fuck your brains out. Is that what you want?" She'd been drunk in the club, and as badly as I wanted this, I was not one to take advantage of a vulnerable woman. "Do you want this? Because I need to know I'm not taking advantage of you when you're hammered."

She licked her lips and looked into my eyes. "We're shifters. The alcohol is already almost out of my system, Wyatt. I'm not drunk anymore. I'm fucking horny."

I let out a shaky breath as I ran my hands down her back and gripped her ass. "Then get ready."

Kira moaned and kissed me again as the elevator doors opened. Frantically, we more or less ran down the hall to the room. Kira fumbled the key in the lock, and finally, the door opened.

I slammed the door shut, then yanked her top off even as I lifted her and tossed her on the bed. I grabbed the tiny shorts molded to her body and slid them off in one quick movement, along with her thong. She gasped as I flipped her onto her stomach, lifted her hips, and buried my face in her pussy.

I slipped my tongue into her, and the taste of her almost had me exploding. Kira clutched the sheets and groaned as I fucked her with my tongue. Sliding into her, then flicking across her clit, then up to circle her asshole, and back again. Over and over. Heat flooded from her pussy, the taste delectable.

"Gods, eat me, make me fucking come, Wyatt," Kira moaned, thrusting her hips back into my face.

I pulled my face and rubbed a finger over her clit. "I'm gonna make you come so hard."

Kira looked over her shoulder at me, eyes half-lidded in pleasure. "Promises, promises."

Growling, I pressed my face to her pussy again and wrapped my lips around her clit, sucking on it. I slid my tongue back and forth as I did and pressed two fingers into her pussy. She started to vibrate under my hands, her orgasm nearing with each second. Her clit swelled under my lips, engorging as I sucked on it.

"Don't stop...holy shit, don't you fucking stop, Wyatt." Kira's voice was barely audible as she buried her face in the pillow.

Obeying, I flicked my tongue even faster until, with a shuddering scream, Kira jerked and spasmed. Pulling my face away, I slid my fingers slowly across her clit and pussy as she rode the climax to conclusion. Rising, I ripped off my clothes. My cock stood erect, bouncing faintly in time to my heartbeat.

Kira, hair messy and sweaty, spun around and looked at me. If anything, that first orgasm seemed to have filled her with more lust rather than dissipating it. She eyed me hungrily, first locking her eyes on mine before slowly sliding her gaze downward. Her gaze stopped on my cock, and she grinned slyly.

"Damn. If I'd known this is what you were working with, I might have done this sooner."

She lunged at me, reflexes honed tight from years of training. I didn't even have time to flinch before she had my cock in her mouth. The warm wetness of her tongue and throat nearly made my knees buckle. I threw my head back and let out an inarticulate moan of pleasure as her mouth slid up and down my shaft. Her free hand cupped my balls as she worked.

Looking down, I gazed at her sleek, muscular body. Her upper back flexed as she moved on my dick.

Wanting nothing more than to touch her, I caressed her shoulders and back with my hands. Her skin was soft and smooth. I wanted her more than anything I'd ever wanted in my life.

Kira sucked the head of my cock, her tongue massaging the tip. It was so fucking good that I nearly went cross-eyed. She pulled my cock out of her mouth and licked her lips, then looked up at me.

"I want this inside me," she said as she stroked my length.

My hands trembled with excitement. Part of me wondered if this was a dream, but the coolness of her fingers sliding along my shaft told me it was very much real. I leaned down, put my hands under her hips, and lifted, toppling her onto her back.

She bit her lower lip and eyed me hungrily. "Don't be gentle. I'm not a fucking China doll."

With a growl of desire, I spread her legs and thrust into her. Her wetness enveloped me, tight and warm. I stayed like that for a moment, simply enjoying the feel of her around me. Kira's eyes rolled back in her head, and her hands clamped onto my shoulders, digging her nails into my skin.

Urged on by her writhing and groans, I thrust into her. Kira bit hard into my shoulder and moaned low in her throat. Her breasts pressed into my chest. Winding my hand into her hair, I tugged gently as I slid out to the tip, then plunged back into her. It was like we were animals, fully given over to the beasts that lived within our minds. I'd never experienced something so glorious.

Kira grabbed my chin and forced my eyes on hers. "I told you to fuck me. Hard."

"Oh my gods," I muttered but did as I was told.

My hips crashed into her as I slammed my cock into her pussy, harder and faster with each thrust, her breasts bouncing with the impact.

"Fuck!" she cried out, throwing her head back into the pillow. "Yes! Oh, gods!"

Grunting and sweating with exertion, I kissed her chin, then murmured, "You like that cock? Is this what you want? Is this how you wanted it?"

"Harder! I'm gonna fucking come."

Rising to my knees, I grabbed her hips and yanked her onto my cock with each thrust. Kira cried out, clutching at the sheets. Her mouth dropped open in a moan that slowly built to a scream as she shuddered to climax.

My own orgasm was near. I leaned forward and licked her nipple, tasting the salt of her sweat as ripples of pleasure coursed through her body.

She grabbed my hair and tilted my head toward her. "Come for me, Wyatt. I want to feel you come inside me."

The words were all it took. Like a grenade burst in my pelvis, ecstasy so strong exploded through my body that I cried out. I'd never orgasmed so hard in my life. It was like my soul was being drained and pouring itself into her. My hips spasmed again and again.

Finally spent, I collapsed onto her chest, heaving breath into my lungs. Her hands were still in my hair, and her heart hammered under my ear. My mind had short-circuited, barely able to believe what had just happened.

I rolled onto my side and looked at her. Kira was on the verge of tears. My post-coital bliss vanished, replaced with icy fear. Had I done something wrong? All I'd wanted was to make her feel what I felt. The last thing I wanted to do was upset her.

When she looked at me, I could see that wasn't it. She opened her mouth to say something but stopped as though frozen with indecision. A tear slipped down her cheek, and without thinking, I reached out and wiped it away. Kira closed her mouth and stared at me.

My heart twisted as I watched her throw up the barriers and walls that had always stood between us. She sat up, squaring her shoulders and lifting her chin. Without a single hint of what she'd been about to say, she got up and started searching for her clothes that lay strewn across the room.

"Let's forget this happened." She didn't even look at me as she spoke.

"Wait, what?" I said, pulling the sheets over my nakedness, suddenly ashamed.

With an overly dramatic sigh, Kira turned, her breasts still uncovered and swaying. "You're my brother's best friend. This was…a mistake. I was pissed off at the world, a little tipsy, and horny as hell. My head wasn't in the right place. It never should have happened."

"Kira? You can't believe that." I gestured to the bed. "What just happened was…" I tried to think of the right words. "It was more than sex. That was *intense—*"

"Wyatt, now isn't the time for romanticism, okay? We fucked, it was good, but it's over now. Forget about this. It'll be easy."

She found her clothes and hurriedly shimmied into her thong and shorts. I could tell she meant to leave as soon as possible. I stumbled out of bed and pulled on my own clothes, managing to get dressed and across the room before she had the door open. I slapped my palm against it, shutting it before it moved more than a few inches.

Kira glared at me. "Wyatt, I need to leave. Zoe's probably worried about me."

"If it has to be this way, then fine. But I won't forget this, Kira. I couldn't. If I must, I will pretend it never happened. It won't be easy, but I will do that because you asked me. What I want to know is why you were crying a minute ago."

Something wavered in her eyes, but it was gone so fast, I might have imagined it. Kira sighed and shook her head sadly, like I was a child who didn't understand something simple.

"Mind your own business, Wyatt. From now on, you won't have to worry about me."

That was it, the clue I'd needed. *From now on.* It meant she had made it onto *The Reject Project.* She was going to be on that awful, godsdamned show.

Kira sighed and yanked the door open. She was down the hall before I could react. I was shocked that my greatest fear had been realized. I ran after her but had to double back to get my shirt. By the time I got to the elevator, the doors were closing. Kira simply stared at me as I ran toward her, but she made no move to stop the doors.

Deciding to take the stairs instead of waiting for the elevator to return, I sprinted down to the lobby, but I wasn't fast enough. The elevator was empty, and Kira was nowhere in sight. I high-tailed it out of the hotel and headed to the club, hoping to find her, knowing that was where she had to have gone. At the door, I flashed my badge again and ducked into the bar, searching through the mass of bodies for Kira. I didn't see her, but her scent was fresh, which meant she was here. The only problem was that the place was even more crowded than before, almost elbow to elbow.

Frustrated, I went to the bar to ask the bartender if he'd seen someone matching her description. There, leaning on the bar counter and nursing a drink, was Zoe. She looked hammered but was still coherent enough to recognize me.

"Hey." She raised her cocktail toward me, some of the liquid sloshing over the rim. "How did all that go? I saw you and my girlie hustle out the door." She hiccupped. "Did she clean your pipes out good?"

"What are you talking about, Zoe?"

Squinting blearily, she poked my arm. "Sorry, buddy. You can't pull one over on a fae. Two people can't hate each other that much without eventually either killing each other or fucking their brains out. My guess is the latter since you're both still alive."

I grabbed her arm and pulled her to the door.

Zoe pointed at my hand and called out to the bar patrons. "Lookie! Mister Grabby-Hands is back for more."

"Where's Kira?" I asked when we were out on the sidewalk and away from the incessant thumping of the bass music.

"She texted me like ten minutes ago, said she was coming to find me." Zoe swayed, and I scooted her over to the wall so she could lean against it. "What happened?" She frowned and glanced at my crotch. "Oh no. Is it small?" She pouted up at me and held her forefinger and thumb an inch apart. "All that build-up, and you've got a little wiener?"

"Zoe?" Kira yelled.

I glanced at the door, where Kira was coming out of the club. She rushed over to us and wrapped an arm around her friend to hold her up. Kira pushed me away from her.

Zoe leaned close to Kira's ear. "Does he have a small pee-pee?" she asked in a loud, drunken whisper.

Ignoring her again, I put my hands out, pleading. "Kira, don't do this. I can't watch you put yourself in danger. I won't be able to save you this time."

Kira snorted in disgust and turned to wave for a cab, tugging Zoe along behind her.

"I'm not the weakling you think I am, Wyatt," she called over her shoulder. "It's too late. My fate is sealed. You'll have to get over it."

Before I could say anything else, Kira shoved Zoe into a taxi, then crawled in beside her and slammed the door. I stared at the red tail lights as they slowly disappeared down the street, my hands clenched into shaking fists.

She was going to die. It didn't matter how well she was trained or how much she wanted to succeed. I was sure she wouldn't survive the show. The showrunners pushed the boundaries because they knew people loved the drama and horror of on-screen deaths. I was intimately aware of how their minds worked. I couldn't let her go into that alone. There had to be a way to stop this.

I paced up the street, pulling at my hair and trying not to put my fist through a wall when the thought hit me. I froze mid-stride, an icy chill sliding down my spine. A myriad of possibilities ran through my mind and were quickly dismissed, but I did have one option to save Kira. It wouldn't get her off the show, but it might give her a better chance at surviving.

It was time to pull some strings.

Flopping down onto the curb, I pulled out my phone and dialed a number I hadn't used in years. It rang and rang, and just as I was about to give up, someone answered.

"Wyatt?" My aunt's voice was a combination of shocked, pleased, and confused.

"It's me, Aunt Denise."

"My goodness. When I saw your name on the caller ID, I thought it was a mistake. How are you? It's been a long time. Your voice is so deep. You must be a full-grown man now."

"Aunt Denise," I said, interrupting her spiel. "Is Uncle Rob there? I need to talk to him. It's really, *really* important."

"Oh, of course," Aunt Denise said. "Let me grab him."

My feet bounced nervously, knots of fear and dread curling and uncurling in my stomach as I waited. When my uncle came on the line, he sounded as surprised and pleased as my aunt had.

"Wyatt? Is it really you?"

"Hi, Uncle Rob."

"This must be important. I thought you said you were never going to talk to any of us again. What can I do for you?"

Sighing, I said, "I need a favor. Probably the biggest one I ever have or will ever ask for. Whatever you want in return, I'll do it."

"Name it," Uncle Rob said without hesitation. "Whatever it is, it's yours."

Chapter 11 - Kira

I'd thought getting cast to be the lead on *The Reject Project* would be simple, but boy, was I wrong. In my head, I'd figured the beginning of the process would be easier than my job as an operative. I couldn't have had things more backwards. At least as an operative, I understood what was happening and why. This was a chaotic blur.

I remembered getting the congratulations call from the mysterious psychic. Then, almost immediately, my emails, texts, and phone blew up. I had multiple documents to read and sign, a publicist who worked on the show had set up a time to film something she called B-roll, and I was supposed to give them all of Zoe's info, too, since she would be my stylist. And that was just from the first three emails.

Before I could do anything, I had to sign a ton of legal forms. By the time I was done, I couldn't be sure I hadn't signed away my firstborn or immortal soul. In fact, everything happened so fast, I didn't have time to get stressed out.

Going out that night had been my idea. I needed to blow off steam. The plan had been to find some hot guy at the club, bang the night away, and then get my head straight for what was to come.

Wyatt had thrown a wrench in that plan.

I was still kicking myself for what had happened. My brain alternated between reliving the amazing things he'd done to me and being disgusted with myself for succumbing to his charms. Of all the people I could have had a one-night stand with, I had to go and choose him? It was more about him being in the right place at the right time, but still, it was ridiculous.

Thankfully, Wyatt hadn't pushed the issue, nor had he shown his face when I went back home to say goodbye to my pack. Due to the inch-thick non-disclosure agreement I'd signed, I couldn't tell them why I was leaving, but Mom and Dad knew. They'd figured it out when I told them I was moving to Fangmore, though I never explicitly confirmed their suspicions. Most of the pack elders hadn't bothered to show up for my departure, which hurt. I wished it didn't hurt, but it did. Everyone probably assumed I was being quietly cast out in disgrace. Part of me wanted to scream and rage at them for what they thought, but my actions on the show would have to speak louder than any words I said to them now.

Tears streamed from Mom's eyes as she hugged me goodbye. "Will they let you call us?" she asked as she pulled away.

"Not sure, Mom. I'll call if I can, okay?"

She nodded and blew her nose as she backed away. Dad stepped forward and put his hands on my shoulders. The look on his face was one I'd always been desperate to see. There was love there, and sadness, but the main emotion in his eyes was pride. I'd never seen him look as proud as he did right then. Not even when I'd walked toward the mating circle before everything had fallen apart.

He pulled me into a tight hug. "You're doing the right thing. You'll do great. I know it," he whispered in my ear.

The other pack leaders who attended gave me some cursory goodbyes, but their bored expressions and listless words told me they didn't give a damn that I was leaving. It made me wonder what they'd do if I told them exactly why I was leaving the pack lands. Would they change their tune and beam at me with pride? Or would they simply look at me with sadness and start consoling my parents on the death of their daughter? A death they'd be sure was coming.

"Let's get out of here," I whispered to Zoe as we walked away from the house.

Zoe's eyes flicked to the tree line. "We can, but you've got company."

Following her eyes, I saw the familiar form of my brother Kolton's wolf sprinting out of the forest toward us. He shifted as he drew upon us, a heavy backpack slung over his shoulders.

"Hang on, buttface," he said. "You aren't going anywhere without me."

I gaped at him, then looked at Zoe. She had a guilty look on her face and refused to meet my eyes.

Gritting my teeth, I snarled at her. "You knew he was gonna do this?"

Zoe, still unable to look me in the eyes, shrugged. "He's your brother."

Whirling on Kolton, I shook my head. "No. Not happening."

He was already walking toward Zoe's car. "Too bad you think that because yes, it is."

Before I could say anything else or grab him by the hair and drag him away, he'd already tossed his backpack in the trunk and climbed into the back seat.

"You've got to be kidding me," I hissed.

Zoe walked toward the driver's side door and waved me to come along. "Look on the bright side. Now you have a stylist *and* a bodyguard. Cool, huh?"

I had too much to worry about to drain my patience or energy arguing with Kolton. Who, other than me or Wyatt, was the *most* stubborn person I'd ever met. I opened the trunk, tossed my two bags in, and slammed it shut.

When I was in the passenger side, I turned to point a finger at Kolton. "I don't need to hear you complaining about the show or trying to talk me out of it, got it? I've already signed a shit-ton of legal documents, so it's set in stone. Copy that?"

He sighed as he buckled his seatbelt. "Yeah, yeah. Got it. You know my stance. I can't tell you anything you don't already know."

Content for the moment, I turned around and buckled my seatbelt.

Zoe smiled at both of us. "Road trip!"

Her smile faded when she saw that neither I nor my brother seemed excited about the drive.

She pouted. "Fine, then. Be that way," she grumbled and pulled away.

The chaos only got worse when I arrived in Fangmore City. No sooner had I arrived at the penthouse hotel room they'd reserved for me than I was called to the studio headquarters for a short interview that would air on the show's premiere. After that, I was sent to a company-owned clinic where I was subjected to every physical you could think of. The last time I'd been poked and prodded this much had been the night I'd spent with Wyatt. No matter how hard I tried to get that night out of my mind, it kept popping up.

All through the physical tests, my mind drifted back to him. I remembered his green eyes, filled with fire as he pleasured me. His muscles as our limbs twined together. It was all that occupied my thoughts as I did endurance tests, strength tests, lung capacity tests, and a multitude of others. It was like his eyes were following me through the entire process. It drove me crazy and made it hard to focus on what I was supposed to be doing.

"Kira? Kira? Hey?" Zoe called out.

I blinked myself back to reality. I was sitting in the luxurious hotel room, totally zoned out. I tried my best to stop thinking of Wyatt, of his tongue and the way it had felt between my legs.

"What?" I asked peevishly.

"Kolton has to leave."

Snapping fully back to reality, I twisted around. "Huh? Why?"

She tilted her head to the door. Glancing over, I saw two massive fallen angels standing there, gazing at me with emotionless eyes as Kolton cursed and stuffed his things into his backpack.

"Why does he need to go?" I asked as I stood.

The largest of the two stepped forward. "Only the contestant and her stylist are allowed in the room from here on out, Miss Durst. He'll get the chance to give you a final goodbye before the show starts."

"It's fine, Kira," Kolton called over the shoulder of the silent disgraced angel. "I'll see you soon."

A few seconds later, Zoe and I were alone. My shoulders sagged. As much as I hadn't wanted Kolton to come, I'd grown used to him being here the last week. Now that he was gone, it was like the one final strand connecting me to the pack had been severed.

"Well, this sucks," I said.

"Yeah. I kinda wondered when it would happen, though. I knew it would only be a matter of time," Zoe said.

My friend was still her usual chipper self. Now that it was set in stone that I was going on the show, she'd resigned herself to being my official stylist. It made me nervous that she'd be so entwined with the show.

"Aren't you worried, Zoe? You could be in danger, too," I said.

She made a dismissive gesture. "Hardly. In thirty years, no stylist, staff member, or host has ever been harmed. I'll be totally fine. You're the one *I'm* worried about. Is your head in this? You've been in a bit of a daze since we got here."

Not wanting to get into the subject of Wyatt, I shied away from the question. "Worried is all. It's really happening, isn't it?"

"Sure is. Can we get started on your wardrobe? I had the studio send over a bunch of fabrics to try out."

"Why not?"

Clothes didn't excite me as much as they did Zoe, but I let her do her thing. Taking swatches of fabric, she magically created dozens of different outfits. Most were amazing, but she skewed into experimental territory a few times. The craziest of the creations was a green velvet-and-tulle dress. The nearly transparent tulle fabric was all that covered my chest, basically exposing my breasts for anyone to see.

"Oh! That is so hot!" Zoe gushed.

Looking down at my visible nipples, I shook my head. "Absolutely not."

Zoe's face fell. "What? Why?"

I waved my hand over my chest. "Because everyone can see my tits, that's why. Are you crazy? I'm gonna be on TV."

Zoe sighed and rolled her eyes. "Gods, you shifters are such prudes. Fine."

The next outfits were more suitable, and I let her have creative freedom as long as my nibbly bits weren't overly exposed. She loved stuff like this, and this would be the chance for her designs, makeup, and hair talents to be seen by the whole world. Still, my head wasn't in it. I was just along for the ride.

Zoe must have noticed. She was humming happily at a dinner gown she'd just created, then looked up and saw my face. Something must have clued her in because her smile vanished.

"Ugh, I'm such a bitch. I'm sorry," Zoe said, running to me and wrapping me in a hug. "Are you okay? I get excited about clothes and stupid stuff. I totally forgot where your head must be."

I wrapped my arms around my friend and hugged her back, unable to say anything. The words were stuck in my throat. This was all happening too fast. The danger seemed to be getting more real with each passing day. My confidence in my skills was waning, and all I could think of were all the people who walked onto the show thinking they knew exactly what they were going to do but ended up going home in body bags.

"I'm scared, Zoe." My voice trembled. It was the first time I'd admitted that to anyone. Even myself.

Zoe clutched my shoulders and looked into my eyes. "No matter what happens, whatever crazy games they make you play or complicated or dangerous things you find yourself in, you'll be fine. It will work out." She smiled at me. "None of those people are as tough as you. Right?"

I laughed. "If you say so."

We hugged again, and I was more than grateful to have her at my side. If I had to be here alone, I'd have probably gone out of my mind with fear.

Releasing me, Zoe raised an eyebrow and grinned. "You shouldn't think of the bad stuff. Think of all those hot, strapping young alpha wolves who are gonna try everything in their power to win you over. I'm gonna love watching you fall helplessly in love with one of those dudes."

"Good luck with that," I said. "I'm playing this game to win, but I don't give a shit about the mate blessing. This is all about the Moon Goddess and the favor she grants. I'm in this to protect my pack and stop a war. Whatever drama happens along the way is just that—drama. I'll play the part, but my pack is all that matters."

Zoe shrugged. "Sure, but you can have a little fun along the way, right?"

Her talking about other men made my heart ache a little. It took a few minutes for me to understand why. Wyatt. I couldn't get him out of my mind. That kiss, his hands on my body, the taste of his skin. And he hadn't so much as texted since the night I left him outside that club. Either he had never really cared for me, or I'd done too good a job pushing him away.

I scolded myself for even letting those thoughts seep into my mind. I was probably never going to see him again. Besides, there was a very real possibility that I'd be dead in a few weeks.

A knock at the door pulled me out of my thoughts. One of the fallen angels who had removed Kolton came in when Zoe answered the door.

He nodded to me. "Miss Durst, I came by to tell you this is a one-hour call. You have sixty minutes until we bring you down to meet the crowds and start officially filming."

My eyes bugged out of my head as a cold sweat suddenly drenched me. "One hour? It starts in one hour? Are you serious?"

He nodded again. "We'll be back when you're ready." To make sure I was absolutely aware, he held up a finger. "One hour."

Once the door was closed, Zoe turned, her eyes frantic. "We need to hurry."

The next hour was a frenzy. Zoe and I packed away the clothes she'd made me, then she did my hair, twisting her fingers through it to enhance the blond accents and add a few curls. Waving her hands over my face, she applied the makeup, accentuating my eyes and lips. Magic swirled around me for almost forty minutes.

At last, she had me put on a maroon strapless dress. Sexy and form-fitting but chic enough not to be trashy, the dress packed a punch. It would make for a fantastic first impression. A glance in the mirror caused me to smile despite myself. I looked good. *Really* good, actually. I almost felt like I was ready to face whatever insanity was in store for me.

Another knock on the door. From outside, we heard the angel's muffled voice. "Miss Durst? It's time."

Zoe squeezed my shoulders and looked me dead in the eyes. "You'll do great." She shoved a matching maroon clutch into my hands and escorted me to the door.

As I walked behind the two angel bodyguards, I pulled my phone from the clutch and glanced at it.

Part of me hoped Wyatt might have sent me a text. But there was nothing. With a sigh, I handed it to Zoe.

"Turn that thing into a magic bracelet or something. I don't care," I said.

As soon as the elevator opened to the lobby, I heard a hissing roar, undulating and piercing at the same time. It took a second for me to realize it was the sound of a crowd cheering and screaming outside. Through the giant glass front doors of the hotel, I saw thousands of people lining the streets of the capital.

"Holy shit," Zoe whispered.

"Yup," I said, my mouth going suddenly dry.

"This way, folks," the fallen angel said.

I was terrified, but my feet followed the gigantic figures in front of me. Zoe slipped her hand into mine, and I squeezed it hard. A moment later, the doors opened, and a flood of noise enveloped me. Strobing flashes from cameras blinded me. Hand-drawn signs waved and swung through the air, but everything moved too fast for me to read them. People were yelling and screaming and reaching over barricades to try to touch me.

"Here she is, everyone!"

The voice was a familiar one. I'd heard it for years every time Zoe and I watched *The Reject Project*. It was the voice that had tempted me into this madness. Von Thornton stood on a massive stage in the middle of the city square. He was dressed in a solid white suit, bright stage lights illuminating him beneath the full moon high in the night sky. He held out his arms and beamed at me.

Again, he spoke, his voice amplified by some fae spell. "Our newest irresistible underdog." He beckoned to me. "Come on up here, beautiful. Let the people get a look at you."

One of the angels touched Zoe's hand. "Ma'am, you can't go with her."

I shot Zoe a panicked look as her hand slid out of my grasp. Then, like a tidal wave, I was rushed forward. Later, I couldn't even recall going up the stairs to meet Von. It was like the final twenty yards happened in some sort of fugue state. One moment, I was down on the street with Zoe, the next, I was thirty feet in the air, on a massive stage with one of the most famous people in the world.

As I walked the last few steps toward Von, the crowd surged with noise, screaming loud enough to make my eardrums rattle. Von walked toward me. He was a gorgeous man, but it was disconcerting. Almost too perfect. His vampiric good looks and mannerisms made my shifter skin crawl, but this was a job—I had to view it that way.

And just like that, a switch flipped in my mind. This was just another operation. As long as I kept telling myself that, I could do anything. I was the best deep-cover operative Tranquility had. I was a hell of an actor, and this was about to be my biggest assignment.

Von reached forward to take my hand, and with a bright smile of my own, I extended my hand and took his. He raised it and turned to the crowd, sweeping his free hand around to gesture toward me like I was some magnificent piece of art.

"I present to you, Miss Kira Lana Durst. Rejected mate of the Eleventh Pack."

The crowd erupted. I hadn't thought it could get louder, but it did. The cheers lost all coherence and became pure vibrations of sound pulsing against me.

Von led me to a director's chair in the center of the stage, opposite his famous red-velvet armchair.

Once I was seated, he took his place and crossed a leg nonchalantly over his knee as the crowd grew quiet.

"Well." Von arched a perfectly groomed eyebrow. "This is something, isn't it?"

I could see right across the city. There were people as far as the eye could see. Sure, the show was popular, but I'd never anticipated this. I'd never been a big enough fan to watch the season premieres. This was insane.

"Um, yes, it is," I said.

The crowd chuckled along with Von, and I tried to ignore all the cameras. The main film crew manned a camera directly in front of me and Von. I could almost hear the lens zooming in on me. Thank the gods Zoe had made me look glamorous enough for what was happening.

My hands were twisted in my lap, fingers gripped together to keep my fear at bay. Out of the corner of my eye, I saw Zoe waving frantically to me. A faint smile played on my lips, letting her know I'd seen her. She threw her arm around Kolton and pointed to him, which had my smile growing wider. Kolton looked worried, but I waved, acting like I was waving to the crowd. The thousands of people cheered again, but Kolton only scowled back at me, obviously unhappy about something.

"Well, let's get down to business, shall we?" Von said. "You are Kira Durst, daughter of the alpha of the Eleventh Pack." He looked at the crowd and held up a finger. "This next part is interesting." He pinned me with a stare. "You were rejected less than three weeks ago?"

The crowd emitted a combination of gasps, applause, and "aww" sounds that irked me. I didn't want pity, but I had to play the part.

"That's correct, Von," I said.

"Kira, this is your first time in front of a crowd like this. As our only female contestant this year, can you tell our audience a little about yourself? Give us the Kira Durst story."

I stared blankly into the camera. What was I supposed to say? A hundred things flooded my mind. Should I talk about being a Tranquility operative? Should I try to explain why Jayson had rejected me? Or should I use the platform like some beauty pageant contestant and ask for world peace?

Thankfully, the arrival of a massive car pulling up at the base of the stage saved me from having to answer. Instead of a stretch limo, it was a stretch SUV.

Von sprang to his feet. "Hold that thought, Miss Durst. It looks like our alpha contestants have arrived."

Every eye suddenly spun away from me and angled toward the car. Even Zoe and Kolton looked over to see the contestants. Everyone taking their eyes off me gave me a moment's relief, and it was like I was suddenly gloriously alone. Taking a breath to compose myself, I got up and stood beside Von.

One by one, men got out of the car, each as gorgeous as the last. Every one of them could have been a movie star or model. The crowd, especially the ladies, screeched as the men—all attired in tailored tuxedoes—waved.

I did my best to hear all the names as they were called out and file them away in my memory, but the screams, flashing lights, and my nerves made that impossible. I'd have to wait until later to try and get them all straight.

The men looked up at the stage and tried to catch my eye as I smiled and nodded at whatever the hell Von was saying. I didn't really care for the intent and greedy way they looked at me. Like I was nothing more than a prize to be won.

After the eighth man stepped out, Von raised his hands and addressed the crowd. "We have a bit of a last-minute change regarding our tenth and eleventh contestants. The eleventh contestant was delayed and will join us on Bloodstone Island. And due to unforeseen circumstances, our tenth competitor had to drop out." Murmurs of confusion rippled through the crowd. "Yes, yes. Very unfortunate. But we have filled that slot with a very eligible alpha from the Second Pack."

A leg, clothed in black, extended out of the car, followed by a hand and arm. Von was beside me, calling out the name of the final contestant, but I didn't need to hear it. The man looked up to the stage and locked eyes with me, giving me a cocky grin.

Wyatt Rivers' intense green eyes gazed up at me.

Chapter 12 - Wyatt

I would have given my left arm to have a camera when Kira saw me stepping out of that limo. Her face was priceless. There were about a million cameras catching her face, though, so I was sure I'd be able to find a good picture. Maybe I'd hang it up in my room for posterity's sake. The combination of shock, horror, confusion, anger, and disbelief was something I'd want to look back on forever.

Taking my place beside the other guys, I straightened and smoothed out my tuxedo. Unlike most of the others, I ignored the flashing lights, screaming fans, and general chaos of the premiere. I was focused on Kira and what was about to happen to her.

On that gigantic gaudy stage, Kira was still looking at me with wide-eyed bafflement. I could practically hear her brain short-circuiting. No matter what kind of shitshow this ended up being, I at least had this one moment where I'd one-upped her in a way she'd never expected.

I cocked an eyebrow and gave her the cockiest grin I could manage. Her face clouded. But she was a good actress, I'd give her that. That beaming, perfect smile of hers reappeared a moment later as Von Thornton put his arm in hers. I hoped she knew I was doing this for her. After everything that had happened, Kira had to realize I wouldn't allow her to throw herself to the wolves—literally and figuratively—without me being there to pull her from the fire.

It had surprised me that my uncle had gone along with my request. He was fairly high up in the network's chain of command and one of the main executives at *The Reject Project*. He had the power to pull any strings he wanted. I'd assumed I'd have to give a kidney before my family would even consider talking to me after we'd been estranged for so long. The warmth with which my uncle and my aunt had welcomed me was strange, but I wasn't one to look a gift horse in the mouth.

Uncle Rob had been hesitant to put me on the show and confused about why I was all gung-ho about it after all the years I'd spent decrying the show at every turn. I'd given him a line about wanting to bring some respectability to my name...and mentioned that I might know the new female lead.

"Well, that makes things spicy, doesn't it, Wyatt?" he'd said.

"Can you do this for me, Uncle Rob?"

"All right. If there's anyone on Earth I can be sure about getting out of this thing alive, it's you, Wyatt. But if anyone asks, I had no idea you were going on the show, got it? I'm not gonna be answering uncomfortable questions at Thanksgiving."

"Got it. Thank you."

That had been that. A few days later, I was whisked off to Fangmore City to be prepped for this moment: the reveal of the eligible alpha bachelors. Now, I watched Von Thornton lead Kira back to their seats in the center of the stage.

She looked stunning. It reminded me of how she'd looked that night. Beautiful and amazing, asking me to do things I'd only thought about doing to her in the deepest recesses of my mind. As the other male contestants walked up the red-carpeted steps to join her and Von on stage, I wondered if she was remembering the same things I was. My blood ran hot at seeing her, but I had to keep my cool. Gods, I hoped she wouldn't tell Von she knew me.

Plenty of people watching the show would know we were colleagues and had a history. Uncle Rob had made sure the network would sweep most of that under the rug, but if worse came to worst, it would add another element of drama. That was fine, but if that revelation happened, I wanted it to be once the show had truly gotten underway. There was still a chance, however small, that other executives might step in and remove me, but their hands would be tied once the actual filming started.

The flashing cameras temporarily blinded me as I tried to get a look at Kira's expression. Unable to focus on her, I glanced at the crowd and quickly found Kolton. He was right where he'd said he would be. He nodded gravely. He'd been the only person I'd told about this. As a close relative of the female lead, he'd been put up in a nice hotel, though not as nice as Kira's. He'd literally been throwing up from worrying about his sister. When I broke the news that I was going on the show to help protect her, he'd wept with relief. He'd spent the last few days thanking me profusely, but I could see his worry had returned. Why shouldn't it? Now, not only his sister but his best friend were going to compete in one of the most dangerous shows in the world.

Kolton raised a hand, waving but not at me. He was trying to get Kira's attention. My heart thundered. What was he doing? Kira spotted him, and I watched as the two siblings made eye contact. Kolton glanced at me, then back at Kira, shaking his head slowly and deliberately. The message was clear. Don't tell anyone she knew me.

Kira didn't answer overtly, but from the set of her jaw and her shoulders, I had to believe she was agreeing. Well, I hoped so, anyway.

Von gestured to the line of alphas, including me, who stood to the side of the stage. "Now, Kira, don't they all look delicious?" he said, flicking his tongue across one of his long incisor fangs.

That elicited more wild cheering from the crowd. Kira smiled and made a show of sliding her gaze up and down the line of men. She barely paused at my face before moving along.

"They are nice to look at," Kira said with a laugh.

The audience shrieked again.

Von laughed and leaned forward. "I think the ladies in the crowd agree. Am I right, ladies?"

My head was starting to ache from the raucous crowd. How the hell could they be so excited about this? It was noxious. Ridiculous. Like cocks strutting around hens in a farmyard. But no matter my true feelings, I made sure the confident smile stayed put on my face.

"Kira, are you ready to sink your claws into these hunks over there?"

She leaned forward and put a conspiratorial hand on Von's thigh. "Oh, I think it would be more fun to sink my *teeth* into them."

I bit back a cackle. The tone she was using was the same sickly-sweet voice she slipped into during a sting. That perfect amount of pouty flirtatiousness turned men's heads into jelly and made it easy for her to get whatever information she could out of them. Everyone else in the crowd, including Von, thought she was a hundred percent serious. The host clapped his hands, and dozens of whooping catcalls erupted from the crowd.

Von stood again and grabbed a microphone from a small table beside his chair. "Let's get to know our men."

He walked over to the far end of the line. None of the men had engaged in conversation on the drive over, each of us lost in our thoughts about what was coming. Now was my chance to see how each man reacted. Did they dodge questions, did they lie, were they submissive, confident, cocky, or aggressive? My operative training might help me determine the biggest threat.

At the moment, they all were my biggest threat. Each of them was eyeing Kira like they wanted to eat her for dinner.

"We'll start backwards based on the pack hierarchy and work down to the First Pack alpha."

As Von moved down the line getting names, I listened and logged the information in my mind. Ryan from Tenth Pack, a quiet sort and a little intimidated, if I wasn't mistaken. A young shifter named Leif from Eighth Pack, who kept glancing toward another alpha down the line—perhaps they knew each other. A meaty, muscle-bound alpha named Nathaniel from Seventh Pack, who was the definition of a dickhead.

Then another guy named Garrett, who was smiling a lot but didn't look comfortable being here.

As Von drew closer to me, my eyes finally took in the guy beside me, and I was in for another shock. I knew him. It had been a long time, and his body and hair had changed, but his face was still familiar. Mika Sheen of First Pack. His long dark hair was tied back in a man bun. He turned, his eyes locking on mine. Recognition flashed there, though his face was devoid of emotion. We'd been kids the last time we'd seen each other.

All Mika gave me was a nod of acknowledgment before turning back to watch Von. I wasn't sure if he would be a threat to me. He came from money and had always been privileged, but even as a kid, he had a tortured soul that wasn't easy to break. If he was here, he had to be a reject in some way, but that didn't track with what I knew about him. This contest was getting more complicated by the moment.

Von continued his path. A greasy and selfish acting alpha named Omar from Sixth Pack. Tate from Fifth Pack, who made me nervous for some reason I couldn't put my finger on. A quiet guy named Abel from Fourth Pack, who seemed to be genuinely happy to be on the show, more so than most of the others. J.D. from Third Pack was full of energy, even wrapping Von in a bear hug. On first impression, he looked like a good enough person, even if he did act a bit like a frat bro. He was the one Leif had eyeballed earlier. I wondered if there'd be drama or fighting between those two during the show.

Even as I tried to memorize all the names, faces, and pack allegiances, I felt like I'd failed. The men all blended together. Once we got to Bloodstone Island, I'd do a better job of getting a bead on each of the contestants.

Then, like magic, Von was in front of me. I could sense the frenetic vampire energy radiating off him. His face was perfectly unblemished. Centuries of experience had made him the greatest showman on earth. But I was a Tranquility operative. I could see through people. When I looked into his eyes, I saw the truth. No matter how well he played it off or how wide his smile, he had a secret. He was bored out of his mind with his life, and this show was the only way he could find any excitement or drama. It explained why he'd stuck with it for so long.

The microphone was under my chin. Kira, Von, and the thousands in attendance stared at me, waiting for me to speak.

Clearing my throat, I leaned forward. "Wyatt Rivers, Second Pack."

Von threw an arm over my shoulders. "Greetings, Mister Rivers. Now, Wyatt, what should Miss Durst know about you?"

The other men had either flirted with Kira or aggressively told them how much they wanted her. I decided to keep things similar—and mess with her a little.

"Well, Von, she needs to know that I protect what's mine, and she'll be mine soon. I'm possessive, in a good way, and she needs to be ready for me to stay by her side. The only way I'm letting her get hurt on that island is over my dead body."

The crowd oohed and aahed at that. I caught sight of Zoe standing beside Kolton and decided to go for a laugh.

"Also, Von, she needs to know that...I do *not* have a small wiener."

Kira's head jerked back slightly at that, and a red flush crept up her neck to her face. Her smile grew tight and forced. Shrieks of approval and laughter rang out from the crowd.

Von guffawed and slapped me playfully on the chest. "Oh, stop! You dirty, dirty boy. We're gonna have trouble with you, I see."

Von moved on to Mika. I'd gotten under Kira's skin in a big way, though she wasn't letting it show. I looked at her and gave her another cocky grin.

Once the introductions were complete, Von moved to the center of the stage and finished the show with a bunch of flowery, poetic words about fated mates and new chances and us all having the opportunity to be worthy of the Moon Goddess Heline's blessing. It was cookie-cutter stuff, nothing that really mattered. All bullshit to me. The Moon Goddess cared about one thing, and that was herself. I was getting antsy and ready to get out of the spectacle.

After finishing his lengthy spiel, Von took Kira by the arm and led her down the steps toward two waiting limos. They were separating the guys into two groups. One group would leave in the limo in which we'd arrived, and the others would ride with Kira and Zoe.

I could already see how the groups were going to break up. I wouldn't be going with Kira and have the chance to talk to her. I looked around and caught sight of Kolton. I gave him a nod, hopefully conveying that I'd do my best to protect her.

Two massive fallen angels ushered Zoe through the crowd to Kira at the base of the stairs, then hustled them toward their limo. Von slipped into the limo I'd arrived in, and the contestants started to slip into the cars. The shouts, screams, and cacophony of noise faded as I climbed into the limo.

We pulled away once Mika had gotten seated. Von was all charm, smiles, and non-stop chatter as he pulled a few bottles of champagne out of a leather-covered cooler. He passed the glasses and champagne around. My nose wrinkled at the coppery smell as he popped the top.

All the men were smiling and drinking. They laughed at Von's jokes and told their own, but I could tell each of them was doing the same thing I'd started doing on the stage. They were measuring each other, weighing who would be a threat or obstacle.

Mika was beside me, the only one other than me who was silent. I was being silent to gather intel, but Mika looked miserable. The cocky smile was gone as he stared into the bubbling glass of champagne in his hand, not drinking. He'd been the same as a kid—always upset or gloomy about something. Time hadn't changed that aspect, from the looks of it.

"Why the fuck aren't we in the limo with the chick?" Nathaniel grumbled.

"Right? I need a chance to let her see what she could have," Tate said.

A few others made similar remarks. It set my teeth on edge, but it let me know where things stood. Most of these alphas were in this for reasons *other* than finding a new fated mate.

"My name's Ryan," the man across from me said, leaning forward and extending a hand.

I looked at his hand like it was the strangest thing I'd ever seen before coming to my senses and reaching forward to shake.

"Um, Wyatt. Nice to meet you."

Ryan gave me a nod. "This is exciting, right?"

Grinning, I said, "Something like that."

"What did you say you did for a living?" Ryan asked.

"Law enforcement," I said. It was close enough to the truth.

Ryan's eyes widened in surprise. "You're a cop?"

I nodded. A few other alphas in the car overheard me. Nathaniel laughed in disgust. "Oh, great. We got a pig. You gonna tell us what's legal and what isn't on Bloodstone Island, Mister Policeman?"

In response, I grinned and held eye contact as I sipped my champagne. He looked away first but tried to cover it by waving a hand at me like he was bored.

By the time we got to the airport, I was confident I could take any of the men in the car. All of them were from established packs, most came from money, and none had really had to work hard for anything. None of them had ever survived in the wild as a lone wolf.

I had.

Still, I was a little scared of how off-balance some of them acted. Things might get intense during the show. You could never anticipate what people would do when pushed to the limit. Some might be so desperate to get their fated mate and redeem themselves with their packs that they could put Kira in danger. I had to not only keep an eye on her but on every one of these men, too.

Chapter 13 - Kira

Thank the gods Zoe was smart enough to keep her mouth shut about Wyatt. When she climbed into the car with me, her saucer-like eyes said everything that needed to be said. A grim nod from me was all the answer she received. She understood.

Zoe's frenetic energy was even more elevated than usual. Probably exacerbated by the revelation that Wyatt was on the show with me and the general anxiety she and I shared. Whatever it was, she was a bouncing ball of chaotic spirit. She was talking a mile a minute, introducing herself and asking everyone questions. The other men were nervous, and so was I. All we wanted to do was sit and contemplate what was ahead, but Zoe's voice was like a dull hum over everything that made introspection nearly impossible.

It took all I had to keep my pleasant smile and bright-eyed happiness in place. Gods, Wyatt. For the life of me, I couldn't figure out how he'd done it. The male contestants had been picked more than a month ago, well before I made my desperate attempt to get on the show. Had he gotten someone in the council to pull rank with the network? That didn't make sense.

The council had washed their hands of me. No one would go to bat like that for something so inherently dangerous and stupid.

To get my mind off Wyatt, I swept my gaze across the four guys in the car with me. I needed to get an idea of the type of men I was dealing with. They were all handsome and well-groomed. Makeup artists and hair stylists had probably gone over each of them with a fine-toothed comb before they arrived at the premiere.

They were all glancing furtively at me, eyeing me like they were starving, and I was the last piece of bacon. They all exuded confidence and charisma. I found it strange that any of them had been rejected by their mates, but they were here, weren't they? All except Wyatt, I assumed.

With an embarrassed smile, I leaned forward to address them. "Guys, that was wild, right? I'm so sorry, but in all the chaos, I didn't really manage to memorize your names. It was too much to keep straight. Do you mind?"

"Oh, thank the gods," one of them said with a heavy sigh. "I'm glad to hear that since I can't remember your name, either."

The two of us chuckled while the others shot him annoyed looks.

He slapped his chest. "J.D. Short for Jordan Darkham, but I go by the initials. Third Pack."

The man had a big, easy smile and was clearly used to using it. Something about him reminded me of a golden retriever—lovably goofy and eager to please. I was worried for his safety already. This show did not reward people like him. You had to have a bit of a ruthless streak to survive, and from what I could see, this guy had none of that.

J.D. threw his arms around the two guys sitting on either side of him and grinned like an idiot. Both men flinched in surprise. The one on the left glanced at J.D. with surprise, color rising in his cheeks, while the other snarled and shrugged the arm off his shoulders.

The pissed-off guy glared at J.D. "My name is Omar, and if you touch me again, you stupid little pup, I'll rip off your fucking arm."

I wrinkled my nose in distaste. What a purebred dickhead. If my eyes and ears didn't deceive me, there was a narcissist if I ever saw one. I filed that info away for later.

The other guy sat, J.D.'s arm still around his shoulders. Red-faced, he smiled at me politely. "I'm Leif." He glanced at my outfit and smiled. "That dress really is amazing. I love it."

"That settles it," Zoe said. "He's my favorite. He has good taste."

The final contestant in the car was sitting in the corner away from most of us, quiet but with a faint smile on his lips as he gazed out the window at the scenery whizzing past.

"What about you, mister?" I asked, hoping my voice sounded sufficiently flirtatious.

Pulling his eyes away from the window, he smiled at me. "Sorry. I'm being rude. Abel from Fourth Pack. Can I ask, have any of you been to Bloodstone Island before?"

"Holy shit, what a stupid question, bro. Are you serious?" Omar glared at Abel. "No one sets foot on Bloodstone except feral shifters, vampires driven mad by eternity, and every other vile creature you can think of. Everyone knows that." He rolled his eyes at Abel. "At least anyone with half a brain. It's where people go to die. I hope you boys are ready for that, because I'm taking this sexy lady home with me. You all can have fun rotting on that island with whatever monsters the Tranquility Council left for you."

Zoe's eyebrows shot up to her hairline, and she curled her lip in disgust. She had the same opinion of Omar that I'd already developed. "Unpleasant" was an understatement. He also seemed to be completely oblivious to the fact that his demeanor was a major turnoff. I could see why his mate rejected him.

Staying in character, I ignored the little back-and-forth and smiled brightly. "Really good to meet you guys. Though, I agree with Omar that the island is not an ideal place to spend time." I chuckled. "Hopefully, we all have our wills up to date and tombstones picked out."

Leif shrugged. "Well, I prefer to be cremated. If there's a volcano on Bloodstone, just toss my corpse in there."

J.D. laughed like it was the funniest thing he'd ever heard. At least some of the guys weren't as pessimistic as I was after the big send-off. That giant spectacle had had the air of some kind of goodbye. The odds weren't in our favor. Some of these men *wouldn't* make it off the island alive.

The thought had me peeking out the back window of the limo at the other car following us. An anxious buzzing danced across my skin. Wyatt was back there. Right behind me, like always. I was going to rip him a new one once I got a moment alone with him. When I was done with him, the monsters on Bloodstone Island would seem like puppies.

Unbidden, the memories of our night together flashed through my mind—his fingers inside me, his tongue on my skin, his lips at my ear. *You damn well can have a good time with me*. Those words and the way he'd shown me exactly how much of a good time I could have with him rattled around in my head.

"Already got your eye on someone?" Leif asked with a grin.

Blinking, I forced myself back to the present. "Huh? Sorry?"

His grin broadened. "Those red cheeks...looks like you're blushing. Maybe one of us has already caught your eye?"

I laughed off his comment. "I'm only thinking about how exciting all this is. I don't know any of you well enough to take a liking yet. We've literally just met."

Omar's jaw clenched at that. He'd obviously assumed he was too good a catch for me not to have already realized he was the goddess's gift to women. Abel deflated a bit as well, though not in a self-important way. If anything, he appeared to be insecure, especially for an alpha. What was his story?

I wanted to feel bad for him because he looked sort of dejected, but I cautioned myself. These guys knew the risks when they signed up, just like I had. They were all hoping for a fated mate. It wasn't my fault that they'd turned to this show out of desperation. I had too much to worry about on my own end. None of this was about love or lust for me. My one goal was to protect my family and prevent a war. That was all I had my eyes on.

Ten minutes later, the limos pulled up to a helipad near the coast. Three helicopters sat on the tarmac, surrounded by pilots and more bodyguards. One was a huge demon with two-foot-long horns curving out from his forehead, his thick muscles barely contained by his suit.

Zoe pointed out the window. "We're gonna be on TV again."

Glancing out, I saw luminescent orbs floating near each aircraft—magic drone cameras taking in every scene as we made our way to Bloodstone Island. I wondered if those things had followed us the entire drive.

We parked beside the helicopters, and Von Thornton leaped out of the limo Wyatt was in.

He raised his arms, gesturing to the helicopters. "I hope no one is afraid of heights."

A small chuckle ran through the contestants. I felt Wyatt's eyes on me, hot and insistent. Like he was begging me to look at him. I bit the inside of my cheek and forced myself not to look at him. I didn't want to give him the satisfaction.

"Ladies, you'll be in this chopper with me, J.D., Leif, and Mika," Von said, stepping toward the craft in the front.

I breathed a sigh of relief that I wouldn't have to share a flight with Wyatt. I was still trying to process everything. The longer I had to prepare myself without him in the vicinity, the better. Despite my best efforts, as I buckled myself into my seat, I looked out the door and watched as Wyatt got into the farthest chopper.

"How long is this flight?" I asked Von.

"Not long, my dear. Not long at all," he replied with a grin.

I frowned. Bloodstone Island was one of the most remote places on the planet. If I remembered correctly, it was hundreds of miles offshore. It should have taken at least an hour to get there.

The helicopters were enchanted so that the spinning blades above us made almost no noise. The air swept around us with a faint *whoosh* as we took off. The helicopters cruised above the trees, and a moment later, we were over the open ocean headed toward the horizon, the night sky inky-black above us. The stars twinkled, and the massive white face of the moon shone down on us.

The air rippled, the stars shuddered, and even the lunar surface became distorted. My ears popped, and suddenly an island was visible in the distance. I gaped at it, looking over at Zoe in question.

Her face was ablaze with admiration. "Damn. That's some good magic. Temporal displacement of this many people and these giant helicopters is *not* easy."

Von heard our conversation and patted me on the knee. "*The Reject Project* only employs the best fae spellcasters. We spared no expense."

Behind us, the floating cameras sped along, keeping pace with the aircraft as we descended to the island. It was huge. Much bigger than it appeared on TV. I glanced down at the choppy waves of the ocean. This far from the mainland, we were in the realm of the merpeople. Huge clans of the mysterious ocean dwellers were said to reside this far out. I wondered if I'd catch a glimpse of one at some point.

As we drew nearer, more of the island took shape. Dense, shadowy jungles became visible, along with a small chain of volcano-shaped mountains. Maybe Leif *would* get his wish. It was beautiful in a savage sort of way. But along with the beauty was something sinister. The island was cloaked in danger. The land basically screamed that it was dark, mysterious, and terrifying.

Shaking my head, I tried to get a grip on myself. Everyone knew the place was dangerous. The challenges would be difficult and life-threatening. I'd have to use all my training and every ounce of my instinct and ability if I ever wanted to step foot on the mainland again. I was here to win. Nothing would stop me.

The choppers landed gracefully on a massive helipad, and that was when I caught sight of it. Reject Mansion—an enormous, sprawling estate built into the side of the coast. I'd seen it a million times while binge-watching the show with Zoe, but TV didn't do it justice. It was one of the grandest houses I'd ever seen.

We all offloaded from the helicopters, and Zoe squeezed me tight and squealed in delight. Her fears and worries vanished for a few minutes as she fan-girled at the sight of the mansion. She bounced on her toes as we made our way toward the building.

The floating cameras followed our little group as we traversed the path that led to the stairs up to the front door. A small group emerged from the mansion and met us halfway up the stairs—fae staff members and a burly vampire security guard. They had a quick, hushed conversation with Von before leading us the rest of the way up the steps.

I clung to Zoe's hand as fear seeped into my chest. No amount of positive self-talk would dispel it. Shit just got real. I wished I could keep her by my side the entire time, but that was not a realistic hope. She was here as my stylist, not my bodyguard or companion. At least not in the eyes of the show and its staff.

"Everyone, smile," Von said in a sing-song voice.

The hovering cameras swept around to take a group photo of us as we neared the front doors. We all stopped and gave the cameras our best sexy, serious pose. I was sure we all looked glamorous, with our perfect outfits and hair, our sexy smiles and sultry looks against the backdrop of the beach. The only problem was that this was the last time we'd all be photographed alive. Many of us would never get off this island.

I couldn't stop myself from glancing over my shoulder toward Wyatt. He was at the far end, thumbs hanging from his belt, looking cocky. Almost as though he felt my eyes touch him, he turned and looked back at me. His arrogant stance was a show, another act for the cameras. His eyes were dark and intense, filled with the same fear I had in my own heart.

Chapter 14 - Wyatt

A couple of witches moved the cameras around at Von's direction, getting more images of the contestants. I was working on staying calm and at ease, but nothing could have been further from the truth. In the short time I'd been involved with the show, I'd come to the realization that every single person attached to it was insane, off their rocker, ready for a padded room. That was the only thing that made any sense. Everywhere I looked, there was nothing but smiles and laughter. Didn't they understand what was about to happen to us? Didn't they care that many of us wouldn't get off the island alive?

I didn't want to blame Kira for all this, but I didn't know where else the blame should go. Why had she been so damned insistent on going through with this? For the millionth time, I wished I'd had the chance to ask her and Kolton to join my pack of lone wolves. It would have meant a drop in status and the loss of their home, but anything would have been better than this.

Yet here I was, in a tuxedo, standing on Bloodstone Island, a fake smile plastered on my face, basically looking down the barrel of my own death. I stood to the side with J.D. and Abel, two of the few guys I'd found to be semi-normal. Across the patio, Kira was smiling brightly and taking a picture with that douchebag Nathaniel. The guy had his arm around her, his fingers perilously close to her breasts. Trying to cop a feel, like some asshole high-school kid who didn't know better.

When Kira looked my way, her smile never faltered, and her eyes remained joyous. Only I knew her well enough to see how furious she was with me. If she hadn't been such a good actress, her anger would have been obvious to everyone.

After nearly an hour of photos, video clips, and mind-numbing small talk, Von walked up the steps to look down on us like it was a stage.

"All right, everyone. If our servants and staff could back away and give us a moment?" he said with a wave of his hand.

Von's fangs seemed more sinister here. Something about Bloodstone made everything look more dangerous and predatory. From the way he looked at us, I had the distinct sense that he would enjoy watching whatever happened.

"Welcome, guests," Von said. The witches had moved the cameras around to get a good shot of him addressing us. "Bloodstone Island is not to be trifled with. A more dangerous place you will not find. This is Reject Mansion, the only safe place on the island. Each night at dusk, powerful spells activate. Witches, fae, and warlocks have developed these spells. When the wards go up, you are safe. Be sure to be here before nightfall. Once the protections are up, there is no passing them, and they will not drop until sunrise.

"The inhabitants of Bloodstone Island are numerous, and all of them are dangerous. Most of them are nocturnal hunters. It may sound melodramatic, but if you are caught away from the mansion after dark..." Von shrugged. "We've probably seen the last of you."

A nervous chuckle ran through the crowd. Glancing to my left, I tried to get a look at Kira, but there were too many people between us. All I could see was Zoe, who looked both entranced and terrified by what Von was saying.

"Now," Von went on, "being that our little show has been on air longer than any of you have been alive, you know how this works. But in case you need a refresher, I will enlighten you."

He pointed out the cameras. "Ninety percent of the show is live-streamed. Everything you do will be watched by the entire world. Exhibitionists, get ready, because it's your time to shine." Von laughed. "Each week will cycle through an *official* episode. This episode will consist of one game-like challenge, one romantic date, and one fight for survival that everyone must complete. Also, if things get extra exciting, as I dearly hope they will, each week will wrap up with an arena match. That juicy little tidbit will unlock the mating chamber. This is where our lovely Miss Kira Durst can pick one of you lucky gents to...how should I put it? Try out each week? Shift the gears? Ride the pony, shall we say? You know where I'm going with this, don't you?" His fangs glittered.

I clenched my fists and inhaled through my nose to keep from shifting and ripping the fucking vampire limb from limb. Each and every second, I was reminded why I hated this show. I couldn't believe they were *still* doing the mating chamber. I hadn't watched this thing in over a decade, and this was a fresh reminder of why. Death, blood, and fake romance weren't enough, so real-life porn was added to the mix to make it *really* titillating. I'd hoped the mating chamber had been phased out. But why stop something that guarantees ratings, right? I did a poor job hiding my snarl of anger.

All the shifters around me looked like they'd anticipated the mating chamber and were looking forward to it. Keeping my cool, I took a step over to look at Kira. If she was bothered about the mating chamber, it didn't show. She was laughing along with Von.

If it killed me, I'd make sure not a single person set foot or paw in that chamber with Kira except me. I didn't care how smiley and nice some of these guys looked. I didn't trust a single one of these fuckers near Kira. None of them could be trusted with her safety, not even Kira herself. She might be playing a game, but I wasn't.

Von clapped his hands together, his smile getting even wider somehow. I wondered if his head would split apart if it went any further.

"Ladies, if you would be so kind?" he asked.

A small cluster of witches stepped forward, each holding a small wooden chest. I watched them move through the crowd, stopping at each contestant and staff member. When the young witch stepped up to me, she pulled a bracelet from the chest, took my hand, and wrapped it around my wrist. The item was surprisingly comfortable, and I could barely even feel it on my arm. She murmured a few words, then moved on. I tried to slide it off, but it wouldn't budge an inch.

"My assistants are outfitting you with special armbands. Please don't attempt to remove them, as they are attached to you via magic," Von said. "They will not be released until the end of the show or the end of your life. Whichever comes first.

"These gorgeous little beauties act as trackers for our enchanted cameras. That way, they can find you anywhere when we are rolling live or recording extra footage for some of our special broadcasts and weekly updates. As of now, since we have cameras rolling, your band should be green."

A small gem in the armband blinked green. Beneath it was a small screen and a few buttons.

"This is how you will know cameras are recording. If the light is white, we are not actively recording. These bands are also the only way the showrunners will send you messages. You'll notice a small screen available for text messages.

"We at *The Reject Project* want you, as our contestants, to be part of the action. There is a small button to the right of the screen. If you aren't recording, and some type of action is about to unfold, please don't hesitate to hit that button. It will signal the enchanted cameras, and they will rush to your location. Just make sure you don't accidentally hit it as you're pulling down your pants in the bathroom. Can you say awkward?" Von laughed like he'd told the funniest joke in history.

"The device can also signal for emergencies and a few other items. I'm sure you'll get accustomed to it in no time. I have no doubt this will be an exciting and adventurous experience. The cameras will eventually become commonplace, and you'll forget they exist. I, and the entire world, can't wait to see you all on season thirty-one of *The Reject Project*. Each of you is capable of winning, and I have no doubt you all have a shot as long as you try hard enough.

He paused. It felt like he was waiting for some type of applause, so the group clapped dutifully. I did my best not to roll my eyes.

"Are you men ready to have a real get-to-know-her talk with Kira?" Von asked.

Everyone chimed their agreement. I couldn't even blame them. Unless they were all out of their minds, they had to be ready for this smarmy, creepy vampire to shut up and get a move on. I wanted to settle into the mansion and prepare for the next day. I was also desperate to pull Kira aside and give her the talking-to I'd been planning since I'd heard she'd done this stupid thing.

Von held up a finger. "Ah, that would be fun, but...you'll all get to know each other better at the extra fun live-stream premiere tomorrow. For now, Kira still has to prove herself as a worthy mate to all you sexy alphas."

Prove herself? I didn't like the sound of that. A chill ran down my spine as a witch stepped forward with one of the vampire guards and took Kira's hand, leading her toward the mansion.

Once Kira was out of sight, Von turned back to us. "Don't worry, gents. You'll see her again very soon. Please follow our island security team to the right."

Von pointed toward the jungle to the side of the patio. Three security guys came forward. One looked like another vampire, while the other two had the scent of shifters but not wolves. Bears, I thought. I didn't have the chance to delve into the complexities of smell as the three men and a small group of witches unceremoniously hustled us into the jungle along a small path that could only be walked single-file.

We were no more than fifteen feet into the forest when we all froze in our tracks, our noses in the air, growls rumbling from our throats. I could scent a myriad of things all around us, each one as dangerous as the next. Most of the men here had probably never run afoul of some of these things and wouldn't recognize the scents. I, however, had dealt closely with the things that walked the night. I scented a gorgon, a chimera, at least one feral shifter, and, if I wasn't mistaken, a wyvern.

The stories *were* true. Bloodstone Island really was as dangerous as they said. Even with my training and experience, the sheer number of creatures was enough to douse my guts with cold fear.

"Onward, boys. Mustn't keep the camera waiting," Von said as he pushed to the front. "Don't bother shifting if you're scared. No need. The island is carefully controlled and monitored for the challenges and tasks. *This* is one such special occasion. I assure you, everyone is safe. Come, come. Don't dally." Von strode ahead of us, completely unconcerned.

Hadn't he just made a huge deal about how dangerous it was to be away from the mansion at night? He'd made it sound like the showrunners were controlling more than they let on. Despite what my nose and instinct told me, I kept moving, following the fucking vampire deeper into the jungle. The path ended after a hundred yards at a spectator area on the edge of an amphitheater.

There was still no sign of Kira as we took our seats. I looked over my shoulder, trying to see the path we'd come from. Maybe she was being brought behind us for some grand entrance.

Almost as soon as I had the thought, a spectacular flash of fae magic fluttered around us, and with a quiet *pop*, Kira appeared in the center of the amphitheater. She was no longer wearing the fancy dress but something that resembled her Tranquility ops gear. My blood pressure shot up several notches when I saw the pistol in one hand and what looked like a silver bowie knife in the other. Not good. Not good at all.

After getting her bearings, Kira looked up into the seats and caught my eye. She gave me a hard look that told me exactly what she wanted: for me to stay in my seat and not get involved. I could almost hear the threat of violence if I disobeyed. If anyone else saw us exchanging glances, they didn't let on. I gripped the armrests and clamped my teeth together, flexing my jaw.

She didn't want me to interfere lest it make her seem weak. But nothing she said could keep me from jumping in if something crazy was about to happen.

I glanced around the amphitheater. Witches, fae, and cameras surrounded us. Even if I disobeyed her wishes, I'd never be allowed to go to her. I'd be stopped by one magic spell or another before I even made it ten feet. All I could do was hope Kira's training would help her survive whatever fucked-up scenario the showrunners had cooked up.

Several of the other alphas were leaning forward in their seats, confused and concerned for Kira. Mika, Abel, and Ryan all eyed her warily. Mika was on the edge of his seat. J.D. and Leif had their brows furrowed, looking more baffled than worried. Nathaniel and Omar each had an equally cocky look of amused disinterest. None of them looked worried enough, though. Even the ones with the most concern on their faces looked eager to see Kira prove herself. It irked me. I wanted to knock their heads together.

J.D. leaned toward me. "I hope she finishes this test quick. I'm freaking starving, man. I want to get back to the mansion and hang out a bit, get settled."

Staying in character, I glanced at him and plastered a remarkably realistic smile on my face. "For real. I could eat a horse right now."

J.D. grinned and bumped his fist gently on my chest. "My man."

The guy had the disposition of a giant puppy. Gods only knew why he'd signed up for the show. Someone like him didn't stand a chance to survive this. Hopefully, he'd get lucky. I didn't hate him the way I was already starting to hate others, like Nathaniel.

I didn't dwell long on the man, my gaze intent on Kira and the stage, trying to see what they were about to throw at her. My anxiety increased with each passing second.

As though some member of the show read my mind and heard my request, another flash of magic rippled the air. An instant later, a huge tiger appeared on the stage opposite Kira. Its shoulders were bunched and thickly muscled. Yellow eyes locked on Kira as it opened its jaw, saliva dripping from razor-sharp fangs. A hungry growl rumbled in its throat as it stepped toward her.

Fuck.

Chapter 15 - Kira

I felt a little disrespected. An entire island full of the most dangerous paranormal creatures known to the world, and they send a zoo animal after me? A big angry cat would be incredibly difficult for a human woman, but I wasn't any random woman. The producers were well aware of my background, so surely they realized it.

My frown leveled out as I caught the scent of the new arrival. I stiffened. This wasn't a normal tiger. Several alpha men who hadn't caught the scent yet stood, whooping and whistling in encouragement. They yelled and chanted for me to attack the animal.

Except, it wasn't an animal. It was a tiger shifter. Feral by its scent and behavior.

Several men shouted at me to shift, which meant my little disability hadn't been revealed yet. Even if I could shift, I was certain the showrunners had cast some spell that would prevent it. I'd have to figure another way out of this. I did *not* want to kill another shifter on the fly, but dying didn't sound fun, either.

If I bit the big one on day one, the showrunners wouldn't bat an eye. With death around every corner on *The Reject Project*, they always had a few women waiting in the wings. Sentimentality was not a word associated with this show. They'd toss my body in a bag and call up the next female in line. It happened a lot. In fact, when the prize mate died, the show's ratings went through the roof. But I'd be damned if I let some other woman take the prize. I had too much at stake.

Tired of waiting for me to react, the tiger shifter snarled and leaped at me. The orange-and-black fur streaked forward faster than any natural animal. With its claws extended, the shifter swiped at the air by my face. The only thing that saved me from having my throat opened was my reflexes. I bent backward, pulling my face out of range, then danced back to put space between the shifter and myself.

I regained my balance just as the cat lunged again, swinging both paws forward to catch me in some kind of deadly hug. I rolled forward beneath its legs. Before I'd even stopped moving, I fired the gun. There was a hissing yowl as the bullet tore a small chunk of flesh from the tiger's hind leg.

My eyes darted around, searching for an opening. Some of the men were still cheering and yelling.

"You know," I said, loudly enough for everyone to hear, "if I'm going to fight another shifter, I'd prefer it be hand to hand, not claws to gun."

The cheering died as the realization sank in that I wasn't fighting a regular animal. I was fighting something faster, stronger, and smarter than that.

A voice I recognized as Omar's called out, "Shift and fight it!"

The tiger and I circled each other, eyes locked. Blood oozed from its hind flank. Lifting the silver knife, I bared my teeth in a snarl.

Von Thornton appeared at the side of the amphitheater stage, a floating camera trailing him.

"This is a tiger shifter who has gone feral," Von said, his eyes twinkling with mischief. "As we all know, once a shifter's internal animal has taken full control, they are no different from animals."

I spared a glance toward the vampire. Von raised an eyebrow, obviously amused by my hesitancy to kill a fellow shifter. I thought about cursing him, but that idea vanished when the cat struck again.

Wyatt's voice rang out, high and clear. "Kira, jump!"

I leaped backward, nearly somersaulting. Two of the tiger's claws snagged on my fatigues, ripping the fabric slightly. Heart hammering, I spun around to frame the tiger in my sights again. I cursed myself for letting Von distract me.

"Let go!" Wyatt shouted.

I spared the barest of glances toward the audience. J.D. and Abel were holding Wyatt back. It seemed to be taking all their combined power to keep him from rushing to my aid. *Idiot.* He had to know the staff wouldn't let any of the men interfere. Seeing the distress on his face, I was a little surprised that he hadn't already shifted. Maybe the weird magic bracelets prevented it. The showrunners would want to be in control of as much as possible, and I wouldn't put it past them to neuter the men in that way.

The shifter attacked again, but this time, I anticipated where he would swipe. I side-stepped and lashed out with the knife. My blade dug a thin trough into the beast's side. It turned, its ears flattening as it roared at me. A deep and terrifying sound burst from its throat, loud and harsh enough to make me wince.

Yellow teeth shone in the moonlight as a gaping jaw expanded like a tunnel of teeth, showing what awaited me if I failed.

This didn't feel right. I didn't like the idea of fighting a feral shifter. It could happen to any shifter. When a shifter grew sad, anguished, desperate, lonely, or distraught enough, the animal side could fully take over. When that happened, they were too far gone to ever come back.

The men were all shouting at me to shift, begging, demanding, and asking. All but Wyatt. His voice was notably absent for obvious reasons—he knew my story. I didn't need to shift. I'd spent years honing the strength and speed of my shifter abilities in human form. I could be powerful and explosive without transforming into a wolf.

The shifter charged again, madness swirling in its eyes as it came at me. Learning its lesson the last two times, it dived in low instead of coming high. He came at me, and the whole world slowed down. Adrenaline sped up my reflexes to the point that everything but me was in slow motion.

The tiger went for my knees. If those claws struck, they would slice me to the bone, and I'd bleed out before any of the fae medics could get to me.

At the last second, I jumped, jerking my hips to do a backflip. I landed exactly where I wanted—on the beast's shoulders, right above its skull. Letting my legs slide down its chest between its forepaws, I flexed my thighs, pulling the paws backward as I wrapped my arm around the beast's throat and hauled back, cutting off its blood and oxygen supply.

With its front legs effectively useless due to my legs pressing them back, the creature kicked hard with its hind legs, trying but failing to claw at me. The six-hundred-pound beast thrashed around, but I twisted its head. It tried to spin backward and crush me with its weight. I forced it to stay on its belly, and finally, after what felt like years and my arms were shaking, the tiger's strength began to wane. Then, blessedly, it slumped to the ground, unconscious.

Heaving in lungsful of breath, I disentangled from the creature. The arm I'd used to choke the beast was like rubber, the bicep ready to cramp from the exertion I'd placed on it. I glanced into the crowd and saw a mixture of reactions on the faces there. Most showed shock and awe that I'd beaten the beast without killing it. Others looked annoyed that I'd gone the bloodless route. Wyatt looked as white as a ghost but gave me a grudging nod of respect. I couldn't help but smirk about that. Did he have that little faith in me? He should know better after all these years.

A slow clap started from stage left, and I looked over to see Von walking out as he applauded me.

"My goodness, ladies and gentlemen. Look at this beauty," he said, sweeping a hand toward me. The floating cameras followed his gesture. "I hope the alphas were all watching that. Miss Durst is a very worthy mate indeed. She looks just as good taming the wild beast as she does taming our hearts."

Every word out of his mouth pissed me off. After battle, the last thing I wanted was to be displayed as some sexy little thing to be won. But instead of spitting on the floor at his feet, I plastered a thin smile onto my face and bowed dramatically toward him.

The witches returned and led me back to the mansion, taking a different path than what the alphas took. That was a blessing since I was in no mood to answer the obvious questions about me not shifting. It wasn't their business, anyway.

They led me to what would be my room for the duration of the show. I'd thought the hotel suite was luxurious, but this room was fit for royalty with its thickly woven wool carpeting, mahogany wood floors, ornate carved cherry-wood fireplace, and wainscoting. Chandeliers and candle-tipped lights cast a golden glow over everything.

I didn't get a chance to inspect the rest of the room because Zoe nearly tackled me as I crossed the foyer.

"Holy shit, Kira." Zoe wrapped her arms around me and squeezed so tight, I thought I would suffocate.

"Can't breathe. Zoe, can't breathe," I gasped out.

She pulled back and tracked her gaze over hurriedly over my figure. "I watched the whole thing on TV. The tiger...are you okay?"

My legs and stomach were smeared with tiger blood. "I'm fine. This isn't my blood; it's his. I need a shower."

Zoe helped me undress. After a quick shower, I found Zoe had laid a new outfit out for me on the bed. It was a flowy, flowery, low-cut dress that *screamed* tropical vacation. I put it on. It felt weird dressing like I was on a cruise when I'd been fighting for my life less than thirty minutes before. It was mental whiplash. The juxtaposition of the five-star resort with the life-threatening island of death and torture made it seem like I was living in a dream. Or a nightmare.

I was sliding my feet into a pair of dressy sandals when there was a knock at the door. Frowning, I looked to Zoe, who shrugged.

I walked over and opened the door, stifling the scream of surprise. Von Thornton himself stood outside my door, so close to the threshold that we were almost nose to nose. Gods, he was creepy. Vampires and shifters had histories that dated back centuries. Most disputes had been settled in the ancient past, but something about them had always made my skin crawl.

"Dear Kira, I have come to escort you down to your get-to-know-you session with the alpha contestants." He reached out and put an icy hand on my arm. "First, I have to say, I was *very* impressed with your performance earlier. If I had to guess, a *lot* of tiger shifters will be in your corner after your display of mercy toward one of their brethren."

Shrugging his hand off my arm, I said, "Thanks, but I'm still not happy about you throwing a feral at me with no prior warning."

Von tittered out an obnoxious little chuckle. "Oh, my lovely young thing, you'll get used to the brutality of Bloodstone Island soon. Everyone does." He shrugged. "Or they die. Only two options, really."

Before I could even think of how to respond to that, the vampire stepped into the room, wrapped an arm around me, and leaned in close like a conspirator. I could smell the metallic tang of blood on his breath.

"I shouldn't do this, but I'm going to give you a little friendly advice. When you finally start interacting with the alphas, stay impartial for as long as possible. Give them each some nice long looks, flirt away, and make them all think they have a shot. Even if you are initially drawn to two or three of them, we want the audience to be on the edge of their seats, wondering who you'll choose. We can plan how we want the drama to play out later on. Reevaluate, if you will. Amping up the excitement is a never-ending job."

I looked at him, taken aback. It suddenly became very obvious that the *reality* of reality TV was tenuous at best. It was really only a step or two away from a scripted fantasy show. Hell, would they even let me choose who I wanted, or was that preplanned as well? I'd find out.

I nodded politely. "Thanks. Will do."

Clasping his hands together, Von grinned at me. I struggled not to glance at his pointed fangs. "Fabulous. I'll be at the end of the hall when you're ready to go."

Von stepped out and closed the door behind him. I groaned and leaned my back against it. Behind me, Zoe peered from around a corner, her face twisted with disgust.

"You know," Zoe said, "I used to be a huge fan of that guy. All vampy Dracula, sexy and stuff. But after being around him? Ugh, no thanks."

Chapter 16 - Wyatt

Despite myself, I was impressed with the mansion. The place must have cost millions to build. It looked like every castle, manor, estate, and villa I'd ever seen on TV rolled into one. The colors were deep, dark, and rich—lots of crimson, gold, and dark green. Had they tried to make it look like some kind of glamorous haunted house on purpose? Probably. All part of the show. A modern house with a bunch of glass, stainless steel, and sleek lines wouldn't inspire the same kind of gravitas that this one did.

We were in a large parlor that overlooked the ocean. I'd taken a seat in a plush armchair near the window so I could enjoy the amazing view. The bright moon reflected off the waves. Part of me hoped Kira would come down soon so she could see it. The island sucked, but this was beautiful. I wanted her to see it.

The other men started murmuring behind me. Turning in my chair, I saw Von leading Kira down the stairs, her arm in his. I glanced at the bracelet on my arm and saw the light was white. We weren't being filmed.

Hundreds of pounds were lifted off my shoulders. Being on camera all the damn time was stressful. That, and trying to keep it hidden that Kira and I knew each other. Every word I uttered, every look I gave, had to be analyzed and thought through before I committed. It was exhausting.

I stood and joined the others as they welcomed Kira. Scanning the group, I was pretty sure I'd gotten all the names memorized. Not only that, but I'd started categorizing them based on what kind of threat I thought they posed to Kira. The *idea* of the show was that we were all trying to win her as our fated mate and have a happily ever after. Many of these guys probably only liked the *idea* of being with Kira forever, enjoying her body along with all the prize money and other gifts that were up for grabs. They'd be selfish in their pursuit of her and might even turn dangerous if it became obvious they'd have no chance with her.

Ryan, Abel, and the walking puppy dog J.D. were no threat whatsoever. They were too good-natured and acted like they were happy just to be here. I didn't sense any ill will or subversive tendencies in any of them. I had a bad feeling they'd have a hard time surviving here.

Leif, Garrett, and Mika were fine, at least on the surface. Mika was dark and brooding, and I had no clue why he'd been rejected or what had made him desperate enough to come on this show. Garrett and Leif were quiet, but Leif was always staring at J.D. If I had to guess, J.D. had pissed him off in some way. Those two could duke it out somewhere and leave Kira alone, but I needed more info on both of them before I could be sure of them.

The three I was most concerned about were Omar, Tate, and Nathaniel—all varying degrees of asshole. Omar was angry that Kira hadn't shifted to kill the tiger, like she'd somehow personally disrespected him by not shifting. That was going to be interesting when it came out that she didn't shift. Was he bigoted toward latent shifters? Maybe.

Tate was an enigma and hard to read, which was frightening. He kept eyeing the other competitors like they were puzzles to solve. What worried me most was the calm and clever way he carried himself. I could see what was lurking behind his eyes, but could anyone else? Maybe, maybe not.

Nathaniel was a meathead. A walking hard-on who only knew how to talk about Kira's tits, the tits on the witches, the tits on the production assistants—he seemed to have a fetish for the word "tit." It was like the worst clichés about frat boys made up the guy's DNA. Of course, as soon as the cameras rolled or Kira appeared, all comments about his favorite word vanished. He was smart enough to know how to win.

After making the rounds and saying hello to everyone, Von escorted Kira to another room where a table displayed a huge spread of snacks ranging from aged cheese and meat to caviar. It looked like he was doing a short interview with her, a camera hovering in front of them. Most of the guys had moved over to the fireplace, sipping cocktails around the roaring flames.

Omar glanced over his shoulder through the doorway at Von and Kira, then shook his head. "I don't get it. Was she trying to be cute by not shifting? It was fucking stupid. I mean...what the fuck?"

"Can you stop dwelling on that?" Leif said with a weary sigh. "She won, didn't she? She put the tiger down. What more do you want?"

"I want my future mate to act like a shifter, okay?" Omar growled.

Leif rolled his eyes and changed the subject. "Anyway. Why do you think the last contestant wasn't at the premiere? Isn't he supposed to meet us here? That's weird, right? I can't remember that ever happening before."

In the hustle to get to Bloodstone and then watch Kira fight for her life, I'd forgotten there was one more competitor. I bit my cheek in frustration. One more person I'd need to get a read on. Another guy to categorize and assess. This was far more annoying than I'd anticipated.

Ryan shrugged. "Maybe the guy was busy with some personal pack stuff? Had to settle all that before he came out here."

"Came out here to *die,*" Leif added.

I chuckled. Leif understood what was at stake here.

Nathaniel slammed a cocktail and sat the glass on an end table with a bang like a gunshot. "Nah," he said. "Dude's probably getting the last of the gonorrhea cured by some fae doctor before he comes out here." He laughed at his crude joke. "Gotta get the oil change done, right?"

We all ignored him. Abel raised his wrist to show a blinking yellow light. "Countdown to cameras," he said.

Omar stood and slicked his hair back; the rest of us rose and straightened our suits. I despised this freaking bracelet. It was a powerful magic item. Even though I knew the risks and what it would mean to interfere, I'd seen Kira in trouble and had immediately tried to shift to help her. But I couldn't. This little piece of jewelry could be activated to keep me from being able to shift. The damned vampire hadn't really touched on that. It made me trust that bloodsucker even less than I already did. What other information was he holding out on?

As soon as the light on the bracelet turned green, a few of the guys I'd put in my "danger zone" turned on the charm. Smiles flashed, biceps bulged, and eyebrows cocked like the arrogant pricks they were. I did the bare minimum to let them think I was excited to be there but nothing more. I wasn't happy to be here. I was here to protect Kira and keep her safe. Nothing else.

Kira hurried back into the seating room, looking somewhat embarrassed. "I'm so sorry. You guys were waiting for me, and I've been doing interviews. I apologize."

She was doing everything she could to keep from looking at me. I wanted to laugh at how obvious she was being. Obvious to me, anyway. The viewers would probably think she didn't find me attractive. They'd lose their minds if they knew what had gone down between us in that hotel.

Kira led us back to the seating area, where we took seats in the big circle of chairs. Servants passed out wine, champagne, cocktails, and snacks from the big buffet in the next room. I made a point to take the seat directly to her right.

A red flush of irritation crept up her neck as I sat beside her, but her face remained impassive as she spoke to the other alphas. She looked far too good for someone who had been fighting for her life against a tiger shifter less than an hour ago. If I was honest with myself, she looked good enough to eat.

"Well, this is much nicer," Kira said. "All those flashing cameras and screaming fans make it hard to have a conversation."

Kira was a good actress. She was always on point during sting operations and deep cover projects, but I knew when she was nervous. She kept touching a spot on her collarbone, a nervous tic I wasn't sure she realized she had. She only did that when her stress level was through the roof.

I leaned in close. "Kira, I want to say you look gorgeous tonight. My name's Wyatt, if you didn't remember from earlier." I slid my eyes up and down her body, enjoying the act. "You really do look amazing." I gave her the cockiest wink I could manage. "I may go feral with my desire for you."

Kira's eyes widened as I spoke, doing her best to tell me to shut up non-verbally. Her face was scarlet, her jaw working as she ground her teeth. I could see she was having an epic battle in her mind, with one part telling her to play the happy contestant, the other part telling her to slug me right in the nose.

Instead of striking out at me, she gave me a demure smile and turned to address Abel, who sat opposite her.

J.D. smacked me on the shoulder. "Nice job, bro. That was smooth. You already got her to blush. Way to get in there first and make an impression."

"Why don't we all introduce ourselves again?" Kira said. I was pretty sure she'd just flubbed Abel's name and looked mortified about it.

"I'll go first," I said as nonchalantly as I could.

Kira turned toward me. Her bright smile and sexy stare barely concealed the flames burning deep in her eyes. She was probably imagining driving spikes into my head.

"Go ahead," she said with a grin.

I addressed the entire crowd. "Wyatt Rivers. Second Pack. I work in...uh...law enforcement."

"Thank you," Kira said, the slightest hint of condescension in her tone.

One by one, everyone introduced themselves. When it was Omar's turn, I had to school my face to not show my disgust as he fawned over Kira and praised her for how amazing she'd done in the tiger challenge. He even went so far as to say she had a kind heart for allowing the shifter to live. I caught Leif's gaze across the room, and he mimed putting his finger down his throat. All Omar had done since Kira's challenge was complain about how dumb she was for not shifting in the fight and not killing the tiger. Now he was telling her she was wonderful.

Next was Nathaniel. I knew what was probably coming from that guy, but I wasn't prepared for how heavily he turned on the charm.

"My name's Nathaniel. I'm sure you remember that, though," he said, winking at Kira. "I work in finance." He rubbed his thumb and forefinger together. "Big money, you know? Enough about me, though. Can we just, like, talk about how sexy this woman is?" He looked around at all of us, waiting for someone to disagree. When everyone gave a general chuckle of agreement, Nathaniel nodded to himself. "See? That's what I'm talking about. Kira, you may be the hottest woman to ever be on this show."

Kira didn't blush at the compliment. She shrugged and pulled an I-don't-know-about-that face. "Not sure I agree, but thank you for the compliment, Nathaniel. Can I call you Nate?"

The color drained from his face, but he did his best to recover. "Uh…well…you see, that's not my name. My name isn't Nate, it's Nathaniel."

"Mmhmm," Kira said coolly.

I covered my mouth with a hand to hide my smile.

"I really did like how you handled that tiger shifter," Nathaniel said, trying to hide his panic at his misstep. "It was sweet of you to have mercy on them. It shows you have a kind heart," he said, mimicking Omar.

"Oh my gosh," Kira said. "Don't call me sweet."

"Then what should I call you?" I said, breaking into the conversation.

I wiggled my eyebrows at her. Knowing the cameras were rolling, Kira forced herself to smile and laugh.

"Don't get cheeky. It's a little early." She swatted my arm playfully but hard enough to sting.

Nathaniel glared at me, but I gave him an easy smile.

Leif spoke up. "How old are you, Kira?"

"Twenty-three," she said.

That started a cascade of personal questions from around the room. What did she do for fun? Where did she go to school? Did she play sports? What was the Eleventh Pack like? It went on and on. I got a bit bored since I already knew everything about her. Kira answered everything politely and asked questions in return.

"Any siblings?" I asked, wanting to get back into the conversation.

Kira turned toward me and gave me a half smile. "Yes, actually. I have an older brother. His name's Kolton."

I grinned at her, sweeping my hand dramatically toward one of the floating cameras. "Well, say hi. I'm sure he's watching."

Several other alphas laughed, and Kira went a bit pink in the face again. She turned to the nearest camera and gave it a sad little wave.

"Hey, big brother."

As much as Kolton hated the show, he'd be glued to the screen for every episode until his sister was home safe. He was probably sitting in the hotel right now, glaring at all these other alphas like I was.

Ryan, one of the nicer guys and from the Tenth Pack, spoke up. "I'm sure your brother is really proud of you."

"Yeah," J.D. added. "Anyone I know would be proud as hell of me for fighting and *beating* a tiger shifter in my human form." He put a hand to his mouth and called out. "Yo, Von! These little canapés are fine, but I need real food. Can we have dinner or what? It's almost eleven."

Von appeared, his bright smile looking as shimmery as usual. But if I wasn't mistaken, he gave J.D. a dark glance for trying to summon him like a servant. Vampires did not like being belittled. I commiserated with that. If some kid whose great-grandfather hadn't been born yet when I was in my second century of life tried to tell me what to do, I'd be pissed, too.

"Come, everyone. Dinner awaits," Von said.

Dinner was probably the fanciest thing I'd ever had in my life. Sea bass, truffles, foie gras. There were even specialty dishes that had elements from creatures across the world.

One dish came out with pan-fried kappa eggs. I'd helped take care of a kappa infestation on the outer edges of the Eastern Wilds a few years ago. Staring at the jiggling eggs on my plate, I recalled the humanoid reptile-like creatures crawling out of the water and mud to attack us. Grimacing, I pushed the plate aside.

"Problem, sir?" one of the servers asked.

"I'll...uh...save room for dessert," I said, trying not to look at the eggs again.

"Of course. Very well." The server swept the dish away.

While I waited for the next course, I noticed my bracelet had changed. The green light was flashing instead of solidly on, then a moment later, it changed to white. The cameras floated away. All around the room, I watched everyone relax a little at having a break from the cameras. None of them looked as relieved as Kira. She was hiding it well, but she was absolutely exhausted.

As dessert was served, Von returned from feeding in another room. I didn't want to think about what he'd been feeding on.

"Well, well, we have had a busy evening, have we not?" Von said. "Once you are done with your meal, our house stewards will see you to your quarters for the duration of your time on *The Reject Project*. I think it would be good to try and get to bed soon. There will be"—he tilted his head, obviously thinking of the right word—"noises outside. They typically start around midnight, sometimes as early as sundown, but nothing to worry about. The sooner you get to sleep, the better, though. The noises can keep you up."

There were smatterings of conversation when everyone stood, but I only had eyes for Kira. I was desperate to get a moment alone with her. We needed to discuss everything that had happened since getting to the island. And I had to explain what I was doing here. But the other guys were sticking too close to her. Mika and Tate had Kira cornered in a conversation. Kira was tired and irritated, but she kept up her act.

I stood at the far end of the dining room, watching her talk to the guys. She never once glanced in my direction. She'd been through a lot, and I didn't want to push things any more than I already had. Leaving the dining room, I found one of the stewards to take me to my room.

The room was large and held eleven beds. All the alphas would be sharing. So much for privacy.

I sat on the bed and took a moment to finally let things set in. I was on Bloodstone Island. This was really happening. And both Kira and I were in terrible danger.

I wondered if I'd ever get any sleep. Maybe I'd stay up until every last one of these guys fell asleep. That might give me a chance to sneak out and find Kira.

Chapter 17 - Kira

"Here's your room, dear," the witch said as Zoe and I walked down the hall.

I skidded to a stop and turned to see what she was talking about. My room was at the very end of the hall. The woman was looking at Zoe, not me.

Shaking my head, I said, "No way. She's staying in my room with me. She's my friend. My stylist. It'll be fine."

The witch gave me a placating smile but didn't back down. "Unfortunately, only the female contestant is allowed to sleep in that room." She held a hand up to hold off a question, even though I hadn't even opened my mouth. "And before you ask, this isn't sexism. In the seasons when it's a single male reject and a bunch of female wolves trying to win him over, it's the same thing. The main contestant always sleeps alone."

Zoe crossed her arms and cocked her head. "Always?"

The witch rolled her eyes. "You know what I mean. Some trysts may happen during filming, that's to be expected—but no crew members or support staff are to stay with the lead contestant." She turned back to me. "And even though she's your friend, she's still designated as your stylist. Therefore, she's considered support staff."

"No," I said firmly. "Absolutely not. I want her with me. We only got here a few hours ago, and I'd like to have someone who knows me to help me get settled."

I wasn't asking, I was demanding. The witch could hear it in my voice. I did everything but growl at her. I would not be dissuaded. I'd fight the bitch right there in the hallway if I needed to.

The woman looked ready to argue further, but something in my face must have told her to think again. Finally, the woman sighed with annoyance, then glanced up and down the corridor as if she was afraid someone would hear her.

She held up a finger. "One night, got it? Since it's your first night, she can stay with you to get you comfortable, but after tonight, you're on your own. I'll have to tell the director and Von about this, but I'll explain you were"—she looked me up and down scornfully—"being difficult."

I gave her a sickly-sweet smile. "Thanks for that. Come on, Zoe." I grabbed my friend by the arm and hauled her down the hall, leaving the witch behind us.

"Her magic smells weird," Zoe whispered with a crinkled nose.

"She probably needs a good lay," I said absently as I pulled her into my room.

Once the door was locked, I let out a low growl and stomped my foot on the ground. My childish display didn't give me the catharsis I wanted. Instead, deciding to take a page out of the angry-man textbook, I punched the solid wood door. My strengthened shifter bones didn't break, and the skin didn't tear, but it still hurt like a bitch. Not only did it hurt, but I felt no better. Why did men do that? Punching inanimate objects was so stupid. Now I was angry, hurt, and feeling dumb.

"Are you okay?" Zoe asked. She was looking at me like I'd lost my mind.

Cradling my hand, I turned around. "No, I'm not okay. Not with fucking Wyatt here."

Zoe chewed nervously on her lip. "Yeah, that was a crazy surprise. I found out about three seconds before he showed up. Kolton found me in the crowd and told me. I would have warned you, but...well, you saw how wild it was there."

It had been wild. The premiere felt like it had been days ago, but somehow it had only been less than five hours ago. A lot had happened in those five hours. It was stressful enough with the show alone, but now Wyatt was here as one of the contestants.

"How the hell did he do it?" I asked, still rubbing my sore knuckles.

"Get on the show? No clue," Zoe said. "Maybe someone from the council pulled some strings."

I shook my head. "The council might be powerful enough to do that, but they'd need a reason. The show or island would have to be involved in something highly illegal and criminal to send an operative into deep cover. I've never heard even a whisper of anything like that with this show. No, he managed it some other way."

"True." Zoe gasped. "You think he's here to protect you?"

"Doubtful."

"Did you give it to him so good that he's now obsessed with you? Maybe he's on a quest to make you his permanent sex slave."

"Zoe, please, stop. Besides, it wasn't *that* good," I lied.

"Mmm-hmm," Zoe grunted as she flopped into a seat. "Sure."

"I can't believe how obnoxious he was at dinner. Did you see all the little looks he was giving me? And that goofy introduction around the fireplace? 'Hi, my name's Wyatt,'" I mocked. "Ugh. The winking and laughing when I said something he knew I didn't mean. Like, I know I'm acting for this stupid show, but I don't need someone subtly pointing it out. It was fucking exhausting."

Zoe chuckled. "I don't think the contestants are supposed to know each other before the show starts. I can't remember that ever happening. I wonder if the showrunners know? As far as everything I've read, there's no *firm* rule about it."

"I don't care what the rules are," I said. "I'm not giving him a chance to ruin this for me. I'm gonna keep pretending I don't know him. That's all I can do. If there is a rule about it, we both might get kicked off.

Then, I'll be even more ostracized. No, I won't play his little game. As far as I'm concerned, the first time I laid eyes on Wyatt Rivers was on stage at the premiere."

"That's probably a smart way to go about it," Zoe said. "If it got out among the other contestants, it could cause a lot of extra drama. And if there's one thing *The Reject Project* doesn't need, it's *more* drama. You'll have more than enough to deal with as it is. Surviving all the challenges will be difficult. If the other alphas think one of them has an unfair advantage, they may try to sabotage the others. Which is fine and dandy, but sabotaging a competing alpha can sometimes end up putting the woman in even more danger. I think you're making the right decision."

"Thanks." Having her agree with my plan made me feel a little better.

Zoe started getting ready for bed, but I stood at the window, staring out at the jungle beyond. Even through the thick glass and the magic shield, I heard a bizarre keening sound. The volume rose and fell. It was unlike anything I'd ever heard before. It was too dark to see past the magical barrier, and part of me didn't really want to see what was making that noise.

Zoe was asleep on the massive velvet couch beside my bed when I crawled into bed. I stayed awake with the events of the day replaying in my mind. Interviews, flashing cameras, screaming fans, helicopters, tigers, food, flirting, stress...it was all too much. The sheets were hot, I was uncomfortable, and I couldn't get my mind to slow down.

Completely frustrated, I swung my legs out of bed and grabbed a thick robe from the closet. I wrapped it around myself, covering the silk pajamas they'd supplied me, and tiptoed out of the room, careful not to wake Zoe as I went.

With no clue about where I was going, only the deep desire to wander, I padded down the hallway. Thankfully, it seemed all the crew had turned in for the night as well.

The house was enormous. Many of the doors were closed, and I didn't try opening them, afraid of barging in on someone's quarters. The last thing I wanted was to stumble into a room and see Von Thornton balls-deep in one of the young female production assistants. Or worse—sucking her neck.

Instead, I wandered through the house, checking all the open areas available to explore. I found a huge den with a massive skylight that looked up into the stars above. It contained an ornate pool table, a dartboard, a card table for poker, and a few other things that were standard in game rooms. The room had been done so stylishly, it didn't look silly or childish.

The kitchens were dark, but I could see they had also been outfitted in a vintage style. The look was spotless and immaculate, as if transported from the 1950s. I had to admit it was very cool.

As I roamed the halls and rooms, I realized I wasn't wandering aimlessly. I froze as I suddenly understood I was following a scent—a familiar one at that. Pine needles, sawdust, whiskey, and a note of leather. Wyatt.

I rounded the corner of what must have been the third or fourth living room or den I'd found. Standing there, looking grouchy, was the man himself.

"Damn, I waited long enough," he whispered.

My eyes widened, and I glanced at my bracelet to make sure the light was still white. It was; the cameras were off. Realizing we weren't being spied on,

I stepped toward Wyatt, looked into those sexy eyes of his, and slapped the shit out of him.

"What the fuck?" he hissed, rubbing his cheek.

"You know what the fuck. And how the hell are you irritated you were waiting here? There's no way you could've known I was gonna go stumbling around the house at night."

Still rubbing his cheek, he said, "Yes, I did. You might have been terminated, but once a TO, always a TO. No operative in their right mind would be able to sleep in a weird place without getting the lay of the land. Plus, it doesn't take a genius to know you'd have a hard time sleeping." He leaned in and widened his eyes for emphasis. "Because you've finally understood the stupidity of your actions in coming here."

I wanted to scream at him but had to keep my voice low. "I assure you, I am not regretting anything. I'm here to protect my pack from whatever war might be about to break out. With the gods as my witnesses, I'll bring pride back to my pack."

Wyatt snorted. "Yeah, speaking of pride, I can't believe you wrestled that damned tiger shifter. A feral one, no less. It's ridiculous."

He was talking about the show, but something about the way he phrased it made me think he was mad at me. That, of course, made me even angrier. Like I'd asked to wrestle a feral shifter.

"Get over it, Wyatt. This is the game. Like it or not, we're in it. If you can't finally put your bossy-ass ways behind you, you're gonna end up distracting me and getting me killed."

It was almost like I'd slapped him. His face suddenly went gray. "I'm sorry."

The words were quiet and hesitant, but there they were. I was shocked. Wyatt had apologized. My brain did a quick search. I couldn't think of a single time he'd apologized for any of the shit he'd done. Almost everything had been "for my own good," like he never trusted me to get out of a situation. The look on his face told me it wasn't just lip service—he was serious.

"Hang on," I said. There was no sarcasm in my voice. "Can you repeat that? I need to go get my cell phone and record it."

"Oh, shut up," Wyatt said, his apologetic tone vanishing. "What we need to worry about is keeping you safe. Keeping you alive."

"Well, we also need to keep pretending that we don't know each other," I hissed, glancing around the hall again. "I'm pretty sure these guys won't be happy if they found out you know me. They might turn on you and get *you* killed. Or turn on *both* of us, and then they're burying two bodies in the Eleventh Pack lands."

"Technically, I'm not a member of the pack, and you were on the shortlist for getting kicked out. They'll probably bury us on the side of the road somewhere."

"Oh my gods," I groaned. "You are a little fucking ray of sunshine, aren't you?"

"Ease up, it was only a joke."

"No time for jokes, Wyatt. That shit you pulled during the meet-and-greet? Talking about Kolton? That's a surefire way to get someone to realize we're connected. You're best friends with my brother. That alone shows the connection."

Wyatt raised an eyebrow. "We're linked by more than Kolton."

"Oh, right." I put a hand to my head mockingly. "I forgot. There's the fact that for the last five-ish years, you've been my nosy, bossy, pushy asshole of a co-worker. And you keep shoving your big fat nose into my pack's official business and hanging around where you aren't wanted. So, truly, the only reason we are connected is because of Kolton. Nothing else."

The steely look he gave me made me feel weird inside. He could always keep his cool. I, on the other hand, struggled to keep my composure and had a temper. It irked me that he could be so stoic, even now when I was trying to piss him off by being an asshole.

He leaned forward, his voice dropping even lower. "You know, there's another way I'd like us to be connected. Something similar to what happened in that hotel room, maybe?"

Heat and color flooded my cheeks. I scowled and shoved him back, but that only made him smile as he stumbled to regain his footing. That cocky grin pissed me off even more. I stepped close to him and pushed him against the wall, digging my muscles into the thick muscles of his chest. My body betrayed me, and I remembered how warm his flesh had been against mine. The way his tongue had slipped between my legs. The taste of his cock.

I shook my head to clear the images and turned my glare back on him, desperately hoping he had no clue what had just been running through my mind.

"Here's the deal," I said, poking a finger into his chest. "I don't need reminders about how annoying you are every five minutes while those cameras are rolling, okay? Stop baiting me when all eyes are on us. Otherwise, you or I or both of us might let it slip that we know each other. Hell, we're probably screwed, anyway. Who knows how many people who know both of us watched the premiere."

"It'll be fine," Wyatt said. "The studio will sweep external issues under the rug. We're pretty isolated here. If we stay cool, no one will know."

Before I could ask what the hell he meant by that, he wrapped his arm around me, spun me, and switched places with me. I was pressed against the wall, and he was up against me. I wanted to shove him away, but every nerve in my body was short-circuiting. I couldn't do anything except breathe in his scent. It enveloped me, like it had that night in the hotel.

"I'm gonna play it like this," Wyatt whispered, his lips inches from mine. "I'm going to act like this is the first time we've met without all those walls you put up between us, all the anger and shit you've built up to keep me out."

A gasp came, unbidden, from my mouth. Indignation and shock roiled in my head.

"There are no walls up. I don't need to build any walls because all you are is my brother's friend. And all I am is a rejected wolf. The only anger comes from the fact that you're constantly trying to get involved in my business. All I want to do is forget any moments we've shared in the past."

That last part was in reference to that day years ago. The day that changed everything for me, when Wyatt had found me sobbing in the forest, covered in blood and desperate for help. That wasn't where Wyatt's mind had gone, though. I could tell by the look he gave me. He assumed I was talking about the night in the hotel.

He pressed even closer to me, his eyes narrowing. My body continued to do the exact opposite of what I wanted. His body heat was making me wet. That, and the memory that kept springing to my mind of how he'd made me feel with that mouth and tongue of his. I bit down painfully on the inside of my cheek to clear my mind.

"You can act however you want in front of the cameras," he whispered furiously. "You can act however you want in front of all those guys and Von and the audience. But don't think for a moment that I'll ever believe you want to forget what happened in that hotel room."

Any second now, he would smell my arousal, and he'd know that he was right.

"Just shut up, Wyatt, or you're gonna turn me on again." I tried to fill my voice with scorn and sarcasm, but the words were too close to the truth for my liking.

It was too late. His lips were almost touching my collarbone as he sniffed.

He groaned. "Gods, you smell delicious. Like you did that night. I still think about it, Kira. You laid out on that hotel bed, looking the way you did. Give me a few minutes, and I'll have you crying out in pleasure again. Would you like that? I'd love to go back into that room full of alpha assholes with your scent all over me, the smell of your pussy on my lips."

My heart was racing. My panties were soaked, and my nipples were so hard, they ached. I wanted exactly that. I wanted his cock inside me. But that couldn't happen. Not if I wanted to survive this, and because I couldn't let him know he'd managed to worm himself into my head.

"You need to forget what happened between us," I hissed. "That was a one-time thing. I was in a bad headspace, freaked out about coming on the show, and, well, I needed sex, okay? And you happened to be in the right place at the right time. That's all. I was going off to this island and assumed I was probably never going to see you again, so..." I trailed off. I couldn't think straight with him that close to me. Nothing was coming out right.

"You wanted to have what you'd always secretly wanted?" Wyatt finished for me.

"That's not...I mean...no, I didn't say that."

Why couldn't I control my breathing? Of all the times for me to lose control, I chose now?

"You need to survive," Wyatt said, then leaned forward and started kissing my jaw.

I pressed a hand to the wall to keep my knees from giving out. Suddenly, the colors of the room seemed brighter, every sound was amplified, and each touch from him was like a pleasant fire gliding along my skin.

"I know, Wyatt." I was rapidly losing command of myself. "It's all a matter of acting. I...play along. With the game, you know? Fool the people in this game and get through the games to get the prize."

He moved his face across mine, brushing his lips against me in the barest touch, almost like a breath of wind, so close to a kiss yet so far. I gritted my teeth to prevent myself from leaning forward and taking what he'd almost given me.

Wyatt pinned me with those intense eyes of his. "This show isn't a game. It's more like torture right now. And are you sure you can act around me? Can you control yourself?"

He made it sound like a challenge. I wrinkled my nose. "I can. I haven't met a challenge I couldn't overcome yet. Especially not one from you. You haven't left me a choice."

With a dark laugh, Wyatt pressed his lips to mine. I wanted to shove him away, to knee him in the balls, then wipe my face and tell him how disgusting he was. Instead, warmth radiated through my pussy, and I opened my lips to allow his tongue entry, imagining what it would be like to allow another part of him inside me.

Too soon, he pulled away and shook his head. "You've gotten us both into this dumb situation. I'm going to enjoy tormenting you on camera."

I'd be damned if I'd let him do this to me without some reciprocation, a little tit-for-tat for making me squirm like this. I leaned forward and gently bit his neck. He sucked in a breath, and I caught the scent of his own carnal excitement. I grinned to myself.

"Looks like that counts for both of us. You mess with me, I mess with you right back. How about that? You need to remember I can handle myself."

As much as I hated to admit it, I was seconds away from doing something stupid, like dropping to my knees and yanking his cock out of his pants or dragging him into a room to jump his bones. My reprieve was the yellow flashing light on my bracelet. I stared at it wide-eyed and saw that his was also flashing.

"Shit." I shoved him backward.

Our old training locked into place in a millisecond. Wyatt leaned against a wall and crossed his arms, putting a calm but amused look on his face. I adjusted my robe, stuffed my hands in my pockets, and tried to look interested and bemused. Less than a second after we had gotten into position, a small camera drone hummed around the corner.

Surprisingly, it wasn't there to film me and Wyatt. Our absence hadn't been noticed. We were simply in the way of what it was really filming. Two other contestants were out of bed, walking the halls.

Chapter 18 - Wyatt

Kira's scent, the feel of her skin, and the way she looked in that robe almost sent me over the edge. I was pretty sure she'd been close to dragging me to the floor and having her way with me. The look in her eyes had been unmistakable, making my cock throb. So, when I saw Leif and Ryan come around the corner, I was beyond irritated.

Professionals that we were, Kira and I assumed simple conversational stances once we realized the cameras were coming. The calm and gentle smile on my lips hid my sexually frustrated rage.

Ryan and Leif were having a whispered conversation that I couldn't hear. They were deep in discussion and didn't see Kira and me until they were almost right on top of us. They nearly tripped over themselves as they stopped short.

"Hello, boys," Kira said, a charming and innocent smile on her face.

Ryan frowned and glanced between the two of us. "What's going on here?"

Kira shrugged. "I couldn't sleep. Too wound up from the day, you know? I decided to wander the halls and see what the place was like." She tilted her head toward me. "And then I found this stud doing the same. We've been talking. Getting to know each other."

Ryan's brow smoothed, and he smiled, almost like he was relieved. "Got it. Yeah, it's been a pretty crazy night."

Leif didn't look convinced. He continued to look from Kira and back to me. When I met his eyes, I could see the wheels turning in his head. I hoped he'd accept the simple explanation. It was easier to believe I was trying to seduce Kira to help myself win the show than the idea that we already knew each other and had already done the dirty deed before the show started. That's what I told myself, anyway. The look in Leif's eyes, however, told me he was smarter than I'd given him credit for. It made me nervous.

Leif smiled, letting go of whatever internal investigation he'd been working on. Blessedly, he even changed the subject. "Have you guys heard those noises outside? It's weird as hell."

"Yeah," Kira said. "That's part of why I couldn't sleep."

Ryan stared out the window. "I swear to Heline herself that some of those roaring sounds don't even sound real."

As if in response to that, a screeching howl pierced the night. The double-paned glass of the window muffled the sound slightly.

"Manticore," Kira murmured under her breath.

"What?" Ryan asked, his eyes going wide. "Those are real?"

Kira quickly turned from the window, realizing she'd spoken aloud. "Um...uh...yeah, pretty sure. They usually reside in Middle Eastern countries, but some have been known to make their way across the ocean."

"I'm sorry," Leif said. "What's a manticore?"

"Mystical creature. Body and head of a lion, massive wings of a bat, and a big thick tail of a scorpion," I said. "The scorpion tail looks scary, but the venom only disorients you so the jaws and claws can do the rest. Pretty terrifying if they catch you unaware, but their bones are hollow like a bird's so they can fly, which means they're pretty easy to fight off if you know what you're doing."

Ryan and Leif gaped at me, and Kira arched an eyebrow. I guess I'd said too much. My cover was law enforcement. No one needed to know I was a TO. That would make it too easy to connect me to Kira when her career was eventually revealed.

I shrugged. "Took a specialty biology class in college. 'Creatures of the Earth.' Still remember all that stuff."

The guys seemed to buy it. They started chatting with Kira, and I breathed a sigh of relief. The only reason I was here was to keep my best friend's sister alive. Nothing about this would be easy, and I needed to keep my head on straight. As delicious as Kira was, and as tantalizing as it would be to make her back arch in ecstasy again, I needed to get my desire for her out of my mind. She always found a way to get into trouble. If I was going to keep her safe, I'd need to be completely focused on what was happening and what she was doing.

It bugged the hell out of me that she still seemed to despise me. Even when we'd had sex, there'd been a bit of *hate-fucking* involved. It had been hot and sexy. Tonight, before those two bozos showed up, I'd thought the same thing would happen again.

After all this time, I wish she'd let go of our past. I'd never truly understood why she'd pushed me away after what happened. If I had to guess, it was probably her pride more than anything else.

Twelve years, and her irritation and hate for me had only grown like some malignant plant inside her, pushing vines and creepers through her heart and mind. Still, it was her prerogative. I couldn't tell her how to live her life, who to love, and who to hate. If she wanted to bite the hand trying to pull her to safety, that was her decision. I was prepared for that.

"All right," I said, "I'm gonna try to hit the hay again." I gave Kira a friendly nod. "It was nice getting to know you tonight, Kira."

Kira smiled at me. Anyone who didn't know her would think it was a sexy goodnight smile. I knew it for what it was: a sarcastic grin that was about one step away from a *fuck you*. It was all I could do not to laugh.

I said goodbye to the two guys and walked away. As I rounded the corner of the hall, I had every intention of making my way back to bed and sleeping. The problem was, I only got a couple of yards down the hall when an image flashed in my mind: Kira in my arms, bleeding out, the silver knife protruding from her body.

I froze mid-step. I couldn't leave her by herself. Not with two guys I didn't know. Not in a place like Bloodstone Island.

Doubling back, I slid behind the thick curtains of one of the windows in the hallway. It allowed me to hear the three in conversation without them being able to see me.

"Kira," Leif said, "I have to say you are looking beautiful tonight."

"Oh, I don't think so," Kira said. "No makeup, hair's a mess, I'm out here in PJs and a robe. I probably look like a slob."

"No way. If I woke up every day to see you looking like this beside me, I'd count myself a lucky man."

I rolled my eyes. Leif was laying it on thick—really thick.

He and Kira exchanged a little more flirtatious banter before he excused himself to go back to bed. Pulling my toes further under the curtains, I waited for his footsteps to recede. Unless my ears were deceiving me, there was only one set of feet departing, though. Where the fuck was Ryan?

To be safe, I waited one full minute before sliding out from behind the curtain. Peering around the corner, I saw Kira and Ryan walking away. Ryan was far too close to her, his arm brushing hers. At one point, he even put his arm around her waist, and Kira leaned into him for a few seconds before pulling away. The muscles in my jaw ached from me grinding my teeth.

They strolled the halls, and I stayed far enough back that neither of them would pick up my scent. Unfortunately, that distance didn't allow me to hear their discussion. Ryan continued to make small flirty touches to Kira's shoulder, her arm, her hand. If his hand went anywhere near her ass, I didn't think I'd be able to stop myself from sprinting down the hall and maiming my fellow alpha.

After tailing them for nearly ten minutes, the two stopped in front of what must have been Kira's room. They stood outside the door, awkward and nervous, like they were on their first date. I prepared to race down the hall if the jackass decided now was a good time to try for a kiss.

His voice drifted down to my hiding place in the alcove. "It was really nice talking to you, Kira," Ryan said. "I was honestly worried about who I might be here with. You know, who was this possible mate I have to prove myself to. I'm super excited it's you. I can't wait to get to know you more over the next few weeks."

I sighed to myself. That was tame enough, and he actually sounded sincere. Maybe he wasn't some horny bastard trying to get his dick wet on the first night.

"Thanks," Kira said. "It was nice talking to you, too. Now, I've got to get some sleep. I'll be worthless tomorrow if I don't."

Kira stepped into the room, and once I heard the door lock, I turned and did my best to stay silent as I took a shortcut back to my room. I had to make sure I got back and into bed before Ryan, or he might suspect that he and Kira had been followed.

On my trip back, I could still hear the snarls, growls, and yowling from outside. At the bunk room, I opened the door silently and slid in. Everyone was passed out and snoring. I managed to get my shoes and shirt off when the doorknob twisted. I quickly got under the covers and turned my head. Closing my eyes, I began to breathe like I was asleep.

As I lay there listening to Ryan undress and get into his bed, I opened my eyes. The room was lit only by the light of the moon streaming through the curtains. It cloaked the place in a strange, gray shimmer and deepened the shadows.

Over the years, I'd gotten used to being the de facto leader of my little band of lone wolves. It had been a long time since I'd been in a place like this, and with so many strange shifters I didn't know or trust. My territorial nature made it difficult to relax with the scent of all the alpha testosterone seeping into every square inch of the room.

My brain was still firing on all cylinders. I went through a dozen plans to keep Kira close to me and the dangerous alphas away from her. From the little I'd seen and heard about the show, most female deaths happened when some douchebag was trying too hard, trying to impress her or the audience, or making a fatal mistake when their temper or ego got the best of them. That couldn't be allowed. I'd kill any of these men before I allowed one of them to bring harm to Kira.

It was the only thing I could do to save her if it became necessary. The entire island was surrounded by powerful magical barriers. Even a fae as talented as Zoe wouldn't be able to teleport us out of here. Witches, warlocks, and fae had worked together to create the barriers. No, that idea was out. We could try to get off the island another way, but the studio had made a pact with the merpeople who lived around Bloodstone. The studio provided a safe place for their kind and had lobbied to outlaw fishing and charter ships from going near them. In return, the merpeople would violently attack anyone who tried to get to the island to record videos of the show or people who were trying to escape and get back home.

About ten years ago, a couple of guys got cold feet after the first contestant died and used a small boat to get back to the mainland. That hadn't gone well for them. My only real hope was helping Kira get to the end of the competition unharmed. Then I could go home, knowing I'd done everything in my power to keep her safe.

My eyes finally started to close, but I could still hear the noises outside. The danger was much closer than anyone understood. Most of the idiots I was stuck here with didn't understand that we were mere inches away from death.

After less than four hours of sleep, I awoke with a new plan that had come to me in a dream. My best bet wasn't to hide in the background like a wallflower. First off, some would find me creepy. Second, it might make others dislike me or be apathetic toward me. I needed to win the favor of both the showrunners and the superfans. Fans got to vote on upcoming challenges and tasks. If I could sway them all to my corner, it might help them choose things in my wheelhouse rather than stuff I couldn't or wouldn't do. Also, if I was a fan favorite, the directors and producers would facilitate Kira and me being together more.

Even with the lack of sleep, I was wired and ready to get the day started. Ryan and Leif both looked worn down and exhausted. Obviously, they weren't used to going on stakeouts and dangerous missions on only two or three hours of sleep.

Kira had brilliant acting skills, but mine were pretty damned good, too. It was time to put those to the test. If there was any way to protect her, I'd do it.

Even if I had to make a silly fool out of myself for the viewers.

Part of my desire to protect her came from the fact that she was Kolton's sister and that I had feelings for her. The other, more visceral reason was that she never should have had to put herself in this situation. Her pack should have rallied around her instead of ostracizing her. Even her own father had acted like she'd done something wrong when all that had happened was that an asshole had poisoned her. How the fuck was that her issue? No one had even suggested other avenues before they let her come to this gods-forsaken place to risk her life for a stupid fucking show.

The others were getting ready for the day, all of them silent as they did. Many looked like they were suffering from hangovers from all the wine the night before. J.D. was the only one who was acting chipper and ready to go.

"Yo, guys. Sorry about last night. If any of you wants to throw me to a pack of ferals for my snoring, I won't hold it against you," J.D. said as he laced up his shoes.

Leif rubbed a hand over his bleary eyes. "I may take you up on that."

A few of the other guys chuckled. I stood and headed for the door. Mika, already dressed, walked out beside me. He still had that forlorn and downcast look on his face. Since everyone else was occupied, I decided now was the time to ask him what he was doing here. He'd been even more privileged than I was as a kid. Something horrible must have happened for him to be rejected and come on this show.

I tugged his shirt and pulled him aside.

He slapped my hand off. "What the fuck, Wyatt?"

"Shh," I hissed, glancing over my shoulder. "Why are you here, Mika? You remember me; I've known you since we were kids. I know for damn sure you don't need the money, and you couldn't care less about winning Kira as a mate. You've barely said more than a few words to her. What the hell is going on here?"

That broke through his brooding facade. His frown morphed into dejected sorrow and hopelessness.

"The...um...the elders of my pack made sure the show took me."

"What? Why?" What reason would a group of pack elders have to send the alpha's eldest son to a place that risked almost certain death?

Mika stared at the floor. "Because I rejected my fated mate."

I frowned at him. "Huh? Wouldn't that make her the reject, not you?"

Mika glanced around the hall to make sure we were still alone. "Because, Wyatt, the reason I rejected her is that she cheated on me. Fucked another guy, and I caught them. In the act. Butt-ass naked. He had her bent over, screwing her brains out, and...she was fucking loving it, man. Made me want to be sick."

My heart hurt for the dude, but that still didn't explain why *he'd* been sent here. "Bro, that still means she's a cheating bitch of a reject. You have no reason to—"

"It was my father," Mika growled, tears in his eyes. "It was my father who was fucking her. He'd been fucking her since we first met. Nearly a year. Happy now? He got pissed that I rejected her because he wanted to keep banging her. His own daughter-in-law."

A heavy stone formed in my stomach. I knew how fucked-up the upper packs could be. All that power and money did weird things to people, as my own history with my old pack showed. But this? This was a whole new level of fucked-up.

"Holy shit, Mika. What the hell?"

Mika shoved past me, wiping his eyes. "I'm going to get something to eat."

I stared after him. I looked back at the bunk room. How many of the other men had been forced to come here? Kira and Mika might not have been the only ones offered up for sacrifice by their packs. I gritted my teeth. I really hated this fucking show.

I needed to get closer to all these guys, whether I liked it or not. If any of them had similar stories, it could change things. I needed to figure out their motives. Were they here for money, fame, or to get into the pants of a hot shifter chick? Or were there other things at play that forced them to come on the show? I'd have to do some digging.

Cameras followed us as we headed out to the fancy outdoor seating area. The cameras were silent and stayed far enough away that they weren't directly in our sightline, but it still pissed me off that the damned things followed me everywhere.

We took our seats as the sun rose over the trees of the island. There was a massive spread of food ready for us, and several guys had already grabbed plates and glasses of orange, pineapple, or mango juice. My nerves had destroyed any appetite I might have had, but coupled with the lack of sleep the night before, I forced myself to eat a waffle and some fruit to fuel my body for the day.

After eating, I pushed my plate aside and grabbed my cup of coffee when Kira came out the doors. My mouth went dry when I saw her. I wanted to kill Zoe for what she'd dressed her up in. The tight fitness leggings were more than paper thin, showing off every curve of her lower body. A tiny tank top covered a sports bra, revealing the flat skin of her belly.

The other alphas had seen her, and I didn't like the leering looks they gave her. She was fully clothed, but the items left little to the imagination.

Kira moved through the group, giving flirtatious smiles to each guy who came up to wish her a good morning. She went so far as to put a palm on Nathaniel's chest and laugh at a joke he told her. I could almost see his cock swelling in his pants at the touch.

Kira was more genuine when she greeted J.D., Abel, and Ryan. She seemed to actually like those three guys. I had to admit that they, along with Leif, were the ones I'd pegged as the *least* dangerous of the group.

Standing, I eased my way over to the breakfast buffet. Kira was making a plate, and I refilled my coffee and cream. Omar sidled up next to her while I busied myself.

"Let me get that for you," Omar said, taking Kira's plate and adding pastries, fruit, and cured meats to it.

"Oh. Thank you. You're sweet."

I rolled my eyes and glanced over. Omar was sporting a shit-eating grin.

"Did you sleep well?" Kira asked him. "I had a hard time with all the noise outside."

Omar handed her plate back to her, then trailed a finger over her forearm. "I would have slept much better with you beside me, exhausted, covered in sweat, and ready to drift off in each other's arms."

Kira put a hand on his arm and laughed. I grinned to myself. Her laugh was so fake. Even Kira couldn't completely stay in character for something as corny as that.

Kira took a seat at the big table. The only open seat was beside the alpha named Tate. He looked pleased that he'd positioned himself in such a good spot on accident.

Before I could have a word with Kira to get on camera with her, Von arrived with a cadre of more hovering cameras. The floating orbs sped off to capture the morning at a dozen different angles.

Von looked a little ridiculous. He wore a Havana hat and dark sunglasses. Above him floated a bewitched umbrella that hovered and tilted with each movement to ensure the sun stayed off his sensitive vampire skin.

"Good morning, everyone. I trust we all had a fun night?" He lowered his sunglasses and winked at Kira. "We begin today with a glorious challenge that will be highly dangerous." The thought seemed to turn him on. "And it will be exactly what our fans want to see on the first full day on the island. It will test your limits. It will push you to extremes. It will also most definitely thin the pack a bit, so to speak."

The mood at the table shifted instantly. Gone was the jovial feeling of enjoying breakfast. Our lives were on the line, and we were about to undergo something that would more than likely kill one or more of us. The tension could be cut with a knife, and Von reveled in it.

The vampire gestured in different directions as he spoke. "Each of you will be dropped off at a different starting point across the island. It will be your task to race back to the mansion and safety. You must outrace not only your fellow competitors but the feral shifters that have been set loose." Von again lowered his eyeglasses and scanned the crowd with glee. "Did anyone notice your suits from last night were missing this morning?"

We all looked around at each other. It appeared none of us had really checked on the clothes. We'd been too concerned with what we should wear today to think about what to do with the tuxedos we'd worn for the premiere.

Von laughed. "We gave them to the ferals. They have all your scents now. That should make things much more interesting. Along with the ferals, you'll need to be on the lookout for some of my more unfortunate brethren. Some vampires can't handle the doldrums of immortality and go mad. Usually, the Tranquility Council dispatches these poor souls. Those who aren't put down are transported here, and they hide in the jungle under the canopy to guard against the sun's dangerous rays. Also, a multitude of other creepy crawlies can be found in the jungle on your way back. Shadow beasts, chupacabra, poltergeists, and basilisks are only some of what you might encounter. Some of you will not return, sad as that may be. This task typically knocks out one or two people."

Rather than sounding sad, Von could barely contain his excitement. The thought of sprinting through an unfamiliar jungle while outrunning or fighting off unknown monsters didn't sit easily with me. If even half of what Von had said was true, I'd need to figure out how to find Kira out there. Getting close to her as soon as possible meant I'd have a better chance of making sure she got back safely.

"And"—Von held up a finger—"the first one back will win the first romantic date with our lovely Kira Durst."

Heat bloomed in my chest as I looked across the table at Kira. Another reason to get her back safe. She must have sensed my eyes on her because she turned away from Von and looked right at me. I smiled at her. All I got in return was a sigh and a roll of her eyes. My smile turned into a smile.

Chapter 19 - Kira

Wyatt's cocky little grin pissed me off. I could tell he was already thinking about how he'd be the first one to get a date with me. That meant he was pretty sure of himself. But Von's verbiage didn't sit right with me. I was going to be out there, too, so what did I get if I won?

"Wait a minute," I said. "What if I get back first? Who says the female won't beat all these pretty young boys to the mansion?"

Von laughed and shrugged. "Well, my dear, you get to choose who you go on a date with. Though, I think it will be tough to outpace these strapping young alphas. Especially when they know what awaits them if they win. I wouldn't worry too much about it."

With those few words, Von had sealed it. I would break my back to ensure I got back first. One of my weaknesses was my competitive streak. It pushed me to work harder than anyone else and had helped me rise in my career. The way Von had easily dismissed my chances set a fire blazing in my chest. I'd be damned if I let any of these men make it back here before me.

Several staff members swiftly cleared the tables as we all stood and approached Von. Cameras surrounded us, and for the first time since getting here, it all felt real. Even fighting the feral tiger shifter the night before hadn't been like this. It had happened so fast that I'd barely had time to think, much less process the experience. Now? Things were about to really get started.

I took a breath to steady myself as a group of witches approached us. They were going to cast a spell to send us wherever we were supposed to start. Ryan and Leif looked the most queasy and worried. Most of the others were trying to psych themselves up, probably preparing themselves to shift the instant they hit the ground in the jungle.

Nathaniel was walking back and forth, pounding his fists on his thighs and murmuring to himself. "Let's go, bro. Let's fucking go. Who's got a big dick? You do, you've got the big dick. Now let's do this."

I stared at him and shook my head in disgust. It appeared Nathaniel had never gotten past the emotional state of a seventeen-year-old. It amazed me that people like him even existed, and it made me sick that I had to flirt with some of these guys. If Nathaniel or Omar won this challenge, I might throw up.

A witch stepped up to each of us, and a floating camera sped over and took up position behind every competitor. Of course. Gods forbid the viewers missed a moment of the action. What if one of us was transported right next to a fucking kappa or hungry vampire? No one would want to miss a second of the blood and guts.

I'd probably have to answer questions about why I didn't shift. The others would all be in their wolf forms in seconds. Even though I'd learned to channel my inner wolf's strength, no one would accept that I chose to make things harder than necessary. I'd deal with that later. Right now, I needed to concentrate on staying alive and getting back here first.

Von held up his hand and started counting down. "Five."

The witches put a hand on each of us.

"Four."

They started chanting in an unknown language.

"Three."

I could feel the magic building as the spells were cast.

"Two."

My breathing became quick and sharp, almost hyperventilating but not quite.

"One."

I saw fear in everyone's eyes, even Wyatt's. It sent a shudder through me.

"Zero."

A flash of magic shattered my vision into a kaleidoscope of light. The stone patio was no longer under my feet. Instead, I was standing on a thick blanket of rotten palm fronds, matted ferns, and moss. I was deep in the jungle, the canopy so thick that the light was more like dusk than morning.

It only took an instant for me to catch my bearings before I started sprinting. The magical drone hummed behind me, pursuing me. The giant leaves of the jungle flashed past and slapped at my face and arms as I hurtled through the forest. All along the path I'd chosen, I could hear noises through the underbrush. Rattling, hissing, ominous growls. None of them were close enough to be dangerous. The smells were playing havoc with my mind. When the sheer number of scents hit my nostrils, I was shocked and appalled that they'd managed to get so many dangerous creatures on one island.

The air grew cold at the approach of a ghost, causing me to veer sharply to the north. The skin-crawling sensation of a nearby mad vampire tickled my mind. A scream broke through the sound of my running. I skidded to a stop, tilting an ear toward the noise. It was a shout of panic, fear, and pain. The voice was deep like Wyatt's, but I couldn't be sure if it was him.

My brain was working on the logistics of rushing toward the scream when a vampire tackled me. I sprawled on the jungle floor as the emaciated creature tumbled over me and jumped to its feet. Scrambling, I leaped up and backed away, putting distance between me and the vampire. It glared at me through sunken eyes. Its face was a sallow gray, shrunken by hunger, which made its fangs look that much bigger when it hissed at me.

After hundreds—sometimes thousands—of years, vampires went mad. There was only so much life anyone could handle. Once they lost any trace of the humanity they once had, their bloodlust fully consumed them and turned them into monsters like the one before me. This one had clearly lost its mind a while ago. It was naked, and every rib was visible through the skin stretched tight over its bones. It had been male, but its sex organs had shriveled to a small black lump. The only desire the thing had now was to drink the blood of the living.

For all that it looked weak, the thing still had supernatural speed. It leaped forward, soaring through the air faster than I'd anticipated. Its teeth gnashed and snapped at my neck as I ducked aside and pushed an elbow into its chest. It scrabbled at the ground and leaped up again, grabbing me around the waist and baring its fangs toward my neck. Before it could latch onto my throat, I pressed a hand under his chin and shoved its face away. Grabbing its throat with my other hand, I dug my fingers into the skin and summoned all my shifter strength. The creature's spine broke beneath my hands with a snap that sounded like a branch breaking.

I stumbled away as the thing crumpled to the ground. Taking a few deep breaths, I watched it writhe and try to get back to its feet. The broken neck wouldn't kill it, but it would impede its nervous system long enough for me to get away before it could heal.

I ran again, this time picking up my pace exponentially. All around me, I could hear shouts, screams, snarls, howls, and yelps from wolves. My fellow shifters were fighting for their lives.

Before I could orient myself and find the best way to get back to the mansion, another vampire crawled out of a pile of dead palm fronds. Its claw-like hand lashed out, scraping across my sneaker as I leaped back. It rose from its resting place and stumbled toward me. With a growl, I kicked out, striking it in the chest. The thing fell backward, impaling itself on a broken tree branch. The sharp wood pierced its back and shot out through the chest, stabbing right through whatever shriveled heart it had. It screamed in horror and pain, then slumped forward and turned black before my eyes.

Before I could start running again, an icy cloud of air burst across my body, and the ghost was upon me. It manifested in the shape of some horribly tentacled, dripping abomination. The ghosts of murderers never retained their human forms in death and always turned into awful, unknowable things like this—a mirror image of the soul they'd had during life.

I dodged its attack and sprinted away. Without any reliquaries or enchanted weapons, I had no chance of fighting a ghost out here. Running was my only option. Thankfully, it didn't follow me.

Gritting my teeth with determination, I scrambled up a tree to get a lay of the land. When I reached the top, I could see the roof of the mansion in the distance. It was disconcerting how far away it was—three miles, at least. And I'd already fought off two vampires and a ghost in four hundred yards. Gods only knew what awaited the rest of the way.

Climbing out of the tree, I heard someone scream in pain. The scream was closer than any I'd heard thus far, and this time, I recognized the voice. Leif. I chewed my lip as I looked in the direction of his screaming and then back toward the mansion. The decision was simple but not easy. I wanted to win, but I couldn't let an innocent person die if I was close enough to help it.

Growling, I sprinted toward Leif's screams. A few moments later, I burst into a clearing. Leif was on the ground, screaming and clawing at the dirt as a feral wolf shifter dragged him backward toward the underbrush. Leif was in his human form and covered in bites, scratches, and blood. The look of abject panic in his eyes sent a shiver of terror through me. It was the look of a creature that knew and understood it was about to be devoured by another creature. There was no greater fear in the world. None that I'd seen, at least.

Remembering that we'd all been given a silver knife as our only weapon, I pulled it from the thigh sheath and rushed forward. The feral saw me coming and released Leif's foot to lunge toward me. The madness was evident in its eyes. I leaped at it, tackling the beast to the forest floor. It snapped its jaws at me, sending saliva strings slapping into my face. A paw lashed down and cut through my leggings, leaving four bloody gashes across my quadricep. The pain didn't hurt so much as it pissed me off.

Slamming my knife into its side, I felt the blade slide through the skin and flesh like a knife through butter. There was a pop as it cracked through a rib and then a burst of bloody, foamed air when it pierced the lung.

The beast yowled and twisted from my grasp to run back into the jungle. I lost my knife, but I'd managed to get the thing away from Leif and myself. Crawling over to him, I found he was in bad shape. He'd passed out from either blood loss or shock. His body was riddled with deep bites, one right by his clavicle. He'd come inches from having his throat ripped out by the feral shifter.

He wasn't healing fast enough. Shifters healed fasters than most other creatures on the planet. The gouges on my leg had already clotted and formed scabs, but Leif's wounds were still seeping blood. With a sigh, I bent to lift the man into my arms. He was fucking heavy. I'd never be able to carry him to the mansion.

Before I even had Leif off the ground, I heard paws on leaves, panting breaths, and low growls. I tilted my nose to the air, taking in the scents around me. More ferals. All wolves, at least four of them. I'd lost my knife, and Leif's was missing from his belt. No weapon, no ability to shift, and an unconscious body to protect. Fuck. Even my skills wouldn't be enough to survive this if things went bad.

I crouched low and raised my fists, glaring into the forest, ready for whatever was to come. A familiar howl broke through the morning air, and a wolf leaped into the clearing. I recognized it immediately from the torn ear. Wyatt had told me he'd been grazed by a hunter's silver bullet in his younger years. He'd carry that wound forever.

Wyatt backed up against me, lips pulled back from white fangs as he growled at the ferals circling us. Leif moaned, and his eyes fluttered open. Now was my chance.

I grabbed his arm and helped him to his feet. "Fucking run," I growled, throwing one of his arms over my shoulders.

The feral shifters were slowly inching out of the forest, and Wyatt snapped and bit at them, keeping them off us long enough for Leif and me to stumble into the jungle toward the mansion. My leg was still sore, even though it was healing. Leif was barely able to stumble along, but it was better than carrying a dead weight.

After half a mile, my body aching and drenched in sweat, Wyatt reappeared beside us. He was scratched, and his fur was bloody, but he overall looked uninjured. He shifted to his human form and ran his hands over my body, looking for injuries.

"You're hurt," he said, seeing the claw marks on my leg.

"It's fine. Can you take this freaking guy?" I groaned as I tried to push Leif toward Wyatt.

He took the other man in a fireman's carry, then shot me a wicked grin. "Race?"

"Oh, hell," I growled, then took off running.

My body was exhausted, but Wyatt was carrying Leif, which meant I should have still outpaced him. Much to my irritation and dismay, though, Wyatt was right there beside me, the other man hanging across his shoulders and groaning in pain.

The noises around us increased. Snarling, howling, and grunting came from so many different creatures that I couldn't distinguish them from their sound or their scent. All I knew was they were getting closer. We were fast enough to outrun the ones behind us, but they were coming from all directions. We had to change our route three times to skirt one threat or another.

Wyatt hissed a curse as a scaled arm snapped out from the shadows, long curved talons scratching two deep furrows in his arm. I could see the outline of the mansion through the trees. We were almost there. My lungs and legs were on fire. I could only imagine how Wyatt's body must have been groaning under Leif's weight. Loath as I was to admit it, I was incredibly impressed with his strength.

Finally, we broke through the tree line and crossed over the magical barrier into the mansion's grounds. We collapsed to the ground, dry-heaving and sucking wind. I glanced back and saw the feral shifters, vampires, and a half dozen other creatures slink back into the foliage. Close. That had been way too close. I sat on my knees, hands on my thighs as I looked around for any of the others, but the place looked deserted.

Clapping echoed from the top of the steps. Turning, I saw Von walking down, his umbrella hovering over him.

"Well done, Miss Durst. You are a surprise," Von said. "Wonderful job getting back fast—*and alive.*"

Wyatt set Leif down, then scooped me up in his arms, carrying me toward the chairs on the veranda. It happened so fast, I didn't register what was happening until we were right in front of the cameras Von was addressing. It sounded like he was giving the viewers some kind of run-down.

"Put me down," I hissed. "I'm not hurt."

Out of the corner of his mouth, he whispered. "Don't forget the cameras."

I looked back over at Von and realized what Wyatt was doing. The asshole was playing it up for the audience, making himself out to be my big strapping hero—my white knight. I groaned internally and felt my skin crawl, but Wyatt was right. If I didn't thank him properly, the viewers might think I was a cold-hearted bitch. Reluctantly, I wrapped my arms around his neck and rested my head on his chest as he carried me to a chair, gently setting me down.

"Thank you for helping me get Leif back here, Wyatt. I don't know how I could have done it without you." I tried to make my voice as gracious and sweet as I could. The fact that it was true—I would never have saved Leif without Wyatt—stuck in my craw, but there wasn't much to be done.

Wyatt knelt in front of me and checked the wound on my leg as the cameras took in his every move. His body language and facial expression told me he was desperate to give me one of his legendary ass-chewings. He tended to give me those after I did something particularly dangerous. But he blessedly had to keep his mouth shut due to the cameras.

Instead, he whispered, "I'm glad you made it back."

He sounded totally genuine, which surprised me. All I could do was nod at him. "Yeah. You too."

"Looks like you're already healing up," Wyatt said, running his fingers along my thigh, trailing over the thin fabric of my torn leggings.

I glanced around. We were still alone.

"Were we the first ones back?"

Von smiled languidly. "Indeed you were, Kira."

A fae healer was crouched down next to Leif. He'd roused himself and managed to sit up. His wounds were fairly severe, but the healer was removing any infection that might be setting in. Gods only knew what those feral shifters ate out there in the jungle.

Leif pushed himself to his feet and limped over to us. He kept his eyes downcast, probably embarrassed about having to be rescued on his first challenge.

"Thank you," he said with a grimace.

His hand was clamped to his side, blood still seeping from the wound. It looked like the feral had not only tried to rip his throat out but his guts as well.

"Are you gonna be okay?" I asked.

The fae healer took Leif by the arm. "He will be, but even with his advanced healing, he'll need a couple days to get back in order."

She led him up the steps to the mansion to finish treating him. More screams and shouts rang out from the jungle. A moment later, J.D. and Tate came tumbling out of the forest. A massive, slithering, snakelike creature with the head of an eagle pressed up against the magical barrier, turning and sliding back into the trees when it couldn't pass.

J.D. was on his back, heaving air into his lungs. "Holy shit."

Wyatt remained by my side as more and more of the alphas returned. Some came stumbling in, slow and exhausted, while others sprinted in with dangerous creatures hot on their tails. Not one of them was without a mark or bruise, though none looked as rough as Leif had.

At last, Von raised his hands. "Welcome back, gentlemen. Such a wonderful job, and I'm sure a great way to get the blood going in the morning, is it not?" His smile faded, and the fakest frown I'd ever seen replaced it. "Unfortunately, Mister Ryan will not be joining us again. He ran afoul of a dangerous beast in the jungle and has been eliminated from *The Reject Project*. Very unfortunate. I was really getting to like that one."

A sick, hollow spot opened in my stomach. Ryan was dead? He'd been so sweet the night before. There'd been nothing nasty or mean about him. In my mind's eye, I saw Ryan screaming as some awful creature clawed at his body and tore him to shreds in the dark of the jungle.

I buried my face in his hand and refused to look at Wyatt. If I did, he'd see me crying again. And it had been a very long time since he'd seen that happen.

Chapter 20 - Wyatt

Von sent Kira off to get cleaned up, and the males were escorted to a sitting room inside the mansion. Like all the other rooms, it was luxurious beyond belief. My hands were still shaking after what had happened in the forest, and I was happy when servers came to take our cocktail orders. I ordered a vodka cranberry to help calm my nerves.

The others were in various states of shock and anger. Some were pissed that the first challenge had been so difficult. Others were trying to deal with the fact that one of our own had died. Everyone had liked Ryan, and his death was jarring, to say the least.

J.D. was pacing back and forth across the room, running his hands through his hair. He was taking Ryan's death the worst.

"He's dead. Killed. I can't believe this." He kept muttering those and similar words to himself as he paced.

I doubted any of these guys had ever been through something this dangerous. Sure, they'd likely seen tons of death, but I doubted many of them had ever been this close to danger. J.D. was from the Third Pack, which meant his upbringing had been as privileged as mine. When you'd always been insulated from the dangers of the world, it was hard to come to terms with the fact that the universe wasn't a perfect place.

Abel and Mika had taken seats beside me. Abel was nursing a beer, and Mika was staring blankly into the ashes of the cold fireplace. They also seemed to be taking Ryan's death hard, but they were dealing with it better than some.

My own thoughts were with Kira. She'd been devastated to learn of Ryan's death and had struggled to keep herself composed. She couldn't be a blubbering mess for the cameras, but as tough-as-nails as she always tried to be, she had a kind heart. The whole reason she'd pursued a career as a Tranquility operative was so she could protect and save people.

Before I could dwell on Kira's state of mind, a conversation between Omar and Nathaniel pulled me away from my thoughts.

"You got it, bro. Called it big time," Nathaniel said.

"I know. When I put those hundred bucks down, I had no doubt that fucker was gonna be the first to die."

I turned toward the men. Nathaniel pulled his wallet out and slid a crisp hundred-dollar bill into Omar's hand. They'd placed bets on who would die first? I clenched my jaw.

Tate watched the exchange and laughed, then shook his head. "Woulda been nice to win some money, but I'm just happy I got back looking less messed up than most of you. Speaking of, does anyone know how the hell Kira got back that fast? A little surprising since she obviously can't keep her mind on task. Like, how dumb was it to go back for Leif? She could have gotten herself killed."

I clamped my mouth shut and curled my hands into fists instead of telling Tate exactly what I thought of his assessment of Kira.

Surprisingly, Abel, who usually seemed so quiet and reserved, spoke up. "Yeah, Tate. It would be surprising to you. If Kira ran by and saw a piece of shit like you lying there, she'd leave your ass."

Omar snickered. "Please, what are you doing, Abel? Trying to look like Prince Charming?"

"Yeah, get over yourself," Nathaniel said. "Who gives a shit if one of us gets knocked off? It makes it better for the rest of us. I'll tell you, I've got my sights on nestling my face between Kira's sexy legs and giving her the tongue ride of her life."

Omar and Nathaniel high-fived. Abel pushed out his chair and walked over to them, pressing his chest against Tate's. The argument grew heated, and Mika slapped my leg to get my attention. Looking over, he raised the arm with the bracelet. It was green. The cameras had started rolling without us knowing. Instinctively, I glanced around the room and saw the hovering cameras had moved into place to capture the fight.

I had been looking for a chance to make an impression on the viewers, and while helping Kira and Leif had been good, this might be a better chance.

Abel's nose was right up in Tate's face as they shouted insults at each other. Omar and Nathaniel looked like they were ready to join Tate in kicking Abel's ass. I leaped from my chair and pushed myself between the two men.

"Enough!" I pressed them back, holding a hand on both men's chests. "Cool down before you dumbasses get all caught up and shift and start killing each other."

The showrunners would probably salivate over the thought of a knock-down-drag-out fight between the alphas. It would attract more viewers. I might be making a mistake by stopping the fight, but I hoped it would show the audience I was level-headed and could make calm decisions in stressful situations.

"So close," Von said behind us.

I spun and saw the vampire strolling into the room, a huge smile on his face.

"I was hoping for a little blood," Von continued. "Of course, I *always* am. But the Arena Match later this week will give them all gore they can handle. And *technically*"—he made air quotes around the word— "you aren't supposed to be fighting in the mansion. It's against the rules. We wouldn't want any of you getting hurt before the next challenge."

"How's Leif?" I asked.

Von turned to one of the cameras and smiled. "Good news. Our fae healer is taking care of Leif, and I've been given word he'll be back in the game and vying for the hand of lovely Kira very soon."

The vampire spun away from the camera to us with a more wicked smile than usual. "Speaking of Kira, it's time to announce who has won the romantic date with her. Along with that, we have an interesting situation to reveal. Our viewers have already voted that one of you will gain immunity from the Fight for Survival tomorrow. The names of these two lucky gentlemen will be revealed as soon as Kira arrives."

All the men glanced around at each other. I couldn't tell what was the better prize to the other men here. Many looked excited by the prospect of having some quiet time with Kira, while others looked like they were thinking of the best way to game the system.

When Kira came gliding into the room a few minutes later, I took one look at her face and wanted to hold her. Anyone who didn't know her would think she was only tired. I knew her well enough to see the strain. If I had to guess, she was holding herself together with pure force of will. She hadn't known Ryan long enough to truly care for him, but he'd seemed like a good alpha. The guy hadn't deserved to die like an animal in the jungle.

Kira's body language told me she was probably blaming herself, even though there was nothing she could have done to cause or prevent what happened. Even if it hadn't been her on the show, Ryan would still be dead. The only difference would be that she'd be safe at home on the couch, watching it with Zoe instead of living it.

"Ah, good," Von said with a clap and a smile. "Miss Durst has graced us with her beautiful face. Now we can get down to the exciting bits." Cameras hummed and turned in place as they positioned themselves for the best angle. "As for the romantic date, Leif and Wyatt crossed the magical barrier at the same exact time, so there is technically a tie. But seeing as Wyatt was the only one conscious, he has been named the victor of the first challenge."

Despite myself, pride and accomplishment surged through me. I never would have thought I would feel that while on the show. It had been a job, a duty to my best friend and his sister, but now I was fighting the urge to puff my chest out in pride. It had to be all the testosterone in the air. The show did everything it could to promote that macho bravado they wanted all the alphas to project.

Keeping my head, I nodded my thanks and smiled across the room at Kira.

Nathaniel bolted up from his chair, blocking my view of her. "I call bullshit. I challenge Wyatt. I want to claim his reward."

Instead of being taken aback, Von's smile only widened. "Well, this is exciting, isn't it? Nathaniel, you are allowed a physical fight to take his advantage or reward for yourself. As our long-time viewers know, this is called an Alpha Brawl. Very sexy and usually bloody, but..." He held up a warning finger. "Competitors are not allowed to kill one another in the Brawl. That's the only rule, really. Nathaniel, is this something you would like to pursue?"

Nathaniel glared at me. "Hell, yes, I do."

He obviously wasn't used to not coming in first place. It was like he took personal offense that I'd gotten back before he did. This fucker had been laughing about Ryan's death and happily handing over the winnings to Omar.

Gritting my teeth, I held Nathaniel's gaze. "I accept," I growled.

Nathaniel stared me down. He was trying to intimidate me and was probably used to getting other guys—even alphas—to bow to his intensity. All I did was stare right back.

"Fantastic," Von said. "Before we get to the action, we should announce that our viewers back home have voted that Leif will receive immunity from the upcoming challenge. The young man put it all on the line and must have made quite the impression to get the lovely Kira to put herself in danger to help him. His pretty blue eyes must have cast a spell over her."

Kira chuckled along with Von, perfectly playing the part of a hot girl who was free game to any of the alphas. It was as far from the real Kira as could be imagined. A part of my mind twinged with uncertainty. Why had she gone back to help him? Was it simply that she was a good person and had devoted her life to helping people and hunting evil? Or did she actually like Leif?

My mind was suddenly swarmed with unwanted images. Leif and Kira, naked and writhing on a bed of satin sheets. One of Leif's hands clutching Kira's breasts, the other working feverishly between her legs. Kira, her head thrown back in passion, gasping for breath and thrusting her hips toward Leif's hand.

I bit hard on the soft meat inside my cheek. The coppery tang of blood filled my mouth, but I managed to keep my stoic expression intact. That was stupid. There wasn't anything between Kira and Leif. They hadn't even known each other for a full day. Was he even her type? Hell, she'd been fine with Jayson and hadn't dated at all before getting paired with him. Why couldn't a guy like Leif be exactly what she was looking for? I knew exactly what to do to get her to suck in a breath, moan, and quiver in bed, but I had no real clue what she was looking for in a guy. It bothered me more than I'd realized.

"Let's go. I'm ready to wipe that fucking smile off this douchebag's face," Nathaniel said, pointing at me.

I didn't even bother answering him. Instead, I stood and tucked my thumbs in my belt, holding his look and feeling a moment of excitement when his eyes wavered. They never looked away, but his discomfort at being stared down was obvious. I was itching for a fight. Any fight. Dealing with the walking, talking dickhead Nathaniel was exactly what I needed to blow off some steam.

"Hang on." Kira came to stand between us. "They don't need to be fighting."

"Yeah, we do," I said. "This guy thinks he deserves something, and I'm gonna show him exactly what he deserves."

Kira shot a glare at me. I could see all the unspoken words she was trying to relay in that look. All I did in return was smile, raise an eyebrow, and wink at her. I was sure the cameras and viewers would love that. Kira, however, looked even more pissed.

"Come, come, everyone," Von said. "We'll have the Alpha Brawl in the amphitheater."

We followed Von out the door and back to the path we'd taken the night before. Nathaniel walked at the head of the group, flanked by Kira and Von. I chose to stroll along at the tail of the pack. Kira kept glancing back toward me, but I didn't meet her eyes. All I could do was stare at the back of Nathaniel's meaty head in anticipation of the coming fight.

Other than me, Nathaniel was the biggest alpha on the island. Gods, it would be cathartic to take all my anger out on someone. A lot had happened in the last few days, and I needed to get it out of me before I exploded.

My best attribute was keeping my head when everyone else was losing theirs. In one day, I could see most of the others were terrible at that—too many emotions, tons of testosterone, and posturing. Most of them saw Kira as eye candy and a sweet ass they might get lucky enough to nail. My only goal was to get her out of this place alive and well. I never wanted to see her crying and covered in blood again. That image still haunted my mind.

The cameras whizzed overhead, taking up positions all around the amphitheater as the other alphas and Kira got seated. Von led me and Nathaniel to the center of the stage, then turned to the nearest camera.

"Good afternoon. Such exciting times here on *The Reject Project*. Already, we've had the lovely Kira defeat a feral tiger shifter, the group has braved the evils of the jungle, and one of our number has tragically met his end. And now? On only the second day, we have our first Alpha Brawl. Wyatt won a romantic night with the lovely Kira, but Nathaniel has chosen to challenge Wyatt for that most delectable prize."

Von looked at each of us. I gave a curt nod to indicate that I was ready, and Nathaniel gave him the same sign. The other alpha cracked his knuckles and bounced on his toes. All for show. He was trying to intimidate me, and it wasn't working.

"No weapons," Von said. "All you have are your human and wolf forms and whatever fighting skills you bring to the brawl. Remember, killing is expressly forbidden and can be punished with expulsion from the island. That means you need to fight hard, but not *too* hard. Proceed," Von said, slicing his hand through the air.

The vampire backed up quickly to join the others. Nathaniel raised his fists into a fighting stance and walked toward me.

"You screwed up now, motherfucker," Nathaniel said. "Shoulda just given me the date. Shit, how is she gonna enjoy herself with a cunt like you?"

"Nathaniel, do you ever shut up?" I asked, walking forward to meet him.

He didn't respond other than jabbing a fist at my nose. I turned my head aside at the last second. I was a little surprised by how fast he was. My face stayed passive as we circled each other. I'd already read him to the bone. The best way to fight a guy like this was to frustrate him. Once there, he'd make mistakes and give me openings.

Lightning-quick, Nathaniel juked in, slashing his left hand in a cross and then swinging his right upward in an uppercut. I slapped the crossing hand away and took a quick step back, allowing the uppercut to flash past my face less than an inch away. He was fast and knew how to fight, but he didn't have my training. My hands remained relaxed at my sides.

"Are you gonna fight or not, pussy?"

I cocked an eyebrow. "Oh, we're fighting? I thought you were dancing with me. Is that not what was going on? Listen, buddy, if you're looking to get a blowjob tonight, you'll have to dance *and* buy me dinner. I'm not the kind of guy to put out on the first date."

Laughter erupted from the stands. I didn't dare glance over to see Kira's reaction.

The laughter sent a spike of heat into Nathaniel's already pissed-off mind. His face went red, and he lunged toward me, shifting as he did.

I took two steps back and shifted into my wolf form. Nathaniel's jaws snapped shut right in front of my nose. I shot forward and slammed my head into his side, feeling his ribs flex painfully. Nathaniel yelped in agony and stumbled back before snapping at me again, this time catching my back paw in his teeth. I snarled as he pulled me to the ground with a twist of his head. In a moment, he was on top of me, fangs clicking together in front of my throat. My forepaws were on his chest, pressing him away.

He was strong, maybe stronger than I was. That was disconcerting but not totally unexpected. In his human form, he was a lumbering oaf, so it didn't surprise me that his wolf was thickly muscled and had more mass than I did. I rolled out from under him and snapped my teeth, nicking a bit of skin on his side. Fur tore away, blood trickling from the wound. Shaking my head, I tossed the fleck of skin away. Then we attacked each other again, head-on.

The fight was brutal and seemed to drag on forever, but it couldn't have been more than four or five minutes when Nathaniel finally made a mistake. He clamped down on my back leg again and swung me around, tossing me to the side of the stage. Instead of jumping atop me to get the advantage and bite down on my throat or belly, he turned to the alphas and Kira and raised his muzzle to release a howl of victory.

Before I'd even come to a stop where he'd tossed me, I was back on my feet, running full speed toward him. He had no idea I was right behind him when I leaped onto his back, forcing us into a tumble of snapping, growling, and salivating teeth. He latched onto my shoulder, but I jerked and yanked myself out of his grip. In two quick movements, I flipped him on his back, straddled his chest, and locked my teeth onto his throat, squeezing hard enough to cut off the air supply to his brain.

Barely getting myself under control before the bloodlust pushed me past the point of no return, I eased the pressure on his throat and pinned him to the ground. Exhausted and bleeding, all Nathaniel could do was whine and paw ineffectually at my chest and face. If I wanted him dead, all I had to do was snap my jaws fully shut and tear his throat out. The fight was over.

Von leaped to his feet, applauding like a madman, and the other guys joined in. Kira wasn't clapping. I'd expected her to look annoyed or pissed at me, but that wasn't what I saw as she stared at me across the stage. There was heat and desire in her eyes. Apparently, my wolf and fighting prowess had impressed her. Or, maybe she was excited that I'd saved her from a night of inappropriate jokes, ass-touching, and a desperate attempt to get into her pants.

My cock went hard, the testosterone and adrenaline from the fight making it worse. I wanted Kira but couldn't have her. And the cameras were picking up the way we were looking at each other. Several had zoomed in, catching the fiery stare for the entire world to see. The spell was finally broken when Von stepped on stage and gestured toward me.

"The winner of the Alpha Brawl, Mister Wyatt Rivers. Well done, sir. You may release your challenger," Von said.

Letting go of Nathaniel's throat, I shifted back to my human form and stood to my full height. A few scratches and bite marks marred my skin, but overall I was in better shape than Nathaniel, who lay moaning on the ground now that he was back in his human form. I grinned at Kira, letting her know I'd seen the way she'd looked at me.

The guys came down and grudgingly congratulated me. Most of them seemed surprised that I'd defeated my rival that easily. Nathaniel was an impressive physical specimen but lacked the killer instinct to win a fight against someone like me.

J.D. wasn't even grudging in his admiration. "Dude, you are freaking strong. Holy shit, man, that was fantastic." He pumped his fists like he'd just watched his favorite boxer win a match he'd bet his life savings on.

"This is bullshit," Nathaniel groaned as he finally sat up. "That wasn't a fair fight."

"What part wasn't fair?" Mika asked in disgust.

Nathaniel slowly got to his feet and gestured toward me. "He...well, he..." He shook his head, and his face went red. "You wouldn't understand unless you were fighting him, but he fucking cheated."

Von raised his eyebrows, and I could tell he was doing an epic job of keeping himself from rolling his eyes. "Yes, *anyway*, it's time for Wyatt and Kira to get ready for their romantic evening." He looked from me to Kira and smiled gleefully. "And hopefully, we'll get lucky and see some more pining looks. It looks like Kira enjoys a man who can take what he wants, hmmm?"

Kira, face flushed, glanced away from me. So, Von *had* noticed the way she'd looked at me. I could see that it bothered her. I wasn't sure if it was because she'd been caught or if it was the fact that it was me she'd been looking at that way.

Maybe I'd get a chance to ask her tonight.

Chapter 21 - Kira

When I got back to my room, I was a mess. They'd kept us out there for hours doing interviews about the day's events. All that would be spliced into the show when it aired later that day.

All I'd wanted was to go back to my room. So much had happened, and it was only the first day. Ryan was dead, Leif badly injured and almost dead, Wyatt and Nathaniel fighting over me like two stupid jocks. It was all more intense than I'd thought it would be, and much more than I'd bargained for.

"You look like shit," Zoe said as I walked in.

"Thanks. You're a delight to look at as well."

"Sorry," Zoe apologized.

I pushed a stray hair out of my face and flopped onto the makeup chair. Zoe started getting me ready for my "romantic date" with Wyatt.

"Looks like you haven't decided whether to cry, shout for joy, or throw up," Zoe said. "If it's the last one, can I get a three-second warning so I can get out of the splash zone?"

I shook my head in disbelief. Everyone knew people died here. It happened multiple times each season. Still, part of me had felt like we were all in a dream or on a fake TV show.

"Zoe, Ryan's dead. I can't believe it."

Zoe stopped working on my hair and sat beside me, putting a hand on my thigh in comfort. "I heard. He seemed nice. I'm sorry."

"This is much more brutal than I thought it would be. You're right, he was nice. I think that's part of why his death is hitting me so hard. We had a really good talk last night. He walked me back to my room, and I think he was interested in me. Like, as a person, you know? Not some prize to be won, like how a lot of these guys look at me. He was a really, *really* good guy. He didn't deserve this."

Zoe looked at me questioningly. "Does that mean you were interested in him? In that way?"

It only took an instant for me to find the answer to that. I sighed and shook my head. "No. Not really. He was a good wolf. Honest, sweet, and kind, but no, he didn't appeal to me like that."

Zoe took my hand in hers and squeezed hard. I turned to look at her. She had a pleading look on her face.

"Kira, people die on this show. If you freeze up every time someone gets taken out, you're only putting yourself in danger. You've got to move past it. Don't even blink when they die. I'm sure the guys are great, but you're my best friend. They could all die horrible deaths, but as long as you come home safe, I'll be fine."

It was easier for her. She didn't have to spend time with the guys. She hadn't made connections with them.

I shook my head. "You don't get it. Ryan was a real person. He's gone now. Forever. He deserved better."

Zoe released my hand and slapped her palms on her thighs. I could tell she was frustrated about something.

"Are you mad at me?" I asked dumbly.

"No," she huffed. "I have to tell you something. It's either gonna piss you off, break your heart, or some combination of both."

Now I was confused. What the hell was she talking about?

"Spill it," I said.

Zoe took a breath, then said. "It gets sort of boring in here while you guys are out doing what you do, so I've been chatting with some of the staff. The witches, the other fae, the security guys, the production crew, the whole nine yards." She shrugged and rolled her eyes. "I may or may not be trying to get laid, but that's beside the point. When Ryan died, everyone was talking about it. Some of the production assistants spilled the tea on Ryan."

"Like what?"

Zoe sucked in a lungful of air, then let it all out in one rush. "He lied about being a reject. He never got rejected. He already has a mate...*had* a mate back home. They made up the reject lie to get on the show. If he won, he was going to turn down the fated-mate blessing and take the prize money. The showrunners found out but let him stay because they thought it would cause a shit-ton of good drama if he got to the end and turned his back on you."

I felt like she'd slapped me across the face. I blinked a few times before I could speak. "What the hell are you saying?"

Zoe's face dropped, and she looked miserable. "I'm saying that guy you thought was super sweet and

nice and really into you was a dick who wanted to
string you along and then leave you high and dry.
That's what I'm saying."

"No way. That can't be true. Are you sure?" I
wanted it to be a lie, but I could see how serious she
was.

Zoe nodded. "Yeah. We got to talking. Most of
the guys on the show have their own baggage and
reasons for wanting to be here. All I can say is almost
none of them are looking for the perfect mate. Which
means you need to be really careful. If these guys
don't give a shit about you, that means they might be
just as dangerous as this damn island."

All I could do was sit there for a few minutes
and think about what Zoe had just revealed. Ryan had
a mate back home? He'd been so charming and flirty
with me the night before. I felt dirty and nauseated
just thinking about it. I still didn't think he deserved
whatever fate had taken him out in the woods, but he
most certainly didn't deserve any more of my sadness
and pity.

Zoe was right—I needed to worry about my
own survival. I wasn't here to get a mate, either. Did

that make me as bad as Ryan and the others? I
supposed it did.

"What other rumors or drama have you heard?
Spill it, sister."

Zoe quickly looked away. "Uh…oh jeez. Let me
get your next outfit first, then I'll get into it."

She grabbed the clothes I'd be wearing. Once
she started working, juicy tidbits of info started
tumbling out.

"So, neither Mika nor Leif wants to be here.
Their packs forced them to come as some kind of
severe punishment."

"Punishments for what?" I asked, gaping at
her. What could be that bad?

Zoe shrugged. "No idea about Leif, but the
rumor is that Mika had a falling out with his father
when Mika rejected his fated mate. No one really
knows anything more than that. Kinda weird, though.
His dad is the alpha of the First Pack. The most
powerful pack in the world, and Mika was set to
inherit that. It's crazy to think about.

"I did hear that Tate guy is legit. He's
absolutely desperate for a mate. His died
unexpectedly, and it broke the poor guy's heart. All he

wants is a new fated mate. Though, it seems like he doesn't give a shit who that is, as long as he gets one. Basically, he's still in love with his dead mate, and if he gets you, there will be, like, zero passion or love."

"Good gods," I said. "What else?"

Zoe bobbed her eyebrows. "Omar. What a piece of work he is. He'd already gone through an official mating ceremony when he lost his mate."

I gasped and put a hand to my mouth. "Dead? Like Tate's?"

Zoe barked a laugh. "Um...no. See, he's got what the ladies call a wandering dick. He had a pretty intense taste for vampires." She shook her head. "A lot of guys do. Vampires look eighteen but have the sexual experience of centuries under their belt. His mate was supposed to be away for a few days on business. She got home early and found our boy Omar in an orgy with six vampire chicks."

"No!" I whispered.

"Yes. It all came out in the background checks. I'll be honest, after seeing and hearing everything over the last two days, I don't know if I'm still a fan of this show. It's all really fake and staged. I liked the idea that at least some of this was real, but..." She shrugged sadly.

All these guys, and most of them were fake. It irritated the shit out of me that it was looking more and more like Wyatt might be the only good guy, the most honest guy in the whole group.

I groaned. "And Von told me to 'remain impartial.' Said I should let them all think they were *winning* me over. How do I even act remotely interested around these guys? Especially a creep like Omar?"

Zoe scoffed and waved that question away. "Ignore the immortal sadist. Take it from a fan—if you want to get the audience on your side, forget about ninety percent of these dudes and focus on one or two. You're already well on your way. Keep it up."

"Keep what up? What are you talking about?"

Zoe frowned at me. She looked like she thought I was lying. When she realized I had no clue what she was talking about, she rolled her eyes and grabbed the TV remote.

She turned the TV on and switched channels to *The Reject Project*. The show was popular enough that it had its own channel that ran reruns of past seasons, in-season discussions, challenge breakdowns, as well as interviews with past cast and crew members. The channel was currently showing highlights of the day so far. Zoe fast-forwarded, then paused.

Wyatt was holding me in his arms, carrying me away from the forest. We were caked in dirt, smeared with blood, and shiny with sweat. The cameras had caught us as we'd been looking into each other's eyes—Wyatt looking down at me with concern, me looking right back at him.

My cheeks flushed red as I looked at the screen. I hadn't realized we'd been that close, gazing at each other like that. I'd been irritated with him at that moment. I hadn't been injured and hadn't needed to be carried. I'd been about to bite his head off and tell him to put me down, but without context, the image looked like two people on the verge of falling for each other.

Shoving the thoughts out of my mind, I laughed and pointed at the screen. "This? That's what you want me to do? Snuggle up with Wyatt and make the viewers think I want to bump uglies with him?"

Zoe shrugged. "I mean...you've *already* bumped uglies with him. Why not keep the charade going?"

"Because, Zoe, he's *Wyatt Rivers*. There's no way that's gonna work. He'll drive me fucking crazy. Hell, he's already driving me crazy, and we've been here less than twenty-four hours. We hate each other, and that's not going to change."

Zoe sat on the bed and studied me, a knowing smile on her lips. "Sure didn't seem like you hated each other when he swept you out of the bar the other night."

I stared back at her, unblinking. "I thought you were hammered that night? I kinda hoped you'd blacked out and wouldn't remember."

Zoe laughed. "Fae can hold their liquor pretty well. Plus, no matter how drunk we get, we don't black out. We remember everything. I remember how flushed your face was, how intense Wyatt was when he looked at you. I remember all of it." She raised an eyebrow at me.

I was appalled that she recalled so much of that might. She'd barely been able to stand when I found her out on the street, talking to Wyatt.

"Also, you still haven't given me the good dirt about Wyatt," Zoe said.

"What dirt?"

Zoe held her palms so they were roughly six inches apart. "Bigger?"

"Huh?"

She moved her hands another three inches apart. "Bigger than this?" she asked with a gasp.

"Oh, for fuck's sake, Zoe. Stop it."

She pouted and lowered her hands. "It's important information."

"That night was a spur-of-the-moment thing. I was coming here to maybe die, and I needed some stress release. That's all that was. A night of..." I paused and gave a defeated shrug. "Good sex, I'll admit. I was desperate to get my mind off everything for a while, and Wyatt happened to be there. Nothing more. I let myself forget what a bossy, domineering asshole he was for one hour. I put all that out of my mind, used his body to get what I wanted, and then we were done. I've already forgotten how it felt if I'm being honest," I lied.

Zoe wasn't buying it. She leaned closer. "Sure. I saw you afterward. The afterglow, how angry you were at Wyatt. I know you, sister. You got mad at him because he made you feel something that night."

Before I could respond to that little bombshell, Zoe changed the subject. "Well, no matter what's happened in your past, I'm glad Wyatt is here looking out for you. He may be the only one who really gives a shit what happens to you. From what I've seen, the other guys are desperate, horny, or idiots. Some of these guys are so hell-bent on winning and beating the others, they'll forget to protect you. Wyatt won't have that problem. He'd throw himself into a pit of ferals and vampires before he let you get hurt again."

"Well, the showrunners obviously don't give a damn if I live," I said. "They threw me to that tiger within the first hour." I tried to remember the rules of this stupid show. "Remind me what happens if I die or get hurt badly enough that I have to go home? What happens to the prize?"

Zoe scrunched her face in disgust. "That's one of the parts I hate. If the lead contestant dies, they pull in a new one. Whoever came in second in the casting process is on standby. *The Reject Project* goes hard on the whole the-show-must-go-on thing."

It was strange to think of a young woman sitting at home, knowing that if something bad happened to me, her chance to shine would come. Hell, she'd probably been rooting for the feral shifters and vampires to do me in.

Zoe finished my makeup and hair for my date with Wyatt. I was not looking forward to it, but I had to play the part. I needed to get my head in the right space to be flirtatious and giggly on camera. I felt queasy just thinking about it.

"Done," Zoe said. "Oh, you look hot. Wyatt's going to have a boner in a second when he sees you."

"What is your morbid fascination with Wyatt's genitals, Zoe?"

"Because, silly, those weird-looking things are fascinating."

She took my hand and helped me stand. I gave her a hug. "Thanks, Zoe. I don't know what I'd do without you here."

She laughed. "No clue." She leaned her lips close to my ear and whispered, "Don't forget, you can request the cameras to be turned off for some alone time if you want."

I pulled away from her. "Thanks."

When I stepped out my door, one of the fallen angels I'd met in the city was standing outside. Recognizing him, I said hi, but he simply grunted and led me toward the stairs and down to the lower level. The cameras zipped in and around me to catch me walking into the dining room. One of them even did a full body reveal, starting at my feet and slowly moving up the silk dress to my face.

I wasn't led to the big dining room that we'd all enjoyed the night before. Instead, the fallen angel led me to a small, intimate dining room. A fire roared in the fireplace, and outside, the sun was just sliding below the horizon. I hadn't realized it was getting that late.

Wyatt was already there and stood as I entered. No one else was anywhere in sight. A camera flitted into the room and positioned itself on the wall for a good angle.

Wyatt straightened his suit and grinned at me. I was struck again by how well he cleaned up. The crisp suit, his freshly washed and styled hair, those amazing eyes staring back at me.

He looked at me in astonishment. Zoe had done a good job with my dress, hair, and makeup, and it showed on his face. Giving myself a little internal fist pump that my appearance could take him by surprise, I walked toward him. Wyatt's face quickly morphed back to the extra flirty version of himself. Gone were the simple smile and bright, inquisitive eyes. He'd slipped back into the persona he projected for the cameras.

It should have irritated me, but it didn't. It was the smart thing to do. I was pragmatic and understood what was at stake. It would be nice to be ourselves, but the cameras were always around. If we wanted to survive this, we had to play our parts. I winked at him and smiled like the seductive little minx the viewers wanted me to be.

Wyatt hurried around the table to pull out my chair for me and helped me into my seat. He rounded the table and took his seat.

"Any idea what we're having?" I asked. "I'm starving."

"Glad you asked," Von said as he stepped into the room, that bright, creepy smile on his face "Wyatt. Kira. I'm glad the viewers and I will get to watch you two get to know each other better."

"Um, thanks," Wyatt said.

Vin clasped his hands together and leaned down close to Wyatt. The hovering camera followed him and got a close-up view of the two men.

"Wyatt, I think this would be the perfect time for you to ask Kira about her rejection story."

A cold hand clenched around my stomach. The last thing I wanted was to talk about that. Not with Wyatt, and not with hundreds of millions of people watching. I'd known that I would eventually have to talk about it. The show was called *The Reject Project* for a reason. But I never thought it would happen at the end of the first day or with this man—the person who'd been there to see the embarrassment, shock, and shame on my face. It would almost be like telling the story while looking into a mirror.

Smiling thinly, Wyatt nodded to Von. "Great idea," he said, but I could pick up the annoyance in his tone.

Von, ever oblivious, grinned and took a step back. "Enjoy your dinner. The chefs of The Reject Mansion have a glorious seven-course meal planned for you." He wiggled his eyebrows suggestively. "*Lots* of aphrodisiac dishes are on the menu. I leave you to enjoy each other."

Without another word, Von left the room.

The next several seconds were uncomfortable and awkward. We couldn't talk as though we knew each other with the cameras on us, and I had no idea how to start a fake getting-to-know-you conversation. Thankfully, we were saved by the quick arrival of a server dressed in a black tuxedo.

"Good evening, my name is Ricardo, and I will be your waiter for this very special meal. Let me pour you some wine. I will return in a moment with your first course."

Ricardo poured dark red wine into our glasses before vanishing and returning moments later with a plate of oysters.

"Oysters from off the coast of the Thundering Shores. Two topped with house-made chimichurri, another two with horseradish and lime granita, and finally, two topped with shredded pears that were pickled in a champagne vinaigrette. As accompaniments, house-baked onion and poppyseed crackers. Enjoy."

Once he was gone, I looked at Wyatt and raised an eyebrow. "I don't even know half the words he just said."

He laughed and shrugged, lifting his first oyster. "Bottoms up."

Hesitantly, I followed suit, amazed at how good it was. The texture was weird, and I made the mistake of trying to chew, but otherwise, it was surprisingly delightful. Like a pleasant and more decadent sip of ocean water along with the delectable seasonings.

After we finished our second oyster and had sipped some wine, I knew I needed to get things going. I needed to make this look like it was the first time we were having an intense conversation.

I put my glass down and leaned my elbows on the table. "So. My rejection."

Wyatt was in the middle of a sip of wine, and his eyes darted toward me. Surprise was written all over his face. He must have thought he'd have to drag it out of me.

He put the glass down and dabbed his lips with his napkin before speaking. "Right. Do you mind if we talk about it?"

Shaking my head, I bit into one of the crackers. "Not at all. It is what it is."

"Well, when did it happen to you?"

"A little over two weeks ago," I said, then swallowed my final oyster.

Wyatt, ever the good actor, did a great job of looking shocked. "Two weeks? That's all? I can't believe you aren't still in mourning."

I smiled shyly at him, playing it up for the cameras. "Well, if it hadn't happened, I'd never have met all you amazing guys."

Wyatt ate his last oyster, then asked, "How long were you together?"

"Five years. He rejected me about two minutes before we would have completed the official mating ceremony. He was with the Ninth Pack, and the pairing would have strengthened my pack and ensured their safety if any troubles came up. I'm sure you've heard the rumors about possible war, aggressions, things like that. For whatever reason, he and his pack found me wanting. So he dumped me and left me at the altar."

I flinched as Wyatt tossed his fork on his plate so hard, I was afraid the china would break. He locked his eyes on mine. "Sounds like this ex-mate of yours was a dick. A damned idiot who needs to pull his head out of his ass. I think he'll end up regretting this for the rest of his pathetic life." He leaned forward and gestured to me. "Look at you. Beautiful, sexy, smart. A hell of a fighter. You're amazing."

My face went hot as I blushed under his heaps of praise. Gods, he was really laying it on thick.

"Well, I'm not sure I'm that great."

"Bullshit," Wyatt scoffed. "In fact, I'm glad that douchebag doesn't get to have you. If he could give you up that easily, he never deserved a single second of your time. You were patient for such a long time, and he rejected you like that? You're a hundred times better than he is—no question. No matter what happens here, you need to know that you deserve better than that guy."

His words were impassioned and intense and nearly took my breath away. Wyatt was staring at me with hungry and imploring eyes. It was almost like he was begging me to believe that what he was saying was true and not a show for the cameras.

Before we could continue, Ricardo returned with a new course. "Continuing our romantic foods theme, I present roasted artichoke hearts with shredded and fried sweet potatoes bathed in a strawberry, fig, and balsamic glaze." He bowed his head before leaving the room again.

I took a few bites before speaking again. "I'm glad you think so highly of me after such a short time. I still have to believe there really was something wrong with me that made him reject me like that."

Wyatt swallowed and waved his hand at me to stop. "Don't do that. Don't talk negatively about yourself. If I had to guess? This rejection sounds like normal pack politics. His shitheel of a father probably found him a better match in a higher-ranking pack, and then they cut you loose. You deserved better. Did you ever get the chance to confront this so-called *mate* about this rejection?"

I cleared my throat. Things were getting *real*. It didn't feel like we were on a show. Wyatt sounded sincere. Did he actually believe these things? Ever since Jayson rejected me, all I'd experienced was shame. Shame, anger, and self-loathing. Nothing I said to myself ever got those emotions out of my head. A small part of me continued to believe that I was at fault, that I'd somehow ruined the mate pairing. Hearing Wyatt sticking up for me and trashing Jayson and his family should have been petty and childish, but it lifted my spirits and made me feel less broken.

"I never really had the chance," I said, my voice softer than I wanted, but I couldn't get myself to speak up. "I didn't want to. After he rejected me and pretty much ruined my life, I knew I didn't want to deal with him. Part of me realized that I would never want to be with a man who had never truly been there for me in the first place. I still feel some indignation, which I know I need to let go of, but..." I hesitated for a moment, again scared at how real this conversation was getting.

"But what?" Wyatt asked, his voice as soft as mine.

The words were already forming in my mind, and I understood what they'd mean when they came out. I didn't want to say them. I didn't need to, and it would make things weird, but there was no stopping it.

"But...I don't need to linger on him. He's in the past, and he never really wanted to be with me. Why should I pine for him when there are plenty of people in my life who would go through hell to be with me? To be near me. To protect me."

I grabbed my wine glass with shaking fingers and looked at Wyatt over the rim. The look I gave him was soaked with meaning and intention. I couldn't believe I'd said that. When he gazed back at me, I knew he'd picked up on what I was saying. His eyes lit up with fire and, possibly, understanding.

I hoped the cameras didn't pick up the blush painting my cheeks.

Chapter 22 - Wyatt

The entire dinner, I'd been focused on keeping things light and jovial. In a word? Easy. Kira and I were in a dangerous spot—any wrong misstep could spell disaster. I wasn't really worried about the outside world, certain that our connection had already been figured out, but I didn't want to let on to the other contestants that Kira and I were colleagues. As co-workers and acquaintances, it could be assumed that I had an inside track on getting Kira to fall for me. That could prove dangerous.

We all knew how dangerous this show was. If one of these guys got it into his head that he had no chance and was being screwed over, he might do something that got Kira killed to add a new female to the mix.

My main concern was to keep the conversation flowing and sounding believable. That was where my mind was when she'd said what she said. Then she started speaking, and all my thoughts and carefully planned acting flew out the window. Her words slammed into me, and I tried to figure out if she was being serious or if it was all part of the act. It didn't help that she looked gorgeous. My mouth almost watered just from looking at her. My brain wasn't working right with her sitting there like that.

I finished the food in front of me to give myself a moment to process what she'd said. I liked that she hadn't felt real heartbreak over Jayson. That tool didn't deserve Kira's pain. He'd missed out, and it was good that she'd left him behind.

After a few bites, I looked at her and saw that she was looking back at me. She wasn't giving me an expectant or questioning look. It was like she understood that I was trying to process everything and was fine with it. Was her meaning what I thought it was? Should I pursue that line of questioning, or should I do what I'd originally planned and talk about banal, simple topics?

Before I could come up with a plan of attack, Von and our waiter reappeared. I'd had enough of this vampire to last me a lifetime. Leaning back in my chair, jaws clamped in irritation, I gave him the biggest and brightest smile I could manage.

"How are things going?" Von asked.

I looked at Kira. "Seems to be going well. Kira?"

She nodded, her eyes never leaving my face. "Yes. I think so, too."

"Pause," Von said with a wave of his hand.

My bracelet suddenly stopped shining green and turned white. He'd turned the cameras off. They sat motionless in the air, waiting to be turned back on.

"This chemistry is wonderful," Von said as the waiter cleared our plates. "But I think we need to give everyone at home a better look at it." He glanced back and forth at us. "This whole sexy pining thing you two have going on hasn't gone unnoticed. A huge contingent of our viewers has already started rooting for you two. You are totally getting shipped. It's all over our message boards, our fan club page, and on social media."

I frowned and shook my head, my smile faltering. "Um...I'm sorry? Shipped? What is that?"

Kira snorted a laugh, and I snapped my gaze back to her. She grinned at me. "It's when fans of a show want two characters or contestants to get together. Come on, Wyatt, get with the times."

Her gentle prodding should have irritated me, but I enjoyed the way she'd said it, and the grin on her face when she spoke.

"Correct," Von said as he rolled his eyes. "They even gave you a cute little ship name. Kwyatt. Pronounced *quiet*, you get it?"

I really didn't, but he seemed so pleased with himself that I let it go.

"Can we get back to dinner?" Kira asked.

Her tone was nonchalant, but I could hear the undertone of annoyance at Von's constant interrupting. If the host noticed, he either ignored it or didn't care.

Von clasped his hands behind his back and leaned forward as though to whisper a secret to us. "Kira, we may have to get you cue cards. I hate to say it, but you aren't very good at this. You haven't asked Wyatt about his rejection story. We need to have a two-way conversation to give the viewers what they want."

Kira's smile grew even bigger, and I could tell she was desperately trying not to break a leg off the chair and stake Von through the heart with it.

"I'm sorry. I'll do better with that," Kira said through gritted teeth.

"Fabulous. I'll leave you to it."

Von vanished back out the door, and I watched him go. My discomfort was like a heavy wet blanket draped across me. The thing I never really wanted to talk about was about to come out.

Kira rolled her eyes at me before the camera turned back on. The look on her face told me all I needed to know. She didn't think I had a rejection story, assumed I'd made something up to get on the show. But she'd still go along with Von's suggestion and ask. She was probably excited to hear what story I'd come up with.

"So, Wyatt? I've told you my story. Let's hear yours."

I sat my wine glass down and blew out a breath as I prepared myself to talk about something I hadn't mentioned in years.

"My story isn't quite like yours. It's not typical. But it still changed my life."

Something in my voice must have tipped her off. The sexy smile she had for the cameras slipped a little, and her eyes narrowed slightly. She could sense I was telling the truth, and she was probably floored that there was a story at all.

"Explain that?" Kira said. She wasn't concerned with acting anymore. Her tone was all business. She wasn't angry, but I could see the operative peeking through. She wanted the story.

Folding my hands on my lap, I said, "To start with, I became connected to my fated mate much earlier than usual. It was well before I should have been able to connect to her—years before I was old enough to do the blood tests. It was a mistake. Because of that, my life never got on track. I ended up leaving the situation as fast as I could."

It was vague, and Kira could tell. She raised her eyebrow in the way she did when she knew someone wasn't telling her the whole truth. To my surprise, she didn't press me for more info.

"Do you regret it? All the decisions you made that led you here to this island? With me?"

I grinned at her. "The only thing I regret is that I didn't find a way to be on a remote island with you sooner. I just wish it wasn't one this dangerous and that I had you all to myself."

Kira huffed out a breath and rolled her eyes again. She didn't look upset at my flirting attempt, which made me feel good. Before we could speak again, the server brought out the entrees: a gorgeous steak with roasted potatoes and seared asparagus. We ate in silence.

Later, over dessert, we talked about the challenges we'd already gone through on the island. I was thankful she didn't pry further into my rejection. I didn't want to get into it in front of millions of people.

As we were standing to leave the table, Von joined us again. It was getting exhausting having him interrupt us so often.

The cameras stopped, and he leaned in the door right as we stood and waved a hand to us. "We need a kiss or a hug or something. Come on, guys, you know what the crowd wants," he hissed at us and then ducked back away, turning the cameras back on.

I didn't give a damn what the crowd wanted, but I knew what I wanted. Not even hesitating, I leaned forward and kissed her. Kira made a tiny squeal of surprise as my lips pressed into hers.

I expected her to allow a few moments of kissing for the camera, then push me away and be all huffy about it once the filming stopped. Kira had made it abundantly clear that she wanted to forget about our one-night stand. Instead of pushing me away, though, she pressed against me. Her lips parted slightly, allowing my tongue to slide into her mouth. Kira ran her hands up my back, then tangled her fingers in my hair.

It didn't take much for me to realize what I'd known deep down for years. I'd never wanted a single night with her in a hotel. There'd always been more, and even that night hadn't been like this. It was as though a flip had been switched. My hands slid across her hips and up her back, pulling her close. I was being swept away in her. All thoughts of the show, cameras, hosts, and contestants vanished. It was just Kira and me.

Too soon, Kira pulled away and smiled shyly at me. That was not like her at all. Then she shrugged and glanced at the camera.

"That was a really nice way to end a date, Wyatt. I had a great time tonight. Thank you. I guess we should get some sleep."

"You are correct, Kira," Von said as he stepped back into the dining room. "Everyone needs their rest for tomorrow. Our viewers, I'm sure, are aware of what awaits you all in the Fight for Survival test we have in the morning."

Von stepped over and ran a finger down my lapel. "Hopefully, Mister Rivers here can sleep after that sexy kiss you two shared. Looks like sparks are indeed flying at the Reject Mansion." He smiled at the camera once more. "Until tomorrow, friends. And remember, everyone loves an underdog."

Von waved a hand, cutting the recording. He spared us a glance as he walked out. "Lots to do before tomorrow. I'll be up helping the team edit footage for hours. Ugh, such is life. You two should head off to bed. Great job. See you tomorrow," he called over his shoulder as he strode off into the depths of the mansion.

I was watching Von and all the cameras round the corner when a hard yank on my hand had me stumbling backward.

"What are you doing?" I asked Kira as she dragged me along with her.

"Shut up," Kira grunted.

"Well, damn. All right, then."

Kira pulled me down a hall I'd never seen. She tried two different doors until she found one that was unlocked. The room wasn't decorated like the rest of the mansion. Instead of high-end wallpaper, carpeting, and antique furniture, it looked more like a doctor's waiting room: white painted walls, thin gray carpeting, and a couple of couches and padded metal chairs. I figured it was some sort of sitting room for the staff, but it looked like it barely got used.

Before I could inspect the room further, Kira flicked the lock and spun to face me. The look in her eyes sent an electric jolt through my body. The need and desire in her eyes made my cock grow hard immediately.

"Kira?"

She rushed forward and fell into my arms, kissing me with more urgency than a few minutes before. Her breasts pressed into my chest as her hands clutched desperately at my back. I wrapped my arms around her, and she moaned into my mouth as I cupped and squeezed her ass.

I lost myself in her. All these years, I'd had an inkling of how much I wanted her, but that had all been kept hidden. I'd stuffed it down and brushed it off as only wanting to be near her to protect my best friend's sister. Tasting her tongue and lips, feeling her hands on my body swept all that away. That night at the hotel hadn't been a mistake. I'd wanted her then, I wanted her now—I had always wanted her. I was nearly drunk with relief at having her in my arms. It was like she was a drug, and I needed more.

Kira's fingers were already working at the buttons of my suit. Not taking my lips off hers, I hurriedly shrugged out of my blazer, letting it tumble to the floor, and slipped the straps of her dress off her shoulders. It pooled around her feet, leaving her wearing nothing but a flesh-colored thong. Breaking the kiss, I looked down at her body, taking in every glorious inch of her, then looked into her eyes and growled low in my throat.

Kira kept her eyes on mine as she unzipped my pants, reached inside, and took hold of me. My breath hissed out of my chest in a sigh of happiness and pleasure as her hand slid up and down my shaft. Need and desire erased all conscious thought. Seconds later, I was on my knees, slowly tugging her thong down her legs.

She sank onto the couch, and I ran my fingers over the creamy skin of her thighs. I trailed kisses from her knees up to her thighs, moving ever closer to her pussy.

"Fuck," Kira whispered, throwing her head back against the couch.

I slid my tongue across her opening, and she sucked in a breath, arching into my face. Gripping her ass, I put my mouth on her, lapping at her sweet folds, then entered her, fucking her with my tongue. With each thrust, she moaned. The taste of her made me dizzy with desire. My cock was painfully hard and throbbing as I worked at her. I wanted her, but I was going to make her come at least once before I allowed myself inside her. I wanted to feel her body shake and quiver under my hands as I brought her to climax.

As I circled her clit with my tongue, Kira's back arched. Glancing up, I saw her eyes roll back with ecstasy. Her fist was pressed into her mouth, teeth clamped down on her skin. I reached up and gently pinched her nipple as I slid a finger into her pussy and sucked on her clit. That sent her over the edge. She bucked against my face as she came, her grunts of pleasure muffled by her hand.

She was still breathing heavily as I raised myself over her, my cock sliding along her thigh toward her pussy. Barely coherent after her orgasm, she pressed her hands against my chest.

"We...we have to be quiet. I don't want anyone to hear," she said, trying to catch her breath.

I leaned down and kissed one nipple, then the other. "Why?"

"The other alphas can't know. They'll think I'm a slut or something."

I chuckled as I slammed into her. Kira's eyes went wide, and her mouth dropped open. Once I was fully seated inside her, I leaned down and bit her playfully on her shoulder.

"You mean I can't mark you as mine?"

She quivered under me. I hadn't started moving yet, but her face was pure ecstasy.

"No marks. No...no marks." She dug her nails into my chest. "I need you to fuck me."

"Yes, ma'am," I said with a smile.

I pulled almost all the way out, then thrust back into her. Kira let out a gasping groan. Seeing her like that, being inside her, was one of the greatest moments of my entire life. I kissed her, and she twisted her hands into my hair again as my thrusts quickened. I caressed her breast, flicking a thumb back and forth across her nipple. Kira wrapped her legs around me, pressing her heels into my ass and urging me to go faster.

"Yes...oh, fuck..." Kira whimpered as she looked down to watch my cock slam into her.

I lowered my head to her breast, sucking her nipple and kissing her skin while grinding my cock deep into her. She draped her arms around my neck as I fucked her. She was soft, wet, and warm. It was like I was in a dream. Everything was hazy and surreal. I didn't want it to end.

Pulling out of her, I flipped Kira over on her belly and entered her from behind. My chest pressed into her back as I kissed her jaw, our breath and sweat mingling as I moved inside her.

"Wyatt, I'm getting close. I'm gonna come." The words left Kira in panting bursts.

I increased my speed, the muscles in my legs and ass bunching as I fucked her deeper and harder. I didn't even care about my orgasm—I just wanted to give her everything I could. I wanted her to scream and moan, to call out my name.

Kira buried her face into the couch and let her cries of pleasure leak out in gasps and groans. I heard her catch her breath, then scream. She convulsed beneath me as an earth-shaking orgasm enveloped her.

"Wyatt...Wyatt!"

She screamed my name into the couch cushion, sending me over the edge. Pleasure blasted through my body, starting at my balls, then running along my dick to the head and all the way up my spine. No orgasm had ever hit me so hard. My body quaked as I continued thrusting into her, both of us riding the cresting and falling wave of passion and release.

The orgasm felt like it might never end. Finally, after several seconds, it ebbed, leaving me in a fuzzy, blissful state of relaxation and happiness.

My pants still around my ankles and my dress shirt hanging open, I wrapped Kira in my arms and rolled over, cradling her against my chest. A massive goofy grin was plastered on my face, but I didn't care. I couldn't care about anything but the woman in my arms.

Chapter 23 - Kira

As I lay in Wyatt's arms, I was overcome with emotions. His scent was intoxicating. With his arms wrapped around me, I'd never been more content. For the first time since I'd been on the island, I felt safe. It was like being swaddled in a warm blanket on a cold, wet day. It was difficult not to sigh with happiness.

He'd given me the best sex of my life. Twice. Mind-blowing, earth-shattering sex that turned my brain to jelly. As my thoughts slowly coalesced back into the correct format, I understood that I needed to say something. This couldn't happen again. As much as I wanted it, I couldn't allow it. There was too much at stake.

We were in danger here. As much as I wanted Wyatt pressed against my body every night, it would be the worst thing for both of us. Lives were on the line here. We couldn't forget that simply because the sex was fantastic. Knowing Wyatt the way I did, there would be no persuading him. I'd need to be harsh. I'd have to push him away. To save him, if nothing else.

Twisting around to look him in the eyes, I leveled a firm, serious look at him. "That was fun, but it was because we both needed to release some stress."

Wyatt's eyes narrowed. "Kira–"

"Stop. Let me finish. We needed that, and we both wanted it. It was good. It was fucking amazing, but we're adults. Sometimes this happens. There's no reason to bring it up again. Just like we don't need to talk about what happened in the hotel room."

Wyatt pushed himself up on his elbow, pulling his arm from around me. I felt a strange sense of loss when he moved his arm. I shoved that down deep, not wanting to think about what it might mean.

"Kira, why did you throw yourself at me a few minutes ago if you wanted to forget about it as soon as it happened?"

He sounded hurt. Hell, why shouldn't he? Were the roles reversed, who could say I wouldn't be pissed and hurt? That was not what I wanted, but bigger things were at stake here. My pack *needed* me to win. Their safety was paramount. My feelings were secondary to the fate of an entire pack.

"In fact," Wyatt said, fully sitting up and pulling away from me, "if all you needed was to get your rocks off, why not go somewhere else? There are nine other freaking guys in this house right now who'd give their left nut to fuck you. If what we did was simply stress relief from being on the show, I guarantee you could walk into that damned bunk room, and at least three guys would have their pants off before you could finish asking. They'd probably fight to the death for a chance. So why me?"

I huffed and sat up straight. I didn't want to say what I was about to say, but I had no reason to hold back. Not now.

I rubbed a hand across my face. "I will admit that as annoying and nagging as you are, with all the obnoxious stuff you do and sticking your nose in my business, I feel safest with you. I don't feel safe with any of those other guys. Not at the moment. It's probably just because of our shared history or something, but that's the truth. You're the only one I would have felt okay doing this with. All right?"

Wyatt raised a skeptical eyebrow. He didn't smile. "You feel safe with me?"

Changing the subject, I gestured to the door. "And another thing. That whole story out there. Was that true? Or was it for the cameras?"

"What story?"

"The rejection thing. Have you been rejected?"

The question hung in the air, heavy and expectant. A pained expression crossed over his eyes. So, it was true. How had I never realized it before? Was this why he'd been so angry that Jayson had rejected me?

Wyatt hung his head. "They wouldn't have let me on the show if I didn't fit the bill somehow. The rules aren't *that* strict, but you can't simply walk on. And some of the people who run the show...they know my history."

I wanted to ask more questions, but the analog clock on the wall caught my eye. It was getting late. I checked my bracelet. Thankfully, it was still glowing white. No cameras on the way. Yet.

"Shit. We need to hurry. People are going to start wondering why we aren't back in our rooms," I said, grabbing my clothes.

"Why do you care?" Wyatt asked. "Doesn't this, like, cause more drama or something?"

I froze where I was, suddenly realizing my nakedness, but I refused to cover myself as I turned to look at him.

"Wyatt, you need to go find an employee shower or something. You have to wash my, you know, *sex* scent off yourself. If you get back in that bunk room with my scent all over you, the other guys might turn on you. Do you really want all of them gunning for you tomorrow? Seriously? You're good, but you can't fight odds like that. I don't..." I paused and blew out a breath. "I don't want you dead, okay?"

Wyatt's shoulders sagged, but he nodded. "All right. Fine."

He quickly dressed as I shimmied into my dress and thong. Once we were fully clothed again, I pressed my ear to the door in the door to listen for footsteps. When I didn't hear anything, I unlocked the door and opened it a crack. The coast seemed clear.

"Okay. You're good," I said, nudging Wyatt toward the door.

"Kira, I wanted to say–"

"No time, Wyatt. You need to hurry. I think there's a staff breakroom one hallway down. I passed it last night. There's probably a shower there." I checked my bracelet one last time to make sure it hadn't changed color. Seeing it was still white, I pushed him out the door. "Go. Hurry."

"Fine. I, uh, I guess I'll see you tomorrow."

He left without saying anything else. It was all I could do to wait five minutes to leave the room myself. I didn't want to risk us being seen too close to each other. I hurried down the hall to the stairs that led up to my room on the third floor, my shoes in my hand—I didn't want any noise from my heels. Every few feet, I checked that I wasn't being followed. Anyone could be out and about—the show staff, Von, those damned magical cameras, or even one of the other contestants.

Had I spent more time looking forward than looking back, I might have seen him. Instead, I rounded the corner and almost ran right over Leif. I slammed into his chest and stumbled, almost falling backward. He shot out a hand and grabbed my wrist to keep me from falling onto my ass.

"Leif? What the hell?" I said as I righted myself.

"Kira?" Leif looked confused.

He took me in, a smile stretching his lips. I'd done all I could to straighten my hair and smooth the wrinkles out of my dress, but I must have looked exactly like what I was: a woman who was minutes out from a sexual tryst. I ran my hand through my hair again, feeling my face going red.

"Uh…listen, Leif. I'm not sure what you think happened, but–"

He snorted, then tugged on my hand. "Come on. We need to get you back to your room. Hurry."

His nonchalance surprised me. I followed him as he rushed me down the hall to the last set of steps that led to my suite. Despite my worry about the other guys' reaction at finding out I'd had sex with Wyatt, Leif seemed genuinely amused. Maybe I'd gotten lucky, and he was one of the only guys who didn't care.

Leif spun the doorknob and pulled me inside. We sank against the door, both of us breathing heavily.

"What the hell is this?"

I nearly jumped at Zoe's voice. Glancing up, I saw her staring at us, arms crossed and an incredulous look on her face. She stepped forward and looked me up and down, her eyes stopping at my hair and then shooting down to my shoes. Shit, I forgot I'd tucked my thong inside a shoe.

Zoe looked at the two of us, eyes darting back and forth. "Did you guys do the dirty?"

Leif laughed out loud—a genuine laugh. Zoe and I stared at him as he brought himself under control.

He waved a hand. "No, no, no. Not me. I wasn't that lucky."

How could he be this blasé? It was like Leif was enjoying my and Zoe's confusion. He wasn't acting like someone who'd almost died mere hours before.

"Are you all right?" I asked. "From earlier?"

His smile dimmed, but he nodded. "Yeah. I'm good. The fae healers did a great job on me. I'm a hundred percent. I guess I should be thanking you."

"Anyone would have done that," I said.

He gave me an approving stare. "No, they wouldn't. Not here. You could have left me for dead, but you didn't. The same goes for Wyatt. I'm more surprised that he helped. I'm an obstacle for him."

Waving that comment away, I said, "He's not the typical...well...what I mean is, from what I've noticed this far, he isn't one of those big-headed asshole alphas. He probably had his own reasons for helping me save you."

Leif sat down in an armchair near the door. "This place is way more stressful than I thought it would be."

Zoe raised an eyebrow and studied him. "What's your story, Leif? Something doesn't track."

Leif glanced up at her, not a trace of his smile remaining. "Is it that obvious?"

"Sweetie...come on now."

"What the hell are you guys talking about?" I asked.

Ignoring me, Leif leaned his elbows on his knees. "My reasons for being here aren't typical. It's all because of my blood test. You see, I was really looking forward to finding my fated mate. I did the test as soon as I was old enough. The problem was, I was matched with this female shifter in another pack. She was terrible. Like an absolute disaster of a person. I refused the mating."

"That's not weird to me," I said. "If I had to do it again, I'd probably refuse my douchebag of a fated mate, too."

Zoe sighed in exasperation. Leif chuckled and looked at her. "Is she always this oblivious?"

"On most things?" Zoe said, "No. I think her head's a bit out of the game at the moment. The show's got her so stressed, she can't think straight."

Heat crept up my neck. "Can you two please remember that I'm *in the room with you*? What the hell are you talking about?"

"I was hoping," Leif said, "that instead of a female shifter, the blood test would pair me with a certain gorgeous male shifter. One who happened to get on this show." He shrugged. "I sort of followed him here."

"Oh," I said. Wow, was I a dumbass.

Looking back on it, Leif had been the least flirtatious with me. His few attempts had seemed forced and awkward. Now that I knew, it made perfect sense. He had no desire to be with me. I felt more than dumb; I felt blind.

"I'm sorry, Leif." I had no idea what I was apologizing for, but I was confused about how to proceed.

"It's fine. I thought I'd been doing my best to fit in with the other guys. No offense, Kira, you are beautiful but not really my type, you know?"

I chuckled. "Right. So, who's the lucky guy? Who did you follow here?"

Leif's mouth snapped shut, and he chewed at the inside of his cheek. He looked like he was thinking about whether he should say anything.

Zoe gasped and clapped a hand to her mouth. "It's J.D., isn't it? That's who you want to bang."

Leif didn't answer, but his cheeks flushed, and he winced in embarrassment. It was all the answer we needed.

"I knew it!" Zoe shouted in triumph. "I thought I saw you making googly eyes at him at dinner last night."

Leif nodded. "Yeah. It's him."

I smiled at Leif. "That's great, but why come out here? Everyone knows the show is super dangerous. The odds of *two* male alphas getting out alive are really low."

"I understand that. Part of me coming on the show was to help make sure J.D. got home alive. I don't know if you've noticed, but he's kind of a goofball. He's not built for this."

Putting my back against the wall, I said, "I can't promise anything, Leif, but you both seem like nice guys. I'll do what I can to make sure you both get home safe."

"Thanks," Leif said. "I appreciate that. But don't go out of your way for me. Worry about J.D. Going home would end pretty badly for me. Things didn't, for want of a better word, *go well* with my pack when I refused my pairing."

I shrugged. "That's no reason to run off to your death. You could join an unofficial pack or be a lone wolf."

Leif scoffed. "I think I'd rather take my chances on Bloodstone Island."

I was getting irritated with his flippant rejection of the idea. I wanted to defend lone wolves and the outlier packs. I was about to retort when Zoe's eyes locked on mine, the warning clear. She knew what I was about to say, could see it in my face. Except Leif didn't know about my knowing Wyatt before the start of the show. Besides, there was really no use arguing. Hell, I'd had the same feelings toward lone wolves until...well...when had I changed my tune? Was it when Wyatt gave me the best orgasms of my life? Maybe. Probably.

I shook my head to clear it. "I need a shower."

I headed to the bathroom and stripped off my dress. I sighed with relief as the steaming hot water sluiced over my skin, taking Wyatt's scent with it. I hated to admit it, but washing his scent of me sent a twinge through my heart. Part of me wanted his smell on me. That made me a little uncomfortable, and I finished showering as quickly as I could.

After drying off and putting on a robe, I went back to the bedroom. Zoe and Leif were still sitting and talking.

Leif saw me and stood. "I should probably head back now. Maybe I can alleviate any concerns the other guys might have about Wyatt taking so long to get back."

"Is it weird?" Zoe asked. "Staying in the same room with everyone? It's gotta be like summer camp or something, right?"

Leif gave us both a pained expression. "To be honest, it's kinda miserable. Most of the guys are annoying as hell, especially once the cameras stop rolling. Kira, let me tell you, you've got good taste. You've picked one of the few guys who makes it bearable here."

He opened the door and waved goodbye to us. After he shut it behind him, Zoe rounded on me, pinning me in place with her stare.

"So," she said, tilting her head to the side. "Wyatt?"

Running a towel over my hair, I walked away. "We aren't doing this, Zoe."

"Correct. Because you've already been *doing* something else, or should I say some*one* else."

"It was another mistake, Zoe. Simple as that. I was horny and needed to relieve some stress. Wyatt simply happened to be in the right place at the right time again."

"Really? Would that story be the same if you'd been on a date with Leif?"

I laughed and rolled my eyes. "Of course not. He's gay, Zoe. Mine isn't the type of body to get him hard, if you know what I mean."

Zoe scrunched up her nose and waved her hands in the air. "Yeah, I know, but that's not what I mean. Don't you think it's time to admit something to yourself?"

I dropped the towel on the floor. "Admit what, Zoe?"

She put her hands on her hips. "Admit that you actually *aren't* upset that Wyatt followed you here." She gestured vaguely to the door. "What Leif is doing for J.D. is the same thing Wyatt's doing for you. He's putting his life on the line to make sure you get home safe."

"Well, yeah, Zoe. What Leif is doing is romantic. What Wyatt is doing is...I don't know—"

"Romantic?" Her tone dripped with sarcasm.

"There's not a romantic bone in Wyatt's body. No."

"Is that a fact or just what you're telling yourself?"

Outside, strange squeals, squawks, and screams came from the jungle. They did nothing to improve my mood.

"I'm not sure, okay?" I hissed. "Are you happy? I don't know. All I know is that I can't, under any circumstances, let Wyatt get killed here. You know me. You know what that would do to me. I have to find a way to get him home."

Zoe seemed put at ease by my honesty. She leaned away and crossed her arms, looking out the window with a grave expression. I had no clue what she was thinking. I let her be as she stewed on whatever was bouncing through that fae head of hers.

Finally, she turned back to look at me. "You know, there's usually one or two chances to send someone home."

A tiny ember of hope sparked in my chest. "Seriously?"

Her shoulders sagged. "You barely paid any attention when we watched this together."

"Zoe, focus. What chances?"

"Sorry. Right. Every season, the *lead* mate—that's you—gets a few chances to send one of the contestants home. Most lead mates use it to get rid of people they don't like or aren't compatible with. But you could, in theory, use it to send Wyatt home safe and sound. The problem is that those types of prizes are very hard to win. It's usually offered in one of the more dangerous challenges."

A chance. That was all I needed. If I was given the chance, I would send Wyatt home. Once he was out of harm's way, I could focus on winning. If I constantly worried about what might happen to him, I'd be worthless here.

"I'll keep my eye out for that reward," I said.

Ryan dying was awful, and I didn't want any more of these alphas to die if I could help it. But most of all, I didn't want Wyatt to die. The thought of him getting hurt or killed sickened me. It was all I could do to keep the images of his broken, bleeding, or gutted body out of my mind.

"Let's go to bed. I'm exhausted."

"I bet you are," Zoe said with a knowing smirk.

Ignoring her, I glanced at the door. "Did that witch come back again? The one who said you could only stay here one night? I thought you had to go to your own quarters."

Zoe shrugged. "One of the director's assistants likes to flirt. I made some sexy eyes at him over lunch, and he pulled some strings. Pretty easy."

Snorting, I slipped off my robe and slid under the covers. Zoe turned the lights off and tucked herself into her makeshift bed. I was beyond exhausted, but the day's events weighed on me, making sleep hard to find. The Fight for Survival was tomorrow. It would be difficult, and there was no guarantee that we'd all make it out alive.

I tossed and turned for over an hour. Eventually, Zoe's soft snores filled the room. Nothing would get me to sleep. Right before I decided to give up and maybe go for another walk around the mansion, I looked across the room at the floor right inside the bathroom. The dress I'd worn to dinner was puddled on the floor.

I hesitated for a split second before I slipped noiselessly out of bed and padded over to scoop it up. I felt like a childish idiot as I hurried back to bed, but I was too tired to care. Once I was back under the covers, I lifted the dress to my nose and inhaled deeply. Wyatt's scent drifted off the dress and into my lungs. It enveloped me in a warm feeling of contentment. I let out a small, almost imperceptible moan of delight at the smell. I pulled it close to my chest to snuggle it, drifting off to sleep in seconds.

Chapter 24 - Wyatt

When I opened my eyes, I knew I hadn't slept enough. The night before had been...interesting, to say the least. A faint smile crossed my lips as I remembered.

I swung my legs out of bed and sat on the side of my bunk. My stubble rasped as I ran a hand across my face to wake myself up.

The room was already alive with activity. Nathaniel had already showered and was in front of the mirror, doing his hair. Leif's bed still held a lump, showing I wasn't the last one up. The rest of the alphas were in various stages of waking, dressing, or making their beds.

My eyes narrowed. We were missing two people. Omar and Tate weren't in the room. We'd been instructed to remain in here until the show staff or Von himself fetched us. I hadn't followed those rules at all, and neither had some of the others. Still, I wasn't a fan of those two, and I didn't like that they'd gone off on their own. Something about them and Nathaniel sent off alarm bells, and I wouldn't be able to calm down until I knew exactly what they were up to.

I grabbed the closest clothes—a pair of sweatpants and a T-shirt—and yanked them on before shoving my feet into my shoes.

"Why are you in such a hurry?" Nathaniel asked.

I glanced up at him. He was still working on his hair.

"I didn't know it was any of your business," I said.

He turned and shot me a shit-eating grin. "Someone's in a pissy mood. What happened? Did you try to slip the ole salami to Kira last night? She shoot you down? Not surprising. She probably likes guys with"—he grabbed his crotch and squeezed—"a little more under the hood, you know?"

Ignoring the crude remark, I headed out the door and followed Omar and Tate's scents. The farther I got from the alpha den, the stronger the smells got. The scents were mixing and hard to differentiate, but they were definitely together.

I saw the film crew come down a hallway, so I quickly hid in a small coat closet. They carried trays of food and looked to have come from another of the hidden staff areas, like the one Kira and I had found. Last night came rushing back, and my cock grew hard again as the mental pictures flashed through my mind. That wouldn't help me track these guys down, so I shook the memories of Kira's taste from my head and ducked back into the hall once the staffers were gone.

A few minutes later, I started to get a little nervous. Omar and Tate's scents were leading me closer to Kira's room. Why the hell would they be going there? Surely they wouldn't try something as dumb as approach Kira off-camera.

Their voices caught my ear right before I rounded the corner.

"That's what I'm saying, man. It only makes sense. Me and you. Together. That's how we survive this thing today," Omar was saying.

I froze and turned my head in the direction of their voices.

Tate sighed. "I get it, yeah. The Fight for Survival is dangerous, but if we form an alliance, won't the other alphas target us in the next challenges?"

"Well, yeah, but that's why we'll keep it under wraps."

So that was what was happening. They were treating this like any other reality game show. I wondered if these guys had ever even watched this show. Invariably, when these alliances were formed, one person almost always got stabbed in the back by the other. It was ridiculous.

I stepped out from around the corner and walked toward them as nonchalantly as I could. Tate was about to respond when he saw me strolling toward them. Surprise flashed over his face. When Omar glanced over to see what he was looking at, his lip curled.

"Can we help you with something?" Omar asked.

I shook my head and grinned. "You two should have stayed in bed. If you want to catch Kira's eye, you'll need a *lot* more beauty sleep. So, what are you two plotting? Anything fun?"

"None of your fucking business. Besides, shouldn't you be the one still in bed and nursing your ego after Kira sent you packing last night?" Tate said.

"Right," Omar added. "The only reason you won the first date with Kira was that you gave into her soft and weak side by rescuing that dumbass Leif. It's cute but not what someone like Kira *really* wants. She needs a man who knows how to make the hard choices. Prissy little bitch like you doesn't have a chance of getting into those panties, bro." He stood taller and pulled his shoulders back as he glared at me.

"For real," Tate scoffed. "Like, what the fuck were you thinking? You should have left Leif there to die. Thin out the competition." He, too, stood tall, then flexed his muscular arms with a growl.

They were playing the alpha game, trying to intimidate me and establish dominance over someone they thought was beneath them. It was a silly game spoiled alphas often played. These guys were used to getting their way. They likely came from powerful families.

My smile went from friendly to grim as I stepped toward them. As a lone wolf, I'd learned how to fend for myself without the power of a pack backing me. Along with that, I'd learned how to deal with pricks like this who thought they could steamroll other shifters. The stare I gave them spoke of how dangerous I could be when necessary.

"I know your brains are pretty small, but the two of you need to remember that Kira has the power here. You forget, she doesn't need to pick the last wolf standing. If only one of us survives today, and it's someone she doesn't want, she can simply refuse the goddess's blessing and take the money. She'll live rich and happy for the rest of her life, not giving a damn about whether any of us gets left behind to go feral."

Realization and fear flickered in their eyes. They knew as well as I did that the refused rejects and survivors the prize mate didn't pick were often left behind on the island. It was one of the many things I hated about the show—how bloodthirsty and uncaring it was for everyone involved. But now, these two saw our precarious position. You couldn't simply hope to out-survive the others to win. The prize mate had to actually *want* you.

If Kira refused to take them, they could be left behind to be eaten by whatever monsters lurked in the jungle, or they'd slip into madness and go feral. Then they would be the monsters the next season of rejects had to outwit.

"I can tell you're getting the picture," I said. "What you two need to worry about is not *winning* the game with alliances. You need to worry about protecting Kira with every ounce of your being. If you aren't on her good side, she'll leave your asses here to rot." I jabbed my finger into Omar's chest. "And you're wrong about Kira. She isn't soft or weak because she saved Leif. That shows that she's the exact opposite. The fact that she saved Leif and put herself in danger to do it means she's tough as hell. If you cross her or piss her off, I guarantee she'll leave you to die."

Omar and Tate looked unsure, but they'd stopped trying to intimidate me. Omar looked the more wary of the two. Tate looked less certain of what I'd said.

His face twisted into a scowl. "Bro, you had one fucking date with Kira. You're sitting here acting like you know so much about her. Like you *actually* know what she'd do. Get the fuck outta here."

I couldn't tell them that I *did* know what Kira would do. There was no doubt in my mind that Kira would do all the things I'd said. If one thing about her was true, it was that she could hold a grudge. If any of these guys crossed her or did something awful to a contestant she liked, she'd cut ties and not bat an eye as they screamed for help. It was as simple as that.

Rather than give away my secret, I shrugged and grinned at him. "I got a pretty good read on her during our date last night. All I can say is you should try not to be assholes if you can avoid it."

Before either of them could retort, our bracelets started blinking. Several floating cameras came careening around the corner, followed by the rest of the alphas. J.D. was in the lead and smiled when he saw us.

"Damn, there you guys are. Come on, I'm freaking starving. Let's grab some chow."

Omar, Tate, and I exchanged a few more dark looks as we followed the group dining area. A hellacious feast awaited us. My stomach grumbled as I smelled the food. I wanted to wait for Kira. I couldn't get her out of my head. Especially not after last night.

Not knowing when she'd join us, I went ahead and piled food onto my plate. There was no way of knowing what they had planned for us in the Fight for Survival, but either way, my body needed fuel.

As I began eating, I felt I was being watched. Popping a piece of cantaloupe in my mouth, I looked up and found the person who'd been eyeballing me. Leif. He quickly lowered his eyes. Throughout breakfast, I kept catching him looking at me. It seemed like he was sizing me up, and that sent a spike of anxiety through me. I wasn't completely sure Kira didn't have a thing for him. I didn't want him to believe I thought he was a threat, so when I was done eating, I waved to get his attention.

"How are you?" I asked. "Fully recovered yet?"

Leif looked surprised I'd asked. "Um, pretty much, yeah." He laughed to himself. "The healers here have a lot of experience in bringing people back from the brink of death. The fae acted like it was silly that I was even in the medical room in the first place. Like I should have brushed it off and kept going." He shook his head in disgust.

"Well, I, for one, am glad you're okay," J.D. said from farther down the table, jumping into our conversation. "Kira was amazing yesterday. I mean, she saved you while in human form. That was after defeating that feral tiger the same way." He looked around at everyone else at the table. "This girl really is something. I'm not sure about you guys, but I feel pretty lucky to be here. If she chose me as her mate, I don't know if I could imagine anything better."

Several of the others nodded and mumbled their agreement, but Leif grumbled quietly to himself and stabbed at his food. Was he upset that Kira had saved him? Was it some sort of macho bullshit that made him feel like less of a man? If that was the case, it pissed me off a little. If anything, he should be singing her praises even more than J.D. was.

I was about to lean over and question him about it, but Nathaniel joined the conversation.

He tossed his fork down with a clatter. "You know, that's the second time she's done something dangerous and didn't shift. That's weird. I wonder why she doesn't shift. Like, is her wolf deformed and ugly or something? Maybe she's embarrassed to show it." Nathaniel threw his head back and groaned. "Gods, I hope her wolf isn't ugly. I don't want to spend the rest of my days with some fugly wolf."

A moment later, Kira strode into the dining room. Everyone leaped to attention and stood to greet her. Nathaniel's face was blazing red. I wasn't sure if Kira had heard him, but she was smiling easily at the group. She was perfect for the cameras that followed her. Zoe must have spent extra time on her that morning because she was absolutely glowing. Try as I might, the little boy part of my mind tried to tell me it was because of last night, but the adult part of me scoffed.

Nathaniel fell all over himself, trying to get Kira a plate of food. A few other guys grabbed her juice, water, napkins, and silverware. Gods, they were all so pathetic.

Tate took a seat next to Kira, and as she tried to stab at a piece of sausage, he deftly slipped her fork out of her hand and speared it himself.

"A lady as lovely as you shouldn't have to feed herself," he said, raising the fork to her lips.

I had to bite my lip to stop myself from snorting in laughter at the irritation that flashed across Kira's face. She leaned her head away from the fork, looking for all the world like she wanted to be anywhere but here.

"Maybe you should worry about stuffing your own face, Tate," I said.

Tate dropped the fork and turned to me. His neck was scarlet, the flush of anger creeping upward to his cheeks. He pointed at me and had barely opened his mouth to tell me what he thought of me when Von walked in.

"Good morning, everyone. I trust we had a great night," Von said as he swept his gaze across the room.

"I know the lovely Kira and sexy Wyatt had a great evening, hmm?" Von looked at me expectantly. For a moment, I wondered whether he knew what had gone down after dinner.

I gave him an awkward smile. "Uh…yeah, it was great, actually. Really fun."

"I had fun as well," Kira said, her voice clipped and perfectly pitched—exactly how she thought the showrunners wanted her to act.

Von clapped. "Well, I have some exciting news. The final contestant is on his way. He was unfortunately delayed, but he will arrive on Bloodstone Island later today to meet all of you."

With everything going on, I kept forgetting that another alpha would be joining us. What made this guy special enough to get a free pass to miss not only the first couple days of the show but also the first dangerous challenge? He was getting to jump in without risking his life as much as the rest of us already had. It made me a bit paranoid.

"The final edits for the first episode were fantastic," Von went on. "It aired last night, and all I can say is wow. It looks amazing. You have outdone yourselves with drama, danger, sexiness, and tension. We already have fan groups forming. I thought you'd like to see." He nodded to a TV on the wall.

The screen came alive and showed crowds of screaming fans outside the studio headquarters in Fangmore City. Hundreds and hundreds of fans, all holding up signs or wearing custom shirts. I squinted as I tried to read the signs. *Leif + Kira Forever*, read one. Others said *Underdogs love J.D.* and *Omar is HOT!* The camera panned over to a group of ladies wearing matching shirts that read *The Kwyatts.*

The camera approached this group, and I heard one of them shout, "Kira! Kira! You need to pick Wyatt. He's the one for you. Pick him. Pick him!"

I grinned and cut my eyes over at Kira. Sensing my gaze on her, she looked at me. I smirked, warmth rushing through me as she blushed.

The other alphas had their own fans in the crowd. Even Mika smiled when he saw one woman kissing a cut-out of his face.

Von turned the TV off and turned his attention to us again. "As fun as that is, this is no time to linger on your newfound fame." The smile on the vampire's face didn't leave but became more sinister. "Not when you're about to be thrown into the Fight for Survival."

If I didn't know better, I would have thought the temperature in the room had dropped ten degrees. The mood shifted quickly from joviality to tension and fear.

Ignoring the change, Von went on. "The Fight for Survival will take place in Dark Swamp, north of Reject Mansion. This fight will test your very limits. You'll have to navigate your way out of the swamp. The swamp is home to ghosts—many ghosts. If, at any time, you disturb one, a specially designed magical shield will erupt and trap you in with the specters to fight for your lives."

Von described the challenge like it was an amusement park attraction, and we'd each be handed a bottomless bucket of popcorn and told to enjoy ourselves. The other guys glanced around nervously.

Kira kept her eyes glued on Von as he described the event.

Von's eyes gleamed with exhilaration. "These aren't any old ghosts. This isn't Aunt Beatrice moaning and groaning through the halls of Grandpa's house. No sir, these are deadly ghosts that have been captured and placed here by some of the best Tranquility operatives in the world. Each ghost has at least one confirmed kill and can possess contestants. Your fellow competitors may very well become your enemies during this challenge. Once possessed, contestants have been known to accidentally kill each other. Isn't that exciting?" He was nearly vibrating.

His disregard for our safety and his desire to see us fight for our lives made me sick. His hunger for sadistic drama had me more worried by the second. If Kira died, he'd probably be stoked about the ratings boost. Not only that, but I didn't trust any of the other knuckleheads in the room to keep Kira safe. When the shit hit the fan, the only person who would be looking out for her was me. As I watched her, I promised myself I'd stick by her side like glue during the entire fight.

Chapter 25 - Kira

My heart was racing so fast, I thought it would give out. In all my time as a Tranquility operative, ghosts had given me the most trouble. They were nearly impossible to stop without a trained operative exorcist or some kind of enchanted weapon to disperse them. The threat of being possessed was freaking terrifying. I'd watched an operative have his body taken over by a ghost in my first six months, and it had been horrible. The guy had started attacking the other operatives. We'd had to put him down before he killed any of the others.

My anxiety was skyrocketing when Von, basically reading my mind, added, "Enchanted weapons will be available at the location."

A small sigh escaped my lips. We wouldn't be totally defenseless.

"These weapons will banish the ghosts for a time, though not forever. Which means speed is of the utmost importance in getting back to the mansion."

"Sounds like fun," Nathaniel said, cracking his knuckles like the dumb moron he was.

Von pointed at him and laughed. "That's what I like to see. Bravery, a cocksure attitude, and excitement. Those will all be necessary if you want to survive and, let's not forget, give our viewers a good show." His gaze slipped back over to me. "Speaking of a good show. Kira, are there perhaps any of these gents you want to send packing early?"

The conversation Zoe and I'd had last night sprang to mind. Was that what Von was alluding to? Doing my best to remain impassive, I shrugged.

"Maybe," I said as I straightened in my seat.

Von's eyebrows flew up. "Ooooh, I thought that might be the case. Well, if you so desire, there is an additional bonus for you, Miss Durst. A glowing gem has been hidden deep within Dark Swamp. If you find that *and* survive the challenge, you will be able to send one of these men back home.

"Maybe one of them is simply too much for you to handle, or perhaps you'll take pity on one of the men you think is too beautifully gentle to survive the game. Either way, they will be sent packing. They will not receive any prize money or be reimbursed for their time in any way. What they will get is the chance to go home alive and live out their days as a reject or lone wolf, however they like. For some, it might be the greatest reward. For others, a terrible indignity. Remember, Kira, choose wisely."

If I could get that gem and send Wyatt home, he'd have no choice but to go. The showrunners and security here would force him onto a chopper, and he'd be flown back. He could pull whatever strings he could at that point, but he'd never be able to get back here. Bloodstone Island was probably the most secure location on the planet. I could finally get him to safety and focus on surviving and winning this game.

I did my best not to look at him, even as I felt his piercing gaze on me. My heart thudded wildly. I'd do whatever it took to get that stupid gem. I couldn't let on about my plan. He'd be beyond irritated with me if he knew I was planning to send him home.

The other alphas squirmed uncomfortably. We'd barely gotten to know each other. None of them would feel safe, knowing I'd have free reign to send them home. I hated the thought of it, but it meant I would probably have an easier time during this challenge. They'd be falling over each other to *save* me or *protect* me.

On second thought, there was the possibility that I'd be in even more danger. If they got too desperate to keep their place on the island, they might do something dumb that got me hurt or killed. I'd have to keep my head on a swivel.

"Now, if everyone is done with breakfast, you're free to head back to your quarters. Some protective clothing has been provided. Get dressed, then meet me out on the veranda," Von said. "Kira, your stylist will have your protective gear as usual. See everyone soon."

Back in my room, Zoe was already getting my clothes ready. As soon as she saw my face, she knew something was up.

"What's up?"

I grinned at her. "If I find a green crystal or gem or something in the swamp, I get to send someone home."

Zoe clapped her hands to her mouth. "No shit? Wow, it's really early for that kind of reward." Her eyes darkened. "You said the swamp? Dark Swamp?"

I nodded. "The one and only."

"That place is full of ghosts, and not the *Casper* variety. That's one of the most dangerous places on the whole island."

My breath huffed out of my nose in exasperation. "Thanks. I needed to hear that."

Zoe flopped her arms up and down in an exaggerated shrug. "Sorry, but it's true."

"They're giving us enchanted weapons, though. That means there'll be a fighting chance. Come on, help me get my stuff on."

Once I was dressed, Zoe braided my hair tightly to make sure it stayed out of my face. The boots had zippers that attached them to the legs of the pants. I didn't want to lose my shoes in the sucking mud of the swamp.

Zoe put her hands on my shoulders and looked me in the eyes. "Watch out for yourself out there."

"I will. See you soon."

Before I could even turn toward the door, Zoe yanked me to her chest and wrapped her arms around me. My spine popped, she held me so tightly.

"Come back alive. Please," Zoe whispered.

Surprised, I returned her hug. "I will." I chuckled ruefully. "Or die trying."

Zoe broke the hug and swatted my shoulder. "Don't be a bitch. I'm serious."

I softened at the tears in her eyes. "Sorry. I'll be careful. I promise."

After one more big hug, I finally got to the door. One of the massive fallen angels escorted me to the veranda, where most of the alphas had already congregated. Von stood beneath his floating umbrella. If I wasn't mistaken, he'd caked quite a bit of sunscreen on his face and hands. It was sunnier than it had been yesterday, which made sense, but the sunscreen made him look even paler than usual.

Mika and Abel were the last to arrive. Our bracelets started flashing green. The cameras were rolling.

"Good day, my friends," Von said, opening his arms wide toward us all. "Today is a very exciting challenge. Again, as we have so many times in the past, we are returning to Dark Swamp. Many of our viewers may already know this legendary location, but a little background for those who are unfamiliar with it. The thirty-five-acre swamp is home to three dozen ghosts. These ghouls are very dangerous, and while they have no substance, they can inflict damage. They can tear the flesh and break the bones of our contestants as easily as any of the creatures on the island. As a defense? All they will have is their wits, their speed, and a single enchanted weapon each. But don't forget, this is Bloodstone Island, and all other manner of beasts may find you in the swamp.

"To win today, you must either traverse the entirety of the swamp and return to Reject Mansion unharmed or survive an entrapment zone. Success in a full-fledged battle will enact a return spell for those who survive."

He swept a hand toward us again, and a group of witches and fae stepped forward and started handing out the weapons. I stifled a groan when I saw them. Simple steel clubs with a magical orb attached to the end. The Tranquility Council gave operatives projectile ghost-deterrent weapons. These clubs would require us to get much closer than I wanted. It would be like trying to fight a bear shifter with a baseball bat, but it was better than nothing. I smiled brightly as the witch handed mine to me.

"Now, our cameras have already made their way to the location, and when our contestants are ready, our team will teleport them to Dark Swamp."

Von looked at our group expectantly. "Anyone have any objections?"

"No!" Nathaniel shouted. "Let's get this show on the road. I'm ready to kick some ghost ass!"

"Very well," Von said, nodding to the team of spellcasters.

The witch who'd given me my weapon placed a hand on my shoulder. In the blink of an eye, I was no longer at Reject Mansion. The bright sun that had been overhead was gone, replaced by steely gray clouds that made it look like late afternoon rather than late morning. I could sense that the guys were fairly close to me but still spread out.

The humidity made it hard to breathe, almost like we were underwater. I was already drenched in sweat, my skin clammy beneath my clothes. Faint wisps of steam or fog obscured the ground, making it difficult to see where it was safe to step. The place gave me the creeps.

No one looked like they wanted to make the first move, so I took it upon myself to get us started. Keeping my eye out for that glowing gem, I moved forward, careful to make each step calculated and safe. Wyatt was right by my side, because of course he'd find a way to be near me. If I had to guess, he was hoping he could save the day. Along with him, Mika, Leif, and Abel were closest, and they fell in line behind me, following my lead. The other alphas moved in, flanking us.

Not fifteen steps in, I froze and squatted, trying to hide in the fog. The others crouched when they saw what I'd seen. Up ahead, a group of ghosts floated across the misty ground of the swamp directly in front of us. I grimaced in disgust as I took in their horrifying appearance. One was a man who looked like he'd died by being ripped nearly in half—his transparent form didn't do much to obscure the awful wounds. Behind him was a woman with large swaths of charred flesh and melted skin, as though she'd been burnt alive. Finally, the third was the ghost of some creature I'd never seen before. It had six long insectile arms hanging limply at its sides. A huge jaw full of razor-sharp teeth hung open, mist drifting between its knife-like fangs. Even with us only a dozen yards away, none of the three figures looked in our direction, which told me they were probably blind.

They drifted by us, and I had to suppress a shiver as the temperature dropped. My skin crawled.

I'd seen my fair share of ghosts, but these were far more terrifying than any I'd come upon before.

Once the three specters were gone, I moved forward again. Inching along the swamp, I swept my eyes across the ground in search of the mysterious gem. As I scanned the ground for the stone, Wyatt moved even closer to me. His hovering annoyed the hell out of me, but now wasn't the time to get into it. Maybe later, I'd get him alone and tell him to give me some room—not that it would do much good.

The group spread out, but Wyatt stayed close to me. I was being overly cautious, but I definitely didn't want to set off one of those magical barriers. Fighting a ghost was bad enough, but fighting one in close quarters sounded like a living hell. But my caution was obviously getting on some of the other alphas' nerves.

"Holy shit," Nathaniel whispered to Omar. "If we go any slower, we'll be fucking going backwards."

I glanced over my shoulder at the men and saw Omar nodding to Nathaniel. "For real. I want to get the hell out of here as fast as possible."

"Hey," I hissed at them.

Omar and Nathaniel's heads snapped toward me, their faces red with shame.

"Calm down. I'm trying to get us out of here alive."

I glared at them as I said it. From the corner of my eye, I saw Wyatt trying to hide a grin. I ignored it and turned around to find a safe passage through the swamp's sticky mud, shallow pools, and twisted vines. Mangrove trees dotted the entire expanse, and it was from behind one of those that the next ghost appeared.

It slid alongside J.D., who gave a pathetic little squeal of terror as he flopped onto his ass and gaped at the ghost passing above him. The entire group froze as we waited for the ghost to attack. My gaze locked on J.D., wondering if the spirit would lunge at him and try to kill the man.

I breathed a sigh of relief as the creature paused for a moment and then slid past. J.D. looked like he'd been seconds from pissing himself, and he slapped his hand to his chest.

Leif crouch-walked over to him. "Are you all right?

J.D. nodded at Leif. "Yeah, man. I think I'm good."

"Oh my gods," Nathaniel said, rising out of his crouch. "We're going to be here until fucking nightfall."

The big man took a few steps forward, obviously trying to take the lead and get us out of the swamp faster. I watched in horror as the giant, clumsy man caught his foot on a mangrove root and stumbled forward. He fell face-first into the swamp, grunting hard. There was a weird sound like a breaking lightbulb, and the next thing I knew, Wyatt was tackling me to the ground as massive magical walls shot up out of the mud and trapped us in.

A banshee wail almost burst my eardrums as half a dozen ghosts appeared out of thin air and rushed toward us. Had Wyatt not tackled me, one of them would have crashed right into me. I was thrust onto my back into the mud, sinking deeper into it under Wyatt's body. Around me, all hell broke loose.

To my horror, we were not only trapped in the magical bubble with ghosts but with three six-foot-long baby basilisks that writhed out from under a knot of roots. Pushing myself up to my hands and knees, I heard J.D. scream and saw him swinging his enchanted club at the serpentine beasts as they snapped their poisonous jaws at him.

Tate and Abel shifted on instinct, stupidly dropping their weapons as they did. I had no clue why they would do that. The wolf form of a shifter was even less of a match for a ghost than the human form. Without hands, they couldn't wield the only weapons that would work against them.

My fingers tightened on my club as a ghost came flying like a jet toward Wyatt. Its arms were outstretched, ready to attack him or slip into his body to possess him. I leaped up and swung my club, slamming it into the ghost right before it got to Wyatt. There was an electric crackle as the orb at the top of the club made contact. The specter shrieked and flew through the barrier. It kept going, getting as far away as possible.

"Thanks," Wyatt grunted as he swung his own club at what looked like the ghost of a dragon shifter. The abomination looked like it had died mid-shift. It slashed its ghostly claws at him.

He would be fine, but the screams coming from my right sounded panicked and horrified. Spinning, I found Nathaniel on his back, kicking and punching at a group of ghosts that had him pinned down. One of the spirits lashed out, and blood spurted from the claw marks it left on Nathaniel's chest. He screamed even louder when he saw the blood. It didn't look deep, but it had to have been agonizing.

My feet got stuck in the mud as I sprinted to help him. Yanking one boot out of the muck, I kept trying to rush to him, but two more ghosts appeared, passing through the barrier like it was nothing more than air. They rocketed straight toward me, hands open, claws out, jaws hanging wide as they screeched.

Backing away, I swung my club but missed. Beyond them, I watched as two spirits grabbed Nathaniel's feet and dragged him toward the barrier.

"Help!" He sounded more like a child than a grown man.

He clawed at the muddy ground, digging furrows with his fingers. My fight ended when I cracked my club into both ghosts with one swing, sending them fleeing from the magic. I sprinted to Nathaniel, desperate to save him. No matter how much of a dick he was, he didn't deserve to be torn apart by ghosts.

The creatures had him halfway through the barrier when I wrapped my hand around his mud-caked wrist. The ghosts were so strong, they pulled me along with him. The spell must have been designed to allow them to pull us out, because Nathaniel's feet slipped past the barrier into the swamp beyond.

He clutched at my wrist like a drowning man. His face was covered in mud, but his eyes were white orbs of panic as he looked beseechingly at me. "Please, Kira. Save me. Please!"

I never had the chance to answer him. The specters yanked on him one final time, and his wrist slipped from my grasp. Horrified, I watched as the ghosts tugged Nathaniel deeper into the swamp. I scrambled forward but slammed into the barrier, busting my lip on it. I slapped my palm onto it, but the thing was as solid as steel. Nathaniel's screams grew even more chaotic until they died off completely.

He was gone. Killed by the ghosts. There was nothing more I could do.

A battle raged behind me. I needed to help the ones I could. When I heard Wyatt's scream, I turned to rejoin the battle.

He stood above the corpses of the basilisks, his club covered in their greenish-blue blood. But that wasn't what he was screaming at. He was yelling at J.D. and Tate, who were locked into a wrestling match and trying their best to kill each other. Their eyes were solid gray. Fuck. They were possessed. They weren't actually trying to kill each other.

Wyatt was doing a decent job of pulling them apart, and I was fairly sure he didn't need my help. He and I were the best trained out of the whole group, and others needed me. Mika stumbled away from a ghost and swung his club at it, his other arm pressed to his stomach. Blood oozed from an awful wound there.

I lunged towards him, my foot catching on something, and I went flying face-first into the mud again. Enraged at the indignity, I turned to see what the hell I'd tripped on, then gasped. Jammed deep into the mud and wedged beneath a root was a pulsing green crystal. It had to be the gem.

Forgetting everything else, I grabbed it and pulled it free, then jammed it into a pocket on my cargo pants and zipped it shut for safekeeping.

Leaping back to my feet, I helped Leif dispatch the ghosts that were trying to drag Mika out like they had Nathaniel. We fought for what seemed like hours. Wyatt had successfully forced out the ghost possessing Tate, who was unconscious in the mud. Now Wyatt was wrestling with J.D., trying to touch his enchanted weapon to J.D.'s chest to force the ghost out.

A slimy green kappa came crawling from the mud to join the fight. The enormous frog-like creature let out a wet hiss and slashed at Abel with its webbed claws, digging deep wounds into his back all the way down to his ass. Screaming in agony, Abel fell forward. I leaped over him, bringing my club down on the beast's head with a bone-breaking crack.

Finally, heaving with exertion, we were done. I was on my knees, gasping for breath as I took in the damage. Wyatt had dispelled the ghost from J.D., and the guy looked like shit. His face was pasty, and Leif was at his side in a second to help him up. Wyatt had Tate, Mika, and Abel together, checking over their wounds.

A bright flash of light blinded me for an instant. The swamp vanished, then I was on my knees on the mansion's veranda. The others were with me, and healers rushed forward to help the injured contestants. I wiped blood and mud from my face as Von stepped forward, applauding.

"Marvelous job," he cooed. "I truly think the Fight for Survival might be my favorite challenge. You all could not have done better."

The cameras whirled around us, capturing us at different angles and zooming in on our injuries.

My throat was sore from screaming and yelling during the battle, and my voice rasped when I called out to Von. "Where's Nathaniel? Did he make it?"

Von's face fell into what I thought was his best attempt at sorrow. "Unfortunately, our good friend Nathaniel has been eliminated. May he rest easy, knowing that like Ryan, *The Reject Project* will send his family a small financial prize for their wonderful performances. Their stories will live on in the lore of *The Reject Project*."

Great, I thought, a little money to help you forget your loved one died on a fucking TV show. It appalled me, and I was tempted to say something that would knock the damned vampire down a notch or two, but that was when I felt the lump in my pocket. I'd almost forgotten I'd found the gem.

Getting shakily to my feet, I tore the zipper open, jammed my hand in, and pulled the rock out. I tossed it at Von's feet. If nothing else happened today, I'd at least ensure one person made it off this show alive. One less shifter to suffer through this damned hellhole of an island.

Von looked down at the muddy rock and raised his eyebrows. "Oh? What's this now?"

"The gem," I spat. "I got it."

"And?" Von asked expectantly.

"I choose to send Wyatt Rivers home."

Chapter 26 - Wyatt

As soon as Von had mentioned the gem this morning, I suspected Kira would use it to get rid of me. She was so driven to get me off the island, she'd do anything. I didn't know whether it was because she still couldn't stand me or wanted to send me to safety. It pissed me off either way.

I pressed a hand to my side as I helped the healers take Mika. Blood oozed from his midsection at a disconcerting speed. J.D. also looked like hell. I needed to get over to Von and Kira to say my piece before that vampire granted Kira her wish.

Once the guys were taken care of, I limped quickly toward them. "No way! I'm not going anywhere."

I stepped right up to Kira and stared into her eyes, daring her to say it to my face. Kira stared back, her eyes hard and determined. She really did want me to go home. It hurt that she wanted to continue without me.

Von practically squealed with glee. "Oh, the drama. I *love* it."

"You'll need to choose someone else, Kira, because I refuse to leave."

Two cameras zoomed through the air, catching my eye. One took position right next to Kira and me to capture us glaring at each other. The second got a nice closeup of Von.

Sweeping a hand toward us, Von spoke into the camera. "Poor Kira. All she wants to do is save one of her precious alphas. It seems Wyatt has other ideas." He held up a finger. "I think he understands the one true purpose of this competition: earning your fated mate."

Kira's eyes bulged, and she turned, her eyes flashing. She probably wanted to tell the vampire to shut up, but she managed to clamp her lips back together before she started spewing curses at him. Instead, she composed herself and got her emotions under control. I didn't like that. It meant she was about to try a different tactic.

In a calm and collected voice, she said, "Von, I have truly loved getting to know Wyatt. He's been amazing and has done so much already." Kira glanced over at me sweetly. I could almost hear her saying *checkmate* in my mind. "In fact, Wyatt has stolen the show a bit. I think he's proven himself, and it's time for him to bow out and give some of these other alphas a chance. I'd love to get to know some of the other guys better. I'd rather Wyatt go home alive than keep putting himself in danger here. I want him to live. If he stays, I feel like his fate is sealed."

She might have been playing for the cameras, but I didn't give a shit about them. I stared her down, feeling fire dancing in my eyes.

"You can give that stupid crystal to someone else," I growled. "I'm not leaving, so get over it. One of the injured alphas should go. They can heal properly at home. Stop being dumb, Kira. You know it's the right thing to do."

In hindsight, my use of the word "dumb" was not my smartest move. It looked like someone had lit a bonfire in Kira's eyes. Her nostrils flared, and she clenched her hands into fists. I knew her well enough to know that I was about seven seconds from having my nose broken. For once, Von's interruptions were welcome.

He clucked his tongue. "Oh, dear, this is unfortunate."

"What is?" Kira growled, her eyes never leaving mine.

"Well, you see, the gem can only be used once, and there is a no-transference policy."

"I don't care about transferring it. I've already made my decision," Kira huffed.

"And Wyatt has refused. Usually, when the expulsion gem is used, the alpha jumps at the chance to get home and away from danger." Von gestured toward me. "But brave and strong Wyatt here has declined. He can't be forced to go if he doesn't want to."

Kira turned her furious glare on Von, her composure finally cracking. "Then what the *fuck* is the point of the damned crystal?"

Von wagged a finger at her. "Now, now, don't get upset. There will be other opportunities to gain expulsion gems and send someone home to safety. Unfortunately, none of those will be useful for Wyatt. Once refused, no other gem can be used on him, and the current gem is now useless."

Fuck. I glanced back at the injured alphas. Mika was coughing up blood as the fae healer ran her hands across his body. J.D. and Tate were nearly catatonic from having been possessed. Why hadn't Kira sent one of them home? That would have been the smartest thing to do.

Kira looked as upset as I felt. She took a step toward Von. "Wait a minute. That wasn't part of the deal. You never told me there were stipulations to using the gem."

Ignoring her, Von swept a hand in front of the hovering camera in front of him. It, along with the others, flew back toward the mansion. My bracelet went from green to white. He'd shut off the recording.

"All right, everyone," Von said. "Best to get you all healed and cleaned up. I want everyone to look their best. The eleventh...er...I suppose now the *ninth* contestant will be here soon. Chop-chop, let's get moving, people." He turned and walked back into the mansion.

The other alphas wandered toward the house. Most of them looked exhausted or traumatized by the fight in the swamp. The healers had carried Mika and Tate off on floating gurneys. The last ones left were Abel, J.D., and Leif. J.D. still looked pretty rough. I'd had to fight him tooth and nail to expel the ghost from him. He was leaning on Leif as they walked to the mansion, but they detoured and came straight for me. Kira looked like she wanted to rip into me, but she'd have to wait until we were alone.

Abel walked up to Kira and put a hand on her shoulder. "Hey, I'm sorry about Nathaniel."

Kira grimaced. "Yeah. It sucks."

"Take it easy, okay?"

"Will do. Thanks." When Abel departed, she looked relieved.

"Hey, Wyatt," J.D. said as he and Leif limped over to me. "I wanted to thank you for what you did for me."

"No problem, man. You'd have done the same for me," I said.

J.D. chuckled. "I'd like to think so, but...I don't know. Thanks again."

"Yes, thank you," Leif chimed in. "I can't thank you enough for what you did. It was amazing. Thank you."

Leif sounded even more appreciative than J.D., which was strange. I couldn't remember doing anything much to help him. I'd spent most of the fight trying to help Tate and J.D. I nodded at them as they hobbled off to the medical wing of the mansion.

With the cameras off and all the others gone, Kira no longer had to keep up the facade. She slammed her palms on my chest, sending me lurching back a few feet.

"You idiot. What the hell are you thinking?"

"Me?" I barked. "What about you? What are you thinking?"

Kira jammed her fists onto her hips. "I was thinking that I was doing you a fucking favor. I was trying to get you off this stupid island in one piece, but no, you had to go and screw everything up."

"I never asked for that. The only reason I'm here is to keep you safe. How can I do that if I'm hundreds of miles away on the mainland?"

Kira let a lungful of air explode out in a sigh of frustration. "I can't believe you." She started muttering under her breath, but I could hear every word. "Bossy, overbearing, macho bullshit. What do I do now?"

"What we do now is stick with the plan. My bossy, macho ass is staying, and I'm going to make sure you get back to the Eastern Wilds safe and sound. If you don't make it off Bloodstone, I'll never be able to live with myself."

Looking at me with an irate desperation, she said, "It's not your burden to sacrifice yourself for me."

"I've never seen it as a burden," I snapped. "Stop trying to think you're weak because I want to help you. You aren't weak. You never were, and you never will be. If you were weak, you couldn't have handled that tiger shifter or the ghosts and monsters we took on. I've known you long enough to know what you're capable of. But even the strongest people need help sometimes. It's not a sign of weakness, so please stop making it seem that way. Get over the fact that I'm here to stay."

Some of the heat in her face faded as I spoke, and she rubbed a hand over her face. She looked exhausted. Kira had done more fighting than most of the guys. I should have realized how tired she was. It had been a tough fight, and I didn't like thinking how close we'd all come to ending up like Nathaniel. I hadn't liked the guy, but psychotic ghosts were capable of horrifying things. No one deserved the fate that had befallen him. Kira probably blamed herself for his death. That, more than likely, added to her exhaustion.

I reached forward and gently touched her chin. Instead of pulling away, Kira allowed me to tilt her head back. Her eyes were rimmed with red, and I knew I was right. She was taking all the blame for the deaths of Ryan and Nathaniel on her shoulders. In all the time I'd known her, she'd made it obvious that nothing ate at her more than failure. Whether it was warranted or not, she was always hard on herself.

"Stop it," I murmured. "It's not your fault. I was there, too. I could have tried to save them as well."

Kira rolled her eyes. "No one could have saved Ryan. We weren't anywhere near him."

"Okay, fine, but I was right there with Nathaniel. I should have helped. If you want to beat someone up about it, do it to me, not yourself. I won't even fight you on it because I don't want you feeling like they died because of you. They knew the risks when they signed up."

Kira looked away from me. "That's fine, but what if something happens to you? Who gets the blame then?"

Her words ricocheted through my mind. Kira was *worried* about *me*. I wasn't sure if that made me happy or terrified. I didn't want her worrying about me when she needed to focus on staying alive.

"Doesn't matter," I said. "Like I said, we all knew the risks. I'm not here to win. My only goal is to make sure you win and get out alive. That's it."

"You're a really loyal friend," she whispered. "Doing all this for Kolton."

It was like she'd kicked me in the stomach. Even after everything, she still thought this was about me protecting my best friend's sister. I wanted to shout at her that I wasn't doing this for Kolton, but perhaps it was safer for her to think that instead of knowing the truth. If she knew the real reason, her head might not be in the game. I couldn't risk her getting hurt because I wanted her to know the truth—that I wanted to save her for *me*, not Kolton.

"I need to go get cleaned up," I managed to say. "You should, too. We don't want Von getting pissed at us."

Kira gave a barely imperceptible nod. "Yeah. You're right."

I watched her trudge up the steps into the mansion before I followed. I was still peeved that she'd tried to send me away, but what made it all the worse was that she couldn't see what I felt for her. She truly couldn't believe that I was doing this for more than my friendship with her brother.

To anyone else, it would have been clear what was going on. Was Kira really that blind? Or was she forcing herself to ignore what was obvious? As much as she wanted me to go, I wouldn't. I couldn't stay away from her if my life depended on it.

Chapter 27 - Kira

"You've got to calm down. Seriously." Zoe was doing her best to pick dirt and twigs out of my hair.

"I can't, I'm too damned pissed—ow, shit!"

"Sorry," Zoe squeaked, brandishing the tangled twig she'd ripped out of my hair. "This one was really in there."

Wincing, I rubbed at my scalp. "It's fine. Do what you've got to do."

Zoe sighed and kept poking through my hair. "It's still bullshit."

"What? The crap Von pulled with the gem?"

"Yes," Zoe barked. "I think they're making up rules as they go. That's never been part of the deal. It's always been simple. The lead chose an alpha to leave, and he went, whether he wanted to or not. Now, the whole glowing gem thing is new, but it's still the same basic idea. I hate to say it, but I'm probably never watching this show again."

I didn't speak again until Zoe had all the crap out of my hair. She leaned me back into a shampoo basin. I could see her face as she rinsed and washed my hair.

"I'm still shocked by how brutal it was out in the swamp. It was like being back at work on a terrible assignment. The fact that the showrunners put untrained people out there is crazy. I'm surprised anyone lives. I don't want to think about what might have happened if Wyatt and I weren't there."

"I know. I saw," Zoe said.

"When?" I asked, surprised she'd seen it.

Zoe rolled her eyes. "There's nothing else to do here. The only show that plays is *The Reject Project*. There's zero Wi-Fi or cell service. They don't want the staff accidentally leaking storylines before the episode airs. I can teleport, but the other fae informed me I wouldn't be able to while I was here—some fancy spell they conjured. So, my choices are to watch the show, read a dusty old book, sleep, eat, or flirt with the cute people working on the show. And everyone who works here is boring. So, I watched the live feed of you guys out there."

"How'd it look?"

Zoe shrugged, her brow furrowing. "Well, the episode will be more dramatic. They'll edit it to make it all climactic and add music and stuff, but the live feed?" Zoe massaged conditioner into my hair. "It kinda looked like a bunch of monkeys humping a football. I mean, no offense, you and Wyatt did great, but those goofy magic clubs they gave you? And the way some of the *macho* alphas screamed like little bitches? Ugh, it was not a good look. The directors and editors are gonna have to work some magic to make that look entertaining. They'll probably focus on you and Wyatt, and Nathaniel...uh...well, you know."

Nathaniel. He hadn't been my favorite person. He'd been an arrogant and cocky asshole, but that didn't mean he deserved to be ripped to pieces by ghosts. No matter what Wyatt had said, I still felt like it was my fault he'd died. If I'd held onto him longer, led us in a different direction, or one of a hundred different things, he'd still be here. What Wyatt was right about was me needing to put it behind me. I couldn't focus if I was beating myself up for something in the past.

"All I can say," Zoe went on, "is I'm glad you and Wyatt made it back okay."

"Ugh. Damned Wyatt," I growled. "He should have just accepted his ticket home. He's too dense to understand I was doing him a favor."

"I'm not surprised, actually."

"What are you talking about?"

Zoe turned the water off and started toweling my hair. "Listen, I hate to break this to you. But…" She leaned down to whisper in my ear. "You two have been bumping uglies."

My jaw tightened. "You know that was a…well, not a one-time deal, but you know what I mean."

Zoe snorted. "Really? Is that why you two have been trading those sultry, ooey-gooey looks? I can see you two doing that shit when the cameras are on, you know. Which means everyone on Earth sees it."

I gave her a stern look but was secretly mortified. Everyone on Earth? Tens of millions of people, or more like hundreds of millions? All thinking Wyatt and I were drooling over each other? It was mortifying.

Ignoring my cold look, Zoe said, "Kira, you're my bestie. You kick ass. I'll never say different, and I'll fucking cut anyone who argues that fact. But one thing you are terrible at is seeing what's right in front of your stupid face."

Rolling my eyes, I said, "And what is that?"

"That Wyatt is more than just your brother's friend and a colleague. You're fighting so hard to win this show, but you're fighting even harder to ignore that simple fact."

"It's not a hard fight, because he isn't," I argued.

"You make my case for me. Stop pretending this guy is here to annoy you and boss you around. He is risking his own life to keep you safe and help you survive this.

"I don't know why you've got this big hang-up about him. Is it because he's a lone wolf? I have to be honest, that shit makes no sense to non-wolf shifter types like me. Like, he's a wolf shifter. Why does it matter if he doesn't have a pack? Really weird, but that's beside the point. What I'm getting at is he's a good alpha to have in your corner. And from the way you've been checking him out, he must be good at something else, too."

"Zoe." I jerked my head around to gawk at her. "No. We aren't going there."

Zoe raised an eyebrow. "Mm-hmm. You're blushing, Kira."

I threw my towel at her. "Can you shut up and help me get dressed?"

She did, drying my hair, getting me into my new outfit, and removing and then applying my makeup. When she was done, I checked myself in the mirror. I looked great.

Turning back to her, I put my hands on her shoulders. "I'm really glad you're here. I'd go crazy if you weren't with me. I've got all this chaos and danger swirling around me, not to mention a bunch of horny alphas. I don't know if I ever properly thanked you for being my stylist. So, thank you."

"Aww," Zoe said. "She does have a heart."

"Very funny. I'm gonna go get lunch, you asshole."

Chuckling, I gave her a quick hug before I left the suite. Thankfully, there was no guard at the door this time. I was getting really tired of having a suit-clad block of muscle escort me everywhere.

Once I was downstairs, I was greeted with a nice sight. It seemed that all the guys who'd been hurt had been healed.

Mika was staring at a salad, and apart from his typical moodiness, he looked completely fine. Tate was munching on a sandwich, and J.D. was talking to Leif near the buffet. I was so glad J.D. was okay. The possession had wiped him out. He was one of the few alphas here who was a good guy.

He leaned closer to Leif and laughed before draping his arm across his shoulders. Leif's eyes widened, and he looked my way, catching my eye.

I raised a questioning eyebrow and grinned. In response, Leif gave me a single stern shake of the head that told me to drop it. Whatever was going on there would take a little more time to develop.

Acting like I hadn't noticed them, I grabbed a plate and piled it high with pasta and salad, then turned to find a seat. The first thing I noticed was Wyatt sitting alone, an empty plate in front of him. He was looking at me, his eyes dark and stormy. Apparently, he was still pissed at me for trying to send him home. Well, I was still pissed at him for *not* going home. I couldn't think of another reason for him to look so angry. That was fine, though. Let him be mad. I was secure in the knowledge that I'd been doing the right thing and he'd been an idiot for passing up the opportunity.

Finding a seat near a window far away from Wyatt's gaze, I started eating but didn't get far. My bracelet flashed from white to green, and I barely suppressed my groan. Back on stage, it seemed. From behind me, I heard the faint *whooshing* of the cameras returning. When I turned my head, I was greeted by Von Thornton's shimmering white smile.

"How is everyone feeling after the big outing?" he asked as he stepped into the room.

The big outing? Is that what he called it when a man died, and the rest of us came damn close? The people running this show were completely out of touch.

Still, I grinned back at him and gave the camera a thumbs-up. It made me die a little inside.

"I'm so sorry to interrupt your lunch, but our final contestant has arrived, and I couldn't wait any longer to introduce him."

"Okay, let's meet this guy," Omar called.

Von nodded to him. "A man who isn't afraid of a little competition. I like that. Without further ado, I present the final contestant on this year's season of *The Reject Project.*"

Von stepped aside, and the newest contestant entered the room. My fork fell from my suddenly numb fingers, and a pit formed in my stomach. Jerking my head toward Wyatt, I saw him looking at me, his lip curled in disgust. He gave me a slight shake of the head.

Gavin Fell, Jayson's little brother, shook hands with Von. Panic flared hot in my chest. Gavin? Seriously? The man who had been moments away from being my brother-in-law was the final contestant? Would he tell everyone that he knew me? Or worse, would he tell everyone that Wyatt and I knew each other?

I picked my fork up absently, gripping it like a weapon. I was overwhelmed with the urge to rush Gavin and attack him, and I barely managed to tamp it down. I was still furious at his family for what they'd done to me. I was only on this fucking island because of Jayson and his father.

Before I could do anything but stare at him dumbly, Gavin addressed the room. "Hey, everyone. It's great to be here. I'm sorry I'm late, but I've been watching the live stream. So, I understand you've lost a few contestants already." He bowed his head. "I'm really sorry to hear that. I'm sure they were great guys."

J.D. stood and walked straight toward Gavin, arms open wide. "Let's go, my man. Bring it, big guy. Bros hug, and you're one of the bros now."

Gavin's eyes widened as J.D. wrapped his arms around him and pounded him on the back. He seemed taken aback by the warm welcome. His eyes slid over to me and locked on my face.

I needed to make a move before things got even more awkward. I had to keep up the act. With every fiber of my being, I hoped and prayed that Gavin wasn't here to somehow derail my chances at protecting my family.

Standing and straightening my clothes, I plastered a massive fake smile onto my face and strutted over to Gavin, sticking my hand out to shake his.

"Gavin? I'm Kira. Nice to meet you," I said. I sounded calm and confident, but an icy trickle of fear slithered up my spine.

He disentangled himself from J.D. and turned to face me. He looked a lot like Jayson, but I barely knew Gavin. He hadn't been around much while Jayson and I had been *dating*. He was always away at school. When he was around, he was always scowling at Jayson or off by himself. He'd been reserved and quiet. The last time I laid eyes on him was at the disaster of the mating ceremony. He'd looked entirely disinterested to be there. Now he was looking at me with a fire and intensity that puzzled me.

Gavin took my hand in his. "Good to meet you, Kira." There was a mischievous glimmer in his eye when he spoke.

That look made my stomach somersault. More lies, more secrets, more things I had to keep covered up. This show was getting more stressful by the second.

Gavin pulled my hand up to his lips and kissed my fingers. "*Very* good to meet you, I should say."

From behind me, I heard Omar grumbling something, obviously unhappy with the affection Gavin was showing me.

Von, on the other hand, looked thrilled. "Here less than five minutes and already trying to sweep Kira off her feet? Aggressive. It's fantastic."

I quickly pulled my hand away, trying to lighten the tension filling the room. Even though my back was to him, I was hyper-aware of Wyatt watching.

"I'm sorry you missed out on the fun so far," I said. "We fought ghosts this morning. Um, if you don't mind my asking, what kept you from joining earlier?"

It was my best attempt at subtlety. He had to have a good reason. Why else would the showrunners allow a contestant to join this late?

Gavin looked me dead in the eye. "Yeah, well, it wasn't a great time. The producers allowed me a few days to get everything in order."

"Get what in order?" I asked sweetly, not understanding what he was talking about.

Gavin glanced over his shoulder at the hovering camera, then back to me. "The alpha of my pack, my father, was murdered. My brother and I have been dealing with the fallout."

It was like I'd been kicked in the chest. His dad was dead? Someone had murdered Jayson's father? Alphas were never murdered in cold blood like that. I was so astonished that a shocked squeak escaped my lips. A smattering of murmurs broke out around the room as the other alphas processed the information.

Ignoring all of us, Gavin looked into my eyes and said, "Being away from here was inconvenient because all I want to do is win *The Reject Project* and take you as my fated mate, Kira."

His sincerity freaked me out a little bit, to be honest. I could practically hear Wyatt's teeth grinding.

Smiling at Gavin, I said, "Well, I wish you my best. Maybe you will." I raised my eyebrow at him seductively, hoping the cameras got a good shot of it. It made me feel a little dirty, but the show had to go on.

Von saved me by interrupting the conversation. "Along with introducing Gavin, I came to give you all an update. Since we've already had a couple of eliminations this week, the Arena Match will happen tomorrow. I'm sure all of our alphas have had that day circled on their calendars since meeting the lovely Kira.

"Two contestants will enter the arena. Whoever wins will get to spend a magical night with Kira in the mating chamber." Von waggled his eyebrows suggestively.

If I was nervous before, I was now on the verge of a panic attack. The other alphas were all studying me. Some, like Omar and Tate, were staring at me like I was a piece of meat to be devoured. Others, like J.D.

and Abel, looked nervous. Wyatt was the only one who wasn't looking at me—he was staring at Von like he wanted to rip him to pieces.

I cleared my throat and touched Von's wrist. "Forgive my ignorance, but how are the contestants chosen?"

Von laughed and put an arm around me. "Oh, dear Kira, by fan voting, of course."

"Fan voting?" I asked.

"Yes. Our audience gets to have a say in how things go down." He touched his finger to the tip of my nose. "But don't worry your little head. I'm sure you've grown attached to your alphas by now, and I want to let you know that the Arena Match is not necessarily a duel to the death. It is, however, very exciting." He released me and clasped his hands together. "Our viewers are voting online right now. The final tally should be ready later today. Take the afternoon to relax. I'm sure you all need it after this morning's *fun*."

Von waved a hand over his bracelet. The cameras shut off and floated away. "Whew. What an exciting day already," he said. "I'll leave you all to get to know our new contestant. We'll let everyone know when the votes are in."

Von left us all alone. I expected the others to disperse quickly once he was gone, but all the guys hung around. I knew why within seconds. They wanted to get dirt on Gavin.

J.D. was the first to launch into questions. "So, what pack are you from?"

"Ninth," Gavin said.

"What's the location? I've never met someone from the Ninth Pack."

Gavin sighed. "Eastern Wilds, same as Eleventh Pack."

He didn't seem excited to answer questions. While J.D. continued to badger him, Gavin stared across the room at Wyatt and Leif, who were standing together. Every few seconds, Gavin's gaze swiveled toward me, and I couldn't miss how he looked at me. The only way to describe it was *lustful*, and that made me even more uncomfortable. Had there been something stewing under the surface all the years I was promised to his brother?

"Will you or your brother be alpha now?" J.D. asked.

Gavin shook his head. "I'm not allowed to be alpha. My brother Jayson will take that role."

Jayson was alpha of the Ninth Pack? That was weird to contemplate. Their dad had always been such a strong presence—of course he had after being alpha for nearly forty years. He'd taken over the role at eighteen, becoming one of the youngest alphas in shifter history. The idea of anyone other than him being the alpha was difficult to get my head around, especially when I envisioned Jayson in the role.

I didn't like that Gavin had mentioned how close in proximity our packs were. That might lead to questions about whether he and I had history. There were already too many threads connecting me and Wyatt; now I had to deal with Gavin as well. I needed a degree in logistics to keep these relationships hidden for the duration of the show.

As though he'd read my mind, Tate spoke up. "You said your pack is near the Eleventh Pack? Isn't that your pack, Kira?" He turned to look at me as he said it. Looking back toward Gavin, he said, "Have you ever met Kira before?"

Gavin looked from Tate to me, then across the room to Wyatt. His face didn't change, but the look in his eye was a direct challenge. For Wyatt's part, he remained as calm as he could, only crossing his arms.

After a moment, Gavin looked back at Tate and shrugged. "I won't lie. I did notice Kira a few times from afar. It would have been hard to miss her living in such close proximity."

Tate's eyes narrowed. "Interesting."

Several other alphas had the same look on their face. It was what I'd feared when Wyatt ended up on the show. None of them liked the thought of one of the guys having a perceived upper hand.

Sensing the mood, Gavin added, "Having knowledge of her before the show doesn't grant me any favors. It was all in passing. She probably doesn't even remember me. I mean, it's not like we worked together or I was friends with her brother or something, right?" He laughed.

The other alphas chuckled, but the rocks in my stomach now had knots around them when Gavin glared at Wyatt again. The two shifters had a stare-off, and the tension was so strong between them, I knew the others would notice it soon. I had to put a stop to it quickly. I couldn't remember a time when I'd been that uncomfortable. The others seemed oblivious to what was going on between the two men. Everyone but Leif, who was glancing back and forth between them.

He caught my eye and mouthed, *What the hell?,* nodding at Wyatt and Gavin.

"I think everyone needs to go ahead and finish lunch," I said, desperate to cut the tension. "We all need our energy. Go on, boys, get some grub."

Thankfully, the others did as I suggested. The alphas who'd already eaten headed back for dessert, and the others filed away to get their first plates.

I nearly jumped out of my skin as Wyatt brushed up against my hand. "That's a funny surprise, isn't it?" he whispered.

"I'm not talking to you right now," I hissed.

"Why?"

Why? Was he really that dense? "Because you should be on a helicopter home. This whole thing with Gavin would be less difficult if you were home safe. That's *why.*"

I sat back down and picked at my food. Wyatt went out of his way to piss me off by taking the seat next to me. Ignoring him, I concentrated on my food.

J.D. sat next to Gavin and continued to pepper him with questions.

"What's your wolf look like? Color, I mean?" J.D. asked.

Gavin frowned. "Why would you care about that?"

J.D. leaned forward. "Bro, this place is crazy. You never know if we might get surrounded by feral wolves out in the jungle. I want to figure out what everyone looks like. That way, I don't accidentally hurt one of my buds, you know?" He shook his head. "I'd be freaking heartbroken if I hurt one of my guys here. I especially don't want to hurt Kira. I need to figure out what her wolf looks like, too. She hasn't shifted yet, but when she does, I need to make sure I don't attack her by mistake."

Gavin frowned and put his fork down at J.D.'s words. My mouth went dry with fear as the confusion on Gavin's face deepened. "What do you mean?"

J.D. looked equally as confused. "What do you mean 'what do I mean?'"

Gavin shook his head like he was trying to clear it. "You won't have any trouble knowing who Kira is in battle. She's fairly well-known in the Ninth, Tenth, and, obviously, Eleventh Pack. She's a latent shifter. She doesn't have a wolf. She can't shift."

Every sound in the room stopped. I clamped my teeth together and looked at Wyatt. From the expression on his face, he was ready to leap across the room and kill Gavin.

Chapter 28 - Wyatt

I pretty much hated every single member of the Fell family, so I already disliked Gavin Fell before he set foot inside the mansion. He was a wrench in the works, a pain in the ass, and a variable I wasn't ready for. At the best of times, I'd have been pissed off to see him walk through those doors. But the smart-ass little comment and the way he stared at me made it even worse.

He was goading me, and then he nonchalantly told everyone that Kira couldn't shift. What was he thinking? I didn't know what he was trying to do, but whatever it was, the mood of the room had gone off the rails. Everyone was silent and staring at Kira. Some of them looked confused, and others looked outright angry.

I slowly got to my feet, unsure how things were going to go from there. I didn't think Kira was in danger, but I didn't want to take the risk.

Kira did exactly what I thought she'd do. Noticing the looks the guys were giving her, she lifted her chin and told everyone exactly what was going on.

"He's right," she said indignantly, glaring at Gavin.

His face clouded over as he realized he'd made a misstep. He looked surprised that everyone didn't already know. His ignorance wasn't enough to quell my rage. Unless you were *absolutely* certain about something like that, you kept your damn mouth shut. It showed me he was just as much of an idiot as his older brother. Which meant he was a threat to Kira.

Gavin raised his hands in surrender. "Kira, I didn't think–"

"No, you didn't," Kira said, cutting him off. She turned to address the rest of the room. "I don't shift. That's correct."

I liked how she judiciously used the word *don't* instead of *can't*. No one other than me knew her secret. None of the other alphas caught on to the wordplay, though.

Omar groaned and rolled his eyes. "We're out here risking our lives to what? Win a damaged mate as a *prize?*"

Tate looked equally pissed. He'd crossed his arms and was staring at the floor, shaking his head in disgust. Abel and Mika wore matching confused and disapproving frowns. I moved closer to Kira, ready to tell them all to shove their condescending looks up their asses. Before I could, Leif beat me to the punch.

"Can you all get over yourselves?" Leif looked at the others like they were stupid. "She's done pretty damned good in her human form, hasn't she? How many of you could have survived what she has so far without shifting?"

"Hey," J.D. said to Kira, "it's not a huge deal. I mean, your wolf is probably taking a little longer to manifest than others. The same thing happened to one of my cousins. You'll be fine."

"She's not gonna be fine," Omar snapped. "She's twenty-fucking-three years old. If her wolf hasn't manifested by now, it won't. She might as well be a human, for goddess's sake."

His tone held nothing but disgust. I took a step forward and growled at him, but Kira pressed a hand to my chest to hold me back. She shot me a sharp look and kept her chin up when she turned back to Omar.

She raised her eyebrow. "I'm faster and stronger than a human. I've learned to focus my energy. But even if I wasn't, I wouldn't care if I was a human. What's wrong with being human, Omar? Do you have a problem with them? You're being awfully judgy about non-shifters when I hear you like to get cozy with vampires."

At the mention of vampires, Omar's eyes swelled in rage. I had no clue what Kira was talking about, but she obviously had more information than I did. He jumped to his feet, snarling at Kira.

Before he could do more than snarl, Gavin slammed a shoulder into him, a deep growl emanating from his chest. The two men squared up and pressed their chests into each other. They were seconds from a full-fledged fistfight. I needed to defuse this before it came to blows and before the damn cameras came jetting back into the room.

Sprinting over, I shoved the two men apart. "Enough! If her not shifting hasn't come up yet on the show, it shouldn't matter. She beat a feral tiger shifter and saved pretty much every one of your asses in the swamp, all in her human form. I'd call that pretty impressive. She saved Leif, and she would have done the same for any of you here. Maybe you could be a little grateful, huh?"

"It *would* be easier if some of you *let* me save you," Kira said, looking pointedly at me.

She needed to get over that. What's done was done. Before I could retort, Von rushed into the room. For the first time since meeting him, he looked irate.

"What's all this?" he asked, gesturing toward me, Gavin, and Omar. I had a fistful of their shirts, and the two other men were staring daggers at each other.

He shook his head and clucked his tongue, obviously annoyed. "Were you all not told earlier? Make sure to summon the cameras to capture all the drama." He ran a hand through his hair and sighed. "Is it possible to redo whatever happened? Make another attempt for the show?'

"No," I barked at him. "Nothing was going on, and no, we aren't going to play games to get you ratings."

Omar slapped my hand away and grinned. It was a dark, dangerous look he gave me.

"You know what, Von? I think we do need the cameras back. We need to have another challenge." He looked from me to Gavin, then Kira, and back to me with a smile. "A challenge where we can only survive if we shift. Our precious little *mate* isn't up to snuff, in my book. Might be better if she got knocked out of the show so we can bring in a replacement. That's always good for ratings, isn't it?"

On this show, getting knocked out meant getting killed nine times out of ten. He was literally saying he wanted Kira to die so he could get a chance at a new and *better* mate.

I was about to tear his throat out when Kira pushed me aside. She stepped right up to Omar, looking up at him as he was almost a full foot taller than her. Von had summoned the cameras back, but Kira didn't seem to care.

"I'll do any challenge you want, Omar. I'd be more than happy to complete any task involving shifting, and I'll complete it any way I see fit. I may not be able to shift, but at least I'm not a narrow-minded dick who got sent here for breaking his fated mate's heart by going balls-deep in some vampire chick."

"Oh, snap!" J.D. said and put a fist to his mouth to cover his grin.

Leif looked mortified and pointed at Omar. "You got rejected for being a cheater? You *actually* cheated on your fated mate?"

That was a big no-no in our culture. The fated-mate pairing was a sacred thing that was not to be defiled. It was part of why Gavin's brother had rejected Kira. He'd refused to believe the drug had made her sexually attack me. Cheating on a fated mate was tantamount to spitting in the eye of the Moon Goddess herself. The others knew the same thing, and the whole room was looking at Omar with differing levels of disgust and disappointment.

Unrepentant, Omar gave a low growl and swept his eyes across the room, daring one of them to say something. Von clapped his hands to get our attention.

"Now this is exciting," Von said. "I think I have an idea that everyone, especially our viewers, will love."

I groaned. From the little time I'd spent on the island, I had figured out a few basic things. One of them being that if Von said that something would be *entertaining* to the viewers, it meant it would be dangerous as hell.

"Our votes have already come in for the Arena Match," Von went on. "Wyatt and Leif were the two winners, but this exciting turn of events has me thinking a brand-new challenge may be in order. What if we do something that will really push you all to your limits? Put you under duress and truly reveal all this delicious drama within the group."

Von ran his tongue along his long canines. "I need to discuss this with the rest of our team. I think you all need to get ready. What I'm planning will take place at night. You've got a few hours." He turned to leave, and I heard him whisper to himself, "This is going to be *amazing*." He was in a much better mood than when he'd arrived.

Omar was still glaring at Kira, and I stepped in front of her, blocking his view. His eyes met mine, and I narrowed my gaze, hoping he could read the threat in my eyes. All I wanted was one chance. If he did or said anything I didn't like, it was on.

The other alphas had started filing out of the room. Tate passed me, giving me an incredulous frown. "You know, for someone who's so sure Kira can handle herself, you're awfully protective. Seems dumb to me, but whatever."

"You know he's right," Kira said when he was gone.

I turned to see her looking at me in that way she did when she wanted to get her point across. "What?"

"I *can* take care of myself. I don't need you playing the hero. Jumping in like this only makes me look weak."

"Hang on," Mika said, holding up a hand. "Kira, no one here thinks you're weak." He glanced at Omar and winced. "At least nobody with a brain. I don't think that's what Wyatt was implying when he came to your defense."

I was a little surprised to hear Mika speak up for me. He'd been more or less a brooding and silent shadow the whole time. I appreciated him trying to explain to Kira what I thought was obvious.

Omar scoffed and walked out, bumping his shoulder into mine and growling as he left the room. He didn't even bother glancing at Kira. He was going to be trouble. He'd blatantly said he wanted Kira dead so the show would bring in another female. One way or another, Omar would have to be dealt with.

Leif walked over and wrapped Kira in a hug, squeezing her tightly. I was already pissed off, and seeing one of the other guys touching her nearly sent me over the edge.

"Don't let what he said get to you," Leif said. He pulled away and gave Kira a reassuring grin. "His opinions don't matter, and there's nothing in the world that would make me think less of you."

I pressed my lips together in a thin line. Was Leif using this whole thing as a way to move on Kira? It sounded like he was practically confessing his love for her.

When Kira smiled back at him, my annoyance only increased. It wasn't her fake smile; it was genuine. She swung her arms around Leif and hugged him back. All I could do was stand there with my fists clenched, wondering if I did have anything to worry about from Leif. If I voiced any concerns, I'd look as petty and stupid as Omar. When Leif finally left, I released the breath I'd been holding.

Now, we got to go and try to get ready for whatever horror Omar had brought down on our heads. It would have been bad enough simply doing the Arena Match, but to be honest, I had no fears about my chances fighting Leif, especially not after the way he'd been flirting with Kira. A one-on-one fight was easy to understand and plan for. Now? That damn vampire had gotten something in his head that was probably a hundred times worse and way more dangerous.

Before I could say anything to Kira, she stormed off. So far, this day had been about as shitty as it possibly could have been. I couldn't think of a way it could have gone worse.

Gavin had left only a few seconds before Kira did. If I hurried, I could catch him before he got to the alpha den. If nothing else, I was going to try to get some answers. Why was he here, what were his plans, and last of all, was he going to put Kira in danger?

He was walking down the corridor toward the den when I caught him.

"Hey, Gavin?"

He turned slowly and looked at me like I was something to be scraped off the bottom of his shoe. "Wyatt."

"What are you doing here?" I asked.

Ignoring my question, he said, "You know, all these years, I always thought you were hunting Kira. I never thought you'd go this far to win her over, though."

I growled. "We aren't talking about me. I asked you a question. What are you doing here?"

"None of your business. Besides, I should be asking you the same thing. You're a lone wolf. No official pack. I thought every alpha had to be aligned with a pack to be cast."

"It's not an official rule, more a guideline they can overlook when they want to," I said with a shrug, hoping he didn't press for more details.

Gavin sneered. "Well, isn't that lucky."

Stepping even closer to him, I looked him in the eye. "You know, I've never liked your family. The Fells have always acted like they were better than they are. You guys pretend you're as important as the First or Second packs, but you're out there in the Eastern Wilds, just like Kira's pack. Your family ruined Kira's life out in the real world, and I'll be damned if I let you ruin her chances here. Do you understand me?"

Gavin took a step back and raised his hands. "I get it. She got screwed over. I understand that."

I narrowed my eyes. I'd never thought Gavin would admit to any wrongdoing by his family. I kept my mouth shut, waiting for him to explain.

"You can drop the whole protector act, Wyatt. I'm not here to hurt Kira."

"Really?" I waved back toward the dining room. "You didn't make things much better for her in there. It looks like you're trying to hurt her."

That struck a nerve. I watched his eyes waver, and a wince of embarrassment flashed across his face. "That...was a mistake. I fucked up, okay? I assumed everyone would know. I didn't out her to be a dick. I'll apologize to Kira about that. I'll even apologize for the shit my dumbass brother pulled. She and I can hash it all out when I get some time alone with her." His cocky smile returned. "Which I am *really* looking forward to, by the way."

Gavin kept grinning at me as he took a few backward steps, then spun on his heel and walked away. The asshole whistled as he went.

I stood, rooted in place, as he vanished around the corner. He'd left no doubt in my mind that I'd have to watch out for him. Things were getting more dangerous by the second. Omar and Tate were bad enough, but now I had a member of the Fell family here, planning to do gods only knew what to Kira.

My mind was going a thousand miles an hour as I finally started walking toward the den. I needed to get my focus back. My anger at the others couldn't cloud my judgment when it came to Kira. Whatever challenge they cooked up for us tonight, I'd need to be on point. Kira was pissed at me for not going home, but the more I saw, the more I realized I'd made the right decision. No matter what it took, I'd keep her safe tonight.

Chapter 29 - Kira

I was seething. Slamming the door behind me, I stomped into the room and collapsed onto one of the couches, covering my eyes with my arm.

"Looks like things didn't go well at lunch?"

I moved my arm a fraction and looked at Zoe, who was sitting in a chaise lounge beside the dark fireplace. She put aside the book she'd been reading and walked over to me.

"What happened? You look pissed."

"You could say that," I said.

"Is the new guy a dick? I saw the helicopter arrive a little while ago, but I couldn't get a good look at him."

I let out a defeated and desperate sigh, then said, "It's Gavin, Zoe."

"Gavin?" She frowned at me, then her jaw dropped. "Jayson's brother? *That* Gavin?"

"The one and only."

"Oh, holy shit." She gasped. "Are you serious? He's the last contestant? That can't be. No way your luck is that bad."

I laughed humorlessly. "Thanks, I appreciate that. But my luck is that bad. He also told the guys I don't shift."

"Whoops. How'd that go down?"

"About as well as you'd expect. Pretty sure Omar's gunning to get me killed so he can get a new piece of ass on the show." I put my arm back over my eyes. "This is a disaster."

Zoe put her arm around me. "It's okay. You're strong. Screw those guys. If Omar wants you dead, then make sure he kicks the bucket first."

I let out a laugh that sounded perilously close to a sob. "Is that what it's come to? Is that what I am now? I'm going to go out there and actively try to kill people? All I ever did as an operative was try to help and save people. It's not in my DNA to do something like that."

Zoe nodded. "Okay, true. You aren't the type. Maybe what I'm saying is that if there comes a time when you have the chance to, say, save either Omar or Wyatt, you mosey on over and save Wyatt and let Omar fend for himself. Something like that."

"That might happen sooner rather than later."

"What do you mean?"

"Von walked in and saw Omar, Gavin, and Wyatt at each other's throats. It gave him some big ideas to change the original challenge for tonight. He's going to come up with something that lets the alphas get their aggression out or something. If I had to guess, it's gonna be dangerous as hell."

Zoe's eyes bulged. "Holy shit, they really are looking for ratings. The Arena Match was already announced on previews today. If they change it up at the last minute, viewership is gonna skyrocket."

"I'm very happy for them," I said flatly.

"Let me get you ready. That way, you can get your mind off it. Did they say what you should wear?"

I shook my head. "All Von said was 'get ready.'" I shrugged.

"All right, we'll go with the same survival gear you used in the swamp. Can't go wrong with that. It'll give you a little protection, anyway."

Zoe got my gear ready, then helped me get dressed. She must have used magic to clean them while I was at lunch. The garments were no longer caked in mud, dirt, and blood. Before she could work on my hair, there was a knock at the door.

"Who is that?" Zoe asked.

"No clue. I'll check."

By the time I made it to the door, I was even more irritated. As I unlocked the door, I swore that if it was Von, I'd chase his ass down the hall with a sharpened stake.

It wasn't him, though. It was one of the witches.

She smiled at me as the door swung open. "Oh, good. You've already gotten prepared," she said when she saw my attire.

"Yes, for tonight. Can I help you with something? I was hoping to rest a little before the challenge."

"Oh no, Miss Durst. Unfortunately, there will be no time to rest. Your challenge starts now."

Before I could do or say anything, the witch's hand shot out and closed around my wrist. There was a momentary flash of light, then darkness.

The next thing I knew, I was staring at the floor, looking down between my knees. My head was groggy, and I felt dizzy. Blinking, I tried to orient myself. I was tied up. That was the first thing I noticed. I was bound tightly in some kind of rope. I was sitting on a stone or rock, water all around me. I was in some sort of pond. The air was moist, and the sky was nearly dark. It had barely been past lunch when the witch came for me. Now, the sun was already down. She'd not only teleported me but kept me knocked out for hours. Zoe was probably *pissed* that it had happened right under her nose.

My first instinct was to panic, but that would do me no good. Instead, I took a few deep breaths and tried the ropes. Whoever had tied me up knew what they were doing. There was nowhere to get slack to free myself. The pond was deep enough in the jungle that I couldn't even get my bearings. Once the stars came out, I might be able to figure out where I was, but that wasn't a guarantee.

The weird sounds of the night started to ramp up. The screeches and howls, hisses, squawks, and growls combined to create a cacophony of terrifying noise. Something about the sounds stood out, though. I squinted, trying to stare off into the foliage. A grinding sound, right there under the dull roar of everything else. It was obviously mechanical in nature, which made no sense.

My nerves were shot, and being tied up had me on the verge of panic. Thankfully, while my feet had been bound, they'd neglected to tie my knees or the rest of my legs, so after a few tries, I was able to get to my knees, then up to my feet. I hopped around the small rock I was imprisoned on and inspected my surroundings. I did my best to tamp down my anger, fear, and stress. My inner wolf was making herself heard, too, which was rare. I'd spent years pushing her deep into the recesses of my mind, only using her strength and speed to my advantage. The fact that I could feel her raging inside my mind meant a lot. She understood exactly what this signified. We'd been tied up and placed on a platter as some kind of *reward*, a prize for whoever won tonight's challenge. Neither of us liked the idea of being a trophy.

I hopped closer to the water. Maybe it was shallow enough for me to make it through the water. My wrists were tied, but I was pretty sure I could do a partial doggy paddle through the water to get to shore. Once there, maybe I could find something sharp to cut through the ropes.

With the dying light, I had to lean close to the water. At first, I thought it was only moss or pond scum floating around, but when I got close enough, I realized what I was looking at.

"Son of a bitch," I hissed.

Looking up and scanning the whole pond, I saw what hadn't been obvious before. Little purple flowers floated everywhere. Wolfsbane. The water was filled with wolfsbane. I took a closer look. They'd crushed stems and roots and dumped those in the water as well. The water would be saturated with the poison. Any wolf who got into that water would be in for a bad time. Wolfsbane was toxic to us, and prolonged exposure could burn and paralyze us. No matter how fast I swam, even without my hands tied, my body would lock up. I'd drown before I made it to shore.

Shouts and screams erupted from the jungle, and my head snapped toward the sounds. They were louder than the regular island noises. The snarls sounded suspiciously like shifters. Whether it was the contestants or ferals, I couldn't be sure. A moment later, a screech pierced the night. It could have been an injured vampire or a pissed-off ghost, but again, I had no way to be sure.

Behind me, on the other side of the pond, I heard a deep and menacing growl. Definitely *not* a shifter. I was a sitting duck out here, and I had no way of knowing how close help was. If some other creature that wasn't affected by the wolfsbane decided to paddle over for a quick peek, I'd end up being a fairly easy snack for it. There was no way I could hope for the alphas to get here to help me.

A thought formed in my mind, and there was a moment of indecision before I decided it was worth the risk. Getting back down on my knees, I edged over to the pond and plunged my hands into the cool liquid. I flinched in pain as the wolfsbane stung and burned my fingers, hands, and forearms. Once the rope was saturated enough, I pulled them back out, breathing a sigh of relief as the pain abated to that of a minor sunburn.

My sacrifice was worth it, though. The ropes, laden with water, were looser and easier to stretch. It took nearly five minutes, but I managed to free my wrists. Rubbing them, I basked in my ingenuity for a few seconds before doing the same thing to my ankles. The sensation was equally agonizing, but knowing that it would work eased the sting a bit. In minutes, I was totally free and standing on the rock, letting my body heal. Now, I needed to find a way off this stupid rock.

The moon had already risen, and I could see it reflected in the water as I racked my brain for ideas. It was in the water that I saw the reflection of massive wings gliding silently down from the sky toward me. I frowned, then I registered the shape and knew exactly what was coming. My reflexes kicked in, and I rolled backward out of the way right as the demon's claws raked the stone.

Scrambling to my feet, I took in the beast in front of me. A massive, grinning slab of muscle and fangs stalked toward me, its leathery wings folded on its back. So, this was one of the mad beings trapped on this island. It looked like it had walked right out of hell itself.

Before I could even try to reason with it, the thing lashed, and its three-inch-long talons slashed the air inches from my face. I stumbled backwards and nearly fell into the water, righting myself just in time. If that had made contact, it would have torn my throat out. This beast was trying to kill me. All right, then. It looked like there would be no discussion.

Jumping forward, I sent a kick into the demon's ribs. As large as it was, my kick was strong, and it flinched and clutched at its side, moving backwards. Seizing the opportunity, I rolled forward and drove a punch deep into its inner thigh, forcing it to its knees in pain. Before I could get away, he backhanded me, sending me sprawling back on the rock. Roaring, it lunged at me. I rolled to the right as its claws dug thin grooves into the stone.

I wouldn't have many more chances. It was too big and too strong. There were no weapons or way to flee or give myself more space to work. I needed to end this quickly. Before it could stand back up, I grabbed the thick leathery wings on his back and heaved. I put one leg behind its thighs to trip it, then yanked the beast over, flipping it over my leg. With a screech of rage, it fell into the water.

Ignoring the pain it would cause, I leaped on its back and used my hands to shove its face under. My skin was on fire as the demon thrashed beneath me. Thankfully, it was face down and couldn't claw at me with its wickedly sharp talons. All it could do was splash and try to get its head out of the water. The rock sloped downward, meaning the demon had no way to get purchase. Its hands slipped over the algae-covered rock.

When its movements finally began to slow and weaken, another idea struck me. I yanked its head up and shook hard.

"Fly me off this rock, asshole. Otherwise, I'll drown you."

In the distance, another round of howls, screams, and cackles echoed across the pond. The demon chuckled, a sound like a bucket of rocks being shaken.

"The ferals are coming for you," the demon growled. "Your best bet is to run for haven—if you know what's good for you."

Growling, I shoved his face back underwater. The pain was almost easy to ignore now that I was so fueled with rage. But it wasn't the pain that was the problem; it was the paralyzing effects of the wolfsbane. With a start, I realized my fingers weren't gripping his horns as hard as they had been.

The demon must have noticed, too. In a last desperate attempt to free himself, he flapped his great wings, catching me off guard. One wing smacked me in the face, and my hold gave way. The second wing pushed me off his back, and the thing managed to get on all fours before leaping into the air. The *thwap-*

thwap of his wings was the only sound of his departure.

I sat, cradling my hands to my chest. The pain had completely vanished, but I couldn't even curl my fingers into fists. It would take a few minutes of healing, then I'd be fine, but I might not have that much time.

A group of scraggly, menacing feral wolves came stalking out of the trees, their eyes locked on me like I was a juicy steak. They howled and snapped at me. Even in the distance, they looked terrifying. For a moment, I was happy the pond was poisoned. At least the damn things couldn't paddle over and try to feast on me.

From behind the ferals, another set of howls echoed from the trees. An instant later, two alphas leaped out and began attacking the ferals. One I knew on sight. Wyatt. His muscular wolf was easy to remember. I wasn't sure about the other, but I thought it might be Mika. I'd seen him in wolf form earlier at the swamp.

The two new arrivals snapped and bit at the ferals, pushing them farther back from the edge of the pond. The five ferals were doing their best to separate

Wyatt and Mika, trying to single them out to make fighting easier.

The feeling was returning to my fingers, and I had my hands clenched into fists, wishing I could join the fight and help them. Three of the wolves snapped at Mika, and he lunged at them, his teeth sinking into a throat. He snapped his head back and forth twice, and even from here, I heard the neck snap. The feral shifter's body thudded to the ground, and the two others bolted into the jungle. Mika, in a bloodlust, sprinted after them, leaving Wyatt alone to fight the other two.

Wyatt fought well until one wolf attacked from his blind side. I sucked in a breath as his flesh tore away, leaving a bloody gash. Wyatt yowled, and the second feral took the opening. It grabbed Wyatt by his throat and slung him into the pond.

Instantly thrashing to the surface back in his human form, Wyatt let out a bloodcurdling scream as the wolfsbane soaked into his skin. The wolves on the edge of the pond looked on in silence as Wyatt gagged and spat the poisoned water from his mouth. My nails dug into my palms as I watched him struggle. I was begging him, in hushed whispers, to swim to the edge.

"Swim, Wyatt. You have to swim. Hurry."

If he heard me, he made no attempt to do what I wanted. His arms slowed, and I saw the pain in his face turn to agony, then he began to slip under. His body succumbed to the poison. I was about to watch Wyatt drown right in front of me.

The thought sent a jolt of terror and heartache through me. I shuddered and hit my knees, watching him give a few final kicks before slipping under the surface.

As his face slipped under, his eyes found me. There was the briefest moment of connection between us, and then he was gone. The scream that burst from my throat was like no sound I'd ever made in my life. My wolf, suddenly stronger than she'd been in years, roared, combining her voice with mine. Even the feral shifters flinched at the sound that howled out of me.

Years of control slipped. Barriers I'd built in my mind cracked and snapped apart. The panic at seeing Wyatt in trouble had broken my wolf's deep slumber. In a second, something that hadn't happened in a long time began to descend on my body. I shifted in a burst of pain and newfound power. Even as I changed, I realized something was different. My wolf was stronger than she'd been the last time. It had been years, and during that time, she'd become much more powerful.

Before I could register what had truly happened to me, I was leaping into the pond. My powerful legs propelled me nearly the entire thirty feet to the edge. I splashed into the water, yelping in pain as the wolfsbane soaked through my fur. The pain was secondary. The only thing I could think of was getting to Wyatt.

Diving under the water, I found him. The poison burned my eyes like fire, but I paddled to him and latched onto his collar as I kicked to the surface.

Keeping my teeth on Wyatt's shirt, I paddled to the edge of the pond as fast as I could. The ferals were growling and snarling at me, their lips peeled back, their teeth bared. My body was already not operating properly. My legs were strangely heavy, and my feet did not want to paddle. My jaws were growing weak. If I didn't get to the shore soon, Wyatt and I would die.

Before my strength gave out, my paws found the ground, and I half-dragged, half-pushed Wyatt onto the shore away from the water. He was still breathing when I faced the ferals. I wasn't sure how good I'd be in a fight, but I had no choice.

More barks and howls came from the jungle. More wolves were on the way. I had no way of knowing if they were the alphas or more ferals. My wolf didn't care. She was seething with anger and bloodlust, the likes of which I'd never known. Even as my body struggled against the poisoned water that had soaked into it, she was preparing to tear her enemies limb from limb. When I looked deep into our mind, all I could see was her desire to protect Wyatt. Nothing else.

Sensing their chance was slipping away, the two ferals bolted toward me. I used my body to block Wyatt's unconscious body. I stared as the two wolves rushed toward us, saliva foaming from their teeth, eyes yellow with madness, growls of rage reverberating in their chests.

This was when I was going to die. The two wolves would overpower my weakened wolf, I would fall, and Wyatt after me. Knowing this, my wolf bared her teeth and howled for them to come and do their best.

The lead wolf jumped toward me, clearing the last few feet. His jaws were open, teeth exposed and ready to sink into my flesh.

He tumbled to the side with a thud. A third wolf, a male I'd never seen before, had tackled him. The new wolf had burst from the jungle and attacked the feral. I stared in dumb fascination as the new arrival pinned the feral down and ripped its throat out in two quick jerks. The feral kicked at the mud at the side of the pond, blood pouring from its neck. It flipped over, falling into the pond and sinking below the surface.

The new wolf turned and attacked the second feral, who'd been as shocked as I was by the interruption. In fact, it was nowhere near ready for the attack that followed. The new arrival attacked the second feral with such ferocity, it barely had the chance to defend itself. Before I could even blink, the second feral lay dead on the ground, its throat crushed between powerful jaws.

The wolf that had just saved me spun to face me, and I finally got a look at him. He was huge and heavily scarred. One of the biggest wolves I'd ever seen, almost as big as Wyatt when he shifted. A thick scar ran along his temple, ending in an empty socket. For all the world, he looked like he should have been a feral, but the remaining eye was alive and sane. This was not a feral wolf.

Before I could shift to my human form and ask him who the hell he was and what he was doing, he fled. His gray body vanished into the underbrush, and then he was gone like a ghost in the night.

Safe for the moment, I collapsed onto the mud beside Wyatt. My body trembled as it tried to heal from the wolfsbane poisoning. Wyatt looked terrible. Along with the poison and the awful injury from the feral, it looked like he'd sustained a lot of other wounds in his fight to find me.

I jerked my snout toward the jungle as more battle sounds reached my ears—human shouts, the howls of wolves, the hissing of vampires. A deep, thunderous scream of a ghost was muted by the ear-splitting screech of a banshee across the pond. I needed to get Wyatt out of there. The wolfsbane had soaked into his wounds and was preventing him from healing. I needed to get him to the mansion and the healers.

I tried to shift back so I could carry him to safety, but my wolf flat-out refused. She'd been locked away long enough that she wasn't giving me control. I tried to focus, demanding that she let me shift back, but it was like talking to a brick wall. Instead, now that my legs had regained some function, I stood, grabbed Wyatt by the scruff of the neck like a pup, and started dragging him away.

It surprised me that we were making such good progress, with the pain of the wolfsbane still coursing through my body. With no clue where I needed to go, I tried to follow my nose. There were some faint scents that reminded me of the mansion. With no other plan, I continued dragging Wyatt in that direction.

After what felt like hours, I stumbled into a clearing and dropped Wyatt, my body too exhausted to go on. In the clearing, two sets of yellow eyes approached from the darkness. More ferals? With a deep and weary growl, I forced myself into a fighting stance and prepared for an attack.

Instead, the two wolves padded forward, and I saw Mika along with another that smelled like Gavin. Even in their wolf forms, I could see their bafflement at seeing me as a wolf. Their heads tilted in confusion, but they knew it was me by my scent.

Exhausted and in agony, I took one step toward them and collapsed. Mika and Gavin walked over and looked down at me, concern evident in their canine eyes. The last thing I remembered was the sound of *The Reject Project* theme song blaring across all of Bloodstone Island.

When my eyelids fluttered open, I was met with a surprise. Instead of the pearly gates, I was staring into the face of the mansion's lead healer. The elderly witch tended to me. Still half-unconscious, I realized I was back in my human form.

The witch glanced down and smiled. "Oh, there she is. How are you, dear? Feeling better?"

I sat up slowly. I actually didn't feel terrible. From what I could see, I was basically fine. The healers here were some of the best, after all.

Nodding, I said, "I do. Can I go check on the others?" I was desperate to know who had survived the evening's challenge.

The witch nodded. "That's fine. I think Mister Thornton is hoping for it, actually."

Climbing off the bed, I hurried out the door and down the hall to where I thought the others might be. I'd thought right. I found them in the main sitting room. Despite the late hour, they seemed to be waiting for me. They leaped to their feet as I came in.

Leif, Garrett, Gavin, Mika, and J.D. were all there, but I didn't see anyone else with them.

"Where's Wyatt?" I asked, my voice coming out more panicked than I'd intended.

Leif stepped over and put an arm on my shoulders. "Calm down. Wyatt's alive. He's still with the healers. He was messed up pretty badly." He made an apologetic face. "He nearly drowned in wolfsbane. It's making it tough for even the healers here to help him, but they still think he'll end up all right."

"How did you shift?" Gavin asked, interrupting Leif. "I know you can't shift. It's never happened before. Everyone knows that. How the hell did you do that?"

Before I could respond, J.D. surprised us all by shoving Gavin. He put a finger against Gavin's chest and said, "Back off, bro. Dammit, man. Can't you see she's exhausted?"

Von walked in with the lead healer. When he saw me, his perpetual grin spread into a massive smile. The healer hurried over to me and began casting spells on my remaining cuts and bruises.

I waved her off and looked at Von. "I'm fine. Send her to Wyatt. He needs help, not me."

"She's supposed to focus on you first," Von said, shaking his finger back and forth at me. "You're the star of the show. And what a star you are. You had us all fooled, you little minx." He laughed and shook his head. "You have a beautiful wolf. To think you had us thinking you were a latent shifter when all along we had an alpha *female* here on the island."

J.D. and the others gaped at me in shock. Gavin looked like he was going to faint.

I gritted my teeth and decided to use the show against them.

"Fine," I said. "I want to use the mating chamber with Wyatt. Then the healer can be there all night and help take care of him."

Von sighed and rolled his eyes. "My dear. The mating chamber is a place for steam, passion, and hushed words. The audience wants to see thrusting hips and tangled bodies thrashing in ecstasy. It really isn't the place for bandages and sutures. Come now, surely you—ugh!"

I'd grabbed him by his tie and yanked him to me, pressing my face against his. I was too tired of his dramatics to check the alpha wolf inside me.

"Listen, jackass," I hissed. "Since you're so interested in my alpha wolf, maybe you should know something. She's really fucking hungry, and I think she may be in the mood for some vampire flesh. I may have to let her take a few nibbles if you don't cut the shit and let this healer help Wyatt to make sure he makes a full recovery. Got it?"

The other alphas said nothing, only staring at me as a very disheveled and annoyed Von led me and the healer out of the room. I'd assumed Von would try and put up another fight, but I was pleasantly surprised when Wyatt was wheeled into the luxurious mating chamber. The healer and her assistants laid him on the massive bed and started working on him.

The last thing I saw before I fell asleep at his side was the awful wounds he'd suffered. All of them inflicted on him as he'd tried to save me.

Chapter 30 - Wyatt

Paws hissed over the grass as I ran. At first, I was confused, unsure where I was or why I was running. Then the scents of the forest told me I was in the Eastern Wilds, far from any houses or roads. The sky was the dark purple of dusk, the sun just slipping beneath the horizon.

There was something wrong, though. I was running faster than I ever had before. Then I realized I was racing toward Kira's screaming in the distance.

Realizing it was her voice echoing through the air, I moved even faster. My feet became blurred as I sprinted toward the sound of her cries. They were like nothing I'd ever heard—heartrending, broken, panicked screams of horror. Searching desperately, I found a cave I recognized and slid to a stop as her voice echoed from within.

I remembered this cave. I'd found her in this cave twelve years ago. The memories flooded back. Why would she be in there? Before I could overthink it, I rushed into the mouth of the cavern.

The first thing I noticed was the blood. It was all over. Smeared on the walls, puddled on the stone floor, and everywhere in between. Kira was still screaming. Deeper in the cave. I ran, heedless of whatever danger awaited me in the darkness. All I could think of was getting to Kira.

My eyes snapped open, and I took a shuddering breath. Disoriented, I glanced around the strange room. Cold sweat slicked my skin, and my breathing came in ragged gasps. The room was dark, but the moonlight drifted in, revealing I was on a huge bed, twice the size of a typical bed.

A strip of warmth across my stomach drew my eyes down. An arm lay across my midsection. Kira lay beside me, deep asleep with her arm stretched across me.

Bewildered, I tried to remember how I'd gotten there. I remembered Von telling all of us that Kira was out in the jungle, awaiting rescue. Then we'd all been sent out to find her. There'd been even more terrible creatures than the last time we'd gone out. Mika and I had ended up together, fighting off vampires as we rushed toward Kira's scent. After that, my recollection got hazy.

Closing my eyes, I tried to remember. There were some flashes of a pond—I thought I could recall seeing Kira out there. I nodded to myself as the events returned. The feral wolves had attacked us. The last thing I remembered was one of the ferals tearing a hunk of flesh from my side before I fell into the water. There was a flash of agony, then nothing.

The water had burned like lava as it hit my skin. Wolfsbane. It must have been. A quick glance showed some red smears on my skin where the burns had been. They were faded and no longer hurt. Beside the bed, I saw a tray that held a half dozen jars of medicine and ointment.

Turning to check on Kira, I didn't see any injuries on her face or hands. I gently lifted the blanket, surprised to find she had no injuries on the rest of her body, either—at least what I could see.

Kira's eyes blinked open, awoken by my movements. She scooted closer to me, pressing against my shirtless chest. That was unusual. Usually, we put up a pretty big fight before any touching happened.

"Um, I'm sorry I woke you up," I said.

"It's fine," she murmured. "I'm just glad you're alive and don't look like you're about to die anymore."

She wrapped a second arm around me and smiled sleepily. Her curves pressed against me, and the way she looked had me half-turned on already. There was a stirring between my legs, and I decided to distract myself.

"What exactly happened? I think I blacked out when I hit the water."

Kira yawned and said, "It was bad. You were badly wounded before you even slipped into the water. Then the wolfsbane got into your wounds, and you went totally under." She hesitated and licked her lips. "I...uh...lost control of my wolf. I shifted and jumped out to drag you to shore."

"You shifted?" I asked, dumbfounded.

For twelve years, she'd never allowed her other side out. She'd fought tooth and nail with her inner wolf for so long that it had almost become part of her personality. Never giving a single inch, not wanting to allow what had happened back then to happen again. It had been a secret held between the two of us since that night. She'd driven her wolf back, harshly enough that I'd wondered if she might be causing irreparable harm to her psyche. Letting the wolf out couldn't have been easy.

I touched her arm, barely brushing my fingers across her skin. "Are you okay?"

Kira snorted a laugh and pushed herself up to sit next to me. "Am I okay? Seriously? Wyatt, you're the one who almost died out there. Speaking of, let me see your wounds. I had to twist Von's arm to let the lead healer work on you."

Her fingers traced some of the wolfsbane burns and cuts on my side. A groan escaped my lips as she touched the nearly healed tear in my side, then traced her finger across my abs to touch a cut there. Then, instead of a finger, her entire palm slid across my skin, up to my chest and then down the other side. The look in Kira's eyes showed me she wasn't worried about my injuries anymore. She looked hungry and lustful as she took in the angles of my body.

The tension and chemistry between us always grew into a roaring fire every time we were alone, and it was becoming impossible to ignore. Kira raised her eyes to mine, biting her lower lip as her fingers slipped further down to graze my crotch. My cock twitched. All my fear of the challenge and for her was gone now. She was safe. We were alone. I could show her exactly what I wanted.

Looping my arm around her, I pulled her close and crushed my lips into hers. Without hesitation, Kira ran her hands up my back and opened her mouth to allow my tongue access. This didn't feel like the last time. Something about it was more *real*. She wasn't doing this because she was angry or scared or wanted to release some tension. There was a warmth and softness to the kiss that told me she wanted *me*. The thought sent a shiver of pleasure up my spine as I stripped her clothes off.

Kira sighed and pulled her lips from mine, helping me pull my underwear off. My cock was already rigid when it sprang free from the waistband. Heedless of my wounds, I gently pushed her onto her back, spread her legs, and slid my tongue down her body. She gasped and pressed her hands to the back of my head, pushing me down. I sucked at her clit, running my hands over her body as she pressed her hips to my face, urging me to continue.

The taste and smell of her sent my inner wolf wild with desire. I slid a finger into her, moaning at her wetness. Kira arched her back as I moved my tongue faster across her clit. It went on like that for several moments until I couldn't stand it anymore. I had to have her.

Pulling my face away, I crawled up the bed until my face was directly above hers. Kira brought her hand down between us and grabbed my cock, stroking it as she looked into my eyes. A breath of air escaped my lungs as her fingers worked up and down my shaft. Kira guided my cock down, playfully rubbing the tip against her clit before letting me slide into her.

It was the third time I'd been with her, and somehow, each time was more amazing than the last. This time was less frantic than before. We could take our time and enjoy the moment, and I was happy to see that Kira felt the same. My hips slid forward and back, my cock gliding in and out of her. Wrapping her arms around my neck, she pulled me closer and kissed me again, her lips and tongue warm on my mouth. All the sensations made my head swim.

Pressing myself all the way inside her, I rocked back and forth as I held her tight to me. She pushed her hand down and started rubbing her clit, her breathing growing faster and more urgent. I could feel her body tensing as I thrust into her faster and faster. My own orgasm was approaching, and for once, I didn't want it to happen. I was having too much fun. The look in Kira's eyes as she gazed up at me made my chest ache. She'd never looked more beautiful.

She clenched her teeth as her hand rubbed furiously at her clit while I slammed into her. She let out a moan and began to shiver in ecstasy. Her orgasm continued washing over her, and she reached her arms around me again and clutched at my ass, urging me deeper and faster. It was too much. I gasped and groaned as my release came, the spasms of pleasure running along my cock and balls up my back. Warmth flooded across my body as I finished.

After I collapsed atop her, we heaved in breaths, trying to recover. I wrapped my arms around her and pulled her close to me. I wasn't sure what the future held, but I was going to enjoy this moment for as long as I could.

After cleaning up and lying down, Kira rested her head on my chest and ran a finger along my stomach. We didn't say a word but simply enjoyed being with each other. After some time, Kira looked up at me as though she'd thought of something important.

"I haven't had the time to tell you yet, but do you remember the wolf who saved us?"

I frowned and shook my head. "No. Which of the guys was it? I was passed out."

Kira sat up on her elbow. "It wasn't one of the guys. I've seen all their wolves, and this one wasn't any of them. It was riddled with scars, like it had been fighting for its life for a while. One of its eyes was missing, and there was a big scar where it should have been."

That made even less sense. "You're saying a feral helped you? Why would it do that?"

"That's the weird thing—it wasn't feral. I looked into its eyes. They weren't crazy or psychotic like a feral would be. He was sane, and lucid, and..." She trailed off. After a minute, she let out a little gasp. "I think he might be a past contestant."

I sat up in bed. "What? Is that even possible?"

"Wyatt, they've been doing this every year for over thirty years. A lot of contestants vanish during filming, and they always write them off as dead. But what if one survived?"

My brow furrowed as I tried to imagine why someone would choose to live on Bloodstone rather than go home.

"If this guy had survived, why wouldn't he come back to the mansion? Get sent back to his pack or whatever?"

Before our discussion could go further, I saw Kira's wristband light up. A glance at my own wrist showed that mine was activated as well.

"It's the middle of the night," Kira groaned. "What do they want?"

On the watch's tiny screen, a video began to play. Von Thornton's smiling face came up.

"Good evening, everyone. I know you're all very tired, but there's been a few last-minute changes to our plans. Tomorrow morning, we will be heading back to the mainland for a special meet-and-greet with the mega fans before returning to Bloodstone, so make sure you get a good night's rest."

"Thanks. Glad you woke everyone up just to tell them to sleep," I grunted, even though I knew Von couldn't hear me through the bracelet.

Von held up a finger. "And one last juicy detail. The game is about to change. I hope everyone is ready for it, especially Kira. For the first time, starting next week, there will be a second female contestant on the island." Von winked. "Remember, everyone loves an underdog."

Made in the USA
Middletown, DE
20 September 2023

38830207R00285